D0297777

THE VAMPIRE SHRINK

THE VAMPIRE SHRINK

Lynda Hilburn

Jo Fletcher
BOOKS

First published in Great Britain in 2011 by

Jo Fletcher Books
an imprint of Quercus
21 Bloomsbury Square
London
WC1A 2NS

A CIP catalogue record for this book is available
from the British Library

ISBN 978 0 85738 719 6 (HB)
ISBN 978 0 85738 720 2 (TPB)

10 9 8 7 6 5 4 3 2 1

Typeset by Ellipsis Digital Limited, Glasgow

Printed and bound in Great Britain by Clays Ltd, St Ives plc

To my mother, Virginia Hilburn,
the best person in the world

CHAPTER 1

My involvement with vampires began innocently enough, long before the blood hit the fan, so to speak.

Like most psychologists, I'd been trained to view the world through a diagnostic lens, to hear my clients' stories with my metaphorical ears, searching out the deeper meanings. Thankfully, my tendency to reduce each person to a prevailing neurosis was tempered by my irreverent, dark sense of humour, which kept me from taking myself and the world too seriously.

While I was never as bad as some of my colleagues about believing only in what I could prove – if you can't quantify it, it isn't there – I had seen enough bizarre situations in my psychotherapy work over the years to make me more sceptical than I was comfortable admitting. That said, my private practice had its share of UFO abductees, demonic possessions, satanic-ritual survivors, religious cultists, attached entities – all the newest selections on the menu of emotional and mental pain – alongside clients with all the 'regular' therapy issues.

So when I opened the door separating my reception area from my office that fateful Friday to welcome my new client,

I was only momentarily surprised. Waiting for me was a young woman wearing a long black dress covered by a dark-purple velvet cape. Rings adorned all ten fingers, and a long snake bracelet with sparkling ruby eyes wound its way up her arm from wrist to elbow. She had waist-length light-brown hair with multicoloured streaks, and she wore white theatrical makeup, dark-red lipstick and remarkably lifelike, high-quality fangs.

My mind began to pick out the various category boxes I could assign her into. Hmmm, goth? Vampire wannabe? Acting-out teenager?

Well, well. This ought to be interesting.

'Please come in and have a seat.' I gave my warmest therapy smile and waved my hand in the general direction of the couch and chairs in the centre of my office. 'I'm Dr Knight. Please call me Kismet.'

That's quite an outfit. Spectacular, really. This sweet young thing has a flair for the dramatic. And what's that delicious fragrance? Sandalwood?

She walked in silently, handed me the packet of forms she'd filled out in the waiting room and sat on the end of the couch farthest from where I was standing. Scanning the information, I noticed she'd listed her name as Midnight.

'Midnight? That's a lovely name. Is there a last name?'

'No. I have no need of anything from my human past,' she said, with exaggerated seriousness and a dismissive flick of her fingers.

Okay. Let's not assume the obvious. I chose a chair across from her and picked up my notepad and pen. 'Tell me how I can help you.'

'I'm only here because my family made me come. They can't accept my choices and they're hoping you'll talk me out of wanting to be a vampire. They want you to fix me.' Her voice separated each angry word like little staccato notes.

She gave me the once-over I'd come to expect from my younger clients: the smirking scan that evaluated my tailored light-blue suit and sensible black heels and found them hope-lessly conventional. Then, inevitably, her eyes moved to my dark hair, which was very long, curly and often had a mind of its own. The dissonance between my conservative suit and the unintentional rock-star hair disrupted the inner picture she was constructing of me. My age – I'd not long turned thirty – added to the dissonance. I always enjoyed the flash of confusion that washed over their faces at that point. My inner trickster was never far away.

She hiked her dress up until the hem rested on her knees and crossed her legs dramatically. 'You're not what I expected.'

'What did you expect?' *Freud in drag?*

'Someone old, with her hair in a bun and no makeup. You're not that much older than me And you're pretty. You remind me of that actress – Megan Fox, the one with the long dark hair and blue eyes.' She studied me. 'Or maybe Angelina Jolie, except with blue eyes and less lips.'

Less lips? I knew what she meant, but I ran my tongue over my standard set of two just to verify their existence and tried not to imagine an extra pair on Angelina's face.

'Thank you. Are you comfortable with someone who isn't old and who doesn't have her hair in a bun?'

She frowned. 'I guess so.'

I could see that her need to connect was struggling with her automatic protective defences and the jury was out as to which one would continue the session.

'That's a start.' I smiled encouragingly at her. 'So tell me about your desire to be a vampire. How long have you wanted to be one?'

She pursed her lips and sat silently for a few seconds. Quick flashes of emotion danced across her face as fear, disappointment and resentment gave way to hope. 'Ever since I met Devereux – Dev, as we call him – about a year ago,' she said dreamily.

Ah, connection won. Maybe she'll let me in.

'Why would meeting Dev make you want to be a vampire?'

'Well, *duh*, because he is one.' She rolled her chocolate-brown eyes and made that 'tsk' sound with her tongue against her teeth.

I kept the practised smile on my face and ignored the teenage angst. 'Can you tell me about Dev?'

Sounds like a lost child has convinced her that he's a vampire.

She stared down at the floor, using the tip of her tongue to play with the fangs. 'I don't think I'm supposed to talk about him. He wouldn't want me to. He says it's better if no one believes vampires really exist.'

Of course he does. Oh, I see. Her sharp little fangs fit perfectly over her own canines, with an almost-invisible band holding them in place – similar to braces. How clever.

'Do you believe that vampires really exist?' I tried not to sound as if there was only one right answer to the question.

'Oh, yes.' She nodded and sat up straighter. 'Denver has tons of vampires.'

Tons of vampires? What a bizarre visual . . .

'Really? Midnight, I want you to know that anything we talk about in here is completely confidential. You can feel free to tell me anything you want and it will go no further. I'd definitely like to hear about all these vampires.' I jotted a note on my pad.

Vampires. Well, that's certainly a change of pace from aliens and demon possessions.

She arched an eyebrow. 'How do I know you won't tell my parents?'

Good. Let's get right to the trust issue.

'Unless you're going to hurt yourself or someone else, I will never tell anyone anything that we discuss,' I explained, giving her my ethically required disclaimer.

She paused a moment, watching me, twisting her hands. 'Well, I don't know. I wouldn't want to get them in trouble. They need to hide from the humans.' She licked her lips.

Damn. She doesn't consider herself one of the humans? Is she brainwashed? How confused is she? Her anxiety level just shot up. Shaking hands, dry lips.

'Ah, I see. Let's leave the vampires for later, then. Tell me about you. Are you in school?'

Her mother had left a message on my voicemail saying she and her husband were concerned because their daughter graduated from high school last year and had no future plans. She'd had a 4.0 grade point average, then turned down a scholarship to college and was making reckless choices. Her mother said she thought a boy was involved.

'No. I used to like school but I'm not into that kind of education any more.'

Hmm. What kind of education is she into?

'What did you like about school? Any favourite classes?'

A spark of interest flashed across her features before she wrestled her face back under control and reset her bored expression. She stretched her fingers then slid her hands along her thighs, probably to dry the moisture on her palms. 'I studied art. Painting, drawing. I also write a little poetry.'

'You're an artist and a poet?' I smiled. 'That's wonderful. What great talents to have.'

'It doesn't matter any more.' She lifted a shoulder and shifted her gaze to the clock and then back to my face.

Oh, yes. Practised apathy. Feigned nonchalance. Fear.

'Why is that?'

She tapped a blood-red fingernail on her leg. 'It's a waste of my time to sit in closed-up rooms, listening to boring people talk about boring subjects. I have bigger plans.'

I wonder if she's given any thought to how closed-up a coffin is?

'What bigger plans?'

'I already told you,' she said with an impatient tone.

'Oh, yes, becoming a vampire. What's so great about that? Why would you want to be a blood-drinking dead thing? Do vampires really sparkle in the sun?' I asked, thinking about the latest trendy vampire movies.

Can she find the humour in the vampire craze, or is it deadly serious?

'Wow.' She laughed and leaped off the couch, then paced in the space behind the furniture. 'You are *really* off. Vampires don't *sparkle*. And they're not dead. Well, I guess they're *technically* dead, but they don't look like zombies. That's probably what you're thinking of.'

I followed her back-and-forth motion with my gaze, noting how her purple cape flared out with each turn in her path. She appeared agitated, perhaps even slightly manic. I relaxed back in my chair and breathed evenly, wanting to encourage her to follow my example.

Bipolar?

'The vampires I know are unearthly beautiful.' She stopped walking and took a deep breath before returning to her seat. She met my eyes, her chin raised in defiance. 'Vampires don't feel bad about drinking blood, either. They don't have to kill to eat – they can just take a little. Obviously they're simply higher on the food chain than we are. It's really quite natural.'

'Sucking blood is natural?' I wrote another note.

Sure. They'll sell blood at holistic food stores any day now. Buy a pint of A-positive and get a pair of Birkenstocks or Crocs for free.

'Well, yeah.' She looked at me as if I were the village idiot. 'Every creature has the right to exist. Just because we don't understand them doesn't make them bad.'

Poor, misunderstood bloodsuckers. Midnight is definitely wearing rose-coloured – I mean blood-coloured – glasses.

'So what is it, then? Do you want to be unearthly beautiful? Is that what appeals to you?'

'Of course. Who wouldn't want that?' She flipped her hair over her shoulder. 'But I'm more interested in immortality and being with someone for ever.'

'Anyone in particular?'

She stared at me, silent.

Okay. That struck a nerve. Try something different.

'I can't even imagine what it would be like to live for ever,' I said, twisting the pen through my fingers. 'Can you? What would I do with myself for all those centuries? I already get bored sometimes over the weekend.'

Midnight giggled, despite her attempt not to. 'I guess it *is* hard to imagine. At least I'd have a lot of time to practise my art. My vampire friends talk about some of the things they've done with their lives.'

I wonder if these vampires are imaginary friends. Is she having auditory hallucinations? Is she psychotic?

'What do they say?'

She looked around the room, probably giving herself time to decide how much to share. 'Some of them spent a lot of years just trying to learn how to be vampires. Nobody taught them, so they travelled around the world, figuring things out, trying not to get staked. Others spent the time doing things they loved – that's what I would do. Nobody could force me to do anything.'

'Who is forcing you to do something?'

Silence.

Definitely more going on here than meets the eye. Is she in a dangerous situation or delusional? What happened to derail her? How did she go from straight-A student to vampire wannabe? Time to regroup.

'Do you have a good relationship with your parents?' I played with a button on my suit jacket – a nervous habit I've never extinguished.

'I guess. They don't understand me.'

The teenage lament. I remember the feeling.

'Tell me about your mother. What's she like?'

'There's nothing to tell. She has all these ideas about who she wants me to be. Did she ever ask me what I want? No.

She thinks because she's a lawyer, I should be one, too. Being an artist isn't a good enough career. Money is the only thing that matters to her. All she does is work. She says it's hard for a woman to make partner in a big law firm, so she's a workaholic.'

Poor Midnight. Looking for someone who won't abandon her.

'How do you feel about that?'

'I get where she's coming from, but I don't want that life. She's not happy. I don't see the point.'

'Do you miss her when she works all the time?'

She opened her mouth to answer, then closed it. Sadness clouded her face before she shoved the feeling into the deep freeze. 'Nope. I hang with my friends.'

Lots of bottled-up pain here.

'Do you have brothers or sisters?'

'No. I'm an only.'

'What about your father?' I circled a comment I'd written earlier in my notes.

She paused and studied the carpet. 'He's a drunk. A boozer. That's what he calls himself.'

'An alcoholic?'

'Out of control.' She nodded and brought her gaze to mine. 'A nut-job, an addict. He sees someone like you. That's why I ended up here. They're worried I inherited whatever glitch he has.'

'You mean a substance-abuse problem?'

Crap. As if things weren't challenging enough for her . . .

'Yeah, among other things. He's an alkie. Drinks so much he has hallucinations sometimes. He can't work any more. He's totally paranoid – thinks everyone's out to get him. I'm surprised he doesn't wear an aluminium foil hat to keep the aliens away. Growing up with that has been a real freak show.'

No wonder she has no boundaries between what's real and what isn't. Mental illness runs in her family.

'Do you think you have a problem? Drugs? Alcohol?'

'No.' She frowned. 'I've smoked my share of pot and I like wine, but I'd rather die than be like my father. I keep myself under control.'

She'd rather die . . . Is all this vampire talk just another form of suicidal ideation? Does she have a plan? A quick way to escape from the pain? She's sending out such mixed signals.

'Are there times when you don't have yourself under control?'

She chewed on her lip again, then glared at me. 'Why are you making me talk about this stuff?' Her eyes glistened with the beginnings of tears. 'I'm already sad all the time, except for when I'm with my friends. What's the use of talking about it? Do you want me to feel worse? There's nothing I can do about my family. I want to think about something good. Something positive.' She sniffled.

Yes. This is good.

I met her gaze, grateful that the dam had finally broken and she might share what was really going on. 'I know it doesn't make sense, because all we want to do is avoid the bad feelings, but sometimes talking about them helps. We're afraid to put our emotions into words because they're over-whelming. Frightening. But if we can find a safe place to let our guard down, to vent some of that intensity and purge a little of the negativity, we usually start to feel better. Therapy can help. I hope you'll begin to think of this office as a safe place.'

I don't know if I would have used a safe place when I was in the midst of my own childhood horrors, but it would've been nice to know such a place existed. Maybe she'll open the door.

She stared at me for a several seconds. She looked very young. Mascara-tinged tears ran down her cheeks. The corners of her lips trembled as she said, 'I feel so alone.' Then she covered her face with her hands and sobbed.

I put aside my pad and pen and moved to sit next to her on the couch, hoping I wasn't jumping the gun. We hadn't had much time to develop trust, but maybe enough of a bridge had been created for her to be able to tolerate my encroaching on her personal space. I wouldn't want to push her away.

She cried for a couple of minutes, then raised her face, her eyes scanning for the box of tissues, which I'd kept at the ready. She grabbed a handful, dabbed her eyes, then blew her nose and slumped back against the couch cushions.

'I didn't mean to tell you that. I'm mad at myself that I did,' she said, her tone hostile, still sniffling, not making eye-contact.

I pressed my hand lightly on hers for a few seconds. 'It took a lot of courage for you to tell me how you feel. I know that wasn't easy for you. Thank you.' No matter how many times I've heard similar stories, they're always heartbreaking.

She looked down at my hand, then shifted her gaze to my face, her eyes puffy, voice soft. 'Courage?'

It's nice to meet the real Midnight. I don't think anybody's reached out to her for a while.

'Definitely. But I still need to ask you something,' I said. 'Can you be courageous a little longer?'

'I don't know.' She tensed, her expression radiating anxiety. 'What is it?'

'Are you planning to hurt yourself?'

The question must not have come as a surprise. To her credit, she took a few seconds before answering. 'No. I would never hurt myself, or anyone else.'

'Okay.' I let out the tense breath I'd been holding. 'I'm very glad to hear that. But if you ever start to feel like you might hurt yourself, or you just need to talk, I'm going to give you one of my cards with a number you can call any time. My service will put you through to me. So, let's make a contract between the two of us that you'll call me if you start to feel bad between sessions. Do we have a deal?'

She took a deep breath and nodded, studying me as if she wasn't sure she could believe me. 'All right. I guess I can do that.'

Little girl lost. But strong, nonetheless.

The light caught the ruby eyes of the snake winding its way up her arm and I took a closer look. The detail in the jewellery was stunning. I pointed in the snake's direction. 'What gorgeous artwork. Did you make it?'

She grinned wide, her trusting younger self peeking out from the shadows, and extended her arm, shifting it from side to side. 'No. I haven't tried to make jewellery yet, but I'm thinking about learning. There's a class I can take on working with silver . . .' The grin disappeared. 'I mean I *used* to think about it.'

Good. Both sides of her psyche are still wrestling for control. There's hope.

'You certainly have an artistic eye – your entire outfit is amazing.'

Even through the white makeup I could see her blush. 'Thank you.'

I glanced over at the clock. 'It looks like our time is up for today. I'd like to meet with you regularly for a while so we can get to know each other. Would you be willing to do that?'

'Yeah.' She grinned again, flashing the designer fangs. 'It wasn't as bad as I thought it would be.'

Well, there's something to put on the back of my business card: Therapy that isn't as bad as you thought it would be.

'That's great.' I smiled. 'I look forward to our time together.' I moved over to my desk to fetch my appointment book.

We scheduled our next session and I walked her out into the waiting area, wondering how she'd look without all the makeup. I shook my head and thought about what a miracle it was that any of us survived our teenage years.

Since Midnight was my last client of the day, I sat at my desk, kicked off my shoes and created a case file for her. I hadn't been able to decide on one specific diagnosis yet, but I jotted down some possible options and then added a sheet of informal notes:

Female, nineteen years old. Referred by family. Dressed in a goth costume, complete with theatrical makeup and detachable fangs, in accordance with her reported desire to become a vampire. Client's verbal family history indicates perceived emotional abandonment by both parents: mother to her career and father to alcoholism and co-occurring mental illness. Prior to the last year, she was a straight-A student in high school, studying art. Little support in her family for her artistic skills and dreams. Will explore client's peer system and her current activities in more detail. Although she hasn't disclosed much information yet about this person, it is likely she has been influenced by a young male who is participating in the goth/vampire-wannabe lifestyle, someone who has given her the affection and attention she craves. She presents herself as a rebellious rule-breaker, but that appears to be a mask. Her defences – the costume, her refusal to give details about the alleged vampires she spends time with and her hostile attitude – keep her protected from more emotional pain. But her body language frequently gives her away: beneath the tough-cookie persona is a sensitive, creative, caring young woman, afraid to share her fears. She is articulate and intelligent, but naïve. She often forgets which role she is playing at any given moment. Explore how seriously she takes this fantasy world she has created. How much is teenage drama and how much psychosis? Continue to build rapport and elicit more information about her vampire-wannabe activities. Test her ideas of reality.

Geez. Life isn't weird enough, so we need to suck blood. Why didn't I think of that?

But I had to admit, the topic had already captured my interest. I was, after all, subject to the same rules as any other psychologist: publish or perish. I was due to write another book and the pressure was on. And, if truth be told, my life had become boring. I had accomplished all the goals I'd set for myself and settled into a listless rhythm. After the excitement of always graduating earlier than expected from every academic course I'd ever attended, adapting to the monotony of private practice was less than thrilling. It would be good to have a challenge after my dismal track-record in the realm of relationships.

I turned on my office computer and searched for everything I could think of about the subject: vampires, vampirism, blood, blood-drinking, cults, mind-control, immortal beings, etc. I was inundated with fictional stories about vampires, historical research on blood-drinkers, case studies involving the self-proclaimed undead and websites for wannabes. Talk about an education.

I printed out examples of the most informative sources and spent a good three hours at my desk, reading through psychological reference books, seeking a trail of crumbs. By the time I came up for air and checked the clock, it had become full dark. I usually tried to avoid walking out of my office by myself at night. Too many lost souls wandering the streets.

'Shit, shit, shit,' I said aloud as I gathered the papers and tucked them into my briefcase. I put my shoes back on, found my purse and my car keys, locked up my office and headed out to the elevator.

At that time of night, the building was deserted and the elevator came right away. I rode down holding my keys with the car alarm clicker in my hand and strode purposefully out the front door of my six-storey office building. Luckily I had parked conspicuously beneath one of the streetlights in the parking lot across the street. My champagne-coloured BMW was the only car left, so I figured I would be safe.

Just as I exited the building, I caught a blurred movement out of the corner of my eye and noticed a shadow to my right. I felt the hairs on my arms rise and I froze. My stomach tightened and my breath caught as a male figure stepped away from where he'd been leaning against the wall. He stood there, gazing at me, smiling, almost close enough for me to touch. We locked eyes for a long moment. The light shining out of the front of my building was bright enough for me to notice that he was gorgeous: tall and toned, with long blond hair, dazzling eyes and snug leather trousers.

Hey, wait a minute. Stop ogling the good looks of the guy who's about to jump on you and run!

And I did.

For someone who sits on her butt all day talking to people, I can still move pretty fast when I want to. I am blessed with one of those long, lean runner's bodies, an inheritance from my father's side of the family, and my body fat percentage is on the low end. But thanks to my mother's genetic contribution, I am too well endowed to actually enjoy running on a regular basis.

The fight-or-flight instinct is an awesome thing.

I sprinted over to my car, clicked the lock, yanked the door open, jumped in, secured the door. My heart was pounding out a heavy-metal drum solo in my chest as I fumbled the key into the ignition. My hands shook so badly it took a couple of tries to get the car started. My throat was so dry it hurt.

Once I was safely barricaded in and the reasoning portion of my brain had sauntered back to the party, it occurred to me that I hadn't heard any footsteps following me as I ran. No voices yelling for me to stop. Still shaking, I scanned the area in all directions but could find no threat of any kind.

The handsome mugger or rapist or whatever he was had vanished. Or maybe it had been some regular guy, enthralled by my grace and beauty, and I'd scared him off when I'd bolted. *Yeah, right, Nerd Woman.*

Maybe he was just there waiting for a friend and I'd over-reacted. He probably hadn't really been a danger at all. It certainly wouldn't have been the first time I'd freaked out over nothing.

But I had to admit I'd never seen such a fantastic-looking man in person anywhere before, much less standing in front of my building. What were the odds that such a magnificent hunk of manhood would need to troll the streets for female attention? Of course, as a psychologist, I know better than to judge a book by its cover. Perverts come in all shapes and sizes.

My heartbeat finally began to slow down to something approaching normal. I had to say that was the most exciting thing that'd happened in weeks, which said a lot about the pathetic state of my social life.

I sat there for a few minutes until the adrenalin rush subsided and then shifted into drive. *I need a new office with a receptionist, a doorman and underground parking.* I drove out of the parking lot and steered the car along one of the many one-way streets that confounded the traffic in downtown Denver.

I caught a red light a few streets over, which gave me a moment to check out the nightlife in this popular part of town. I usually left my office before the fun and games started, so the streets familiar to me in daylight were a whole new world after dark. A magnificent old church, apparently converted into a busy nightclub, took up an entire city block. It really was a beautiful building. Such incredible stained glass. Funny that I'd never noticed it before. Groups of party-goers stood on the sidewalk, laughing and talking, performing one illegal act or another. Many of them were dressed in the same kind of costume Midnight had been wearing: so many potential clients all in one place! I briefly considered parking the car, mingling with the crowd and passing out my business cards. There had to be several books' worth of material to be gleaned from the characters hanging out in front of the gothic cathedral. But that would take bravery – or extroversion – I didn't have.

Just as the light turned green and I put my foot on the gas, I saw a tall man with long blond hair step down the entrance stairs. He nodded and waved at me when I passed.

Distracted and unnerved by the events of the last hour, I drove home to my new townhouse, punched in my security code and locked myself into my own personal sanctuary.

I lit an aromatherapy candle, poured myself a glass of white wine, sat down in my favourite chair – one of those huge puffy types with an equally large ottoman – and stretched out, letting my thoughts wander back to the blond man who'd waved at me.

That was just too weird. My mind must have been playing tricks on me. It couldn't possibly have been the same guy I saw in front of my building, could it? Well, wait a minute. That club was only a couple of blocks from my office and if he had been the same man who saw me run to my car, then it made sense that he could have recognised the car again when I passed him. It was merely a coincidence he was at that particular club, and that I noticed the place today.

Just a coincidence.

But the fact that he actually waved at me gave more weight to the notion that I'd overreacted and he hadn't meant me any harm.

Maybe.

Unless he was a sociopath who enjoyed messing with people's minds.

Oh well. No use fretting about that now. I would definitely be seeking a more secure office location. And some pepper spray.

I carried my glass of wine over to my desk, opened my briefcase, and spilled out all the vampire material I'd printed. Then I fired up my computer, clicked on the TV, and prepared to spend the next couple of hours researching possible topics for a new book.

'Allow me to introduce myself. I am Count Dracula,' blared from the speakers.

Startled, I looked up at the TV then laughed. There he was, the sexiest vampire ever: Frank Langella as Dracula, circa early 1980s. He had the best lips – pouty, full, and definitely come-hither – and eyes that wouldn't be denied. One of my college roommates had been a real vampire fan, and she had an extensive collection of bloodsucker movies. This version was her favourite.

I sat back and enjoyed watching Frank's lips for a while, savouring my glass of wine. As the end of the movie approached, I clicked off the TV, because I didn't want to watch those sweet lips get fried by the sun in the film's inevitable finale.

As I drank the last few sips in my glass, I had a sudden memory of the last time I'd watched that movie in college, sitting with my roommates and listening to them scream at the end, rooting for the vampire to break free and fly away. Afterwards they all talked about what fun it would be to invite some dark, window-tapping stranger into their beds.

Hmmm. I linked my fingers together behind my head. Vampires as erotic fantasy material. Listening to my roommates that long-ago night, the budding psychologist in me had been intrigued, but I considered vampires to be horror-movie and comic-book fare. I was not the kind of person who believed in the supernatural or the mystical. I'd found that most things turned out to have mundane, predictable explanations.

Of course, since then I'd taken the required class in Jungian Psychology in graduate school and I knew all about his theory of synchronicities – the interconnection between inner and outer realities based on the idea of a collective unconscious. Jung said that there are no coincidences and the universe functions through an unknowable intelligence. I could even agree with that on an abstract level. Yes, it did seem odd I was experiencing things that appeared to be related on the surface. But contemplating the cosmic possibilities of metaphysics was a hell of a lot different from believing in vampires.

Still. This had been one strange day.

CHAPTER 2

I spent most of Saturday immersed in my vampire research. It turned out there were millions of vampire pretenders in the world, and reading through some of the websites gave me a better understanding of the scope of the illusion. Most of the wannabes were very sad – young people searching for meaning, connection and love in a world where they hadn't found any. Some were simply drawn to the excitement, danger and forbidden fruit. Then there were the walking wounded who had crossed the line between acting out and psychosis.

By the time I woke up at dawn on Sunday morning, I had formulated a plan of action and I was excited. It had been a long time since I'd felt passionate about my work. I was going to become the Vampire Psychologist. Well, Vampire-Wannabe Psychologist, anyway. Starting Monday, I would run ads in all the local newspapers and online classifieds, offering both individual and group psychotherapy for vampires.

Yes, I thought, mentally rubbing my hands together, this had bestseller written all over it. I had found a brand-new dysfunction-of-the-week that mixed genuine mental illness with just enough scary occult sensationalism to make it a bona fide hit. Maybe I'd even get to go on *Oprah* or *Dr Phil*!

While I daydreamed about my impending stardom, my stomach growled in angry protest. When had I last eaten? I tended to forget mundane details such as food, and strolled into the kitchen to forage for something edible. As usual, the refrigerator was cluttered with old take-away boxes, the contents of which were no longer recognisable, along with bottled water and a substance that had probably once been cheese. My kitchen was a potent reminder that while I was exceptionally organised and efficient in my professional life, I was completely oblivious to its other aspects.

Shopping falls into the category of torture for me. Not only do I have all the impatience of my 'Type A' personality to deal with, but being around all those people – their energy, I guess, for lack of a better word – wipes me out. According to my parents, I'd always been 'too sensitive', too receptive to the moods of those around me. I suppose that's why I became a psychologist, but my sensitivity certainly complicated the rest of my life.

I spent most of my childhood thinking I was crazy – or cursed. Normal kids didn't spend time hiding in closets, talking to invisible friends, and picking up bits of people's thoughts. I learned very early to keep my weirdness to myself, to isolate so nobody would notice. It took years for me to integrate my extra senses, to acclimatise to the strange hand I'd been dealt.

And if my psychic 'gifts' weren't stressful enough, I always got teased in school for being a nerd. The 'brainy girl' with no fashion sense. The shy loner with her nose in a book, cowering in the corner. Thanks to my reclusive parents, I was the poster child for Social Anxiety. I just couldn't see the point of worrying about trivial things like parties, friends or clothes when there were so many mind-puzzles to solve. So many mental illnesses to cure. At least, that's what I told myself. I had a moment of feeling sad for the terrified child I'd been, always observing instead of living.

Another stomach growl prompted me to call my local deli for a breakfast bagel. Picking up the phone, I heard the beeping sound that told me I had messages.

I made coffee and poured myself a cup, then punched in the retrieval number to access my calls.

The first message made me grin. It was from Vaughan, the cute chiropractor I'd met when we'd both volunteered to answer phones at the local PBS fundraiser a couple of months ago. I think he'd called me once before, but I couldn't remember if I'd returned the call or simply thought about returning it. He really was adorable, with his light-green eyes, curly chestnut hair, and that delicious dimple. It probably wouldn't hurt to call him back. After my spectacular failures with men, I'd become such a wimp about dating. It was just so much easier to hole up at the library.

Hearing the next voice made my breath catch and my knees go weak. My heart pounded and my palms moistened. I grabbed the counter to keep my balance.

'How can he still do this to me after all this time?' I said aloud.

Dr Thomas Radcliffe. My first love. The man I'd been willing to change my life for. The man I'd thought was the answer to my prayers. The man who had told me I didn't excite him any more and who'd dumped me for an airy-fairy astrologer who wore crystals and smelled of patchouli oil. Even after all this time, thinking about him still made me want to cry. It had been two painful years, and I had only recently started to feel good about myself again. Two long years of going over everything I'd said and done, trying to understand what it was about me that hadn't been quite good enough for him. Shades of my lonely childhood.

'Kismet? Are you there? Tom Radcliffe here. Oh, well, I guess I'll leave a message. I know you'll be sad you missed my call, but I wanted to let you know I'll be in Denver for a conference and we should get together for lunch, catch up and touch base, do some networking. You have my cell phone number. Give me a call.'

'Catch up and touch base? Do some networking? You arrogant ass.' I forced myself to breathe as my heart rate calmed.

He always talked that way. Pompous. Oblivious. I wondered if his vocabulary had expanded to include all the astrological information he surely must be privy to now. Would he tell me that Mercury was up Uranus, and that's why he'd broken my heart? No matter. I had no intention of meeting him for lunch or anything else. The welcome mat had definitely been pulled out from under Tom Radcliffe. He might still have the keys to my libido, but the rest of me wouldn't be going along for the ride any more. I pressed the button to erase his message and called the deli.

After I'd eaten, I brought my laptop over to the table and wrote for a little while. Then I stretched the cramped muscles in my arms and checked the time. Since I had nothing planned for the day, I figured I could either work for a couple more hours, or I could break my routine and do something different

– maybe take a walk in that big neighbourhood park I'd been meaning to explore. Jefferson Park was Denver's equivalent of Central Park in New York City, and it had lots of trees, benches and trails. It was only a couple of blocks from my townhouse.

Yes, exercise. That was the ticket. I looked down at myself. Whether I liked it or not, it was clear that being physically inactive – sitting on my butt all the time – had a downside. I'd promised myself I'd rectify the fitness situation and gain some muscle in other places besides my brain. I changed into a comfortable dark-blue sweatsuit, put on my still-in-the-box walking shoes, and headed out the door.

Denver could be counted on to have over three hundred sunny days per year, and this late-October morning was a prime specimen. Actually, the fact that it was mostly sunny in Colorado was one of the few things I would have changed about a state that was, otherwise, paradise. Coming from the Midwest, I loved a good rainstorm and relished the introspective embrace of a grey, overcast day.

The first thing I noticed was how many walkers, joggers, runners, bicycle riders, skateboarders and pet-walkers were out on the park trails this early in the morning. And, even more interesting, was how many of them were holding Starbucks cups in their hands as they engaged in those activities. I marvelled at the level of physical coordination it must take to run and drink coffee at the same time.

'Kismet? Kismet! Is that you? I thought you lived around here someplace. You didn't call me back.'

My mouth went dry and my stomach churned. The voice was very familiar. Especially since I'd just listened to it on my voicemail. I wanted to pretend I hadn't heard and run as fast as I could in the opposite direction, but instead I turned around slowly and stared into the dark-brown eyes of Dr Thomas Radcliffe, my astrologer-humping ex-boyfriend.

Shit.

This wasn't how I'd imagined our first meeting would be after all this time. In my vision, I was dressed to the nines – painted, polished and gorgeous. He'd be overcome with remorse for his treatment of me and beg me to take him back. I, of course, would kick him to the kerb. But instead, here I was looking like something the vampire had dragged in, wearing a baggy old sweatsuit. I couldn't even remember if I'd brushed my hair before I left.

There was absolutely no justice in the universe because he hadn't changed a bit. He was still classically handsome and impeccably groomed. He could've been a model who'd just stepped out of *West Coast Magazine*. To add insult to injury, he'd finally grown out his thick black hair, which I'd repeatedly asked him to do during the time we were together. There's just something about a man with great hair.

'Tom. How nice to see you,' I lied, silently pleading with my facial muscles to transform what I was sure was a grimace into an acceptable smile.

I'll be damned if I'll let him know he still affects me.

He came over and almost-hugged me, one of those not-quite-embraces – complete with an air-kiss on either side of my face that are so popular among the rich and famous. 'You look just as I remember you.' Which made me want to knee him in the nuts.

He grinned and stretched his arms out to the sides, making

a show of his rippling biceps. 'You just popped into my head the other day and I decided to make it a point to see you when I came to Denver.'

Asshole. I just 'popped into his head'. So much for my fantasy of the daily inner torture I hoped he'd endured as he replayed the loss of me over and over in his mind.

I retreated from his pseudo-hug and made my face as neutral as possible. My gaze slid to his skin-hugging running tights and I noticed he still wasn't reluctant to advertise all his products and services. No matter how obnoxious he was, he did still possess certain . . . arousing . . . attributes. I fought a flood of memories and coaxed my eyes up to his face, straining my brain for something brilliant to say, but instead came out with the verbal equivalent of elevator music. 'You're still running every day?'

'Yes, indeed – got to keep one step ahead of Father Time.' He patted his tight abs.

Dr Cliché. I wonder if this man ever has an original thought.

He tugged on my arm and guided me over to a nearby bench and sat. 'Can we sit for a minute? Now that I've got you here, I'd love to catch up. What are you doing these days? Are you writing? Are you married?'

I reluctantly joined him on the bench. 'Well . . .' I managed to get that one word out before he launched into a monologue.

'Things are going so super for me. My private practice in San Francisco is booming, both because of the success of my last book and my radio programme. You wouldn't believe how busy I am and how in demand I am as a speaker. Did you see me on *Dr Phil*? I was one of the experts for a recent segment. Oprah's people are talking to my people. She's starting a new network – can you imagine what an appearance on one of her shows will do for my books? I live in a fabulous house in one of the finest sections of town and I just ordered a brand-new Ferrari. I'll take you for a ride the next time I see you ...'

I just stared at him as he went on with his manic rant. He didn't seem to notice that I hadn't spoken or that I was gaping at him like he was a nasty squished bug on my windshield. Had he always been this way? What *had* I been thinking? Had I really been so dazzled by his appearance that I'd ignored his self-absorption? More likely, I'd simply been so desperate for any kind of attention that I blocked out behaviours I didn't want to see. I amused myself for a few seconds by mentally thumbing through the list of personality disorders he fitted into.

Hmmm. Definitely Narcissistic Personality Disorder. And with his temper, maybe Borderline as well. Obsessive-Compulsive. Then there's the sex addiction ...

'So, whatever happened to Summer, the astrologer?' I interjected loudly, with what I hoped was an evil grin.

'Who? Oh, yes. She was a sweet thing. Simply adored me. Thought I walked on water. But we were from two different worlds, and she wasn't a good fit for where I was going. We parted the best of friends.'

Yeah, sure. I'll bet. I wonder what her version of the break-up is.

He glanced down at his diamond-studded watch. 'Oh, damn. Look at the time. I've got to hurry back and get dressed for my presentation. Hey, here's an idea – why don't you come to the conference with me, and you can listen to my lecture. I bet you'll really learn a lot from it. What do you say?'

How typical. He's jogging in a diamond watch.

'As tempting as that sounds,' I said sarcastically, which, judging by his solemn head-nodding, he'd totally missed, 'I'll have to pass. I have clients.'

'Bummer! It's a shame you can't attend, but I know how seriously you take your work.'

He said that as if it was a bad thing. He'd always viewed my refusal to join him in the fast lane as a character flaw, as well as a personal disappointment.

'Yeah.' I crossed my arms over my chest. 'It really is a drag that I'm too burdened with my mundane private practice to spend time discussing your superficial – er, *super* – life. Maybe the next time you're in town.'

He gave a quick pout – he actually poked his bottom lip out – patted my arm, then offered his fake 'I'm really just one of the guys' grin.

'I was going to keep this as a surprise for you, but I guess I can tell you now. I expect I'll be seeing a lot more of you as I'm doing a series of workshops in Colorado, and I'd love to discuss the possibility of using your office part-time while I'm here. Could we get together for dinner and talk about it?' He flashed me a toothy California smile.

Welcome to the wonderful world of Tom Radcliffe's ego. Plenty of room for everyone, folks, step right up. Watch out for the smelly little piles. Enter at your own risk.

He stood and began running in place. 'Tell you what – I'll just drop by your house after the conference is over next Friday night. I got your new address from a close friend who works for the APA Directory.'

'Hey!' I frowned. 'You're lying. Clinician contact information is confidential. No way they gave you my address. It's protected – I even paid extra to make sure.'

'Obviously, you don't remember how persuasive I can be. Especially after a few drinks in the right setting. Wouldn't you like to be reminded of my special skills?'

Before I could answer, 'Hell no,' he had jogged away backwards, yelling, 'I'll see you then.'

Suddenly, everything about Tom Radcliffe seemed hilarious. I sat on the bench and laughed out loud. Luckily, no clients were around to witness my temporary joyful insanity. I did have a reputation to uphold, after all. Sitting alone in the park laughing hysterically wouldn't be good for business.

How could I have been in love with such a narcissistic egomaniac? Such a superficial moron? I'd spent the last two years grieving and miserable, and now I couldn't for the life of me remember why. As long as we kept enough miles between us and a bedroom, I might never be tempted to recover the memory.

I had no doubt he'd got my address by seducing an APA employee. Ethics had no meaning in Tom Radcliffe's world. An official complaint was definitely in order.

I smiled through a brisk walk around the park and whistled all the way back to my house. Maybe my life was looking up.

The buzzing of the alarm clock woke me early on Monday, giving me plenty of time to do some writing and organise the online research I'd gathered before I had to leave for my appointment with my therapist, Nancy. I felt so energised by the vampire-wannabe project that by the time I realised I was hungry, it was too late to do anything about it. I'd missed last month's session, and I didn't want to be late for today's.

I drove to the Cherry Creek office and parked in front of her Victorian building.

'Nancy?' I knocked on the wood-panelled door frame.

'Come on in, Kismet.' She walked towards me, a warm smile on her face. 'Nice to see you – it's been a while.'

I strolled into her cosy psychotherapy office and squeezed the hands she'd held out to me in greeting. 'Hi. I'm sorry I had to cancel our last appointment. Client emergency.'

'Not a problem. We both know how it is.' She nodded towards a couple of oversize chairs. 'Let's get comfortable.'

'Yes, let's.' I sank into the soft cushions and sighed. 'I'm glad to be here today. I really need a session, lots going on.'

'Would you like some herbal tea? I just made one for myself.'

'No thanks. I'm good.' I propped my briefcase against the chair.

She sat across from me, Earth Mother incarnate. Full-figured, she wore a vibrant, multicoloured flowing dress, her long, curly white hair caught on top of her head with a jewelled butterfly clip. Bright-green eyes crinkled at the corners. 'That's a lovely suit. What an exquisite colour of blue – it really brings out your eyes. Is it silk?'

I looked down at my trouser-suit and brushed one of my long hairs from the sleeve. 'Yes, it is. I'm glad you like it. We can thank the good taste of the sales clerk for this outfit.' We often began our sessions with light conversation because Nancy wanted to give me a moment to settle before we began – a standard therapy technique. As calm and in-control as I remained when sitting in the other seat at my own office, like any client I always felt a little nervous about what the session might uncover.

'Well, let's get right to it, then. Where would you like to start?'

Nancy had been a psychologist for forty years, and I'd been seeing her for individual therapy for quite a while. She was my supervisor during part of my licensing process. After I completed the requirements, though I no longer needed supervision, I chose to continue working with her just because she was such a skilful and insightful counsellor. The fact that we also had a healthy mother-daughter dynamic in play didn't hurt my personal growth, either. It was never too late for quality parenting.

'I've had an exciting new development.' I bounced my foot absentmindedly.

'What?' She chuckled. 'You finally decided to stick your toe back into the dating pond again?' She lifted her cup and sipped. Nancy constantly teased me about my relationship anxiety.

'No.' I grinned. 'But we can talk about that later. I want to tell you about a new client and an idea for a book.'

'Excellent! Your writing muse has returned? Tell me everything.'

'A nineteen-year-old woman – girl? – I'm not sure what to call her, she's really both. Trying hard to be a grown-up, but immature. Very sweet. Confused. Anyway, she was referred to me by her parents because, according to the mother, she's obsessed with wanting to become a vampire.'

'A vampire?' Nancy replaced her cup on the nearby table.

'I guess that makes sense, with all the books and movies currently flooding the culture.'

'Exactly. Which is why I was so surprised to discover that nobody has written a book on the vampire-wannabe phenomenon.'

'There aren't any clinical texts on the subject?'

'Nothing I could find online.'

'So you're going to write one?' she asked, frowning.

'That's the plan.' I sat back and examined her expression. 'Hey, why are you frowning? You don't think it's a good idea? I would be the first psychologist to tackle the issue – talk show hosts would swarm out of the woodwork to book me as a guest.'

'Yes.' She nodded, her face serious. 'That's what troubles me.'

'I don't understand.' I thrust my hands out in front of me, palms up. 'I've been looking for a topic for my next book and nothing grabbed my interest. You encouraged me to find a cutting-edge clinical issue to study. Well, one dropped into my lap. Why don't you like it?'

She steepled her fingers under her chin. 'Are you sure that's the kind of attention you want to draw to yourself? Think about the therapists who specialise in alien-abduction hypnosis. Their professional credibility has suffered. They're associated with fringe, occult quackery rather than professional scholarship. They've diminished themselves rather than enhancing their standing in the psychotherapeutic community. I'd hate to see that happen to you.'

'Okay.' I nodded and tapped a finger on my leg. 'I can see why you'd worry about that – vampire wannabes and the whole goth-lifestyle situation tend to reek of reality TV. But if I handle the topic professionally, not allowing myself to focus on the sensationalist aspects, I believe this could be a worthwhile project. I mean, wouldn't there be general interest in the negative consequences of our social fixation with vampires? We really can't allow our teenagers and young adults to embrace the notion of the undead without professionals talking about the downsides, right?'

'When you put it that way, I suppose I have to agree a book on the repercussions would be useful. You'd have to make sure your presentation is always impeccable, though.'

I laughed and brought my hands together, as if in supplication. 'Impeccable is my middle name.'

That finally elicited a smile from her. 'I thought you said "Nerd" was your middle name?'

'Very funny,' I said, appreciating her, 'but sadly true. So, you really think the idea has merit?'

'Perhaps.' She raised a shoulder.

Nancy the Inscrutable.

'Of course, I don't even know what I'm dealing with yet. Meeting one wannabe and hearing about others doesn't legitimise a syndrome or disorder. I'll need to do careful research before I even know if the topic is viable. Would you be willing to read the proposal, just to keep me on the professional straight and narrow?'

'Certainly.' She nodded. 'I'd be pleased to give you feedback about this book, just as I did on your others. I'm glad to hear you understand the kind of slippery slope these media-driven topics can be.'

'I do.' I rubbed my palms together. 'And I'm really excited about this idea. Vampire wannabes – who knew? My young client says there are *tons of vampires* in Denver. She's obviously influenced by a wannabe love interest, probably some gorgeous young Robert Pattinson look-alike. Maybe I can get him to come in for therapy, too.' I laughed, feeling more and more confident about the idea. 'Then there are all the *Twilight* Moms, grown women fixated on the books and the young actors. I might have to open up psychotherapy franchises to handle all the vampire wannabes and the bloodsucker obsessed!'

'Well,' Nancy said, shaking her head, 'be careful what you ask for. And don't discount the likelihood that some of these people could be dangerous.'

'Yes, ma'am.' I made the cross-my-heart gesture. 'I'll keep my wooden stakes handy.'

'So.' She smiled. 'Have you been thinking about taking an emotional risk? Going out on a date? Even having a male friend?'

'Crap.' *She never misses.* 'And I was having such a good time talking about vampires. I should know better than to try to distract you from busting my defence mechanisms. You're like a heat-seeking missile for avoidance attempts. Yes, Dr St John, I have been thinking about it. It isn't as easy as you make it sound, you know.'

'Kismet, here's a good opportunity for you to confront some of your childhood demons. You've said your fear of social situations started very early. You never got the opportunity to learn about healthy relationships – your parents are withdrawn academics who tuck their pens into little plastic things in their shirt pockets. Even today they're stereotypical scientists. Their idea of getting together with friends consisted of inviting others to your home for lectures, very cerebral lectures that you were required to attend and give a report on.'

'Yeah.' I paused, thinking about my parents. 'You've got a good memory. I never really was a child – my parents treated me like a colleague rather than an offspring.' I laughed, and reached into the side pocket of my briefcase to pull out a pair of black-rimmed glasses. 'I bought these at a drugstore when I was twelve years old so I could look smart, like their students at the university.' I studied the glasses for a few seconds. 'I don't know why I keep them.' I shrugged.

'Don't you?'

Let's not go there today.

'Not consciously.'

She gave the therapist's nod. 'We can explore that when you're ready. You said your desire to be a psychologist, to actually mingle with other human beings, baffled your parents.' Nancy retrieved her teacup. 'They couldn't comprehend why you'd want to specialise in the messy realm of emotions rather than pure logic, why you'd want to discuss meaningless things like feelings.'

'Yes.' I inhaled a deep breath and released it. 'If my mother ever did anything as time-wasting as embroidery, she'd have stitched that saying onto a pillow – Feelings Are Meaningless. It took me years to acknowledge some of my own emotions without guilt.' Talking about my parents always caused a heavy sensation in my stomach. I returned the glasses to the briefcase and shook off the negative energy from my mental visit to the past. 'I don't wear the glasses any more, and as long as I keep the conversation on psychology, I can make a little small talk at conferences. I've come a long way.'

'You have.' Nancy looked at me with compassion in her eyes. 'You should be very proud of yourself. But, as we've discussed before, if you really want to increase your confidence around men and have a good relationship at some point, you'll need to take the next step. What if you set a goal of walking up to a handsome man and starting a conversation? Can you imagine that?'

'Gak!' I held my hands up, forming a cross with my index fingers as if warding off a vampire. 'Why don't you just ask me to shed my clothes and run down the 16th Street Mall?'

'Really?' Her eyebrows rose. 'You actually see those things as equal? Kismet! What are we going to do with you? I know you had a bad experience with your ex-boyfriend Tom—'

'Tom!' I smacked my palms against my thighs. 'I can't believe I forgot. I saw him yesterday. He's in Denver. It was wonderful.'

'Wonderful? Tom?' She pressed a hand against her chest as her mouth dropped open. 'Please don't tell me you decided to get back together with him. We talked about what a flawed individual he is.'

'Get back together with him? Not in this or any other reality. The wonderful part was the lightbulb that went off over my head. Lightbulb? Hell – it was a red-carpet spotlight! I finally saw him with absolute crystal clarity. I don't know why I couldn't see it before, but that doesn't matter. For the first time since I met him years ago, I felt nothing. Well, revulsion, certainly, but nothing that would make me lose my mind and reconcile. It was a great experience! I wish you could've been there.'

Caught up in my enthusiasm, Nancy clapped her hands.

'Yes! I'm so happy for you. Maybe setting the new goal won't seem so out of the question now?'

I gave a loud sigh and sat back in my seat. 'Even thinking about talking to a good-looking man gives me cramps. I'm such a coward.' Acknowledging that fact felt bad, even to Nancy, whom I trusted.

'You aren't a coward,' Nancy said, shaking a finger in my direction. 'You simply never learned to be social, to make non-professional small talk. You know shy people are totally misunderstood. It's not as if you choose to feel the way you do.' She drank from her cup again and replaced it on the table.

If you really knew me – knew about the weird psychic flashes – you might see me differently. Hearing things other people don't hear. Seeing things, feeling things. My childhood was a strange trip down a demented Yellow Brick Road. I'm not brave enough to tell even you about that. Right now I know you're worried about me. You wish you could go back and heal my childhood and you're afraid I'll never get past the hurtful experiences. I wish I could tell you how scary it is to be like me. I don't want to know those things. Makes me feel crazy. Especially since I can't count on the abilities – they only show up when they want to. Maybe I have more in common with my clients than I think.

'Yes, well.' I kept my voice light and steady, 'talking about it's the easy part. I think it will take a miracle to blast me out of my nerd persona.' I pointed to my feet. 'I'm lucky I remember to wear matching shoes. Hey' – I laughed – 'maybe my client can introduce me to one of her imaginary vampires and he can entrance me with his hypnotic eyes and change my personality. That would be something to write about, wouldn't it?'

She smiled, completely aware of my distracting manoeuvre. 'I have absolute faith in your ability to take on any challenge you set for yourself. And I'm always here to help.'

We consulted on a couple of my long-term clients and talked about an upcoming conference, then I left and drove to my office.

I rode up in the elevator and walked along the hallway. The door to my waiting room was open. The cleaning crew had probably forgotten to lock it again. I wasn't expecting anyone for another hour, at least.

'Midnight?'

My newest client sat, tapping her feet on the carpet, dressed in a floor-length dark-blue dress adorned with sparkling stars, and a burgundy velvet cape. The sleeves were long enough to cover her arms all the way to mid-hand. Black lace-up stiletto-heeled boots completed the outfit.

'Oh, hi, Dr Knight. I hope you don't mind that I came early. I know my appointment isn't until later.'

She doesn't seem upset. But she's acting different . . .

'Is everything okay?'

Her lips spread, showing her delicate fake fangs. 'Yes. Everything's fine.' She held up a large leather portfolio. 'I just couldn't wait. After our meeting I got all kinds of ideas for drawings, and since you sort of inspired them, I wanted to get here early and show them to you.' Her smile crumpled and her gaze skimmed the carpet. 'But you're probably too busy to look at pictures. I should've thought of that.'

She expects me to reject her.

'Drawings? You're willing to share them with me? That's great. Please, come on in – I'd love to see them.'

We walked across the waiting room. She flashed a little-girl smile and stood, clutching the portfolio against her chest, waiting for me to unlock the door to my office.

This is a good sign.

I escorted her inside, closed the door, and set my briefcase on my desk.

'How do you want to do this?' I asked. 'You can display them on the couches and chairs, or however you like.'

'Okay. I'll set them up.' She literally skipped into the room.

To give her some privacy, I opened my briefcase and rummaged inside, looking for my appointment book. Then I turned on my computer, watching her arrange her display out of the corner of my eye.

'I'm ready. Come and look,' she said, hugging herself. 'I'll tell you about each of the sketches. Some of them are just rough outlines, so don't expect much.'

I walked over to stand next to her in front of the longest couch where she'd propped several pencil drawings of people. 'Oh, wow – these are gorgeous,' I said, and meant it. 'You are really talented.'

'Really?' She straightened, obviously pleased. 'You think so? This is a picture of my mother.' She pointed to a sketch of a tired-looking, sad woman staring off into space. Despite the hopelessness of the picture, it was apparent the woman was beautiful – or had been, before life wore her down. I didn't know anything about art or drawing, but even I could tell the work was excellent.

'Midnight, you really have a gift. That's an amazing picture of your mother. I can see the resemblance between you.'

'Yeah.' She studied the face on the page. 'She used to say we were twins born twenty years apart. But she doesn't say things like that any more.' She shifted her eyes to the next paper. 'This is my father. I drew this one from a photo of him when he was younger. When he still cared about anything besides alcohol.' The sketch showed a very nice-looking, smiling man standing next to a vintage Ford Mustang.

It didn't take keen intuition to feel the waves of yearning rolling off Midnight as she stared at her father and mourned what she'd lost.

'He's a very handsome man. You have his eyes, don't you?'

'Yes.' She touched the picture. 'I do have his eyes,' she said softly. 'I wish I had him,' she said on a whisper, probably assuming I hadn't heard.

She grieves for him as if he's dead.

'Who is this?' I pointed to a rough drawing of a pretty young woman about Midnight's age.

'This is my cousin Anne. She lives down in Durango. We get to see each other every few months or so. She's really the one who turned me on to the vampires. Or on to vampire books, anyway.' She laughed. 'She's a *Twilight* fanatic. I can't wait to tell her about all my new friends.'

Ah, the secret imaginary playmates . . .

'You haven't told your cousin about the vampires?'

'No.' She shook her head vigorously. 'I'm not allowed to. Besides, she probably wouldn't believe me.'

Hmm. Maybe she doesn't totally believe, either. Her emotions are all jumbled up.

'Do you have any sketches of your new friends?' I wasn't sure if she was willing to share any of her vampire fantasy with me yet, but it couldn't hurt to ask.

She hesitated, then walked to another couch where she'd laid out several smaller pictures. 'Uh-huh. I've done several of them. I'm not sure I've drawn them as beautiful as they are, but you can get a general idea.'

I joined her and stared down at the renderings: one perfect ethereal face after another. If these were fragments of her imagination, her creative abilities knew no bounds. 'These drawings could be in a gallery, Midnight. They're outrageously good.'

'Thank you.' She smiled shyly and tucked her hair behind her ear. 'But I really can't take a lot of credit for these. All I did was copy what I saw – they really do look like this.'

She would make a remarkable fantasy artist. I hope she just has talent rather than delusions.

A lone sketch sat on one of the chairs. But this one was different from the others: she'd created this portrait with coloured pencils. Staring back at me from the paper was the most beautiful male face I'd ever seen: pale skin, light-blond hair, indescribable eyes.

What the hell? This looks like the man outside my building. The blond who waved to me from the steps of the old church. Midnight knows this man? No way. That's too weird.

I reached down to lift the sheet and heard a deep male voice call my name:

'Kismet . . .'

'What?' The room spun. Feeling suddenly dizzy, alternately cold and hot, I dropped the drawing.

'Dr Knight?' Midnight touched my arm. 'Are you okay?'

'Yes.' I took a deep breath. 'Of course. I just got caught up in looking at your amazing artwork.'

What the hell just happened? That'll teach me to skip meals. My blood sugar must have taken a dive when I leaned over. I'll make a quick dash out for food after Midnight's appointment. Or maybe I'm coming down with something.

'I'm glad you like the pictures. I was nervous about showing you. I don't ever do that. Show them, I mean.'

Breathe, Kismet.

'I love the drawings. And it's great that you trust me enough to share them with me. I appreciate that.' I smiled and pointed at the images. 'Do you want to leave them out while we have our session, or would you like to put them away?'

She thought for a few seconds, then retrieved her portfolio. 'I think I'll put them away for now.'

While she gathered the art, I picked up my pad and pen from an end table and sat in my usual chair, trying to recover from the strange sensations. I practised a few seconds of conscious breathing and felt myself calm.

Maybe I shouldn't keep blowing off my yearly exams. What if I'm pre-diabetic or something?

She started to sit across from me, then moved further away. I wasn't surprised. After taking the huge step of exposing her inner world through her artwork, it made sense she'd need to retreat and reassert her defences.

'So, Midnight, what would you like to talk about today?'

'I want to talk about Dev and the vampires.' She nodded as if she was trying to convince herself, then laughed. 'Hey, that sounds like the name of a band.'

What? Really? No way! I thought this would take weeks.

Surprise must have shown on my face because she grinned. 'You weren't expecting that, were you? You didn't think I'd tell you about them yet.'

'You're very insightful, and quite right – I wasn't expecting it. You told me on Friday that Dev didn't want you to talk about him. Why have you changed your mind?'

Is she questioning the control this boy has over her?

'Well.' She tapped her hands on the arms of the chair. 'Two reasons. One, I've decided to be honest with you because I like you.'

'Thank you. I like you, too.'

'And second, because Dev told me to.'

So much for questioning his control ... But that's okay. Don't jump to conclusions. There's lots of time to tweak their relationship.

'Hmm. I wonder why Dev would ask you to tell me these secrets?'

She unclipped her cape at her throat and shrugged it off her shoulders. 'He said therapy wouldn't do me any good if I didn't tell the truth.'

Maybe this boy has more going for him than I thought. Or maybe this is his way of asking for help. Midnight is certainly fixated on him.

'How does the idea of telling me the truth make you feel?'

'A little scared, because I've never told anyone about this before. But I liked what you said last time about me being courageous. So that's what I'm trying to be.'

That's progress.

'Wonderful. Being emotionally courageous can be a difficult thing. It's great that you're challenging yourself.' I gave her an encouraging smile. 'So, the vampires. Tell me about them.'

I'm picking up strong intuitive feelings about Twilight *and* Vampire Diaries. *I wonder which one most influenced her fantasy?*

'What do you want to know?'

'Why don't you just start at the beginning?'

She nodded. 'Okay. I met the vampires right after I graduated from high school last year. My friends all went down to this cool club that used to be a huge old church in the funky section of downtown – it's called The Crypt. It's only a few blocks from here. We've got the best fake IDs, so we just slide right in. But it's weird – even though we've got the perfect IDs and they let us in, they never let us buy alcohol. If we go up to the bar, the bartender just laughs at us. Pisses me off. What's up with that?'

'Hmm.' I scribbled notes on my pad. It was always a delicate dance to get the words on paper without letting my clients feel abandoned by my split attention. I always wound up with a cramp in my hand after each session from all the fast writing.

Interesting that the club won't sell drinks to her. Maybe they've got in trouble for serving minors before?

She worried her bottom lip with the tip of one of her fangs, as if it gave her time to think before speaking again. 'Anyway, there are several levels to the club and one of them, down in the basement – we call it the dungeon – is private. There are curtains over the doorway, but one time, my friend Emerald and I, we waited 'til the guy who was guarding the door left for a minute and then we sneaked down and peeked in through the crack and saw all these amazing people,' she reported, an expression of awe on her face from the memory.

'Amazing people?'

'Yeah, two different kinds, really. A whole bunch of kids around my age, maybe a few years older, all dressed up, sort of goth, but not really, wearing white paint on their faces and red on their lips. Then there were the others. So beautiful. They wore regular stuff like leather, and didn't have the white makeup on, but they were totally awesome. They looked a little older, maybe in their 20s or 30s, and they all had gorgeous long hair . . .' She stared off for a moment, her mouth hanging loosely open, lost in the vision.

'So they were totally awesome?'

She nodded slowly. 'Totally.'

'And then what happened?'

Am I sure I want to know?

'We were just standing there, scoping out the room, and a hand came through the curtains, opened them, and the hottest guy I've ever seen asked if we wanted to come in. Emerald didn't want to go – she's afraid of everything – but I really wanted to check out all those people, so I said yes. The gorgeous man reached out, took my hand and actually kissed the back of it and said his name was Devereux. I thought I was going to pass out just from looking at him. There was something about his eyes–' She paused and glanced over at me, trying to gauge my reaction before she shared any more details.

Man? Wait! Dev is an adult? *Not a kid? Holy shit. That changes everything.*

The muscles in my neck and back tightened, which happened sometimes when I worked too hard at holding in all the opinions that wanted to tumble out of my mouth. I bit my bottom lip to stifle myself. Often, having to remain silent was the hardest part of my job.

She met a strange man in a bar. A man dressed in leather, who invited her into a private room. What's wrong with this picture?

'And then?'

'Then he sort of led me inside and Emerald followed us. There must have been fifty people in that room, and they were all incredible. Dev walked us over to a table, and he was so polite. He pulled out the chairs for us, like in the old movies, and asked if we wanted something to drink. We both ordered beers – we had to try – but he brought us Cokes, and we just sat there, staring at him. He wasn't drinking anything, and I asked why not. He said he'd already had his fill for the night, and he just kept smiling and flashing us with those psychedelic eyes. I didn't know what he meant back then, but I do now.'

Uh-oh.

'What do you mean?'

'Well, he drinks blood, you know? That's what vampires do. So when he said he was full, he meant he'd already "eaten" for the night,' she explained, her voice light and casual, as if we were talking about the weather.

He drinks blood? Yuck. Did he tell her that or is that fantasy? If he really does, can you say 'mental illness'?

'Do you drink blood?'

That, obviously, was a loaded question, because Midnight started scraping her lower lip against her upper teeth. She twisted the fabric of her dress in her hands and stared down into her lap.

'Midnight? Are you all right?'

'Yeah.' She squirmed in the chair. 'It just feels scary to talk about this.'

'Do you mean because of what your family would think?'

'No.' She hesitated. 'Because of what Dev would do if he found out.' Her voice softened. 'We're not allowed to drink blood.'

Thank heavens for that.

'We'll come back to the blood in a minute. What's your relationship with Dev?' I was becoming more and more suspicious of this charismatic-sounding character.

Catching the drift of my concern, Midnight shook her head. 'He's just a friend. All the girls are after him, but he said we're too young and that he's into older women. We all hit on him, but he never goes out with any of us. He's in charge – the boss, I guess.'

'The boss of what?'

'The vampires. And the apprentices.'

'The apprentices?' I had a sudden vision of several vampire wannabes sitting around a conference table in New York with Donald Trump. A vampire Donald Trump. I fought to keep the amusement from creeping onto my face. My sense of humour was such a challenge sometimes.

'That's what we call ourselves.'

How much weirder can this get? I need to know about the blood.

'Let's go back to the drinking blood part. You seemed to have a strong reaction when I asked you about that. Why?'

She lowered her eyes. 'Dev lets us hang around with him and the other vampires, but he won't let anyone take blood from us and he won't let us drink blood either. He said that only real vampires can use blood the way it's meant to be used. Since we're officially still human, we could get diseases that vampires can't get. He has lots of rules about what we can and can't do if we want to be with them.'

Okay, so maybe the guy isn't totally wacked if he keeps them from the drinking blood thing.

'So what is it you don't want him to know?'

Long pause.

I waited silently and watched waves of conflicting emotions flow across her face as she decided what, if anything, she was going to tell me.

'There's this one guy, Eric, who wants to be a vampire real bad. Dev told him that he isn't ready, that he needs to go out and learn about life before becoming one of the undead, but Eric doesn't listen. He sets up these rituals at his apartment, where the apprentices drink each other's blood. He gave us all these neat little necklaces with tiny knives on them so we can make little cuts in each other's necks and drink,' she said, her voice breathy. 'It would be really bad if Dev found out because he'd be totally angry, and I don't want to do anything to make Dev mad at me.'

My eyebrows crawled up towards my hairline.

The apprentices drink each other's blood? Damn!

I hoped she was simply acting out and all this blood-drinking was imaginary. I needed to find a non-threatening way to convince her that the entire vampire idea was a fantasy.

'Are you afraid of Dev?'

'No. Not the way you mean.'

'But despite Dev's disapproval, you go to the rituals at Eric's apartment?'

'Well, yeah.' She smiled wide. 'It's so much fun. I never would have thought that drinking blood could be so sexual – so romantic,' she gushed.

Blood-drinking as an aphrodisiac?

I tried very hard to keep the neutral expression on my face. 'Sexual? Romantic? What happens at these rituals?'

AIDS! Not to mention viruses, bacteria, and horrors I can't even comprehend. What about infections from the cuts? Red alert, Kismet.

'Well, first we order a pizza or something and drink some wine, maybe get high, just the same as any other night. Then we pick a partner, and after we take turns drinking a little blood – not much, just a couple of teaspoons – we have sex. It's the most amazing feeling. I let Eric cut my boob last week and suck on it. It was so hot.'

My breath caught. *Is this what she thinks intimacy is? Where did these ideas come from?*

'Are you having safe sex?'

'Don't worry about that.' She nodded vigorously. 'I've got a purse full of condoms!'

I tried to visualise a condom big enough to fit over Eric's entire body. I didn't want to come off as sermonising or lecturing because she wouldn't come back, but I had to find a way to communicate to her how dangerous this choice was.

'Midnight, what about the diseases you can get through blood transmission? What about AIDS? Drinking blood is very dangerous.'

'Vampires can't get diseases.'

Hormone-riddled teenage brain at work here.

'Eric and the other apprentices are just regular guys, aren't they? Human?'

Midnight stared into her lap, silent.

Holy crap. What am I supposed to do about this?

'Will you consider holding off on any more cutting and blood-drinking activities until we explore the possible conse-quences more thoroughly?'

She stayed silent for so long that I feared she might leap up and flee the office, but she finally clicked her tongue against the back of her teeth. 'I guess.'

I let out the breath I'd been unconsciously holding. *Whew. Talk about a pregnant pause. Even if she's just humouring me, it's a start.*

'Thank you, Midnight. I appreciate your open mind and your willingness to trust in our work together. So, outside of the rituals at Eric's apartment, the apprentices mostly just dress up and hang around with Dev and his vampire friends at the club downtown?'

She nodded.

'Tell me more about Dev.'

She got that faraway look in her eyes again and lifted out of the subdued mood she'd retreated into.

'He really rocks. So hot. He's over six feet tall. I am so into tall guys. Gorgeous long blond hair, aqua – not blue, not green, but aqua – eyes, and a killer bod. He's always wearing some kind of tight dark leather.' She sighed and drifted off again for a moment.

Hmmm. That does sound interesting.

Chuckling, I said, 'I get the picture. But what's his story? Why is he hanging out at a bar in downtown Denver? What does he do? Who is he?'

'He doesn't talk much about that. He told me once that he's been a vampire for eight hundred years and that he really loves Colorado because the mountains remind him of some place in Europe he lived before he died. He said he's only been here in the United States for about thirty years. Before that, he lived in some country where they speak a weird language, and he has a funny accent. But an amazing voice. He seems to have a ton of money. He has this excellent loft down the street from the bar, which, by the way, he also owns. The loft is so cool. Sometimes he lets us come over and blast some tunes, and he always keeps lots of food around, even though he doesn't eat any of it.'

He's been a vampire for eight hundred years? That's quite a wild story. Why does this supposedly gorgeous, wealthy man hang around with teenagers? He invites them to his loft but has lots of rules for them. Does he see himself as a father figure? Or is he a clever predator?

I shifted my gaze to the clock and back. 'Dev sounds like an interesting man and I'd like to hear more about him, but we're out of time for today. Can you come back tomorrow?'

'Sure. I don't have much else to do during the day when all the vampires are asleep.'

This is much more serious than I thought. If this man actually exists, it isn't going to be easy to convince her that his vampire claim isn't real. She's besotted.

'Thanks for telling me the story,' I said. 'It helps me to know you better. I look forward to discussing the vampires – and Dev – in greater detail.'

She nodded, smoothed her dress then draped her cape on her shoulders. 'It's good to talk to somebody about it. I have to be careful what I tell anyone. Even Emerald.'

Can't even tell her friend? Predators isolate and control their victims, threaten them to keep the secrets.

I walked over to my desk and collected the appointment book. We settled on a time for the next day and she left. I would have to rearrange my schedule to squeeze her in, but it couldn't be helped. Midnight's situation had escalated from troubling to dangerous.

After my last client that evening, I updated files and added progress notes. My attention kept returning to Midnight and my clear sense that she'd got caught up in a sick situation she was unprepared for. The more I thought about it, the greater the realisation that I had no firm foundation for establishing an effective treatment. I didn't know if her vampire tale was completely delusional, and none of the characters she mentioned actually existed, or if she was involved with individuals who were taking advantage of her naïveté for nefarious purposes and encouraging the fantasy. Both choices sucked, no pun intended.

Maybe I could find out if any of the people involved were under eighteen and get social services involved. Role-playing predators. What was next?

Clearly, I needed more resources. Luckily, one of Denver's few remaining independent bookstores, The Torn Cover, was conveniently located a few blocks from my office. I decided to swing by on my way home and check their large selection of psychology books to see what I could find. Since the store would still be open for a couple of hours and I hadn't eaten much during the day, I stopped in the restaurant next door for a sandwich and a glass of wine.

I was halfway through my meal when a very attractive man entered and sat at the bar. Dressed in a flattering dark suit, his wavy light-brown hair skimmed the collar of his shirt and his strong features created an appealing profile. My entire body tensed up. I hadn't been exaggerating when I told Nancy that being in the presence of a great-looking male – in a non-work situation – brought out the worst in me. She knew some of the facts about my childhood, but not all of them. I was a classic example of Post-Traumatic Stress Disorder. My shyness had been a beacon, attracting every predator in the environment, including the popular handsome boys who'd taunted me. Even now, part of me wanted to regress into a stammering adolescent, waiting for the next cruel prank or hateful humiliation.

The table I'd chosen was in a dark corner, so I figured I was safe. Invisible. I wouldn't even have to be polite, and, once again, I'd keep the world from discovering my acute social discomfort. Not that the world cared, of course, but I clung to my illusions. Maybe it was just me who didn't want to face them.

Just as I drank the last swallow of wine, the man turned on his stool, stared directly at me and smiled. He lifted his wineglass in my direction.

Okay. Here's my opportunity to connect with a man. How hard can it be? Just smile back, Kismet. Nothing bad will happen.

My heart tripped and my stomach muscles tightened.

Maybe next time ...

As a psychologist, I knew several techniques to calm anxiety. I'd mastered many of them. And they often worked. But if I could distance myself – flee – that was always my option of choice.

I made a quick, ungraceful exit from the restaurant, bumping a table as I passed, and entered the bookstore. I didn't have the nerve to look back to check the man's reaction to my hasty retreat.

What a wack-job, Kismet.

As usual, I was annoyed at myself for not being able to confront my issue. Once again I'd been ridiculous and childish, reacting as if every man was out to hurt me, and I wasn't strong enough to handle it. I thought about Nancy's challenge – her suggestion that I walk up to a handsome man and just make conversation. I cringed.

Get a grip, Kismet! You're supposed to be an expert at these things. You can do it! Force yourself. Stop being a wuss. Just find a man and go say hello. Pretend he's a client. You don't have any problems talking to male clients. You're good at hiding behind your professional persona. This weird behaviour only happens in your personal life.

Browsing through the bookshelves soothed me, and I soon found myself engrossed in reading the titles on the spines. Determined to deal with my fear, I lifted a new release off the shelf, opened it, and pretended to skim the page while looking around for an appropriate male. After a couple of minutes, I noticed a man in a tan business suit perusing the computer section on the shelf behind me. Giving myself a pep talk, I gathered my will and turned, planning to inch over to where I thought he was standing. I bumped into his back. He'd obviously moved.

'Oh! I'm so sorry – please excuse me.'

He barely looked up from the book he held. 'No problem.'

When I just stood there, he gave me his full attention. 'Yes?'

'Uh.'

He raised his left hand, displaying a wedding band. 'I'm married. But thanks anyway.' He replaced the book on the shelf and strode down the aisle.

Shit. How embarrassing.

My cheeks burned. Feeling like the biggest idiot on the planet and fighting the strong urge to run away, I forced myself to return to my original task: looking for vampire-wannabe resource material. The more I retreated into my psychologist role, the better I felt.

'Excuse me?'

I glanced up at the very pleasant-looking man standing next to me, smiling. My hands went clammy. 'Yes?' *Okay. Just smile. This doesn't have to be a big deal.*

'Do you work here? I could use some help finding—'

'No,' I interrupted, smile frozen on my face. 'I don't. Sorry.' That wasn't the first time I'd been mistaken for a clerk. I was good at blending into the scenery. Chameleon Kismet. Why did I even bother?

That was all the social interaction I could handle. I set the book I'd used as a prop on the table and hurried away.

It was clear that if it were up to me, I'd never have another personal relationship. Apparently I couldn't practise what I preached. Maybe I should just get a dog or a fish, and be done with it.

CHAPTER 3

The next day Midnight arrived for her appointment wearing her white makeup and the fake fangs. Instead of being shrouded in a long cape, she was dressed like that campy TV vamp, Elvira, Mistress of the Dark, in a very low-cut, cleavage-enhancing tight black dress. She glided into the room and bonelessly melted into the chair. She appeared to be in an upbeat mood.

I picked up my pad and pen and sat down. 'It's nice to see you again, Midnight. I can't help but notice that you're smiling a lot today. What's got you in such fine spirits?'

How can she even function wearing those silly fangs?

'I met someone.' Her grin spread wider.

Now we're talking. I settled back in my chair. *Maybe a nice college guy or hi-tech entrepreneur?*

'He must really be something to light you up this way. Tell me about him.'

'He's one of the new vampires who's started coming to the club. His name is Bryce, and he is so hot.' She twisted a spider ring on her left thumb. 'I've seen him hanging out for a couple of weeks, but it wasn't until yesterday that he came over and talked to me. We spent the whole night together, and it was like a dream. The first time I ever had sex with a real vampire.'

What? Sex with a strange vampire wannabe? I struggled to keep the dismay from my face. To give myself a moment to regroup, I jotted down a couple of notes on the pad. *Well.* I gave a mental sigh. *I guess it was too much to hope that the fantasy would start to fade already. I wonder if they'd take away my licence if I locked her in a closet until she passes through this phase?*

I met her eyes. 'You had sex with a stranger?'

Her body language altered ever so slightly, just enough for me to notice that my question had pushed a button.

'That makes it sound bad or dirty. It wasn't dirty. It was beautiful. We just got swept away.' She almost sang the last two words. Still smiling, she carefully smoothed out the wrinkles in her dress, avoiding eye-contact.

I wish someone would throw away the book that we women keep handing down to each other. The one with all the ridiculous reasons why we lose our minds in the presence of some man or other.

'How old is Bryce?' I asked.

She examined the blood-coloured fingernails on her right hand. 'I'm not sure. I don't think he's as old as Devereux – around three hundred, maybe? – but he looks about thirty.'

He's three hundred years old? Well, I did ask.

'Don't you think he might be a bit too old for you? What are you hoping will happen between the two of you?'

'I think he's the one I've been waiting for.'

Waiting for? You're only nineteen. I need some magic words here.

I started to respond, but just then she turned her head and stared out the window, deep in thought. I waited, and after a while she brought her gaze back to me, all the joy wiped from her face. 'Bryce says he'll bring me over if I want.'

'Bring you over?'

'Make me a vampire.'

Okay. She said she wants to be a vampire, and this guy is offering to help her out, but it doesn't appear that she thinks it's a good thing. She's definitely sending out mixed signals. What's really going on here?

I noted she'd raised her chin at the end of her last statement, echoing the attitude of defiance that had also crept into her voice, so I decided to push the envelope a bit.

'I thought Dev wouldn't let you do that. Have you talked to him about your new guy?'

Come on, Dev, be a father figure instead of a predator. It sounds like Bryce wants that job.

'No.' Her fists tightened in her lap. 'He hates Bryce. He already asked me to stay away from him, but why should I? Why shouldn't I have a relationship with Bryce? Who is Dev to make those decisions for me? He isn't my father.'

Ah. Bingo.

'Did he tell you why he wanted you to stay away from Bryce?'

The anger that had started out as a slow leak now flooded the room. Her intensity crashed into me like a wave. I breathed into the tight muscles.

'He said Bryce is one of the bad guys, that he uses people and he doesn't care about anyone but himself. Then I had to sit there while he went on and on about how vampires are no different from humans – there are good ones and bad ones – and how I'm not "mature" enough to know the difference. Who does he think he is? He doesn't care that I've finally found someone who wants me.'

She burst into tears.

And the wall comes tumbling down . . .

I moved the tissue box closer to her and said softly, 'It sounds like Dev hurt your feelings.'

She blew her nose and nodded.

'Why is Dev so important to you?'

'He's the first person who ever paid any attention to me.' She sobbed for a few seconds. 'I hoped he'd change his mind about me being too young for him. I really love him, and he treats me like a kid.'

'That must be very frustrating.'

'Yeah.' She sighed. 'But I know he cares about me. Just not the way I want him to.'

'Is it possible that having a big-brother type of love might be special in its own way? After all, having someone who watches out for you is worth a lot.'

'I never thought of it that way.' She frowned and paused to consider it. 'Maybe I should talk to him?'

I nodded and relaxed my tight shoulders. 'I think that would be an excellent idea.'

Maybe this Dev guy isn't so screwed up after all.

We sat quietly for a couple of minutes.

'Midnight, are you seriously considering becoming a vampire?'

'Becoming a vampire' had started to sound like a euphemism to me, and I was sensing the same vibe I got when a client hinted about suicide without actually saying the words.

'I don't know. Last night Bryce and I took a little blood

from each other. It's the first time a real vampire has bitten me. He did it while we were having sex, which felt great, but I think I must have passed out for a while because I couldn't remember what happened after that. He said he had chosen me because I was ready. I don't want to let him down.'

Let him down?

Bryce was setting off all my inner alarms. I wished I could see the skin on her neck hidden by all that hair so I could tell if she had any cuts or bite marks.

Did he drug her? He's obviously playing into the vampire fantasy. Is he a manipulative slimeball or something even worse?

'I thought we made an agreement that you'd hold off on any blood-drinking activities until we talked about it first? What if Bryce has some kind of illness? Is he worth dying for?'

She scowled. 'I think you're making it a bigger deal than it is. I know I told you I'd wait, but we got so caught up in the moment. Bryce said that if I really loved him, I'd want to share everything with him. I know how that sounds, but at the time it made perfect sense. He just looked at me and I knew it was the right thing to do. Besides, Bryce said if I do decide to become a vampire, any diseases that I might have would go away.'

Shit. We've crossed the line now. I'm legally required to report harm to self or other, and even though Midnight isn't a minor, she's at risk. If I get the authorities involved in this, Midnight will never trust me again. But if I don't . . .

I locked eyes with her. 'Would you be willing to give this some time? Will you promise me – I mean *really* promise me – that you won't make any decisions about becoming a vampire or drinking more blood without talking to me first? It's a very big deal.'

I let the honest concern I felt show in my face, and I watched the suspicion in her eyes soften into possibility as she sensed my sincerity. I really didn't want to bring in the police unless I absolutely had to, and I needed time to deepen our connection.

She heaved an exaggerated sigh. 'Well, if I *have* to.'

Okay. I'll take that. It's better than nothing.

I persuaded her to put off the decision for a couple of weeks and we spent the rest of the session exploring some of her background. 'Tell me more about your father,' I asked, and she did. The hour flew by.

As she stood to leave she said, 'I told some of the other kids about you and a few of them might want to come and talk. Would that be okay?'

'Sure. That would be great.' I gathered some business cards from my desk and handed them to her. 'Just ask them to call to schedule an appointment.'

I walked her into the reception area where she stopped with her hand on the doorknob and turned towards me again. 'Oh, yeah, I forgot to tell you. I told Dev I was coming to see you that first time – that my parents were making me see a shrink – and he was very interested. Well, anyway, he was waiting for me at The Crypt that night, and he asked me lots of questions about you and our session. He asked me what you look like. I told him everything. He said he might drop in to meet you sometime, and that I should tell you.'

Why does he care about how I look? I'm obviously too old for his taste.

'If he'd like to make an appointment, I'll be happy to see him.'

'It would have to be at night.' She grinned mischievously.

'That's perfectly fine – I do see clients in the evenings.' I didn't add that it was one of my least favourite things to do and that I avoided it whenever possible. But if I was going to specialise in vampire wannabes, I guessed I'd have to get used to the nocturnal schedule.

She left and I went back into my office.

I met with a few more clients that afternoon and early evening and had just kicked off my shoes when I heard the door to the reception area open. I quickly scanned my appointment book to make sure I hadn't forgotten anyone. Finding I hadn't, I put my shoes back on and opened my office door.

Sitting in one of the chairs in the waiting room was the very same gorgeous, blond-haired, leather-clad man I'd seen outside my building and in Midnight's drawing.

My stomach lurched and I think I gasped out loud.

He stood when I opened the door and it was fluid motion, as if he had simply willed himself vertical. His body was all lean muscle radiating some kind of primal power. He moved elegantly over to me and gave a slight bow of his head. He offered the kind of smile that made my Inner Nerd want to fan herself and hide in the closet.

Dressed in black, his snug leather trousers, form-fitting silk T-shirt and long leather 'duster' coat gave the impression of high fashion rather than Harley-Davidsons.

I froze in the doorway with my mouth hanging open,

speechless, staring into the most amazing pair of turquoise eyes I'd ever seen.

He picked up my hand gently and kissed the back, his lips soft and silky. 'I am Devereux. Is this a good time for an appointment?'

So many emotions slammed against each other inside me that I didn't know which one to act on first. Fear decided to step to the front of the line and my mind began to weigh options in case the man physically attacked me. He didn't seem menacing at the moment, but he was much bigger and stronger than me, and I hadn't spent nearly enough time in the gym. Hell, I hadn't spent any. Obviously, he had.

My heart raced and I still hadn't formed a coherent sentence or done anything beyond stare at him like a zombie. What was happening to me? My eyelids felt as though they were coated with cement, my jaw sagged open, the air suddenly became thick, and a sumo wrestler was pounding on my chest. The normal background white noise acquired a sharp edge and turned into a persistent buzz, vibrating in my ears. I felt as if I was in some kind of trance.

'I am very sorry.' He took a step back from me and released my hand. 'I have frightened you. That was never my intention – sometimes I forget how intense we can be. You must be a keenly sensitive individual. I will endeavour to control myself. Please accept my sincere apologies.'

You will endeavour to control yourself? I'm the one having the meltdown here.

He lowered his gaze for a moment, and when he met my eyes again, the tension drained from my muscles and I could breathe. It felt as though a switch had been thrown and I was once again in charge of my bodily functions. I could still hear the hum in my ears, but it had diminished in volume. I ran my tongue over my very dry lips.

'You did startle me. I wasn't expecting anyone this evening.'

'Again, my sincere apologies.'

Both times I'd seen this man, he'd caused my anxiety levels to blast through the roof. I wanted to scream at him that it was absolutely *not* acceptable he'd come unannounced to my office, and that his habit of lurking around me was going to earn him a trip to the police station. He was altogether too sure of himself. I wanted him to know he couldn't just stroll in and expect me to drop everything and attend to him. No matter how gorgeous he was.

Instead, I swallowed the irritation, opted for whatever remnants of professional demeanour I could summon, and said, 'Well, Mr Devereux, why are you here?'

'Just Devereux.' He cocked his head and flashed that godlike smile again. 'As I mentioned a moment ago, I had hoped this would be a good time for our appointment. I trust Midnight told you I wished to meet with you?'

His voice was unusually pleasant. The timbre of it flowed through me like a favourite song, as if I were listening to him with my entire body. He had a lilting European accent, sounding almost old-fashioned, like he'd stepped out of another century. Strange how a voice could be so enticing.

I closed my eyes and sniffed the air. What was that wonderful aroma? It seemed to hover around him like an olfactory aura. Maybe he used a special kind of soap or shampoo, something spicy and masculine and unusual.

He brushed a finger lightly along my arm. 'Dr Knight?'

My eyes flew open and I realised I'd been standing there, blatantly revelling in his scent, making sniffing noises. *How embarrassing. What the hell is wrong with me? Come on, Kismet. Talking has always been your strong suit. Just one word at a time. Concentrate.*

'Yes.' I cleared my throat. 'She did mention that you might call to set up an appointment. Would you care to schedule one for later this week?' I inhaled a deep breath and tried to remain professional.

I was so nervous my stomach contracted, my hands were sweating, and my knee twitched. I'd always had a fear of small spaces and something about this situation gave me that same closed-in panicky feeling. He had done nothing obvious to make me afraid, but my entire body felt as if it was waiting for some other shoe to drop. He radiated danger. Almost raw power.

'Would it be terribly inconvenient for us to meet now, since I am here?'

That voice. Maybe he was a hypnotist and he knew how to use it to put people under. It was so soothing, I could stand there and listen to it all night.

I felt myself sliding down that slippery slope again and rallied. I needed to get this guy out of my office before I made a complete fool of myself.

If I'd known I was going to have a mental breakdown today, I'd have pencilled it into my appointment book.

'I was just leaving. It would be much better if we could schedule another time—'

He reclaimed the step he'd given up and stated, as if the outcome was already a foregone conclusion, 'I would appreciate very much the opportunity to speak with you about Midnight. I am concerned about her.'

Through the candyfloss that had taken up residence in my brain, the voice in my head screamed *NO!* but my mouth said, 'I guess I could give you a few minutes. Please come inside.'

Please come inside? Hey, wait a minute – that isn't what I meant to say. Where'd that come from?

I backed away from the door, drawing it open so he could enter, leaving it ajar so he wouldn't be encouraged to make himself too comfortable.

I was about to invite him to sit down when I noticed he'd already seated himself in the chair I normally used. I realised he had no way of knowing that was 'my' chair, but it still annoyed me.

'Would you mind filling out a little paperwork for me?' Force of habit had me handing him a packet of papers on a clipboard.

He took it. 'My pleasure.'

I sat across from him and studied him while he wrote. His hands were artistic-looking, with recently manicured nails trimmed close. He had very pale skin with a lovely translucent sheen to it, which gave him an ageless quality. It wasn't often that I encountered someone with skin lighter than mine. His bone structure brought to mind the word *chiselled*. Perfect features. Almost too perfect.

Midnight was right: his eyes were extraordinary. They were indeed aqua and beautifully shaped with long, dark eyelashes. I was surprised that his eyebrows and eyelashes were dark because his hair was so light, but the combination was very appealing.

His thick, lovely hair flowed down over his shoulders to mid-chest. It looked soft and silky and very touchable. And his mouth . . . Studying his soft, full, generous lips caused a visceral reaction in me. I imagined the feel of them against mine.

What the hell? Take a breath, Kismet. You're in your office. This is a professional situation. Have you lost your mind? What you're imagining is beyond inappropriate. Stop daydreaming about what you want to do to those lips and pay attention.

As I raised my gaze from his mouth to his eyes I found him watching me with an amused expression, apparently finished with the paperwork. Embarrassment warmed my face as I reached for the clipboard. For some reason, I couldn't take my eyes off him long enough to even glance at the forms he'd filled out.

Why am I acting so weird?

I took a slow breath and struggled to regain control of myself. 'What concerns you about Midnight?'

'Before we speak of that, would you mind if I ask you a question?'

'Well, you can ask. I can't promise I'll answer.'

'Do you believe in vampires?'

'What?' Surprise radiated up my spine and I stiffened in my chair. The buzzing in my ears got louder and I was suddenly very thirsty.

He toyed with a beautiful antique medallion on a chain around his neck. 'Do you believe what Midnight has been telling you?'

Okay. Maybe he has a suggestion about how to help Midnight move beyond her vampire fantasy. He might be crazy, but maybe he can help.

To steady myself, I stood and walked over to the small refrigerator in the corner of the room and selected two bottles of water. I set one of them in front of Devereux, opened the other for myself, took my seat and drank deeply.

Breathe. Just breathe. This can't be hot flashes. I'm too young.

'I can't discuss anything that Midnight may or may not have talked to me about – it's all confidential. But generally speaking, I can tell you that I've never seen any evidence to support the existence of vampires or any other supernatural beings.'

'Ah.' The corners of his lips quirked up. 'You are a scientist. Do you wish to see evidence?'

I was getting that claustrophobic feeling again. Maybe this handsome man really was a nut-case and I'd allowed myself to be distracted by his obvious assets instead of following my professional instincts. I switched into the noticeably calm voice I used to soothe disturbed clients. 'Is it important to you that I believe in vampires?'

He threw back his head and laughed with pure delight. 'I have never been called insane in such a lovely way ever before. I can assure you that it is of no importance whatsoever to me if you believe in vampires or not, but I think the information could prove useful to you. What if I told you that everything Midnight has shared with you is absolutely true?'

Oh, geez. He's a loon.

'Since we can't talk about anything Midnight might have said, I can only suggest that you tell me directly what you want me to know.'

'I am a vampire.'

Uh-huh. Of course you are. 'Tell me about being a vampire.'

'As you wish.' Still clearly amused by me, he gave the full weight of those eyes again and my breath caught in my chest. 'Until I can convince you of the truth of my words, I will be the good therapy client and follow the rules.'

He seemed to find me very entertaining. *Hmmm. Inappropriate humour. That's a symptom in several diagnoses. I wonder what he's basing his role on? I've never seen a movie vampire who goes around telling people he's a vampire. Isn't that the point? To avoid the stake-in-the-heart thing? Maybe that's why he hangs out with teenagers: he's mentally unbalanced. Maybe I could just rattle his delusion a little bit.*

'Why do you want me to know you're a vampire? Isn't that supposed to be a secret?'

His gaze was stilled locked on mine. 'I want you to know about me because I have a feeling about you. I believe you have a crucial role to play in my life.'

My stomach clenched and I broke eye-contact. *A crucial role in his life? This sounds like stalker material.*

This was definitely getting out of hand. Maybe I should rework my idea about counselling vampire wannabes. These folks were much more delusional than I thought, and it wasn't going to be as simple as I first imagined. I'd assumed all my pretend vampires would be similar to my alien abductees: creative, needy, acting out and harmless. I hadn't considered the possibility that this subculture might be populated by psychotics. That would require a totally different treatment plan.

No problem. This is good. I need to know what I'm dealing with.

I glanced over at the clock, thinking of ways I could gracefully end the conversation.

'Shall I show you one of my vampire abilities?' he asked, his voice deep.

'I don't know.' My stomach tightened. 'What kind of ability is it?' I half-expected him to tug a long scarf out of his fist or spread a deck of cards on the table.

'Simple telepathy. Allow me to tell you what you have been thinking.'

He repeated back all my thoughts about things getting out of hand, reconsidering how I'd work with vampire wannabes, that he was being delusional, and my wanting him to leave. Word for word.

My body rode a rollercoaster of emotion.

How could he possibly know that?

I immediately felt embarrassed that he'd somehow known what I really thought about him, which was then made even worse by the humiliating possibility that he'd been aware of my earlier appreciation of his physical attributes. But then I got angry. The buzzing in my ears had morphed into a headache and I was rapidly approaching some inner line in the sand. I hadn't given him permission to read my energy or to inconvenience me with his unexpected presence or his sideshow antics. Since I had no intention of taking him on as a client, I felt justified in letting myself have a reaction.

I held on to the arms of the chair so tightly that my fingers blanched whiter than normal.

'That's quite a clever parlour trick. Are you a mind reader? A psychic?' There was more heat in my voice than I'd intended.

Something is very wrong here. I've never had this reaction to any client, ever. I've never got angry at a client before. I've never been so attracted to a client before. This is unnatural. What's happening?

'You are angry. Once again, I apologise for upsetting you. It is my nature to be able to read the thoughts and sense the emotions of others. It has always been that way for me, even before I was born into darkness. I cannot be other than I am. All old vampires have the potential to be telepathic, but not many are as skilled as I am. It is one of my gifts. As you might imagine, being bombarded by constant mental chatter can be tedious, so I've taught myself to pick up an individual's thoughts only if I choose to. I now receive specifically what I focus on and nothing more. I can teach you to shield your thoughts, if you wish.'

'Can't you just stop whatever it is you're doing?' I demanded, much louder than I'd meant to. I couldn't honestly say I believed he'd read my mind, because how could that be possible? I'd never met anyone with keen enough psychic abilities to actually know another's thoughts, word for word. This was new territory. Not being able to explain it made me nervous.

His lips curved, and he gave another bow of his head.

'With most humans, there is little pull to their thoughts. Their minds are filled with ordinary, meaningless details and I can easily turn my attention elsewhere. But your mind is very powerful and you have your own abilities, which you have not yet acknowledged. That is a very strong attraction for me. But I will do my best not to intrude.'

'Thank you,' I said, and stood up, struggling to hold myself together. *What abilities? What's he talking about?* 'We need to stop now.'

'Yes.' He stood as well and smiled at me. 'Of course. I am grateful for your indulgence. Midnight holds you in high regard and I am pleased that she will be spending time with you. She has most likely told you that she is involved with another vampire she met at my club. This . . . individual . . . is dangerous, and I wish to discourage their relationship. She is most upset with me, but I must be firm on this. I hope that as you learn more about him, you will agree with me. Perhaps she will listen to one of us.'

He has such interesting, old-fashioned speech patterns. I feel as if I've fallen into a time warp. Or into one of my old roommate's taped episodes of Dark Shadows.

There were many questions I wanted to ask him since he'd started talking about Midnight, but I didn't want to encourage him or breach her privacy, so I kept my face pleasantly blank and said nothing.

'May I have your permission to come and visit you again?'

Ah, the vampire wannabe is tapping at my window, wanting in.

'Is there something you wish to talk to a therapist about? Because I believe I've made it clear that I can't discuss Midnight with you, so it might be best if I refer you to another clinician.'

'There are many topics I wish to explore, but only with you. Would you come to my club sometime, as my guest?' he said, his voice smooth velvet again. 'It would give you an opportunity to see the world in which Midnight lives.'

What was it about that voice? Why was it causing me to have very un-therapist-like thoughts? It seemed to generate actual heat in my body. I gathered my professional aura around me like a protective cloak. 'I don't think that would be appropriate, but I appreciate the kind offer. If you decide you want to start seeing a therapist, I'd be pleased to refer you.'

I guided him into the waiting area and he turned to me, lifted my hand and kissed it, his mouth lingering just a bit longer than necessary.

His aqua gaze locked on to mine. 'Please allow me to give you a parting gift.'

Before I could answer, he placed his index finger gently on the skin between my eyes and made a circular motion. I jumped as if he'd burned me. The touch had tingled like a mini-lightning bolt.

I gasped. 'What did you do to me?'

'I provided a layer of protection over your third eye – your sixth chakra – so you will no longer be overwhelmed by what I am. Your symptoms should already be subsiding.'

My symptoms? Third eye? I've got to get this handsome madman out of my office.

'Until next time.' He turned and left as quietly as he came in.

I rubbed my forehead, half-expecting to find a gaping wound, and was pleasantly surprised to feel nothing out of the ordinary. In fact, I was almost clear-headed again. I suspected I was right about him being a hypnotist, because he certainly understood the power of suggestion. Regardless of why the fuzziness, buzzing and pain had gone away, I was relieved they had.

I closed and locked both the doors, noticing that my legs were shaking and my knees were dangerously close to bailing on me. I shuffled over to the couch, flopped down, and stretched out along it, then kicked my shoes into the air as I surrendered into the soft cushions. I could still feel his kiss on my hand and I was very aware that my hormones were threatening to run amok.

That was, without a doubt, the weirdest experience I'd ever had. A good-looking man expressed interest in me and I handled it poorly. Gee. What a surprise.

After lying there for a few minutes, trying to figure out what had just happened, I sat up and reached for the information sheet he'd filled out, noticing that he hadn't answered many of the questions. He listed the club downtown as his address and phone number, and under date of birth he'd written August 8, 1172 and October 31, 1201.

Oh, I get it. In keeping with his story, he'd given me both a human birth date and a vampire birth date. Very clever. According to this, he was twenty-nine years old when he was 'brought over'. So something must have happened to him when he was twenty-nine that caused him to retreat into this masquerade. Since he didn't appear to be much older than that, it couldn't have been very long ago.

I suddenly felt sad. What a shame that this obviously intelligent and unquestionably gorgeous man was caught up in such a bizarre pretence. Or, even sadder, that he was mentally ill enough to actually believe he was a vampire. But there was still that business about him guessing what I'd been thinking. How could he possibly have such an extraordinary level of skill? I remembered reading an article about mental illness and enhanced psychic abilities – the intuitive equivalent of a savant. I'd have to do some more research on that topic.

Why had I let him get to me? I was thoroughly ashamed of myself for behaving so unprofessionally – so irrationally.

I treated him more like an appealing male than someone in a clinical situation. I'd never had that kind of reaction to someone in my office. I owed Devereux an apology. First I'd let myself be attracted to him, and then I'd lost my temper. Both those choices were completely unacceptable and very unlike me. It was undoubtedly time for me to schedule weekly appointments with Nancy rather than monthly. I mean, how unnatural was it for a thirty-year-old woman to be a celibate hermit?

If my bad experience with Tom and my dysfunctional childhood had caused me to be so uncomfortable around men that I was incapable of dealing professionally with a sexually desirable client, then I'd better take some steps towards correcting the problem or find another line of work.

I decided I'd call the cute chiropractor when I got home. Nancy was right. I'd have to get back on the horse sometime.

CHAPTER 4

The next couple of days were uneventful. Determined to confront my fears, I summoned my courage and called Vaughan the chiropractor. We arranged to meet for dinner the following weekend. He sounded so pleasantly surprised and delighted to hear from me that I was actually excited about our date. Maybe I'd even force myself to go to the mall and buy something new to wear.

The ads I'd placed in the newspapers and online announcing psychotherapy for vampires had started to draw responses and I'd begun the screening process for setting up appointments and forming groups. I now understood the importance of thoroughly questioning each candidate. After my experience with Devereux, separating the mildly delusional from the profoundly disturbed was imperative.

As expected, the ads attracted calls not only from vampire wannabes but also from people interested in other forms of the paranormal.

Unfortunately, it also included those who defined their lives by hating anything they didn't understand. One such caller was Brother Luther. He left messages on my voicemail, telling me that I was going to burn in hell for consorting with demons and the minions of Satan. I wasn't sure if Brother Luther was affiliated with any organised group or if he was the sole member of his congregation, but he was very enthusiastic and dramatic about his opinions. He spoke with a Southern accent, and he reminded me of the fire-and-brimstone preachers I'd seen as a child while visiting relatives in the Smoky Mountains. I usually didn't take those kinds of calls seriously, and I assumed he was a harmless windbag.

I was still troubled by the way I'd behaved with Devereux. I knew I should call him and apologise, but for some reason I couldn't make myself pick up the phone. Even thinking about him caused me to have that same strange, overwhelming reaction. I was afraid of him yet very attracted to him at the same time, and those conflicting emotions combined to create some terrifying third thing inside my psyche that I just didn't understand. When in doubt, brood. And that's exactly what I did.

When Midnight came in for her next appointment on Thursday afternoon she wasn't wearing her vampire costume and she wasn't alone. I almost didn't recognise her until she spoke to me. Dressed in jeans, Renaissance Fayre T-shirt and running shoes, with her long hair pulled into a ponytail, she was the fresh-faced girl next door. It turned out that underneath all the makeup was a beautiful young woman. Sitting quietly next to Midnight in the waiting room was a thin, frail-looking female with dark circles under her green eyes and tangled black hair.

'Dr Knight, this is Emerald. I brought her with me because

I didn't know what else to do. Something's wrong with her.' Midnight wrapped one arm around her friend's shoulders and propelled her into my office.

They sat down on the couch together. Emerald gave me a vacant stare. I had seen that reaction before in clients who'd been traumatised. It was as if the body was still functioning, but the personality had gone into a dark closet and closed the door.

I stood next to them. 'What happened to her?'

Midnight turned frightened eyes to me, sending out waves of panic. 'When I came home this morning at dawn, I found her sitting out on the front stairs, staring at her feet. I got her inside and sat with her for hours, trying to get her to eat something or tell me what happened, but she wouldn't say a word. I was going to cancel my appointment with you and take her to the emergency room, but then I thought maybe you could help.'

'Emerald?' I moved over to squat down in front of her. I held up my index finger in her line of sight and shifted it from side to side, watching to see if her eyes followed the motion. There was no reaction from her at all. I reached over and touched her hand. It was icy-cold. She gave off no emotions. For all intents and purposes, the walking dead.

'Midnight, is Emerald usually this pale? How long has she been sick?'

'I guess I didn't really know she was sick. She's been complaining about being tired and sleeping a lot, but I've been so into Bryce that I didn't pay attention. I guess I've been a crummy friend.' Tears glistened in her eyes.

Well, maybe it's good for Midnight to focus on her friend for a while, get her mind off the vampire obsession. Even though she's feeling sad, I'm glad to see her expressing her emotions.

Still kneeling in front of her, I touched Emerald's cheek with the back of my hand. 'I'm not a medical doctor, but I think we need to take Emerald to the emergency room. It just isn't normal for a person to have such a low body temperature.' Now that I was close to her, I could see some bruising on her neck and chest. I gently angled Emerald's head to the side so I could investigate and noticed several sets of small puncture marks running down her neck. I pulled back the collar of the jacket she was wearing and found that the wounds went all the way down to the top of her breast. There was a little dried blood on her skin and clothing.

I was just about to say it appeared Emerald had been attacked by some kind of animal when Midnight said, 'Those are vampire bites.'

I was tempted to challenge the claim, but the helpless expression on Midnight's face stopped me. She was truly worried about her friend, and she was blaming herself.

By this time, all I was thinking about was getting Emerald to the hospital. I was in no mood to play 'let's pretend', but I also didn't want to damage the fragile trust that had been built between Midnight and me. Creating a therapeutic bond was a crucial turning point in therapy, and it wouldn't be good to burst the bubble.

'Let's get her to the hospital.' I stood. 'I could call an ambulance, but it'll probably be faster to take my car.' I knew that Midnight usually walked or took the bus to her appointments.

Besides, I wasn't going to let them out of my sight until I knew they were in good hands.

Midnight rose and held Emerald upright while I gathered my purse and car keys. I opened the door and supported Emerald's other side, and the three of us shifted sideways to exit through the narrow space.

'Hey, Ronald,' said Midnight, addressing a sweet-faced young man sitting in the waiting room.

'Oh, Ronald. I'm afraid we're going to have to reschedule our appointment. We have a bit of an emergency here,' I explained, stating the obvious.

Ronald was one of the 'apprentices' Midnight had referred to me and this was to have been our first session. I'd wondered if he'd show up in costume, but he hadn't. His squeaky-clean-looking auburn hair flowed down over his shoulders, and his round copper-coloured eyes were warm and friendly. In fact, the only indication of his alternative lifestyle was his *Theatre of Blood* T-shirt and a pentagram earring hanging from one earlobe.

He stood. 'Can I help?' he asked, with concern in his voice. 'Emerald is a friend of mine. My van is parked right in front of the building.'

Without waiting for me to answer, he stepped out into the hallway, trotted down to the far end and called the elevator.

Nice guy, I thought.

Under other circumstances, I might have hesitated before accepting his help – after all, I'd only spoken to him on the phone before today, and I didn't really know much about him. Since my inner radar wasn't sending me any warning signals, I decided to take a chance and trust him. Besides, if it came down to needing to carry Emerald, I wasn't going to say no to another set of muscles.

I'd imagined that Ronald's van would be something you'd find on an old Grateful Dead album cover, but it was surprisingly nice and very clean. He opened the sliding door on the side and Midnight and I climbed in, holding Emerald, who was fading fast. Her head drooped as if all the muscles and bones had been removed from her neck, causing her chin to bounce against her chest. She made tiny whimpering sounds that seemed to come from deep inside and every few seconds her eyelids fluttered as if she were in REM sleep.

The hospital was only a few blocks away, but we managed to catch every red light and construction detour on the trip. My anxiety rose with each delay.

Ronald's eyes peered at us in the rearview mirror. 'Who do you think did that to her, Midnight?'

'How would I know?' Midnight snarled, her voice loaded with hostility. I raised my eyebrows at her and she answered, 'Ronald doesn't like Bryce and his friends either.'

My eyes shifted back and forth between them. 'Is somebody implying that Bryce had something to do with this attack on Emerald?' The discussion already had me thinking about the call I'd make to the police. As a licensed therapist, I had a legal requirement to report harm.

'Nobody knows who hurt Emerald. Ronald's just being a jerk,' Midnight said. 'He's mad because Bryce chose me instead of him.'

'I'm not the one being a jerk,' Ronald snapped.

Wow. The negative energy is as thick as fog in here. Apparently there are more dramas in the vampire-wannabe game than I know about.

We finally arrived at the emergency room entrance and Ronald pulled the van into the 'no parking' zone, came around to let us out and took my spot holding Emerald, who had slipped deeper into unconsciousness during the ride over. 'Dr Knight, you go on ahead and deal with the red tape.'

Looking as official as I could manage, I hurried to the admissions desk and enlisted the aid of a nurse. A gurney was wheeled over for Emerald and she was taken away.

Since Midnight was the only one of us who had any information about Emerald, she filled out the hospital paperwork while Ronald went back outside to move his van before it was towed. I stepped outside for a moment to use my cell phone to cancel my last client of the day.

After she answered the nurse's questions, Midnight and I sat in the hard orange chairs in the noisy waiting area. The emergency room was filled with people in various states of crisis, and more trauma victims arrived every moment. There was that ever-present hospital smell: a combination of antiseptic, body fluids and fear. I couldn't imagine working in a chaotic environment such as this, where the adrenalin was constantly pumping. I could almost see the tension in the air.

It was times like these when my 'sensitivity' really became a problem and I experienced sensory overload as strong emotions and physical discomforts bombarded me from all sides. I began utilising all the mental tricks I'd learned to help me distract myself from the unwanted sensations and information. I closed my eyes tight and imagined myself surrounded by a circle of white light. That visualization usually did the trick, but this time it barely soothed the chaos. I still felt anxious.

I'd always been overly aware of people's feelings and emotions, but it was usually through clairsentience – just my normal idiosyncrasy. Somehow I simply knew what was going on inside their psyches. It came in very handy in therapy sessions, where I could do a little skilful intuiting and skip ahead a few pages.

I didn't know why exactly, but I had the notion that my discomfort had something to do with the weird experience with Devereux the other night. Maybe the suggestion he'd given me about my *third eye* – as if there was any such thing – had caused me to revisit yet another unwanted ability from my childhood. I had the fleeting thought that it would be helpful to speak with Devereux about this new development, that maybe he'd have some advice. Then the part of me that was already dangling outside her comfort zone slammed the door on that idea. She wasn't fooled. She knew I only wanted to see him again. In fact, I couldn't stop thinking about him.

Somebody help me. I'm possessed by a vampire wannabe.

I turned to Midnight. 'Would you care to fill me in on what you and Ronald were talking about?'

She slumped down in her chair and crossed her arms over her chest. 'I'm sorry I got mad. I'm really stressed out. I'm just so tired of everyone telling me that Bryce isn't good for me or that he's going to hurt me. They don't know him like I do. He would never hurt Emerald – he knows she's my friend. Besides, I think more than one vampire bit her.'

And we're back to the vampire fantasy. I really hope she tires of it quickly. I made a mental note to ask her more about that later.

She relaxed her arms, sat up abruptly, and turned towards me. 'Then there was the discussion with Dev. About you. He told me he came to see you, and he went on and on about how pretty you are, and how your eyes are so blue that they reminded him of the daytime sky he hasn't seen in more than eight hundred years, and your dark hair this and your long legs that, blah, blah, blah. I was so pissed off that I went and spent the night with Bryce just because I needed someone to want me like Dev wants you.'

I opened my mouth to speak, but then closed it because I didn't know what to say. It was normal for clients to transfer their feelings about their parents or some other significant childhood person onto me, but I'd never found myself in the middle of a love triangle before. Clearly this wasn't the time or place to discuss those issues, especially with a teenage client. Apparently Devereux was clueless about the depth of Midnight's feelings for him. Or maybe he was simply a heart-less bastard who didn't care. In the midst of my annoyance at him for his insensitivity, there was still a part of me that'd been pleased to hear Devereux thought I was pretty.

I was saved from having to figure out anything to say about it by the approach of a handsome, official-looking man dressed in scrubs with a stethoscope around his neck. A doctor, I assumed. He had shoulder-length golden hair and dark-brown eyes framed by wire-rimmed glasses, which gave him a professorial, academic look. By this time Ronald had returned and the doctor addressed the three of us.

'Are you the ones who brought in the young woman with the neck wounds?'

We nodded.

'Are you family?'

We shook our heads.

Midnight explained that she'd left a message for Emerald's parents, telling them their daughter was in the hospital, but she didn't expect them to show up because they'd given up on Emerald a long time ago.

'Doctor—?' I said, searching for a nametag.

'Dr Mitchell. Lee. And you are?'

'Dr Knight. Kismet. I'm a psychologist. Can you tell us anything about what's wrong with Emerald? Can we see her?'

'We've stabilised her, but she's lost a lot of blood and she's receiving a transfusion now. This is an unusual case. Emerald should be covered with blood to account for the excessive blood loss, but she isn't. Furthermore, it appears that she has older puncture wounds on her neck and chest in addition to those we're treating today. We're running tests on the wounds to see what kind of animal caused them. Do you have any information about where she was when the attack occurred? Did you see anything?'

I glanced over at Midnight, encouraging her to answer.

She shook her head. 'I thought Emerald was staying home last night and I didn't get back 'til early this morning, so I don't know what happened. I'm so sorry that I wasn't there for her,' she whimpered, tears running down her cheeks.

I put my arm around her shoulders. 'Dr Mitchell, when will you get the results of the tests back? I'd like to know as soon as possible.'

'Is she a client of yours?'

I started to say no, but then I remembered the lost, empty eyes of the vulnerable young woman we'd brought in and decided to lie. I wasn't sure how far professional courtesy was going to get me, and I wasn't willing to be another person who abandoned Emerald.

'Yes. We just started working together.'

'I should know something by tomorrow morning. I could call you when the results come in, if you want.' He smiled and tilted his head to the side.

Was this guy flirting with me? I must have crossed into some twilight zone because this kind of attention just didn't happen to me. First the vampire wannabe gave me jelly knees, and now the handsome doctor was smiling at me in a most inviting manner. I'd bet the combination of the smile and the head-tilt thing always worked for him. I could definitely verify its effectiveness.

'I would appreciate that.' Flustered, I finally managed to pull out one of my business cards and handed it to him. 'Just leave a message any time and I'll call you right back.'

If one of my almost-clients hadn't been lying in the hospital missing several pints of blood, I might have been tempted to pull my own smile and head-tilt out of the garage and take it for a test spin. Nancy would be so proud. But considering the circumstances, I just put my professional face back on and behaved myself.

'She isn't going to be able to have any visitors today, so it would be best if you return in the morning,' he explained, also stepping into his official persona. 'Don't worry – we'll take good care of her.' He winked at me and walked away.

Well, that's it – I've definitely entered a parallel universe. After thirty years of being almost invisible to men, suddenly I'm on the menu. How did that happen?

Ronald went to fetch the van and Midnight retreated in search of a restroom. I sat down in one of the uncomfortable chairs, closed my eyes and circled my head around, stretching out the tight muscles in my neck. After a few seconds I sensed someone behind me and turned to investigate.

A tall, absurdly attractive man inched towards me, madly scribbling in a notebook, totally oblivious to the fact that I was staring at him. He must have sensed he'd reached my chair because he started talking, eyes still on his writing.

'Dr Knight? I'm Special Agent Stevens,' he said, finally making eye-contact. 'I didn't mean to sneak up on you. Seems I really can't walk and do anything else at the same time. I couldn't help but overhear the conversation you had with the doctor. The victim of the attack is your client?'

'Special Agent Stevens?' I took in his jeans and white T-shirt. 'You don't look like a special agent. Who do you work for?'

'Sorry. I'd just got home and changed clothes when I picked up the call that there'd been another attack.' He pulled out his identification from his back pocket and handed it to me.

Federal Bureau of Investigation, Special Agent Alan Stevens. I shifted my eyes from the photo to his face and back again, then returned his ID. 'Why would the FBI be interested in an animal attack in Denver?'

He paused and studied me as if he was trying to figure out if I was serious or not. 'This wasn't an animal attack. I've been tracking these cases all over the country. The local police are involved, too. So, is Emerald Addison your client?'

'You know I can't confirm or deny that.' *Shit.* He'd obviously heard me confirm it to the doctor.

'That pesky confidentiality thing, eh?' He grinned and made excellent eye-contact.

'Uh.' I played with my hair. 'What cases have you been tracking? What does Emerald's situation have to do with them?' It was definitely time to change the topic.

He smirked. 'Oh, so you won't answer my questions, yet I'm supposed to answer yours? I don't think so. But I'd like your contact information, just in case I think of some questions you *can* answer. Could I have one of those business cards you gave to the doctor?'

I gave him one and he fished in his wallet for his. 'Here's mine,' he said. 'If you think of anything that might help me find whoever did this to your client, you can call me. Day or night.'

'Thanks, I will.' *What an odd fellow.*

He locked eyes with me for a few seconds, then shifted his gaze back down to the notebook, began writing furiously again and shuffled a few feet towards the nurses' station. Midnight, who had been standing off to the side, listening to the exchange, joined me and reported that Ronald and the van were out front. We were just going through the door when Special Agent Stevens suddenly reappeared and grabbed my arm.

'Oh, by the way, Doc – watch out for the vampires.'

CHAPTER 5

By the time we left the hospital, the mountain skyline was shimmering in the midst of a breathtaking colour and light show. Brilliant shades of red, orange, blue and purple swirled around and through each other, muting into pinks, peaches and lavenders as shafts of sunlight streamed through openings in the kaleidoscope of colours. Off to the east, faint points of light floating in an indigo void sparkled as the sun retreated behind the towering peaks in the west. Nothing's as magical as a Rocky Mountain sunset.

We were all exhausted and worried about Emerald, and the ride back to my office was a silent one. It appeared my companions had buried the hatchet because Ronald offered to take Midnight home and she accepted. Before they left I rescheduled Ronald's appointment and thanked him for being such a big help. He seemed ill at ease with my expression of appreciation, but gave me a tentative smile. I looked forward to finding out if I could help alleviate the sadness I saw behind his warm tawny eyes.

I wrestled with myself about whether I should go up to my office and work for a while or head home to a glass of wine and a hot bath. Guilt won the match and I rode the elevator upstairs, daydreaming about sinking into an aromatic bubble-filled tub.

I was gratified to find several voicemail messages from prospective clients and I sat at my desk for the next hour returning calls and answering emails.

I had just decided to pack it in for the evening when my office door opened and two of the whitest men I'd ever seen walked in. I don't mean just pale, like the British actors on the BBC, but chalk-white. Unlike the makeup Midnight used, the tone of their complexions hadn't come from a tube. Suffice it to say they weren't sun worshippers.

One of the men was tall, dark-haired, and handsome and the other short, odd-looking, and muscle-bound.

Startled, I asked, 'May I help you?'

How did they get in? I'm positive I locked those doors.

No response.

They ambled in and circled around, prowling through the couches and chairs in the middle of the room, their eyes fixed on me.

The shorter of the two came and sat on the corner of my desk and leered at me. He smiled a closed-mouth smile and reached out a tattooed hand to touch my hair. I jerked away.

He wore a sleeveless T-shirt that showed exaggerated biceps and triceps rippling across his upper arms. His hair was that artificial colour of burgundy so popular with the goths, and it flowed down his upper body like stringy octopus arms. His eyes were so light-blue they were almost white. He reminded me of a demented miniature muscle man – a nightmare come to life.

These guys made my stomach hurt. It wasn't only that they'd invaded my privacy, or that they appeared dangerous, or even that they could assault me at any moment. It was something else, some basic preverbal fear that caused the hairs on my arms to stand up and the warning system in my head to fire a red alert. I kept having the strange, less-than-comforting intuition that death was in the room, and my usually manageable radar was picking up so much fearful information that it plunged into overload and threatened to shut down.

I glanced over at the phone on the far corner of my desk and began sliding my hand in that direction.

The tall man stepped around behind me, put his hands underneath my jaw and pulled my head back, somehow rendering me powerless. He bent down, brought his mouth next to my ear, and whispered, in a very sensuous voice, 'I've heard so much about you, I thought it was time we were formally introduced.' He grabbed the hand moving towards the phone.

'Who are you? What do you want?' I tried not to sound as worried as I felt.

His hand trailed across the hair at the back of my head and he moved to sit directly in front of me on my desk, jamming his legs into the space under the desk with mine.

'No!' I stifled a scream and reacted instinctively, making an unsuccessful attempt to push away. He bent in close, his hands gripping both sides of my chair and effectively blocked any move on my part. I was glad I'd worn a trouser-suit instead of a skirt, because I wanted as many layers between us as possible.

Think, Kismet. Don't let the lunatic know how afraid you are. Don't give him that power.

He lowered his mouth to within an inch of mine and I twisted my head to the side, shifting away from his hot, unpleasantly sweet breath. He grabbed my chin between his thumb and first finger, holding tightly enough that I knew there'd be bruises, and forced my face back level with his. 'I'm Bryce. I believe you've heard of me.'

'Stop it! Let go of me—'

He swallowed my words with his mouth, clamping his lips on mine with enough pressure to cause my teeth to break the skin on the inside of my lip. Then he sucked my lower lip into his mouth and held it between his teeth until I gave an involuntary yelp of pain. Only then did he pull back with an evil grin and gazed at me with his dark-green eyes, which were suddenly magnetic. I tried to look away, but I couldn't. I literally couldn't. It was as if his eyes were pulling me. I managed to briefly squeeze my eyelids shut, but he dug his fingers into my chin again, jerking my head roughly. 'Open your eyes,' he roared.

My breath caught and my eyelids flew up. His eyes were directly in front of mine, the green darker than before, almost black. I fell into them and the edges of my vision blurred. A strange haze settled over everything as part of my mind drifted off on a cloud.

I felt as if my arms and legs were encased in armour, that even thinking about moving would require way too much effort, and that it really wouldn't matter because they were too heavy to lift anyway. Nothing really mattered.

Bryce watched me with a smirk. 'See? You're feeling much more relaxed now. Aren't you sorry you made such a fuss?'

'What do you want?' I mumbled.

I made what I thought was another valiant effort to raise myself out of the chair. Since nothing happened, I could only assume the message hadn't travelled from my brain to my body. My muscles were pudding and my mouth was dry as the Sahara. Maybe I'd had a stroke and was spending my last moments on Earth in the company of a psychopath.

He laughed. 'I enjoy it when you struggle. It excites me. I'm not sure you really want to know what I want. Let's just keep it a surprise, shall we?'

Bryce lifted a piece of his long hair and brushed it against my cheek. 'You really are quite lovely. All that long, dark hair and sexy eyes – I can see why Devereux is attracted to you. I'm here because I overheard him talking about you to my little servant, Midnight. I think he's quite smitten with you, and nothing would make me happier than to keep Devereux from having something he wants or, even better, to take it away from him once he has it.'

'No one has me,' I said, despite the fact that I had no idea what he was talking about and the part of my mind that had floated away was still missing in action. False bravado was one of my favourite defences. Never let the violently delusional know you're afraid.

All this time the smaller man had been laughing and slapping his leg with one hand. I slanted a glance at him and he showed me his top row of teeth, exposing a very real-looking set of fangs. He definitely had the best pair of fakes I'd seen so far. I wasn't sure what kind of reaction he thought I'd have to his cosmetic dentistry, but I obviously didn't give him whatever facial expression he wanted because he lurched at me. I recoiled from his touch.

'I could rip your throat out with these,' he growled.

Abnormally fast, Bryce reached over, grabbed the small man by the throat and threw him onto the floor. 'Leave her alone, Raleigh. I told you – she's mine.'

Raleigh glared at Bryce, making noises that sounded more animal than human. Then he got up off the floor, stumbled to the nearest couch and stretched out, lacing his fingers behind his head.

She's mine? What does that mean? Am I his to harm, or—? This is bad. I wish I could find the 'on' switch for my brain.

I hadn't worked with any physically dangerous or psychotic clients since my residency at the psychiatric ward during graduate school. Now I tried to remember the skills I'd learned for dealing with them. Since I'd seen Bryce throw the small man around like a cardboard cutout, I knew I had no chance of doing anything that required physical strength. I thought my only hope would be to use my tools as a therapist. Maybe I could reason with him. Or maybe I should just keep my mouth shut. I definitely needed to keep a clear head and that had become a problem.

Bryce turned his attention back to me and searched for something in my expression. He leaned in, ran his tongue over my lips and then kissed me again.

I twisted my face away. 'Stop it! Get away from me!'

He angrily shoved my chair back from the desk, stood up, and lifted me, holding me like a child in his arms.

I pushed ineffectually against his chest and kicked my legs, trying to get him to put me down, and for one sick moment I was reminded of a scene from that old science fiction movie *The Day the Earth Stood Still*, where the robot picks up the woman and she can't get away. Bryce felt that cold and alien to me.

I still had little control of my limbs, and I was forced to acknowledge that this situation wasn't likely to have a happy ending. 'Let me go! What are you doing?'

He walked me over to a couch back against the far wall. The motions I made with my arms and legs were pitifully useless. I hated feeling helpless. I thought about all the opportunities I'd had to take self-defence classes and how I'd always come up with some excuse to avoid them. I didn't know if learning to take down a man wearing a big foam helmet would have helped me fight off these two vampire wannabes, but it would have been better than nothing.

'Let's have a therapy session.' He sat on the couch and held me tight in his lap. I kept pushing against him, getting more and more pissed off about whatever he'd done to cause this bizarre almost-paralysis, but his arms were steel bands. The sweet, coppery smell that rode his breath was stronger now.

'What do you want? Why did you come here?' I demanded, trying to sound more confident than I felt.

'Maybe I need someone to talk to,' he replied in a fake whining voice. He opened the top button of my blouse and ran his finger across the exposed skin. 'Maybe I'm just a lonely vampire searching for my soulmate. What do you think?' He laughed, enjoying some private joke, and then he recovered himself. 'Actually, I've already found my soulmate, but Devereux isn't cooperating. In fact, he was obsessed with you, even before you physically showed up. How pathetic is that?'

Devereux? His soulmate?

'But never fear,' he said. 'I will deal with you and show him the error of his ways. He might be angry with me for a while, but he'll come around. Now, let's talk about you. I hear you don't believe in vampires. I thought I'd change your mind. Watch.'

He lifted his top lip so I could see the upper row of teeth and as I watched, his canines grew longer and longer until they protruded a good quarter- to a half-inch below his other teeth. Then they contracted back up into their normal place and extended again, as if he could will them to move in and out of his gums. He grinned at me. 'How do you explain that?'

Shit. Another psycho magician.

'I can't explain it.' I stared at his mouth, trying to figure out how the trick fangs worked.

Keep him talking . . .

'Go ahead,' he leered, his eyes sparkling. 'Touch them.'

Touch them? I wasn't going to stick my fingers in some psychopath's mouth. He'd probably bite me. I didn't want to think about where those teeth had been.

'No. That isn't necessary – I believe you.' *Placate the lunatic.*

'Oh, but I insist.' He grabbed my hand and forced it up towards his mouth, laying the tip of my index finger on one of his fangs. It contracted while I touched it and I was able to snatch my hand away. Maybe my instincts could override whatever he'd done to me after all.

He sneered. 'I'm old enough to have total control of my fangs, but if you get me aroused or angry enough they seem to have a mind of their own. And right now I'm feeling very aroused.'

Breathe, Kismet. Stay calm.

'You don't have to hurt me. Why don't we talk about your feelings—?'

'I don't think so.' He grabbed my hand again and shoved it down into his lap, which was filled with a large erection. 'Let me show something else with a mind of its own.'

Oh no. This can't be happening.

In one quick motion he had me lying flat on the couch with him on top of me, roughly pressing his lips against mine. Bile rising in my throat, I pushed at him again, my muscles finally deciding to cooperate, but he grabbed my wrists, holding them over my head in a vice-like grip as he forced his tongue into my mouth. Terror flooded my brain. After a few seconds, he kissed his way down to my neck and then, with a flash of pain, he bit me.

I screamed and kicked and shoved against him in a futile effort to dislodge an immovable object. I tried to raise my knee to administer the only effective self-defence strategy I knew, but he weighed on me like a slab of cement and I thought that maybe I wouldn't have to worry about him raping me because he'd probably crush or smother me first.

He made loud sucking sounds at the wound on my neck and I started to feel light-headed. Suddenly the pain stopped and I opened my eyes, which I hadn't realised I'd closed. He wasn't on top of me any more. I heard male voices yelling, and the sound of furniture being pushed around.

I sat up, feeling like the morning after, and saw Devereux and Bryce struggling with each other, dancers in a strange ballet. Raleigh was nowhere in sight.

Watching the two of them was surprisingly entrancing and I couldn't shift my eyes away. It was as if they moved in slow-motion. I was fascinated by Devereux's light-blond hair contrasted against Bryce's dark, silky veil. I hallucinated that their hair was flowing out around their heads as if they were submerged underwater and, while some part of me knew that couldn't really be happening, I was lost in the spectacle.

The harsh sound of Devereux's angry words jarred me out of my trance.

'If you touch her again, I will kill you,' he bellowed in an unnaturally amplified voice. 'She is under my protection now. Ignore that at your peril.' He released Bryce, who laughed in his face and then vanished.

Literally *vanished*.

I stared at the empty place where Bryce had been and tried to coax the neurons in my brain to fire in some helpful way. I blinked quickly a few times to clear the fog. Perfect. I'd finally lost my mind.

That didn't just happen. I must be sleeping.

Devereux straightened his clothing, smoothed his hair back from his face and walked over to me. He sat down, opened his arms and I sagged against him, forgetting for a moment that I had my suspicions about his mental state, and allowed myself to be held. I could hear his heart beating and felt his warm breath on the side of my face.

We just sat like that, with him holding me, collapsed and shaking against him, for several minutes.

'Did he hurt you?' Devereux asked. 'I could not live with myself if I failed to arrive in time to keep you safe. I never thought Bryce would risk my anger by coming here. I made a terrible mistake. Please forgive me. I will pay much closer attention in the future.'

'Thank you, I'm okay,' I mumbled, but I didn't know what I was thanking him for. Had he appointed himself my bodyguard? Was he saying that he was the reason I'd been attacked? Since Bryce said Devereux was his soulmate, was this some kind of lovers' quarrel I'd got in the middle of?

'No, it is not a lovers' quarrel,' Devereux said, responding to my unstated question. 'We have never been lovers. Bryce refuses to accept the fact that I do not return his feelings. I am not as he wishes me to be, despite his many attempts to sway me. I have no judgements against bisexuality, but that is not my preference. His irrational jealousy has caused him to wreak havoc in the vampire community. He believes if he takes over the coven, he will coerce me into doing his bidding. He is wrong. He has made a fatal error now by involving you.'

Involving me? That didn't sound good. Devereux stroked my hair, and I surrendered to the calming rhythm of his hand. I didn't know how to make sense out of anything that had happened. I prided myself on my logical mind, and none of the puzzle pieces fit. My body was in shock and the wound on my neck throbbed. I couldn't really have seen someone disappear before my eyes. That was impossible. It was probably a delusion triggered by the attack. But it had looked so real.

I was grateful to find that all my clothes were still buttoned, snapped and zipped. Thankfully, Bryce hadn't had the time to follow through on his intention to penetrate more than my neck.

I'd listened to many rape and assault victims talk about their horrible experiences, but I'd never truly understood how it felt to be at the mercy of someone who meant you harm. I sat there drowning in an unfamiliar mishmash of feelings, second-guessing myself about what I could have done to talk him out of hurting me. Or, at the very least, what I could have done to shake myself loose from the effects of whatever drug he must have slipped me.

Maybe it was some new version of the date-rape drug that could be passed along by body fluids. That would explain why he focused on my mouth so much – he wanted to make sure I got the whole dose. Yeah, that must have been it. Right. Even I didn't believe that.

I knew better than to blame myself for any part of what had happened. I was well aware how damaging it was to blame the victim for her own victimisation. But I couldn't sort out the avalanche of emotions.

I *should* have been able to do something. What was all my training for if I couldn't handle one mentally ill maniac?

But damn it to hell – I couldn't move my arms and legs! What the hell kind of weirdness was that? Were all vampire wannabes closet hypnotists? Had he pressed a nerve in my spine to cause paralysis?

How dare those assholes waltz in here and make me feel unsafe in my own office? Unsafe in my own life?

I'd never thought of myself as someone who'd ever need to be rescued. I didn't like the feeling.

Devereux gently turned my head and inspected the bite on my neck.

Something about what he found made him frown. 'You have lost some blood. You will probably feel dizzy for a while. May I?'

He moved in closer for what I thought was a better view and I felt his tongue brushing against the bleeding holes in my neck. Outraged, I pulled away and yelled, 'What the hell are you doing?' I immediately felt woozy from the sudden movement, but I'd be damned if anybody else was going to snack on me tonight.

'I have stopped the bleeding. One true thing about the vampire legends is that we have a substance in our saliva that helps wounds heal faster. And, of course, blood is a wonderful delicacy and I would never pass up the opportunity to partake. It is my nature.'

Something about the words 'it is my nature' roused me from my stupor. Suddenly it all came back to me. I was in my office and Devereux was one of the lost souls pretending to be vampires. And I'd been attacked by a lunatic.

'I am not pretending to be anything,' he said. 'I apologise for invading your mind, but we do not have the luxury of time. Bryce is indeed a lunatic, and you need to fortify yourself with facts. Facts are important to you, are they not?'

I struggled up from the couch, my face hot with anger, and was just about to vent some of it on Devereux when he stood and picked me up in his arms, all in one invisible movement.

Now, I'm not a small person. In my two-inch heels I could easily reach 5'10', and no one had ever complained about how I filled out my swimsuit. But for the second time in one night I'd been scooped up like a sack of potatoes and made to feel like a helpless infant. I couldn't even remember the last time anyone had the nerve to touch me without my permission, but that seemed to be the name of the game with these people.

I pushed against him and, just as with Bryce, it was impossible to wriggle free. His arms were unyielding. Closing my eyes tight to hold back the waterworks I felt gathering there, I tried very hard not to cry, but I was suddenly so exhausted I didn't know how much longer I could keep everything inside. Part of me just wanted to curl up in his arms and sleep.

'Please listen now.' Devereux moved gracefully around the room, apparently trying to soothe me. 'There is much I need to tell you. We must talk about the dangerous situation you are in. I am grateful you have finally come, but your arrival has inflamed Bryce's irrational thoughts. I must protect you . . .'

I have finally come? What does that mean?

'No.' I shook my head. 'Please put me down. I'm sure you mean well, but this has been a terrible night and I just want to go home. I appreciate your pulling Bryce off me, and you've been very kind, but I've had enough.' What did he mean that I'd finally come? Come from where? The tears I'd been trying to hold back slid down my face and I made a pathetic sniffing sound.

He studied me briefly, lifted my chin up towards him and gently kissed my lips. He pulled back, gazed at me with soft turquoise eyes for a few seconds more, then bent down and kissed me again, lightly at first, then deeper. His lips were warm and silky and, without even thinking about it, I put my arms around his neck and kissed him back.

Hey, wait. I'm kissing a stranger. And liking it. What's wrong with me?

He let my feet find the floor and wrapped his arms around me, never altering the intensity of the kiss. He brushed his tongue along my lip and I opened my mouth for him. Whatever else he might have been, he was one awesome kisser.

Somebody hose me down, I'm going to spontaneously combust.

We reluctantly pulled our lips apart and he enveloped me into a warm hug. I could feel both of our hearts beating out different rhythms. It occurred to me that my sensing Devereux's heartbeat was proof he wasn't a vampire. Everyone knew the dead had no heartbeat.

The ridiculousness of that thought made me want to laugh out loud – or scream. I didn't know which was more upsetting: my granting validity to the possibility of the existence of vampires or kissing a beautiful nut-case. I was in deep shit any way you sliced it.

He stepped back from me and brushed a stray lock of hair from my face. 'I think you have had enough excitement for one night. Please allow me to drive you home. I promise I will be a perfect gentleman.'

I was going to argue that I could drive myself, but it just wasn't true. I could either take Devereux up on his offer or call a cab, and since I needed my car the next morning, the choice was clear.

Well, there you have it: if Devereux was really a vampire he wouldn't know how to drive, right? Don't they all sprout bat wings and fly?

Devereux chuckled softly. I was going to ask him what was so funny, but my body's lack of coordination suddenly captured my attention.

I had intended to walk over to my desk and gather my things to leave, but even that small attempt to move under my own power proved to be too much for my legs and my knees buckled. Devereux caught me and lifted me into his arms again. I'm not saying it wasn't pleasant, but I felt like a limp rag doll and I didn't understand what had happened to cause me to be so lethargic. 'What's wrong with me? Why am I so weak? What did Bryce do to me?'

'He bespelled you and then he drank your blood.'

'What? You're kidding, right?' *Oh, please, no more vampire fantasies. My brain is going to explode.*

'No. I am very serious. Bryce is a master of enchantment. We all have the ability to use our eyes to entrance mortals, but Bryce takes special pleasure in manipulation and control. He is very powerful and, to use psychology terms, he altered your brain waves. That is why you feel so confused: he surely had intended to drain you to near-death, and he would have had I not arrived when I did.'

Reality check.

'Do you mean he used his fake fangs to make holes in my neck and actually sucked my blood out and swallowed it?' My professional self refused to accept what Devereux was telling me. I didn't want him to be crazy.

He raised one of his perfectly arched eyebrows and stared down at me for a few seconds. 'Humans have the most remarkable ability to ignore what they do not wish to see. The stronger the mind, the harder it is to accept what is hiding in the shadows. I would rather we had the time to introduce you slowly to the ideas you resist, but that is not possible now. This situation is not something that will go away like a bad dream. Bryce will not stay away. His misguided feelings for me have gone far enough and I must take action. He is destroying the unity of the coven.'

I started to ask more questions, but he shook his head. 'No, that is enough for tonight.'

He walked me over to my desk, bent down so I could pick up my briefcase and my purse, and we left to find my car.

I must have fallen asleep on the ride to my house because the next thing I knew, we were there and he was lifting me out of the passenger side of my car.

As he carried me up to my front door I asked, 'How did you know where to go? I didn't give you directions to my house.'

'I performed my "little parlour trick". I can do the same with your alarm code if you wish, or you may simply punch in the numbers.'

I gazed up at his face, decided I didn't have the energy to argue, entered the code and unlocked my door. We stepped into my living room and I blurted, 'Hey, I thought vampires could only come in if they were invited.'

The moment I said it, I couldn't believe it had come out of my mouth. Embarrassment warmed my cheeks. I must have had some kind of head injury or something because I'd never make light of someone's delusion if I was in my right mind. I'd just flunked *Being a Therapist 101*.

'I'm sorry. That was very thoughtless of me.'

He laughed. 'I am pleased you are getting into the spirit of things. But that particular bit of vampire lore is false – we can come and go as we desire. Where is your bedroom?'

I tensed. 'My bedroom? Why do you want to know where my bedroom is?'

He stared down at me, the warmth in his eyes replaced by something remote and cold. 'Yes, it is wise for you to be afraid. No matter how much some of us might wish to pretend, we are not human and we do not live by human rules. We are not humans with fangs. But for tonight, allow me to put your mind at ease. As delightful as it would be to take you to your bedroom and make love to you, I am offering only to carry you to the comfort of your bed. I would be lying, however, if I said I do not hope for an invitation in the future.'

'Er, thanks?'

He carried me upstairs to my bedroom, held me easily with one arm while he pulled back the bedclothes and laid me down. Then he removed my shoes, covered me with the blankets and gazed into my eyes. The last thing I remember was that wonderful voice saying, 'Sleep.'

CHAPTER 6

The ground slips from beneath me and I'm falling, tumbling into surreal unconsciousness where there's no air, no life, and I can't breathe. My entire body contracts in terror as I plummet down into something I'm certain will be beyond my ability to withstand. The void pulls me into a darkness so complete there's no comprehension of it. Still falling and falling, with no sense of speed or location, just the continuous, ever-building dread. I'm enclosed, spiralling down some long tube, dense with stifling-hot, thick air. Then, without notice, I'm expelled out into an empty, cold, desolate nothing. My very essence fragmenting in all directions as death whispers to me. The descent lasts for ever as a distant voice shrieks horrible-sounding words I can't understand, echoing in oblivion. The voice crawls over me and through me, penetrating my skin like hundreds of carnivorous insects, and I scream in the darkness, flailing my arms and legs. Is there something even worse than death? Then the shock of crashing down into warm liquid. Blood — sticky, thick, coppery-scented and old — very old. The intensity of the harsh landing keeps me afloat for only seconds before I discover there's nothing underneath me. No foundation, nothing to hold me, no one. I go under, still screaming, gasping and swallowing blood. I'm drowning in the blood and the

*overwhelming hopelessness ... terror larger than I can hold, and
someone is laughing.*

'No!' I screamed. A shrill ringing startled me and my eyes
flew open. I bolted up, heart beating fast and hard. Shaking,
I leaned back against the headboard and noticed all the blankets and pillows from my bed were on the floor. Fragments
of the dream swam back into my awareness, and the feeling
of terror intensified. I knew I was safe in my bed, but the
memory of spiralling down into that darkness pressed against
my chest and I struggled to slow my breathing. Rivers of
sweat snaked down my face and pooled between my breasts.
I distantly observed that I was still wearing the clothes I'd
worn yesterday.

The annoying sound continued to intrude, louder now. A
headache that had started as a dull throb over my left eye
now infiltrated my entire brain and beat a strong cadence
of its own, rivalling what I finally worked out was the telephone ringing. I took some deep breaths, pushed the wet
hair back from my face, and cleared my throat. Rolling over
towards the nightstand, I fumbled for the phone.

'Yes?' I croaked.

'Dr Knight? This is Special Agent Stevens. We met at the
hospital yesterday. I'm sorry, did I wake you?'

'Who?' My brain stubbornly refused to connect the dots,
and the inside of my upper lip had become hermetically
sealed to my teeth.

'The FBI guy from the emergency room. Special Agent Stevens.'

I ran my tongue over my teeth in a vain attempt at hydration
and wound up making dry, smacking noises with my lips.

'Special Agent Stevens? Uh, yes. Okay, I remember. I recognise your voice.'

Idiot. You let the phone ring a thousand times. Of course you woke me. And you'll never know how grateful I am that you did.

Groggy, I squinted over at the clock to see if it really was as ungodly an hour as I imagined it to be, and it was.

I sucked in another deep breath, held on to the solid reality of the phone and forced myself to calm down. I cleared my throat again. 'Why are you calling me at 5 a.m., Special Agent Stevens? And how did you get my home phone number? It's unlisted.'

'I work for the FBI – enough said?'

'So why are you calling?' I reached for my blanket on the floor and spread it across my legs.

'I want to find out if you've heard from your client, Emerald Addison, the one you brought to the hospital?'

'What do you mean? She's still in intensive care, isn't she?'

'Well, that answers my question. No. She isn't still in intensive care. Sometime between 1 a.m. and 4 a.m. she went missing.'

'What are you talking about?' I barked, the pain in my head slam-dancing in heavy shoes. I pressed the palm of my hand against my forehead as if that would keep my skull from exploding. 'The last time I saw Emerald, she was in no condition to do anything. There's just no way she could have got up and walked out of the hospital. What are you doing about it?'

His voice held the verbal equivalent of a smirk. 'It sounds like we're a little cranky when we don't get our beauty sleep, Doc. Even though you're being testy, I'll answer your question anyway. This case is being treated as an abduction or a missing person. Each of those categories has its own protocol, and the local cops are in charge. Since your client was attacked in the same manner as the other cases I'm investigating, I'm being included in the information loop. So far we have zip. I'm hoping you can tell me something that'll give us a lead.'

Okay. He gets points for pulling me out of that nightmare, but cute cop or not, there's no way I'm sharing client information. Even if I knew anything.

I took a deep breath, pushed 'play' on the 'I'm a Professional' tape in my mental repertoire, and began speaking in my therapist voice. 'As I mentioned yesterday, I'm not at liberty to tell you anything about anyone. If there's something general I can help you with, as a psychologist, I'd be willing to do that.'

'Great. I'll be right there. Put on some coffee, okay?'

'What?' I sat up. *The pushy bastard. I didn't expect him to take me up on it – and certainly not immediately.* 'Wait a minute! I need to shower and get dressed. You can't come over now!'

'How much time do you need?'

There was that cocky tone again, the tone that said he assumed I'd be spending hours primping in front of the mirror.

'Give me half an hour.'

'Half an hour. Will do.'

'Hey, hold on – don't you need me to give you directions to my house?'

He chuckled. 'FBI, remember? We've got all those handy little records. See you in thirty.'

I hung up the phone and rolled out of my comfortable bed, still on automatic pilot. Then I stumbled around and turned on the light. I managed to remove all the damp sheets, threw them into the laundry hamper and headed to the shower. It took ten minutes of standing like a statue under the hot spray before the sensation of something crawling on my skin receded, and I felt somewhat normal again.

I stood with my arms braced against the tile walls enclosing the bathtub, willing the hot water to wash away the fearful residue from the nightmare. The sound of the hideous laughter still echoed through my inner world, reverberating like a ghostly memory.

I picked up a bar of soap and revelled in the sensation of it gliding over my skin and began to feel renewed – to come back to myself. I slid the bar over one side of my neck, kneading gently, and when I lathered the other side I was startled by a sharp jolt of pain. Instinctively, I dropped the soap, which hit the bottom of the tub with a loud thud as I explored the tender skin with my fingers.

'Shit!' I stepped away from the water and gingerly slid my finger over the painful area, mentally shaking off another layer of drowsiness.

Touching the wound on my neck brought the horrible events of the previous evening back to me in living colour: some demented maniac had broken into my office and punctured my neck with his teeth.

His teeth! What movie was it where the psycho put on his grandmother's sharpened dentures and chewed on his victims? How the hell did they get into my office? What a miserable night. First the psychopaths, then the dream. Oh yes – and let's not forget cocky FBI agents, although I guess this didn't qualify as 'night' any more.

That nightmare was off the charts. I couldn't remember ever having such a vivid, terrifying dream before – all that blood and existential emptiness. Maybe those assholes coming to my office last night had frightened me even more than I realised. The dream was probably a reaction to their threats and my feelings of mortality. The standard death dream. Or an indication that my brain was turning into scrambled eggs. Well, whatever it was, I'd have to sort it out later.

I hadn't even begun to think about whether or not I should report the attack to the police. There was the confidentiality issue to consider. Bryce was connected to Midnight, and I couldn't involve her, but if I pressed charges, she'd probably be dragged in.

It was definitely time to move my office to a building with security – cameras, doormen, the whole deal. No more uninvited visitors.

My shower completed, I stepped out and wrapped myself in a thick extra-large towel. Enjoying the warm feeling, I went over to the mirror, wiped away a patch of fog and checked out the wound on my neck.

'Damn! What the hell?'

I stared at the carnage. There were two blatant, swollen holes surrounded by a sea of red with purple and yellow blotches. It looked as if I'd been ravaged by a wild dog or something. I opened the medicine cabinet, rummaged around for my antiseptic salve, and read the label to see if it said anything about being an effective defence against human germs. I remembered reading something about the germs in a human's mouth being worse than anything else. I hoped that wasn't true.

Antibacterial? Well, I guessed that would be better than nothing. Was there any such thing as an anti-vampire-wannabe medicine? An analgesic to ward off those pesky undead cooties? I'd probably need to get a tetanus shot, at the very least. Yeah. There I was, thinking about this weird situation as if it was just another day at the office . . .

I dotted some of the medicine on the wound and held an inner debate about the merits of covering it versus letting it breathe. Breathing won. For now.

Touching the bite mark reminded me of Devereux's tongue sliding over my neck and I had a pleasant body rush. Then I remembered the feel of his lips and noticed my nipples were hard and the area between my thighs was growing warm and wet. I took a quick ride down Possibility Lane as I imagined how it would be to feel his hand there.

The human mind really is resilient. What was I thinking about while patching up the leftovers of my very own psychotic Bela Lugosi's munch-fest on my neck? Sex. Sex with Devereux. I definitely didn't get enough sleep.

Still tingling from the mental afterglow, I towelled my hair, sprayed it with a super anti-tangle concoction, and flipped my head over so that my hair hung down in a thick curtain in front of me. I picked through it with my wide-tooth comb, snarling as I struggled with the clumps of hair that refused to play nice.

I stopped when a simple realisation washed over me. It finally penetrated my sleep-clogged brain that I could have told Agent Stevens I was unavailable and would see him at my office later. I could have continued snoozing in my bed. I definitely knew better than to make any decisions before I'd had my caffeine fix. Apparently the events of the previous night plus the demonic nightmare caused me to have an even more intense case of fuzz-brain. The annoyance of my obvious act of stupidity made me fling my head back up with such momentum that the weight of my hair almost gave me a whiplash.

'Ouch! Shit!'

I strode into my bedroom and tugged open the door to my walk-in closet, knocking a picture of the Stanley Hotel in Estes Park off the wall.

Okay, temper tantrum accomplished. Next?

I climbed into my favourite baggy jeans and a University of Colorado T-shirt and headed down to the kitchen, fantasising about that first cup of nirvana.

After I started the Mr Coffee, I checked my office voicemail to see if Emerald had left a message. She hadn't.

I was pouring my first cup of coffee when Agent Stevens knocked on my door. I didn't usually get up that early, but every time I did, I was reminded of how much I loved watching the sun come up. There's that wonderful feeling of a new beginning, of endless possibilities. This morning in particular I appreciated the beauty, light, and warmth of the dawn.

I let him in, then stood for a moment in the open doorway, watching the light reclaim the sky and enjoying the crisp fall breeze.

'Hey, Earth to Dr Knight – where do you keep your coffee mugs?'

I jumped when he spoke and glared at my visitor, who was making himself quite at home. He wandered around the kitchen, opened every cupboard and drawer, and then parked himself in front of my open refrigerator. 'Holy cow! There's nothing in here but take-away food. Don't you know how to cook? There isn't even any milk for my coffee.'

Is this guy for real?

Waking me up before the crack of dawn was bad enough, but inviting himself over and having an opinion about the state of my refrigerator was over the top. My head pounded and I simply had no patience for dealing with this arrogant cop. If it hadn't been for my concern about Emerald, I'd have kicked his tight little butt right out the door.

The longer I studied him, the more my anger dwindled. He looked exhausted, as if he hadn't been to bed yet. He was either wearing the same clothes I'd seen him in at the hospital, or he had a collection of jeans and rumpled white T-shirts. His eyelids drooped, the purple-blue of his eyes looked less vibrant, and his hair was a monument to what happens when you use your fingers as a comb.

Come on, Kismet. Don't go getting all warm and gooey now because the guy's worn out. This is a professional consultation. No caretaking allowed.

'Sit down, Special Agent Stevens.' He eased his long frame into one of my kitchen chairs. I poured him a mug of coffee, carried it over to the table, and joined him.

'You can call me Alan, Doc.'

I pulled another clump of my hair over my shoulder, making sure it still covered the ghastly souvenir on my neck. 'Well, Alan, how can I help you?'

'Why are you counselling vampires? Don't you know how dangerous that is?'

And to think that for the past thirty years I doubt if I've heard the word 'vampire' more than ten times, and now everyone I talk to seems obsessed with it.

I shook my head. 'Dangerous? What's dangerous about helping people free themselves from a destructive delusion? It's my job to uncover faulty thinking.'

He paused and raised an eyebrow. 'That's the second time you've said something that leads me to believe you don't know what kind of tiger you've got by the tail. Are you seriously telling me you think vampires are delusions? You really don't see the big picture?'

Oh, please. I'm not awake enough for this. I can't believe an FBI guy is talking about vampires.

'Can I see your identification again, Agent Stevens?'

He pulled his picture ID out of his pocket and handed it to me. 'You think there's something fishy about an FBI agent discussing vampires?'

I inspected the ID. It appeared authentic, but I really had no way of knowing.

'You read my mind, Agent Stevens.'

'No, I read your face, Dr Knight.'

I handed his ID back to him. 'Don't FBI agents usually work in pairs? Where's your partner, Agent Stevens?'

'I'm temporarily between partners.' He grinned. 'I seem to be an acquired taste – my partners keep asking for transfers. If you're nervous about whether I'm who I say I am, you can call the local police. They know all about me and what I'm doing here. So, will you answer my question now? Why are you working with vampires?'

My neck throbbed, and my patience was gone. The good feeling I'd gained from the hot shower was retreating at the speed of light.

'Special Agent Stevens, I didn't get up this early to discuss fairy tales or cartoon characters, so unless there is some aspect of psychology that I can help you with, I think we're finished.'

'Wow,' he said, slapping his palms on his thighs, 'you really don't know. I figured when I saw your ad in the paper that you knew what you were dealing with, but you're flying blind. You're messing with things you don't understand, and somebody needs to enlighten you. It might as well be me.'

'I don't think that's necessary.' I sighed and stood.

'Wait.' He grabbed my wrist.

My breath caught. I instinctively jerked my arm out of his grip and took a step back. Nobody else was going to put his hands on me uninvited. I glared at him. 'Don't touch me.'

'I'm sorry.' He held his hands up in surrender. 'That was inexcusable. I get overly excited sometimes, especially when I don't get any sleep. I promise to control myself. Please, hear me out. I think you'll be intrigued by what I have to say.'

Please? I stared into his watery, bloodshot eyes and saw what appeared to be sincerity. Or maybe it was simply exhaustion. Something about the determined set of his jaw and his easy smile convinced me to sit back down at the table and give him the benefit of the doubt. 'I'm listening.' I crossed my arms over my chest.

'Thank you.' He mimicked my defensive posture. 'First, let

me give you a little background, to show you that I didn't start out as a believer either. You and I actually have a lot in common – I have a Ph.D. in psychology, too.'

My mouth formed into an 'O'.

It was apparent he saw the surprise on my face. 'Yeah, Doctor Stevens, at your service. I never intended to be a therapist – my interests lie with the criminal mind. So when I was recruited by the FBI's Behavioral Analysis Unit—'

'As in *The Silence of the Lambs*?' I asked.

'Yeah. I jumped at the chance to become a profiler, and I specialise in cases that have paranormal elements. Yep, I can see by the gleam in your eyes that you're drawing comparisons between my work and a certain television programme. It's true. Some clever coworker or another is always putting old *X-Files* posters on my door, and my official nickname is Mulder.'

So, Special Agent Stevens isn't your normal FBI agent. Interesting.

I had to laugh. I'd enjoyed that programme and Agent Mulder's dry, sarcastic sense of humour. Of course, I fancied myself to be more like Scully.

'I'm impressed.' I sipped my coffee. 'So what's a profiler like you doing in my kitchen wanting to enlighten me about vampires?' I had to admit that thinking of him as a colleague rather than only a cop was making him even more interesting to me. I was a sucker for a clever mind.

He relaxed back in the chair and stretched like a cat. The white T-shirt material moulded to his chest muscles and accented the outlines of his nipples. Very distracting.

He saw me notice and wiggled his eyebrows.

What an ego.

'About a year ago,' he said, 'I started tracking a pattern: dead bodies showing up with holes in their necks, drained of blood. At first I did just what you're doing – I wrote it off to some creative form of mental illness. I assumed I was searching for one predator who moved around a lot, or maybe a copycat murderer who had picked up on the vampire theme. As I suspect you've done, I researched everything I could find involving blood-drinking.'

He downed the last of his coffee, carried his mug over to the pot, poured himself a refill, and returned to the table.

Why, yes, thank you, I'd love some more coffee. Hmmm, Narcissistic Personality Disorder? Attention Deficit Disorder? Or just a typical male?

'We're on the same page so far,' I admitted.

He drummed his fingers on the side of his mug. 'I showed up at the murder scenes, checking for similarities, and the cases just kept getting weirder. Some of the bodies had multiple bites that the lab results showed came from different sets of sharp teeth. No human or animal DNA in the wounds. There were never any signs of struggle, though, no needle marks for drugs. It was as if the victims simply lay there and let themselves be drained. Almost like some form of hypnosis or brainwashing.'

He stopped talking, scanned the kitchen and pointed to a bag of cookies on the counter.

'You mind? I haven't had any breakfast yet.' Without waiting for my response, he leaped up, fetched the bag of cookies and returned to his seat.

'Help yourself.' I wondered if he was always this comfortable with strangers, or if he was simply oblivious.

No, I'm sure – oblivious.

'Then something happened to turn me into a believer,' he continued. 'I was in Los Angeles, following some leads about the latest murders, and I was attacked by a vampire.'

He noticed me tighten my lips, and he said, 'Let me finish. I know this pushes all your "this guy needs therapy" buttons, but hang in there with me.' He opened the cookie bag, selected one and took a bite.

He excitedly pointed his finger up in the air and brought it down in a quick dive towards the floor. 'I saw this thing fly down – I kid you not – from the roof of a twelve-storey building. He landed in front of me as if he'd just stepped off someone's front porch. Not a hair ruffled. He came at me with his teeth bared showing these long, sharp canines, picked me up by my neck like I weighed nothing and threw me down on the ground. He was on me so fast I didn't have time to be afraid. I started shouting questions at him, asking him to tell me about himself. For some astounding reason, he stepped back and started answering. At the risk of being boringly unoriginal, it really was an interview with a vampire.'

It sounds as if poor Special Agent Stevens is missing a few of his marbles.

I bit the inside of my mouth to keep myself from smiling. 'What did this vampire tell you?'

He mentally dissected the expression on my face to determine whether I was being serious or sarcastic. He must have decided my question was on the level.

'That's a very long conversation for another day, but what's important is that my education was vastly expanded. He gave me a graduate course in the strange and impossible. I think I must have connected with him at exactly the right time because he was willing to spill all the vampire secrets. Actually, I think he was suicidal. Maybe I should refer him to you for therapy?' he joked.

He ate another cookie.

'Okay,' I shot him a frosty look, 'so let me get this straight. You're honestly trying to convince me to believe that there are such things as vampires – preternatural blood-drinking ghouls – living among us? That they aren't just myths or psychotic humans?'

He stared into my eyes. 'That's exactly what I'm telling you. What's more, I'm prepared to put my money where my mouth is. I can show you. I think the vampires have Emerald Addison. There's a coven in one of the clubs downtown, a former church, called The Crypt.'

That's the club Midnight mentioned.

'The vampire I talked to – Ian, who's probably back in London now – told me that the group and their leader have been here for years, and they keep a low profile. Recently some new bloodsuckers, the ones I'm pursuing, have come to town and they're killers. Ian said that the one he's most afraid of is called Bryce.'

At the sound of his name, my heart stopped and my blood ran cold. I visibly started in my seat, sucked in all the air in the room, and gasped.

Alan jumped in his chair. 'What is it?'

'You just said the name of the psychopath who barged into my office last night and attacked me.'

He pulled out a small notebook and pen from his pocket

and began scribbling down everything I'd just said. 'You were attacked last night? Tell me what happened.'

My stomach knotted at the memory.

'After I finished at the hospital, I went to my office to work for a while. Bryce and a small, creepy-looking man called Raleigh broke in, threatened me, and Bryce attacked me. He somehow punctured my neck and actually sucked blood out and swallowed it. I was sure he intended to rape me, but thankfully he didn't.'

I told the true story right up to the point just before Devereux entered the scene. Lying, I said that while I was passed out something must have scared Bryce and Raleigh off because when I woke up, they were gone. I didn't know why I wasn't willing to talk about Devereux, but I just wasn't. After all, he had rescued me.

Lame story, Kismet.

Alan put the notebook and pen down on the table, stroked an invisible beard, and frowned at me. 'You're holding out. There's more that you aren't telling me. What is it?' He reached over, lifted my hair out of the way, and turned my head, eyeballing the Technicolor puncture marks on my neck. 'I told you that counselling vampires was dangerous. No wonder you look like death this morning.'

Prince Charming has nothing on this guy.

'Gee, you sweet talker, you.'

'Sorry. Tact isn't my strong suit. In fact, being so blunt and thoughtless is why I never seriously thought about being a psychotherapist. I'd be alienating clients left and right. Actually, you couldn't really look bad if you tried.' He grinned, reached over and picked up a renegade lock of my hair and tucked it behind my ear.

'Thanks, I think.' I'd not only been surprised by his touch, but also by the pleasant sensation that lingered where his finger had brushed my skin.

I've definitely got to get out more. I'll bet Denver's started putting hormones in the water. Or maybe Devereux did something to me the first time I met him. I've been acting strange ever since.

Suddenly feeling awkward, I reached into the cookie bag and pulled out a chunk of chocolate-chip heaven and chewed loudly. Too loudly.

The smirk on Alan's face told me he'd picked up on my discomfort and was enjoying it. He slouched down in the chair and lifted an ankle to rest on his knee.

I pushed further away from the table and put way too much effort into brushing cookie crumbs off my clothes.

As usual, my confidence with men is underwhelming.

'You said you can show me – prove to me that vampires exist?'

'Yeah, I can.' He grinned again, obviously enjoying my unease. 'But right now I need to head back to police head-quarters and see if there's anything new on the whereabouts of Emerald Addison. Are you free tonight?'

Smug bastard.

'That depends on why you're asking.'

He got up and filled his coffee cup again, then paced around the kitchen. 'I think it's time for you to find out what you've stepped in. I want to take you to that club, The Crypt, and give you a dose of an alternative reality. How about I pick you up at 10 p.m.?' He reached into the bag on the table and ate yet another cookie.

There's no justice in the world. The man doesn't have an ounce of extra fat on his body. And I've made a thorough inspection.

'Why would you want to go to a place you believe is a vampire coven? Aren't you afraid you'll be attacked again? Why would you want me to go there with you?'

'Whoa!' He gazed down at me, shaking his head. 'For someone who doesn't believe in any of this, you ask a lot of questions. I'll give you a taste of what Ian told me. Becoming a vampire doesn't automatically change someone into an evil monster – that's all fiction. The personality you had before you died is carried over into your new existence. Most important for our purposes, if you were a psychotic human being, you'll be a psychotic vampire. Now, that's a totally different level of psychopathology.'

'I see.' I nodded slowly. *Does he really believe this stuff? Poor guy. They've really pulled one over on him.*

He picked up his notebook from the table and tucked it into his pocket. 'From what I've learned so far, the vampires in the coven at The Crypt are, for lack of a better word, more mellow than the ones I'm searching for. They've been able to stay below the radar for so long because the leader keeps them on a tight leash, and he doesn't tolerate any behaviour that draws attention to their existence.'

'Would I need to take garlic and crosses if I go to The Crypt? Isn't that how vampires are repelled?'

He ignored my sarcasm. Or maybe he hadn't heard it. 'No. I guess that's all bullshit. Ian said religious items have no effect on the undead. Neither does garlic. And I'd personally appreciate if you'd pass on the garlic – I hate the smell of it. But wooden stakes still work, if you want to carry some in your purse.'

'Uh-huh.' *Is he serious? He's an FBI agent? Really?*

Sitting there while he loomed over me had started to make me nervous, so I stood, expecting him to step back out of my way, but he didn't. He remained there, staring at me with those lazy eyes, displaying the same overconfident smirk I'd seen at the hospital.

I raised my chin. 'Excuse me.'

He laughed.

Arrogant jerk.

I waited for him to give me room to move, and when he did, I strolled over to the counter, refilled my coffee mug and returned to sit at the table. I decided to ignore his bad manners.

I inspected the contents of my cup. 'Have you met the vampires at that club?'

'Yeah, I've been over there several times. The head honcho is called Devereux. He's been very cooperative. I'll introduce you.'

At the mention of his name, my body immediately revisited the kiss I'd shared with Devereux and I felt the heat rise on my cheeks. I think it was safe to say that introductions had already been taken care of.

'What about the mythology around vampires drinking human blood? There isn't anything mellow about that,' I said quickly, hoping to divert Alan's attention from what I was sure must have been my obvious reaction to his mention of Devereux. Either he didn't notice or he chose not to comment, because he simply nodded and answered the question.

He paced around the room again. 'Ian told me that the blood issue is highly misunderstood. First, he said it isn't necessary to kill someone. Small amounts of blood from several donors works just fine. As I already said, some vampires – same as humans – have more evil tendencies than others. For those vampires, killing is the thrill. For them, not killing would be like sex without the orgasm. Speaking of orgasms, Ian said that drinking blood is better than sex – which they can have, by the way.'

The image of Devereux invaded my brain and heat coiled up my spine. I concentrated on keeping my face neutral. 'It sounds as if Ian was very talkative.'

'Yeah.' Alan rested his hip against the counter. 'We spent hours together and I took great notes. Then I got more information from the coven at the club. It's been an educational experience. It's also helped clarify who and what I'm searching for.'

'Wait a minute,' I said. 'You told me the vampire leader doesn't draw attention to his group. Why would he volunteer to talk to you? What's to stop you from turning them over to the local police?'

'Think about it: you've been visited by the craziest vampire in Denver, you have clients who sit in your office and tell you about vampires, and I've just spent the last hour trying to convince you that vampires exist, yet you still don't believe. What are the chances anyone would actually think the owner of The Crypt is the leader of a vampire coven? Devereux can tell me the truth because he knows that no one would buy it. And when you see the club you'll understand how easy it is for them to just blend into the fantasy.'

'What about the FBI? Have you told them the truth? Do they know what you're up to?'

'Let's just say that they're under the impression I'm tracking humans who are pretending to be vampires. They might amuse themselves by laughing at my Mulderisms, but the FBI is pretty conservative, and if they knew what I was actually doing I'd be out on my tail. Okay. I'm really outta here now. I'll see you tonight at ten. Oh yeah – thanks for the java.'

With that, he was gone.

CHAPTER 7

It took me a minute to realise I was just sitting there – almost catatonic, my mouth hanging open – staring at the door that had just slammed.

Moving only my eyes, I surveyed the cookie crumbs, coffee drips and crumpled napkins surrounding Alan's empty mug. Then I shook my head and broke into semi-hysterical laughter, the kind of laughter that makes you grab your midsection because it's almost painful in its intensity. I let the crazed frivolity roll through me for a few seconds then started talking to myself, out loud, which in some quarters might be construed as a bad sign.

'I choose Fictional Creatures for $500, Alex!'

Propping my feet up on the chair that had recently been vacated by the firm hindquarters of the oddest FBI agent I was ever likely to meet, I raised my coffee cup in a solitary toast to the memory of his tight jeans exiting my kitchen and loudly sang the theme song from *Jeopardy!*

In my best Alex Trebek voice I said, 'These bloodsucking, undead denizens of the night have taken over the rational minds of the populace of Denver.'

I pretended to press an invisible button on the table. 'What are *vampires*?'

Alex again. 'Yes! Our new winner is Dr Kismet Knight, formerly a respected psychologist, now a permanent resident of Denver Psychiatric Hospital.'

I sang the theme song again, applauded myself and heaved a huge sigh.

'I *definitely* didn't get enough sleep.'

Transfixed by the streaks of colour floating across the morning sky, I stared out the window and drank my coffee. It was exactly one week ago that Midnight walked into my office for the first time, and since then my life had turned into a cliché-ridden afternoon-matinée horror movie in which I was apparently playing a lead role.

I'd fantasised about having more excitement in my life, and I must have inadvertently rubbed some genie's bottle because I'd definitely got my wish. Unfortunately, it fell under the category of 'be careful what you ask for because you might get it'. If I were half as smart as I thought I was, I'd cut my losses and run. I could refer Midnight and Ronald to other therapists and just go back to my regularly scheduled programming. No harm, no foul. Only a madwoman would purposely visit a dance club allegedly run by vampires – vampire wannabes, of course – or listen to fantastical stories told by misguided FBI agents.

Then I tried to imagine never seeing Devereux again and my midsection clenched up. Definitely not a desirable option as far as my body was concerned.

Because there's nothing like being wired and sleepy at the same time, I decided to have one more cup of coffee and jot down some notes for my book. Agent Stevens's fertile imagination had given me lots of ideas for chapters and I'd have to remember to ask him for permission to use the material he'd shared with me. He wasn't a therapist, so there were no confidentiality issues. Maybe I'd even give him credit in the finished manuscript.

The first thing I noticed when I got off the elevator in my office building a while later was a bulging manila envelope propped against my waiting room door. I picked it up, tucked it under my arm and unlocked the doors leading to my reception area and then to my office. I sat down at my desk and inspected the package. There was nothing unusual about it – no address on the front, no postage or writing of any kind. Inside the envelope was some kind of light-blue fabric with extensive stains on it. My gut cramped and goose bumps appeared on my arms. I had an immediate bad feeling and picked up a pencil to lift the cloth out of its container. I'd seen enough cop shows to know about not contaminating evidence, and my intuition told me that I was in possession of something awful.

Using the pencil to spread out the fabric on top of my desk, I could see it was one of those flimsy gowns they use in hospitals, the ones that never close in the back. The stains looked and smelled like blood.

Blood. Hospital gown. My mind went straight to Emerald. Would she have worn this kind of garment?

No. *Get a grip.* There must be hundreds of explanations for this item turning up in front of my door. It probably had nothing to do with Emerald at all. Just a case of someone leaving the package at the wrong place.

Even though I tried hard to delude myself, none of the rationalisations were working and I began to feel nauseated. The smell of the package reminded me of my dream, and I unconsciously reached up to touch the wound on my neck, which I'd covered with a Band-Aid. I had the unpleasant realisation that if I didn't get to the bathroom in ten seconds, I'd throw up on the floor. I made a mad dash and reached the toilet just in time to lose my morning coffee.

Feeling hot and cold at the same time, my stomach completely empty, I went over to the sink and swished some water around in my mouth. It was a good thing I always carried a toothbrush, toothpaste and mouthwash in my purse. I stared into the mirror and reaffirmed Alan's earlier assertion that I did indeed look like death today. Sometimes even the best makeup job wasn't enough. Having such fair skin was a blessing most of the time because I always looked younger than I was, but today I had definitely crossed the line between ivory glow and anaemic pallor.

I shuffled back into my office and rummaged through my briefcase, searching for the business card Alan had given me, and called the number. He answered on the first ring.

'Stevens.'

'Alan, someone left me a bloody hospital gown.'

'Kismet? Is that you? What about a hospital gown?'

'Somebody left a package containing stained blue fabric at my office. Since Emerald disappeared from the intensive care unit, that's too big a coincidence, don't you think? Can you come over and look at it?'

'Yeah. Don't touch anything. I'll alert the local police and we'll be right over.' He hung up without saying goodbye.

I fished the dental hygiene products out of my purse and scurried to the bathroom, where I brushed and swished until I felt almost normal, then headed back to my office.

I sat at my desk, scrutinised the bloodstained material, and wondered again what I'd got myself into. I'd spent the last week bouncing back and forth between fear, confusion and arousal and I was exhausted. I didn't think I'd been of help to anyone, and I certainly hadn't done myself any good.

Staring at my calendar, I realised I hadn't checked my messages, so I punched in the retrieval code for my business voicemail and found several. The first was from Ronald, asking if we could reschedule his appointment because he'd been up all night searching for Emerald. It was a good thing he couldn't make it because he'd be due at the same time the police would likely arrive and I hadn't even taken that into account. In fact, I'd totally forgotten I had a client coming: another indication of my impending mental breakdown. I made a note to return his call later.

I paused the messages and scanned my appointment book to make sure I hadn't neglected any other important business, tapping my pen on the desk. Fran, my seventy-six-year-old UFO abductee client, was scheduled in this morning for her long-standing appointment, but it wasn't going to work today. One of Fran's challenges was a deep distrust of authority figures. I could only imagine what would happen if the police were still here when she arrived. Fran, who weighed no more than ninety pounds soaking wet, had been known to start screaming and flailing at the sight of a uniform, which usually guaranteed problems with whoever was wearing the offending garment at the time. Yes, I was definitely going to reschedule Fran.

After Fran was Spock. His real name was Henry Madison, but he got very upset if anyone called him that. He lived in a perpetual *Star Trek* episode, even going as far as having his ears surgically altered to be 'Vulcan'. He had his costumes tailor-made and shaved his eyebrows so he could draw on the 'correct' ones. Interestingly enough, Spock hadn't come to therapy for any of the reasons one might assume. He'd come because he wanted to explore his poor choices with women. He just couldn't seem to find the woman of his dreams. He suspected mother issues. I thought that was only the tip of the iceberg.

Continuing with the messages, up next was my daily reminder from Brother Luther about the current state of my immortal soul. He usually gave me a portion of the sermon-of-the-week, and kept his remarks very general and impersonal. Today's message had a different tone. He sounded agitated, and he talked a lot about being 'washed in the blood', and made a comment about being a warrior for God. He ranted on until the allotted message time ran out and was cut off mid-tirade. That was the first time one of his messages caused me to feel uncomfortable, and, in light of the other events of the morning, I considered whether or not I needed to tell the police about Brother Luther, too.

CHAPTER 8

Within an hour, my office was inundated with police officers and forensics specialists. They bagged up the manila
envelope and its contents, confiscated the pencil I had used
to move the cloth around, and were in the midst of seeking
clues by crawling inch-by-inch along the hallway in front of
my waiting room door. Alan stood next to my desk, silently
observing the investigation and writing in his ever-present
notebook.

A bulky female officer approached me. She was big the
way that a weightlifter is big, not fat, but solid and muscular.
She must have been six feet tall. Dressed in a no-nonsense
dark-blue trouser-suit, she appeared to be in her late forties,
and the years hadn't been kind. Her grey-streaked hair was
cut very short in a style that required little upkeep, and the
lines in her face had formed themselves into a continuous
scowl. I guessed she'd been someone for whom high school
had been hell, and she'd taken the Gold in the Olympic
Holding a Grudge competition. Not someone I'd want to
mess with, even if she hadn't been wearing a gun at her hip.

She marched purposefully over to me and snarled, 'You Dr
Knight?'

'Yes.' Gazing up at her, I suddenly felt six years old, called to the principal's office.

'Lieutenant Bullock. I need to get your statement.' She pointed with her thumb back over her shoulder. 'Let's go over there.'

I nodded. We walked to the couch and sat, and I told her everything about finding the envelope, taking out the bloody blue gown and calling Special Agent Stevens. She stopped writing and observed me, waiting, I supposed, for me to say something else. When I didn't, she prompted, her voice deceptively even, 'I understand you have a missing client?'

'I'm afraid I'm not able to respond to that question.'

'Why is that, Dr Knight?' She lowered her head ever so slightly. 'You're the one who called us.' Her voice became very quiet and controlled.

Feeling the chill of her frosty gaze, I swallowed loudly and cleared my throat. 'Under the rules of confidentiality, I'm not able to discuss whether someone is or isn't a client. I called Special Agent Stevens because finding a package containing a bloody anything is out of my area of expertise. I thought it might be something he could deal with.'

She held my eyes for a moment. 'Why would someone leave a bloodstained hospital gown in front of your door, Doctor?'

'I have no idea.'

She gave an unfriendly smile. 'Do you know Emerald Addison?'

I sat silently, keeping my face pleasantly neutral.

She moved closer and locked eyes with me. 'I know Emerald Addison is your client. You're obstructing a police investigation by refusing to cooperate. I'll need copies of the records you have on her friends who are also your clients,' she demanded, her voice getting louder.

I tensed. 'Lieutenant Bullock, I can only repeat what I've already said. I'm unable to respond. I'm bound by the rules of confidentiality.' *And Emerald really isn't my client.*

She bolted up off the couch. 'You're starting to piss me off, Dr Knight.'

Whoa. A cop with an anger issue – what a surprise. I met her gaze. 'That isn't my intention, Lieutenant. I'm bound by my professional obligations, just as you are.'

She made a growling sound, paced around in front of me, then stopped and bent down so that our faces were inches apart. She whispered loudly, 'If the blood on that gown matches the blood of the missing girl, you're going to have a lot more questions to answer. Maybe you didn't just find the gown. Maybe you had it all along. Maybe you're hiding something. Maybe I'll get a court order to force you to give me your records.'

Every time she said the word 'maybe' she accented and elongated the first syllable, allowing each repetition to rise in pitch.

My heart pounded in my chest and I felt sweat breaking out on my forehead. First Bryce, now Bullock. No one had ever got in my face and threatened me that way before, and I still wasn't sure how to deal with it. Since I didn't know what to say, I said nothing. That appeared to make her even angrier. I knew she couldn't force me to divulge information, and I assumed she knew that, too.

'Wilson,' Lieutenant Bullock said to the tall, lanky policeman hovering next to her, 'make sure you get all the good doctor's contact information. I want to be able to find her day or night.'

'I have it,' he said, giving me cold eyes.

She squinted at me and snapped, 'Don't leave town.'

Then, like a fiery comet pulling meteorites in its tail, she left, taking all the officers with her.

Alan came over, sat next to me on the couch, and patted my hand. 'Now you know why her nickname is "Bull".'

I flopped back against the cushions, letting my shoulders slump. My mouth was so dry it took me a couple of attempts before I could speak. 'What just happened here? All I did was find something and call it in. I was being a model citizen. Why am I suddenly a suspect?'

'You're not, not really. They're all freaked out because they haven't been able to solve any of the recent murders or find the missing girl. This is the first lead they've had in days. Lieutenant Bullock is taking this case very personally because she knew the first murder victim – he was a friend of hers, and she's a very loyal person. Don't let her get to you. I'll try to run interference.'

'What about the gown?' I angled my head in his direction. 'Do you think it was Emerald's? Why would someone bring it to my office?'

'I don't know. Yesterday after Emerald was admitted to the hospital, I was hanging around in intensive care, hoping to catch a glimpse of her after they cleaned her up. My persistence paid off because during the transfusion, the nurse walked away for a minute and I took a good look at Emerald. The gown in the envelope was exactly the same as the one she was wearing in the hospital. Now, whether or not the blood is hers, only the lab guys can tell us, but my money's on the likelihood that it is.'

He studied his notebook, absently flipping through the pages, then gave me that serious eye-contact he was so good at.

'You were the one who brought Emerald to the hospital, so maybe giving the bloody gown to you was a message. Can you think of anyone who'd want to communicate something to you that way? Any unusually psychotic clients? Anyone wanting to hurt you? Have you received any threats? You said Bryce and his sidekick broke into your office. What about them?' He chewed on the end of his pen, observing my face expectantly.

As soon as he mentioned Bryce and Raleigh's visit, fear invaded my brain, but I wasn't sure how much more I could tell Alan – how much I could trust him. If I implicated Midnight in the investigation, that was definitely a breach of confidentiality. I decided to fall back on an old therapy technique: when in doubt, say nothing. I wasn't actually lying if I simply withheld information. Therapists are required to be discerning. But I did take note that my comfort level with bending the truth had expanded. I mentally added that to my list of things to worry about later.

I kept my expression relaxed and called on my Inner Sociopath. 'No. I don't understand any of this. I can't imagine it has anything to do with me. Do you think Emerald is still alive?'

He studied the carpet. 'I wish I could be more encouraging, but if they've drained her blood again, it doesn't bode well. I'm hoping we can find out more tonight.' He lifted his eyes to mine. 'Are you still up for visiting The Crypt?'

Damn. I'd forgotten all about that. Maybe I could catch Tom at his conference and make sure he wasn't planning to stop by my house. I wasn't inclined to let him use my office part-time anyway, and I knew better than to be alone with him and a bottle of wine.

'Yes, I guess so. I'm not sure what good it will do, but since I'm involved now, I can't just walk away.' And I had to admit I was curious about the place. Right. Who was I kidding? I was curious about Devereux. Imagining the possibility of getting another glimpse of the platinum-haired fantasy object, I drifted off for a few seconds, indulging in a brief R-rated mental interlude.

Sensing Alan's eyes on me, I shook myself out of my daydream and wondered what the FBI profiler had seen on my face to cause the eyebrow-elevated, semi-suspicious expression he wore on his.

I was about to enquire as to the meaning of that expression when I got a strong intuitive hit that he thought I was hiding something. I simply knew the gist of what he was thinking and feeling. Just my usual. Daydreaming about Devereux must have distracted me from my mental stress-a-thon long enough for me to sense the subtle layers and become aware of Alan's energy. It did seem that my ability to psychically know things worked best when I wasn't consciously trying to use it. Yeah, that was helpful. Or maybe it was more accurate to say it worked best when I didn't get in the way.

It didn't seem possible that Alan could know anything about my interest in Devereux, so his flash of distrust had to have something to do with Emerald. But it really didn't matter what he thought, because I wasn't hiding anything. Not really. In fact, I'd never felt more ineffectual and clueless.

Besides, even if he somehow did know about the contents of my fantasy, it wasn't any of his damn business anyway.

He opened his mouth to speak and I stood, surprising him. The best defence is offence. I'd had just about enough intrigue for one morning. I turned to him, straightened my posture, and checked my watch. 'I have a client coming soon, so I need to get ready. Thanks for contacting the police and handling everything – I really appreciate it. I'll see you tonight.'

He remained seated for a few seconds, his face still registering confused surprise.

Shit. Now he really thinks I'm up to something. He's sending out wave after wave of questions. I should've just asked him why he was staring at me that way. Now I've turned it into some big, strange deal. Why does he make me so nervous?

He finally stood slowly, his eyebrows contracted into a V, and offered a tight smile.

'Yeah, tonight, sure. See you then.'

He walked to the door, glanced over his shoulder at me once and left.

'Well,' I said out loud, 'I certainly handled that with finesse and style. Let's hear it for the Queen of Mixed Messages.'

I forced myself to turn my attention back to work and settled in at my desk, intending to grab hold of anything even remotely normal, anything I felt competent to handle.

As I sat there, I remembered that I'd forgotten to tell the police about the phone calls from Brother Luther. It was probably just as well I hadn't, because it was most likely nothing. I'd been so caught up in the drama of the last few days that I was getting paranoid. Plus, telling Lieutenant Bullock something that might prove to be a false alarm was the last thing I intended to do.

Since Ronald had cancelled his appointment and I'd rescheduled Fran, I had some time to myself before Spock was due for his session. I tried writing some case notes but kept getting distracted and staring out the window. I decided to stroll over to the nearby 16th Street Mall, a pedestrian-friendly outdoor shopping area in the heart of downtown Denver, and pick up some office supplies along with a bit of much-needed protein.

I roamed around the mall for a while, checking out the window displays, and then made a beeline over to my favourite food cart. I didn't normally buy food off quirky carts in the middle of shopping malls, but one of my clients had raved about the quality of Maria's breakfast burritos, and because I was a fan of Mexican food, it was a no-brainer that I'd go and sample the goods.

Because I'd emptied out the contents of my stomach before the police arrived and I couldn't remember the last time I'd eaten before that, it was definitely time to refuel. As I gave myself a quick internal lecture about needing to take better care of myself, my mouth was already watering in response to the heavenly aromas wafting from the gastronomical oasis. The charming young man standing at the cart was Juan, Maria's son, and we were on a first-name basis.

'Doctor Kismet! What's it gonna be today? Spicy or mild?' he teased as he scooped steaming scrambled eggs into a soft tortilla. Juan told me that he could tell what kind of mood I was in by the amount of hot peppers I asked for in my burrito. He called it Burrito Psychology.

'Better leave out the peppers today, Juan. I've had a rough morning.'

He gave me a big, friendly smile, displaying perfect white enamel. 'Let me give you a couple of jalapeños on the side. I get the feeling that your day's about to change. Juan knows these things.'

I smiled back at him and paid for the food. 'See you later.' As I left, I noticed that Juan's usual fan club – a crowd of giggling teenage girls – had swooped in on him the moment I walked away. After my bizarre morning, watching them flirt felt good. At least some part of the world was still normal.

Food in hand, I sauntered down the mall and found a seat on a small wall enclosing an unwieldy sculpture of a cowboy-hat-clad man atop a bucking bronco. Another sports symbol, no doubt. Denver idolised its football team. Maybe I should write a book about the psychology of spectator sports addiction. Or maybe not. I already seemed to have enough enemies without stirring up the local Neanderthals.

I sat there, thoroughly enjoying the melt-in-the-mouth taste of Maria's masterpiece, and began to catch snatches of conversation coming from two women sitting at a folding table a few feet away from me. A little sign next to the table proclaimed 'Psychic Tarot Readings'.

'No, that's not going to happen. He's not for you. Let go of him,' said the woman facing me. She was spreading out tarot cards on a colourful tablecloth decorated with astrological symbols. Rings adorned her fingers, her long fingernails

were painted sparkling silver and an intricate tattoo decorated the back of her right hand. She wore a bright-red dress
with a shiny black vest and her long grey hair flowed down
into a pile in her lap.

The woman sitting with her was less than happy with her
reading, because she sprang up, almost knocking over her
chair, and yelled, 'That's bullshit. You don't know what you're
talking about. He's my soulmate and you're wrong.' She
stomped off, muttering to herself about quacks and phoneys.

I didn't want to embarrass the tarot reader by letting her
know I'd overheard the exchange, so I focused on my burrito,
finishing up the last few tasty bites. The sound of laughter
caught my attention and I raised my head to find the woman
staring at me, making hand motions, inviting me to come
to her table.

'If you've finished your breakfast come on over. I've been
waiting for you.'

I scanned the area to see who she was talking to and when
I couldn't find anyone else in the vicinity, I pointed to myself.
'Me? No thank you. I don't believe in fortune-telling.'

She kept smiling at me and I had to admit I was impressed
by her sales technique. Let people think that you had information just for them and they'd probably sit down and hand
over some greenbacks. It was basic psychology.

'No charge. Just come and listen for a few minutes. If what
I have to say doesn't resonate, you can call me names and
walk away.'

Hmmm. This approach must work or else she wouldn't
keep using it, but I couldn't see how she'd make a living by
giving people the option of not paying. She had me, though.

My curiosity was piqued. I wiped my hands on a napkin, folded up the paper that'd held the burrito, and carried it over to the trash can.

The tarot-reader was still staring at me, shuffling her cards, waiting.

Curious, I walked over to her table. 'Why would you want to read my cards for free? That can't be a very good way to make money.'

'It's not my job to worry about where the money comes from. I just follow my intuition and everything seems to work out perfectly. Come on, sit down. I'm Cerridwyn.'

Well, why not? My life had been so weird for the last week that this just fitted right in. Why not let a tarot-reader in the mall tell me that I'd win the lottery, or that I was Cleopatra in a past life? How much more bizarre could it be than my morning so far?

She stopped shuffling the cards and handed them to me. 'Just move the cards around, any way you wish. Put your essence into them.'

I shuffled, her amused but intense gaze never leaving me. Her eyes were a deep, dark purple – living amethyst – and they were surrounded by a network of fine lines that were exaggerated when she smiled. Clearly she smiled often. At first I'd assumed she was old because of her grey hair, but sitting close to her, I could see she was much younger, maybe not even forty.

She reached out for the cards and I stopped shuffling and gave them to her. She inhaled a deep breath, closed her eyes for a few seconds, reopened them, and began laying out the cards in a specific pattern. She gazed into my eyes. 'You have been chosen. From this time forwards nothing will ever be the same for you.'

Well, that was nice and vague. It was right up there with 'You'll meet a tall, dark stranger'.

She chuckled. 'How did one so young become so sceptical?'

Oh, goodie. Another mind reader.

She studied the cards and declared, 'I see you surrounded by men. Two of them will offer you love, one brings danger. But he is only a messenger of the larger darkness. Your refusal to see the situation as it really is will put you and those you care about at risk.'

What?

She was quiet for a few seconds, unfocused eyes staring off into the distance, then she smiled knowingly. 'Ah, you are playing with the vampires.'

I must have let my mouth fall open, because she started laughing. 'You're surprised that I know?'

'Yes. I do work with people who believe they're vampires. You're very good.'

'But you don't believe?'

'No, of course not.'

She seemed to think that was very funny, because she put one hand on her chest and laughed for a few seconds. 'I envy you your journey. If you're brave, your life will become extraordinary. Even as stubborn as you are.'

I let the stubborn comment pass. 'What do you know about the vampires?'

'I'm very psychic. I've always been aware of nonhumans – not only vampires – and of a growing darkness that's pure evil. There are a few places in the world where this evil is manifesting. Denver is such a place. You're to play a key role. Even more important, you're to learn to love and be loved. You'll find the courage to open your heart.'

Cerridwyn certainly had a flair for the dramatic. Pure evil in Denver? Nonhumans?

'Well, I have to say that I was expecting a canned prediction and you've been very creative. I want to pay you for your time.'

She reached across the table and grabbed my hand, her expression suddenly serious. 'There is danger tonight. It's too late for the young woman you seek. Don't be afraid of your own abilities – they will save you.'

The burrito churned in my stomach. I was afraid to ask what she meant by the comment about the young woman, so I just sat there staring at her.

'I hope this reading was helpful to you. Come and see me again when you're ready to ask the right questions and to hear the answers.' She reached into a pocket in her shirt. 'Here's my card. Call me when you find that courage. Remember that nothing comes to you without your invitation, even if you don't realise you're sending it.'

What invitation? What the hell is she talking about?

She handed me her business card, gathered her tarot deck back into a pile and wrapped it in a red silk scarf.

I fished in my pocket for some money, pulled out a $10 bill, set it on the table as I stood and said, 'You've frightened me.' I was surprised to hear those words come out of my mouth because it wasn't like me to share my feelings with strangers – or with anyone, for that matter.

'Good. Being frightened will help you pay attention.'

She palmed the money, tucked it into her pocket and closed her eyes.

I took that as a dismissal and walked back to my office, replaying her words in my mind. The logical part of me tried to take charge, reminding me that there was no solid research to back up the validity of most psychic readings. The majority of so-called readers were frauds. I had to admit that Cerridwyn sounded authentic, but most of her feedback had really only been cosmo-babble, and the strange feeling in my midsection was simple indigestion.

But the instinctual part of me ignored all that and reminded me of the story of 'The Three Little Pigs', and the one little pig who built his house with bricks. What was my unconscious trying to tell me? Was there really a big, bad wolf out there who could blow the house down?

CHAPTER 9

The rest of the day was pleasantly routine. I had several clients scheduled, and the task of concentrating on their concerns kept my mind off the ghoulish madness and bizarre chaos that had penetrated the edges of my life. The key to successful denial is to keep busy.

Overall it turned out to be quite a satisfying afternoon.

Spock had a moment of illumination in the midst of waxing euphoric about the latest *Star Trek* convention he'd attended. It seemed he'd had a close encounter with a protester – I couldn't imagine what anyone would protest about at a *Star Trek* convention – out in front of the building, and it had upset him. The woman was handing out flyers and bumped into Spock, accusing him of being a 'loser with no life'.

He paused in the middle of his passionate diatribe about the injustice of her accusations and said, a horrified expression on his face, 'Is that true? Am I a loser with no life?'

I asked him what he thought, and we had our first authentic, meaningful dialogue about his role-playing.

All in all, a significant session.

Then Wendy, a member of my Fear of Commitment group, came for her first individual appointment to tell me that she'd read a book I'd suggested and had courageously allowed herself to go on a fourth date with a particularly intriguing man she'd been seeing. Since she usually ended every relationship after the third date – thanks to the number of times her father visited her as a child after abandoning the family – this was indeed exciting news.

Witnessing client breakthroughs reminded me why I chose this work to begin with.

Feeling good, I finished up with my last client, went home, poured a glass of wine and crawled into an aromatic hot bubble bath.

I sat in the tub, enjoyed the blissful sensations, played with the bubbles and recalled my talk with Cerridwyn on the mall. How silly of me to take the tarot-reader seriously. It was totally rational that the strange events of the morning had caused me to be anxious. It really wasn't so unusual that she'd picked up my fears about Emerald because I knew my own intuitive abilities often opened me to information from others, whether I wanted it or not.

To my mind, psychic awareness fell solidly into the category of 'normal brain activities', so I wasn't in the least surprised by the wide range of abilities out there. Reading energy was a common human occurrence. Of course, I had to admit that encountering two such talented individuals – first Devereux, then Cerridwyn – in such a short time span was unusual. But Devereux's gifts might be the upside of his mental illness, and while I didn't doubt that Cerridwyn had skills, she was only a mirror – impressive, but not supernatural.

I was just thinking about how great it would be to take a nap when I heard a voice downstairs in my living room.

'Kismet? It's me, Tom. Your door was unlocked. I knocked but nobody answered.'

My heart tripped against my ribs.

My door's unlocked? What's the matter with me? Damn. I forgot to call Tom and cancel. Then the little psychologist in my head suggested, *Maybe you didn't want to cancel.*

'I'll be down in a minute,' I yelled.

I heard footsteps tramping up the stairs and then Tom poked his head into the bathroom, beaming a toothpaste-commercial smile.

Same old obnoxious Tom.

Surprised and highly annoyed, I sat up in the water, pulled a couple of big clumps of bubbles towards me and raised my knees up to my chest. 'Hey! I'm taking a bath here. I wasn't expecting you so early. Why don't you wait for me downstairs?'

Why am I being polite to this jerk?

He ambled over, lowered the toilet lid, sat down and made himself comfortable. 'No. I enjoy having you as a captive audience. Besides, I've seen you naked hundreds of times.'

He was right about that. From the first moment I laid eyes on him during our internship at the psychiatric hospital I was putty in his hands. All he had to do was give me one of those dazzling smiles or glance at me with his bedroom eyes and I'd follow him anywhere. Thanks to my parents, I couldn't tell healthy attention from the opposite.

Okay, so I'd led a sheltered life. I was primed for the picking.

Tom had been the first man I'd had an actual relationship with. Oh sure, I'd fumbled around in the backseats of cars with various high-school and college dates, and I even managed to find a willing participant to relieve me of my virginity when I determined the time was right. But until Tom, I'd been an emotional virgin.

He was eight years older than I and he taught me things about the sexual arts I never knew existed. We spent four years together and amassed quite a collection of sexual aids, books, toys and videos. Unfortunately, while it was all about pleasure and orgasms for Tom, it was all about love for me. He'd been so disappointed that I'd muddied the waters. I didn't have the wisdom then to realise how emotionally unavailable he was.

I gathered more bubbles around me. 'That's ancient history.' I gave a limp version of a sneer. Unfortunately, I realised too late that it's almost impossible to pull off an effective sneer while sitting naked in a foamy tub.

He perched there watching me, making no effort to hide the fact that his eyes were lingering on certain parts of my anatomy and he was enjoying the view. I remembered that wicked expression on his face and I felt a tightening between my legs – as if my libido had sent out an invitation that went into the mail before my brain could retrieve it.

'Is the water getting cold?' He leered at my breasts and smirked.

I followed his gaze down and noticed my nipples were large and hard.

Shit. Apparently my body didn't get the memo about this not-lusting-after-Tom thing. Old patterns . . .

'I always appreciated how quickly your body got aroused,' he said. 'It turned me on to watch you respond to me in such an obvious way.'

He stood, moved a step closer to the bathtub and laid his hand on his zipper. 'Look,' he said, rubbing his hand up and down the front of his trousers, showing me his erection. 'See what you do to me?'

Geez. It had been two years since I'd had sex and my body was screaming *Yes!* Despite his heartless rejection and empty promises, I still wanted him. Even though he was the poster boy for superficiality, I still lusted after him. I was torn between being disgusted with myself and being overwhelmingly aroused. I started to suggest that we move into my bedroom when he uttered the immortal words, 'Tell me how bad you want it.'

Yuck.

I'd been expecting a sensual seduction scene and instead he gave me a worn-out line from one of the porn movies he collected. His words hit me like a cold shower, dousing the flames of my romantic fantasy. All my desire for him immediately evaporated in the crystal-clear realisation that he'd never been who I'd imagined him to be and I'd been fooling myself all those years. Fooling myself? Let's call a spade a spade: I'd been an idiot.

I raised my voice and gave it a cutting edge.

'Very tacky, Dr Radcliffe. Tell me – does that approach usually work for you these days? Are more women responding to "Mr Macho" than responded to "Mr Sensitivity"? Hand me a towel and get out.'

With a shocked expression on his face, he reached over, picked up a towel and handed it to me.

I stood and slowly wrapped the towel around myself, noticing he was still enjoying the show. 'There's some wine downstairs. Go and help yourself. Leave. Now.'

He opened and closed his mouth a couple of times but no words emerged. The colour drained from his face and his expression veered back and forth between confusion and disbelief. He finally turned and silently retreated.

After he left, I stepped out of the tub and stood in front of the mirror. My cheeks were flushed and my eyes shone. At least it was good to have more evidence that my body was still capable of sexual arousal. Over the last couple of years, I'd started to wonder. But it was clear that anything personal between the two of us was finished. I was actually glad Tom had shown up because who knew how long I might have carried the torch if he hadn't reminded me of who he really was?

Love truly was blind.

'If I promise to go back to being Mr Sensitivity, can I come up and talk to you while you put your makeup on?' Tom crooned from the foot of the stairs. 'I'm getting lonesome down here.'

I rolled my eyes. He was trying to con me again, but it wasn't going to work. I had come to my senses. 'Sure. You can come up, but I'm almost done. Bring the wine bottle with you.'

I might need a weapon.

He came upstairs and leaned against the door to the bathroom, lowered the bottle onto the counter by the sink and stood there quietly, sipping his wine.

'I feel as if I should apologise, but you can't really blame a guy for trying.' He shrugged. 'We've got such a long history together. You've become even prettier since we split up.'

'I *can* blame a guy for trying, so feel free to come up with one of your brilliant, meaningless apologies. I'm all ears.'

I'd pulled my hair up into one of those large hair clips so it wouldn't get wet in the bath and now I released it, letting the curls cascade down my back.

He reached out and picked up one of the wavy clumps. 'Was your hair always this long? It's very sexy.'

'Yes,' I said, frowning. I edged away. All his idiotic behaviours were coming back to me. Now that I wasn't at the mercy of my hormones, he was simply an annoyance – not even worth getting worked up about. 'It was always this long. In fact, you insisted I never cut it. Sounds like you're having some memory problems. I'd watch the recreational drug use, if I were you.'

Still playing with my hair, he ignored my dig and inspected the Band-Aid on my neck. 'What's this?' He touched it with one finger.

I smacked his hand away.

'A nasty hickey, if you must know. Nothing I'd want my clients to see.'

'A hickey, eh? Someone marking his territory?'

'You, Dr Radcliffe, are a sexist pig.'

He trailed a finger across the top of my breast and gave me his 'Aren't I a naughty boy?' face I remembered so well.

I grabbed the offending finger and bent it backwards, causing him to yelp with pain and pull his hand away.

What a jerk. I guess you really can't teach an old horndog new tricks. Why am I even being nice to this fool? Is my old self-destructive pattern really that powerful?

'As usual, you've misinterpreted my actions and you're being irrational.' He rubbed his wounded digit. 'Of course, all women are emotional basket cases. Freud was really on to something with his notions of female psychology. Hysterics, every last one of you. I was merely attempting to show you that I still find you attractive. You needn't have resorted to violence.'

Wow. I guess I'm angrier at him than I realised. But he's such an asshole.

I didn't address anything he said because I knew what he was up to and I was already tired of his games. He just couldn't believe that a woman would turn him down – that his routine hadn't worked. I remember being jealous for most of the time we'd been together because Tom just couldn't resist flirting with every waitress, clerk or secretary he encountered. Why hadn't I noticed his pitiful insecurity before? And why had I blamed myself?

He stood silent for a few seconds, watching me. 'I'm sorry,' he said so quietly I could barely make out the words.

'What?' I shifted my gaze to his. He couldn't have said what I thought I heard. He never apologised.

He cleared his throat. 'I said I'm sorry.' His usual arrogant manner had vanished, like dropping a mask. His brown eyes appeared sincere.

I stared at him, my mouth open, frowning. I lowered the mascara wand. 'Sorry? For what?' *What's going on? Is this a trap? Is he setting me up? I'm not sensing anything. Where are my abilities when I really need them?*

He blinked a couple of times and sighed. 'For the way I broke things off with you. I was an idiot. I regretted it immediately, but I always thought you deserved more than me, someone who could really be there for you – especially after what you went through with your parents – so I forced myself to stay away, to let you think what you now think of me. But I am sorry. I don't want you to hate me any more.'

The mascara wand fell onto the counter with a clunk, leaving a gummy black blob. 'You're sorry?' My brain couldn't process the words. I scanned his face and remembered times when we first got together that Tom had been warm and kind. Before he began to buy into the psychology department's promotion of him as the 'next big thing'. Before his ego took over. Times when he really did live up to the potential I saw in him. That's why ending the relationship had been so hard for me. He was the only person I'd ever trusted. But I hadn't seen any evidence of that version of Tom for years. Who was this stranger in my bathroom?

'Yes. I'm sorry. I hope someday we can be friends again. I miss you. You were more important to me than I wanted to acknowledge. I made the decision to focus on my career and I treated you poorly, pushed you away. I do sincerely apologise.' He rubbed his eyes, then cleared his throat. 'But that's about as much self-disclosure as I can stand for one day, so I'm going to stop talking now.'

I watched the mask slip back into place.

We stared at each other for endless seconds, then I reached down for my mascara wand, the surreal spell broken.

I didn't know what to feel in that moment. Sad, confused, shocked? Who knew he could still be human under his shallow, relentless quest for outer success?

'I don't know how to treat you now.' I turned my attention back to the mirror. 'You've blasted my assumptions out of the water. Who are you?'

He gave a talk-show-host smile. 'I'm still the same Tom you've come to expect. Let's just leave it there. I intend to be the most famous psychologist in the world.'

'Okay.' Back to normal. Abnormal? I'd definitely need to take this bizarre development to Nancy. He'd just rewritten my reality. 'A friend is coming by pretty soon,' I mumbled, my face close to the mirror so I could finish putting on my mascara without smudging it. My hands were still a little shaky. I hadn't expected to have such a deeply held truth overturned in a matter of minutes. 'We're going out to a club downtown. I meant to call you and cancel for tonight, but I forgot.'

Right on cue, there was a knock at the door. Sound carried easily in my small townhouse.

Tom turned and raced down the stairs, yelling, 'I'll get it.'

I'd put money on the fact that he assumed my friend would be female.

'Is Kismet here?' Alan asked, giving each syllable a slightly higher pitch, as if he momentarily thought he'd come to the wrong door.

I didn't hear anything for a few seconds and then Tom obviously recovered from his dashed expectations and reclaimed his innate pomposity. 'Yes, of course, please come in. I'm an old friend of hers. Tom. Tom Radcliffe.'

'I'll be right there, Alan,' I called down the stairs. 'Just give me a few minutes. Get him something to drink, Tom.'

I went into my bedroom thinking about the weird conversation with Tom and dressed in the outfit I'd laid out for the evening. Then I returned to the bathroom for some finishing touches to my makeup and hair. I even squirted on a hint of the perfume a friend had sent me from Paris on her last trip.

Not having been to a dance club in years, I hadn't known what to wear, but I figured jeans would probably work. I had an expensive pair that I'd bought a few months back and hadn't worn yet, and the length was great for the high heels on my favourite black boots. I'd be even taller than usual tonight, but I felt like taking up space.

I was glad to have an excuse to wear one of my new shirts. It was the colour of a summer sky, form-fitting and low-cut. I'd had to buy a special bra for this top because none of my regular undergarments were skimpy enough.

Going out also gave me a chance to wear the beautiful Victorian azure-drop necklace and earring set I'd bought for myself as a birthday present last year. They matched my eyes perfectly and made me feel feminine – an unfamiliar experience.

Feeling rather excited about the evening, I came down the stairs and joined them in the living room. Alan's lips spread in a wicked grin. He'd dressed in fresh jeans and replaced the wrinkled white T-shirt with a deep-blue version that matched his eyes.

'Wow, you look great,' he said. 'Positively edible. And you smell wonderful.'

'Yes, you really do,' echoed Tom.

I said a silent 'thank you' to the helpful sales clerk who'd talked me into buying some bright colours and current fashions. Maybe it was time for me to go visit her again.

I felt pretty good and I had to admit I was enjoying the appreciative expressions on their faces. It had been a long time since I'd dressed up on purpose. It was nice to see that my efforts had paid off. Hell, it had been a long time since I'd had two handsome men paying attention to me. A long time? Try never.

Alan continued staring at me and I frowned. 'What?'

'I'm just amazed by the transformation.' He laughed. 'I came to pick up Kismet Knight, Ph.D., conservative scientist and instead I find Xena, Warrior Princess. Not that I'm complaining.'

I laughed too, feeling surprisingly lighthearted. Evidently, kicking Tom's metaphorical butt and his unexpected apology had perked me right up. 'You don't know me yet. Who can say what other personalities might be hiding in here?'

'I'm looking forward to finding out.' His eyes wandered down my body.

I could swear I physically felt the movement of his eyes. *Oh my. Either the wine is going to my head, or my pilot light just got turned up.*

'Ahem,' Tom said, drawing my attention back to him. 'I'm surprised, Kismet. It used to be worse than pulling teeth to get you to attend a dance club with me. You never enjoyed them. What's special about this one?'

Well, well. Is the most famous psychologist in the world jealous?

'We're doing some research. Alan is also a psychologist and he's introducing me to a subculture I'm interested in writing about.'

'Hey, that's terrific. Can I come?' Tom asked.

What the hell's he up to now?

I turned my gaze to Alan and he shrugged. 'It's okay with me.'

'Are you sure, Tom,' I asked him, 'because it will probably be field study – just observation. I remember how you felt about that in grad school. You thought it was boring.'

But I could almost see the wheels turning in his mind as he imagined the sweet young scantily dressed subjects he'd be observing. No. Not boring at all.

'I'm sure it will be fun,' Tom asserted, flashing another of his game-show-host smiles. He ran his fingers through his abundant hair.

Hmm. This could be interesting. A chance for me to hold my own, not only with old-baggage-laden Tom, but also with Alan, a handsome non-client. Am I up for the challenge? Hell, yes!

'Okay. Who wants to drive?'

CHAPTER 10

We wound up taking Alan's Jeep Cherokee because Tom and I had already put a healthy dent in the bottle of wine.

'What kind of subculture are we observing tonight?' Tom asked from the backseat in a disdainful tone.

Alan and I glanced at each other, grinned and voiced in unison, 'Vampires.'

Tom pressed himself against the front seats. 'Excuse me? Vampires? Dracula pretenders?'

His ability to saturate certain words with such arrogance and affectation had to be an art form. Insufferable Tom, once again present and accounted for.

I had to give Alan points for keeping his eyes on the road and not laughing in Tom's face. Half-turning within the confines of my seatbelt, I fixed my eyes on Tom and gave him my best blank expression. 'Yes. Vampires.'

He rested his hand on my shoulder. '*Please* tell me you're not serious.'

I shook off his hand. 'I've stumbled across a group of people who believe they're vampires and I'm going to write about them. I think it's a valid topic for research.'

I sounded way more defensive than I meant to. As if I dared

him to contradict me. I didn't know why I felt the need to explain my work to Tom, but I did. Or maybe I was just trying to convince myself.

Tom moved his head from side to side, exaggerating the theatrical back-and-forth motion, his lips tightly compressed. 'Kismet, Kismet. You had so much potential. You could have gone to California with me and shared the limelight. You could have been interviewed by Leno. You could have taken a meeting with Dr Phil. Now here you are, studying pathetic fringe elements in Cow Town. I had no idea my breaking up with you would hit you so hard.'

I must have hallucinated the human Tom in the bathroom.

I straightened rigidly in my seat, kept my eyes riveted directly in front of me and took a deep breath. My hands automatically fisted in my lap and I bit my lower lip to hold back the avalanche of words gathering there. I wasn't going to allow the only female psychologist in the group to have a public meltdown. I wouldn't let him push me over the edge.

Apology, my ass. Arrogant jerk. Self-centred, obnoxious, smarmy asshole. Once again, his brain is caught in his zipper. Maybe I can push him out of the car at the next stop sign.

My muscles tensed and sweat dampened my armpits. It was all I could do to keep myself buckled into my seat, because I was seriously fantasising about diving into the back and pummelling a little colour into Dr California's face with my knuckles. Maybe give him youthfully puffy lips without him having to go visit his plastic surgeon. Of course, he might have to check in with his dentist afterwards. It was so thoughtful of him to remind me he hadn't invited me to accompany him to the West Coast and that he was now a big shot.

I'd never had a chance to confront him after he dumped me and left town. All those repressed feelings now threatened to break free. No matter how supposedly *sorry* he was now, my anger obviously had unfinished business.

Breathe, Kismet. Don't let him press your buttons.

Alan glanced at me, his tongue pushing against the inside of his cheek. 'Tom,' he quickly interjected, obviously catching my hostile intentions. 'Do you remember a series of murders in Los Angeles a while back? They got a lot of media coverage – several bodies found drained of blood? I'm searching for those killers and I'll find them in the vampire subculture.'

Alan sounded a lot more formal than I'd ever heard him. Psychologists are a competitive lot and we never miss an opportunity to puff ourselves up for each other. Or maybe it was Tom's hyper-pomposity that brought out the pretentiousness in everyone. Regardless of the reason, he did give me a moment to rein myself in. Lucky for Tom.

Oblivious, Tom droned on. 'So what are you, a forensic psychologist? What are you going to do with the killers after you find them?'

Alan ignored the superior attitude Tom displayed in his over-pronunciation of the words 'forensic psychologist', but I heard him sigh.

'I work for the FBI. I'm an expert on serial killers, in addition to other psychotics and I'm the agent assigned to the case.'

'How did Kismet get involved in all this?'

'She's the Vampire Psychologist.' Alan grinned. 'Here we are.'

Our heads pivoted towards the window as we passed The Crypt, cruising for a place to park. Milling about in front of the main entrance were large groups of twenty-somethings: goths, vampire wannabes, heavy-metal gods and goddesses, Lady Gaga pretenders, androgynous individuals covered in body-art and piercings and some reincarnated hippies.

'It appears we're going to be the oldest people there,' Tom noted, with a hint of annoyance.

'Especially you,' I teased, smiling sweetly. Okay. Just because I'm a psychologist doesn't mean I can't be as nasty as anyone else. I knew Tom was sensitive about his age and that he'd avail himself of every plastic surgery procedure possible in order to stave off the ravages of time. Not that I was above a little nip and tuck myself in the future.

We finally found a place to park several blocks away and walked back to The Crypt, the club where I'd seen Devereux on the stairs after my first session with Midnight. It was huge, taking up almost the same space in square feet as it did in height.

The club had its own personality. The closer we got to it, the more ominously powerful it felt. I could hear music throbbing on the airwaves.

The first thing I noticed about the building was its eyes – the stained-glass windows that filled half of each wall. Extraordinary colours and shapes formed pictures and abstract patterns in each window. There were images of angels and demons, religious symbols, Celtic crosses and spirits rising from graves. I could imagine how amazing they'd look with the sun pouring through them. The windows were brightly lit from behind and the rainbow colours splashed down onto the dark sidewalk, bathing everyone in etheric hues. The architecture was gothic, with ornate towers and archways. The upper level had many nooks and crannies, and standing guard at various outposts were large gargoyles.

As we approached the crowd gathered in front of the main entrance, the smell of marijuana permeated the air and I felt a heavy pulsating rhythm moving up through the soles of my feet.

We climbed up the stairs leading to the entrance and passed through the massive double doors, which were made of heavy wood with elaborate carvings. A wall of sound hit me when the doors opened and the intensity of the vibration took my breath away. At the far end of the club, a rock band commanded the aural landscape with screaming guitars, booming bass notes, and primitive rhythms, the musicians cavorting wildly on the large multilevel stage. The acoustics were such that the sound exploded as it poured from the mounted speakers. A smoke machine was pumping out a continuous layer of fog that hovered near the floor. It had a life of its own, curling and twisting like a ghostly serpent.

A bouncer stood inside the door, blocking our entrance to the rest of the club. He was extremely tall, very thin, and deathly white. He didn't seem to give much credence to the idea of personal space because he bent down very close to say, 'Welcome to The Crypt. ID, please.'

His breath was hot with an odd, sweet scent. He reached out a hand with long, dirty fingernails and I jumped back without even thinking and stepped behind Alan while I retrieved my driver's licence from the pocket of my jeans. It'd been a long time since anyone had carded me.

Apparently not offended by my reaction to his hygiene, he spread his lips in what I assumed was a smile, showing discoloured fangs, and waved us inside with a sweep of his arm. 'Enjoy.'

Tom tapped me on the shoulder and pointed at the bouncer. His expression telegraphed distaste. 'Is he one of your clients? It appears he could use a little help.'

I glared at him. 'Very funny. I just might give him one of my business cards. He could be a perfect case study for my book.'

Down, girl. I don't have to justify myself to Tom, or anyone else. This is starting to feel like a nasty little case of sibling rivalry – not that I have any idea how sibling anything would feel.

'Hey, you two – check it out.' Alan pointed to the interior of the club.

The entire place was decorated like a cross between a graveyard and Dracula's castle, and it was big enough to hold hundreds of people, most of whom had already arrived.

We manoeuvred our way over to the main bar, which ran along an entire wall and was shaped to resemble a long wooden sarcophagus. Standing there, waiting to catch the attention of the bartender, Alan leaned towards me and shouted in my ear, 'I forgot to tell you – never look vampires in the eyes. They'll entrance you.'

I started to say something about that being ridiculous, but that was too many words to scream over the music so I nodded and mouthed, 'Okay.'

Judging by the expression on his face, Tom was already in lecher heaven as he scrutinised the nubile, bouncing female body parts on the dance floor. I didn't think a grin could get any wider. He reminded me of the 'Joker' character in one of the *Batman* movies. He turned back to the bar to put in his order and caught sight of the bartender. 'Holy shit.'

She was spectacular: a leather fantasy right out of the centrefold of a men's magazine. Her hair was cut short and it stood up in stubby little spikes all over her head. It was hard to tell under the dim lights, but the colour appeared to be pink, or maybe orange. Her eyes were almond-shaped orbs. She leaned over the bar and plopped her considerable assets in front of Tom. 'What's your pleasure?'

After a few seconds, he finally raised his eyes up to hers and stared, his mouth slowly relaxing and hanging open.

Alan shook Tom's shoulder and snapped his fingers in front of his face. 'Wake up!'

Tom came back to himself with a start, shook himself, and peered at Alan. 'What happened?'

Alan explained. 'Never look a vampire in the eyes.'

We all stared at the goddess behind the bar. She smiled at us, displaying a fine set of fangs.

Tom laughed. 'Yeah, right.' But he looked rattled.

We ordered Bloody Marys – the house special, natch – and went in search of a table.

The interior of the building had many small rooms, raised platforms and cosy hideaways for customers seeking privacy for one activity or another. Miraculously, we happened to be in the right place at the right time and were able to snag an intimate circular booth in a raised area off the main room. The walls enclosing the booth muted the volume of the music and we could talk without yelling. From that vantage point, we could see almost the entire club while remaining unobtrusive ourselves.

Tom, who'd been very quiet since his close encounter with the centrefold at the bar, expressed the need to find the restroom. He started the long process of wading through a sea of humanity to reach the other side of the club. I watched him go, and about halfway across the room he was hijacked by a tall brunette who pulled him onto the dance floor.

'Hello, Alan.' A familiar voice enveloped me, velvet in my ears. I shivered.

Alan rose from his seat. 'Devereux, please join us. It's nice to see you again.'

Devereux sat next to me in the booth, lifted my hand to his lips, and kissed it. He gave a slow blink of his turquoise eyes. 'Hello. I am Devereux, the owner of this establishment.'

The touch of his lips on my hand caused a strong reaction in several parts of my body. I couldn't sort through my emotions fast enough to say anything, so I was relieved when Alan spoke.

'This is Kismet Knight. She's a local psychologist. I've been consulting with her about the missing girl.'

'It is a pleasure to meet you,' Devereux said aloud, while whispering in my mind, 'I am very happy to see you. Alan does not need to know that we have already met.'

I just stared at him and said nothing because I was overcome by a desire to crawl into his lap and cover his mouth with mine. I'd never experienced such a strong series of emotions before, out of nowhere, and until I was sure I wasn't going to make a fool of myself, I sat very still.

What was it about Devereux? Every time he came near, I turned into a hormonal teenager – maybe his pheromones were communicating with mine in some mysterious way. Clearly, either the man was a master hypnotist or insanity truly was contagious. Or, more likely, I'd just been dazzled by the obvious.

No doubt about it, he was a beautiful man – a work of art. There was no other way to describe him. His face was masculine yet soft at the same time and it made me want to touch him, to run my fingers over his pale skin and through his long, silky hair. I shifted my head and tried to avoid his sparkling eyes, not because I feared he'd entrance me, but because I was afraid of what he might see in mine.

'Yes, I desire you as well,' Devereux murmured in my mind, the words caressing some invisible part of me.

Alan's cell phone rang. He lifted it out of his pocket and answered, 'Stevens.' There was a brief pause and then, 'Shit, I'll be right there.' Turning to me he explained, 'They've found a body – I need to go to police headquarters.'

I started to get up but Alan put a hand on my shoulder. 'I'm afraid I can't take you with me, Kismet. You'll have to wait here. I'll come back for you and Tom as quickly as I can.'

I didn't care for the sound of that. I just wasn't the type to sit waiting for someone to chauffeur me around, and leaving me here with Devereux made me anxious in ways I couldn't even understand.

Devereux turned his attention to Alan. 'I will look after Dr Knight and her friend until you return.'

Alan stroked his hand down my cheek then stood. 'I won't be gone long.' He headed for the door.

'He is attracted to you,' Devereux said, nodding in the direction of Alan's retreating form, 'and you to him. But you are also attracted to me. And there are some confused – intense – emotions about your friend on the dance floor.'

I frowned and studied his face. What arrogance! But, more important, how did he do that? He'd been uncomfortably accurate. His psychic skills must be off the charts.

'I thought you promised me you wouldn't try to read me.' *Obviously his abilities are much more reliable than mine.*

'Yes, of course. I apologise. You are quite right. I do not wish to spoil the mystery between us. You look especially lovely tonight.'

'Thank you. So do you.' *Perfect, Kismet. Tell the man he looks lovely. What a dweeb. I suck at small talk.* 'Er, how long have you owned this club?'

The corners of his mouth quirked up in a gentle smile and his eyes softened, as if he sensed my discomfort. 'I purchased the old church when I arrived in America. The vampire craze had been re-ignited by Anne Rice's books and I allowed myself to be convinced that an occult-themed dance club would be a profitable venture. It has proven to be so.'

Hmm. Okay. Good. Maybe he really is just playing a role . . .

'Do you own other clubs?' I looked around the crowded room. 'I imagine it would take a lot of patience to hang out in such a busy, noisy place every night. I don't think I could do it.'

'No.' He shook his head. 'I own no others. The Crypt is unique. And I quite agree with you about the chaotic environment. In fact, I rarely spend time in the main area. If I am here at all, I am likely downstairs with friends and colleagues. Most of my business still takes place in Europe, so I am often there.'

'What part of Europe are you from? You have a very interesting accent.' I studied the lines of his handsome face.

'Ah.' He smiled, gazing into my eyes. 'I have lived in many places – France, England, Ireland, Scotland, Spain, Russia, Germany, South America, and more.' He laughed. 'I even lived in Transylvania for a short time while I did research for the décor of this club. I suppose you could call me a world traveller. My accent remains strong because I frequently converse in other languages. Many of the places I work are non-English-speaking, so there has been no reason for me to Americanise myself. I seem better suited to days gone by than to modern times. It is only recently that I have discovered sufficient motivation to remain in this country.'

There was something magical about the sound of his voice, and his words held me like aural arms. I found myself completely relaxed and at peace in a way I'd never experienced before.

'What motivation?' My heartbeat accelerated.

'You.' He angled towards me, waiting, his lips close enough to kiss. I breathed in the soft, spicy fragrance of him and closed the gap between our mouths before I even had a conscious thought about doing it.

We kissed long and deep, our tongues exploring, melting into each other. It was as if our physical bodies merged together and we shared the same heartbeat – the same life force. Every cell in my body desired him, and there was no one else in the room except the two of us. All the noise disappeared and we floated in a private universe.

When we finally pulled apart, I gazed into his eyes, which glittered like jewels.

Kissing him had been wonderful. Pure pleasure. But why had I done it? How was it that Devereux could override my nerdy shyness? I clearly wasn't myself around him. I didn't know if that was good or bad.

He whispered, 'My gaze will not entrance you tonight.'

'What?' I didn't care about making sense of that. I only wanted to drink him in with my eyes, to touch him, to kiss him again. In fact, in that moment, nothing else mattered. Then I asked myself, *Why doesn't it matter? What's wrong with me?* It wasn't like me to indulge my physical desires in public. Why was I suddenly so uninhibited?

'Why am I so fascinated by you?' I asked, running my fingers along his cheek. *Did I say that out loud? I'm acting drunk, but I've only had a couple of sips of my drink.*

'We have that effect on some humans.' He took my hand in his. 'I am very pleased you feel that way about me. I hope to fascinate you even more.'

I got distracted watching his mouth for a moment.

'Kismet?'

'Huh?' I pulled away from him and blinked a couple of times to rouse myself. 'See? That's what I mean. Why do you have that effect on me?'

'Do you remember when you asked me what Bryce had done to you and I said he had altered your brain waves?'

'I remember you said that, but it didn't make any sense to me. How can someone alter my brain waves just by staring at me?'

'It is about entrainment. I have done a lot of reading on

this subject over the last twenty years. One benefit of living a long time is the acquisition of knowledge.'

'Entrainment?'

'Allow me to explain. Think of an old clock, the kind with a swinging pendulum.' He moved his hand back and forth, as if he was conducting an orchestra. Sharing his wisdom obviously pleased him and I grinned as I watched his enthusiastic presentation. Professor Devereux.

His graceful motions expanded into wider arcs. 'The rhythm of the swing is very strong, very powerful. Then think of putting several smaller, newer clocks on the same wall with the old clock, each pendulum swinging in a different pattern. Soon, all the new clocks will begin swinging in time with the old clock. The power of the old clock overwhelms the newer ones and they join with it. Am I making sense?'

I skimmed my fingertips across the top of the hand he'd rested on the table. I couldn't seem to stop touching him.

'Yes, I know about that. It's like when women all start having their cycles at the same time, as if we get in sync with each other or something. But what does that have to do with you?'

He nodded and held up his index finger, prepared to continue with the lecture. 'Let me put it in musical terms. Vampires . . .' He paused, frowning. 'What is wrong?'

He had seen me shift my gaze down when he said the word 'vampires'. I brought my hands together in my lap. Saying that word reminded me I was taking advantage of someone who might be psychotic, delusional, or at the very least mentally confused. There I was, making out with a virtual stranger and encouraging him by listening to his stories. That felt bad as a woman and as a psychologist. I raised my eyes to meet his, surprised to discover him grinning at me.

He shook his head. 'You are the most stubborn woman I have ever met. It is becoming troublesome that you will not accept what I am. But I will continue to answer the question you asked and you will simply have to humour me.'

He lifted one of my hands, brought it up to his mouth, and kissed my palm with those incredibly soft lips. Even that small contact caused my heart to race and my libido to tap me on the shoulder. His lovely turquoise eyes sparkled, and he somehow managed to appear sexy, angelic, and dangerous all at the same time.

My mouth went dry.

'As I was saying, in musical terms, vampires give off such a powerful energy or tone that everyone entrains with us. The vibrational frequency that emanates from the undead is stronger than any other, and so it overrides whatever was there before. That is without our even looking at anyone. If we gaze into a human's eyes without holding back, it is a form of mind control. We are able to change your brain waves.'

'Are you talking about hypnosis?' *I knew he was a hypnotist! And, apparently, a damn good one.*

He leaned closer. 'It is much more similar to brainwashing than hypnosis because in hypnosis you are always free to choose.'

'So,' I reached over and played with a lock of his hair, 'you're saying the power of what you are is so strong that I'm pulled in whether I want to be pulled in or not?'

'Exactly,' he said, with a quick nod.

'And when you said your gaze wouldn't entrance me tonight, you meant you'd hold back?'

'Yes.'

I slid my index finger along his lower lip. 'Then does that mean my desire to kiss you is only there because you want me to kiss you? That you are irresistible to me because of that power and not because of anything I feel about you?'

He flashed a dazzling smile. 'I am pleased to hear I am irresistible to you, but no. I am old enough to be in total control of my power and I hold back with you so that you can make your own decisions. You kiss me because you desire to kiss me.'

I trailed my fingernail lightly over his cheek. 'Show me the difference.'

He raised his eyebrows. 'What do you mean?'

'Use your eyes. Turn on the full power. Let me have it. I want to know what you're talking about.'

'Are you certain?' He grinned mischievously.

I nodded and stared into his eyes.

A wave of heat moved through my body, my scalp tingled, and my eyelids sank to half-mast. The next thing I knew, I was in his lap, my knees straddling his legs, my arms wrapped around his neck, passionately kissing him.

In my mind he sighed, 'This is how it will be between us.'

'Ahem.'

I heard a sound from somewhere in the distance, but nothing was more important than kissing Devereux's soft, warm lips. Nothing mattered except keeping my body pressed against his.

'Ahem. Kismet?'

In slow-motion, I turned towards the sound. There at the end of the table were three sets of eyes, staring at me.

CHAPTER 11

Tom's shocked face leaned in towards me. 'Kismet?'

Whatever had happened wasn't finished yet, and I was having a hard time concentrating on the fact that I needed to focus on the audience we'd suddenly acquired. I vaguely recognised Tom but couldn't place the women standing on either side of him.

A woman's voice said, 'She's entranced.'

'Do you mean she's drugged? Did this guy put something in her drink?' Tom demanded, his voice dripping anger.

'No. She's not drugged. She's bespelled,' said a different woman's voice.

'I seem to be missing something here. If someone doesn't clue me in right now, I'm going to cause a scene,' Tom yelled. 'Kismet! What's going on? Where's Alan?' He jerked his head towards Devereux. 'Do you know this guy?'

I squinted up at Tom, nodded yes and buried my face in Devereux's deliciously scented hair.

'I do apologise. You must be Tom. We have not been properly introduced yet. I am Devereux, the owner of The Crypt. Please excuse our rudeness in not acknowledging you sooner.

I take full responsibility. We were doing a little . . . experiment
. . . and we got distracted.'

The fog began to clear in my brain and I started to grasp
that I was sitting on Devereux while Tom and two strange
women gaped at me. I remembered making the decision to
leap into his lap, but for the life of me I couldn't recall why
I'd do such a thing.

Devereux whispered in my mind, 'That was wonderful. I
await the opportunity for us to continue our experiment.'

He effortlessly lifted me up and set me in the booth next
to him. The sounds of the room began to swim back into my
consciousness and my eyes rediscovered the ability to focus.
I wanted to ask him a thousand questions about what had
happened, but it didn't appear I was going to have the chance.

'Please join us.' Devereux waved his arm through the air
over the booth.

Tom and the two women sat. His eyes shifted rapidly back
and forth between Devereux and me. 'Kismet, what's the
matter with you? I've never seen you do anything like that
before.'

'Give her a moment,' urged the woman sitting next to him.
'She's not herself yet.'

She turned her attention to me. 'I'm Zoë, Tom's new friend.
I remember the first time I was taken under. It's almost too
amazing for words.'

'Taken under? What do you mean, "taken under"? What
the *hell* is going on here?' Tom glared around the table.

I ignored him and focused my eyes on the woman speaking
to me, and recognised her as the tall brunette who'd waylaid
Tom on his way to the men's room. She appeared very dynamic

with her dark hair, pale skin, and large, distinctive eyes. The lighting was too dim for me to see the colour, but they looked unusual. I became momentarily fascinated by her eyelashes, which were the longest I'd ever seen.

Finally retrieving some of the ability to speak, I mumbled, 'It's nice to meet you.'

Devereux touched my arm and pointed to the other woman who'd joined us. 'This is Luna. She is one of the managers of the club and my personal assistant.'

I hadn't noticed through my brain fog earlier, but Luna was an exceptionally attractive woman. In fact, finding out that this femme fatale was Devereux's personal assistant bothered me way more than a little. I hardly knew Devereux, and a few passionate kisses shouldn't cause me to feel this jealous of another woman. Especially a woman who might not be interested in Devereux at all.

Yeah, right. Not interested in Devereux. Welcome to Denial Central.

Luna's silver eyes studied me like a specimen in a lab. She leaned across the table, shifted from side to side for a better view, and I got the sense she'd have prodded me with a stick if she could.

'So you're the one. You're the human who's caused all the fuss.' She twirled a strand of her long, straight, jet-black hair. 'I expected more. You're very pretty, and I see what he means about your eyes, but I still don't understand the obsession.' She turned to Devereux. 'What is it about her?'

The two of them stared silently at each other for a moment, and then Luna sighed. 'Yes, yes, I know. I'll be good. But I don't have to like it.'

She returned her gaze to me. 'Have Devereux take you on a tour of the rest of the club. I'm sure you'll find it illuminating.' She stood, nodded at Devereux, and walked away, moving like a sleek panther on the prowl.

Devereux said in my mind, 'Luna does not understand my interest in humans. She does not share my desire to remain connected to the human community. She believes it is dangerous for us to risk exposure by allowing ourselves to be known. There is no reason for you to be jealous of her – she and I have never had an intimate relationship.'

I frowned at him and sent the thought, 'I'm not *jealous*.'

His lips quirked. He thought, 'As you wish.'

'Hey, what's going on?' Tom asked. 'Why is everyone just staring at each other? I think I missed the beginning of this movie. Are you going to tell me what you were doing in this guy's lap?'

I lifted my chin and locked eyes with him. 'Even though I don't owe you an explanation and you're sounding ridiculously like a jealous boyfriend, I'll tell you. Devereux and I have a special relationship. We are very attracted to each other. That's all you need to know. I'll sit where I wish, and I'll kiss whomever I choose!' I said, giving him a stern look.

Although it was totally out of character for me to say all that out loud, it felt good to do it.

'Okay.' Tom scrunched down a little in his seat. 'I hear you. I was just worried about you – you've been acting funny all night. Where's Alan?'

'He was called to the police station. There's been another murder.'

His eyebrows rose. 'A murder?'

'Yes, it's the case he's working on. He told you about it in the car, remember?'

'Oh, yeah.' He frowned. 'The vampire thing. So how are we supposed to get home?'

You could always count on Tom to think about himself in the midst of whatever else was happening.

'He said he'd come back for us as soon as he could.'

Zoë reached over, pinched Tom's chin between her fingers, and guided his face to hers. 'Who knows, Tommy Boy, maybe you won't want to go home. The night is young. Come on, let's dance.' She pulled him out of the booth towards the dance floor.

'Don't leave without me!' Tom called back over his shoulder.

'Your friend is an interesting person.' Devereux chuckled. 'Seeing you with me caused quite a storm of emotions inside him. He is concerned that he was wrong to let you go. He is reconsidering.'

'Are you jealous?' I blurted, without thinking. What was I, a fourteen-year-old?

He snuggled in close and enveloped me in that wonderful spicy scent again. His eyes shimmered in the dim light and his voice flowed like music. 'No. I am not jealous. I am certain of your feelings for me. What you and I have is beyond petty human emotions.'

I briefly thought about insisting that I had no feelings for him, but I had no clue what was going on with me. Saying I didn't have any feelings about him would be a lie, and how could I fool someone who appeared to have the ability, whether I liked – or believed – it or not, to know what I was thinking and feeling? Was that every woman's dream or worst nightmare?

Instead I asked, 'If I stare at your eyes again, will I jump back into your lap?'

He laughed, a full-throated sound that washed over me like warm honey. 'No. You may look at me and remain in your seat.'

I locked eyes with him and thought, 'Kiss me.'

'Your wish is my command.' He pressed his soft, warm lips against mine and plunged me once again into that deep, blissful, timeless universe where only the two of us existed. The sounds in the room receded into the background. Everyone else in the club disappeared. He gently teased his tongue into my mouth, exploring me, and I returned the favour. I heard myself making little moaning sounds. He spoke in my mind, 'I want you.'

My body ached with desire for him. Maybe it was the buildup of sexual need during the last two years, or maybe it was my reaction to his incredible kiss, but I couldn't think about anything except having mad, passionate sex with Devereux. And, at the same time, I knew that even having that thought was totally abnormal for me.

We reluctantly pulled apart.

'Come. Let me show you the rest of my club.'

He stood and held his hand out to me, and I took it, feeling both anxious and excited.

I slid out of the booth, rose up on my toes, and scanned the room. 'I should tell Tom where I'm going. Not that he deserves it. It'd serve him right if I just left him here to fend for himself.'

Devereux cocked his head. 'The two of you had a disagreement?'

'Sometimes, even though I know better, I let his arrogance get to me. In a sick way, he's sort of like family. He's one of the few people I ever trusted.'

'Ah. Well, not to worry – Zoë will tell him you are with me.'

'What do you mean, Zoë will tell him? How will Zoë know?'

'I have spoken to her, in her mind, and she will convey the message. Come.'

Is he saying they all have such outrageous psychic abilities?

We walked down the set of stairs that led from our cosy booth into the central part of the club. Devereux held my hand and guided us through the crowd, which seemed to flow aside magically, creating an impossible path through the jammed-in bodies. We wound our way near the sarcophagus-shaped bar where the Leather Goddess was entertaining a group of slack-jawed males who were enthralled by her bartending talents. At the far end of the bar was an old-looking wooden door. Seated on a stool in front of the door was a large, muscular man with long grey hair, dressed in standard biker gear.

When we approached, the biker guy jumped up off his stool, quickly pushed it aside and opened the door. Either this fellow had ingested too much caffeine, he was naturally nervous, or seeing Devereux triggered an anxiety attack, because he stared at Devereux with wide eyes. I could almost feel his adrenalin pumping. This guy was afraid.

Devereux said, 'Thank you, John,' as we walked through the entryway and the door closed behind us. We were standing at the top of a long, wide staircase that descended down into the bowels of the club.

'Why was that man so afraid of you?'

He placed his hand on the small of my back. 'Some humans seek out that which terrifies them so they can be afraid, which is the only way they know to feel alive – much like watching a movie that causes one to feel fear. John is addicted to vampires.'

Listening to Devereux talk about vampires again definitely took the edge off the lust that had been there just moments ago. It was becoming clear that I'd have to accept his vampire fantasies or I wouldn't be able to see him. And seeing him had become non-negotiable. I'd never felt so *attached* to anyone so quickly before. It was as if I not only needed to touch him, but I wanted to crawl into his soul. Very strange.

I still hadn't made sense out of all the things Alan had told me about Devereux being the leader of a vampire coven. In fact, the information had been replaying in my mind all day, eating away at my logical explanations. Alan was a psychologist, after all. Why would he lie to me? Was he caught up in the delusion as well?

Truthfully, I simply didn't want to think of Devereux as being mentally ill. Why couldn't he just call himself a psychic, which seemed to be true? Why bother with the absurd vampire role-playing?

We walked down the stairs, which led to a long hallway with many doors along each side. I was reminded of Midnight's comment about the lower level being a dungeon by the stone walls and the heavy doors, which looked as if they'd been created to keep screaming prisoners locked away.

A cool dampness pervaded and I was almost surprised to see electric lights instead of torches lining the walls. But even though the place resembled a mediaeval castle, it really couldn't be that old because the church itself had only existed for just over a hundred years. Yet there was an ancient feel to it.

Some of the doors were open. As we passed I could see offices, meeting rooms, storage rooms, a lounge area with a movie-screen-size television and the velvet-curtain-covered entrance to the special gathering place Midnight had told me about during her first session.

Devereux stopped in front of that room and pulled back the curtains. He nodded at me to check out the large group of people gathered inside. 'I will introduce you to some of my companions later. Right now I selfishly wish to keep you to myself. You are a precious gift.'

I wasn't used to men paying such attention to me, so I didn't know what to make of all the emotions that swept over me as he said those words. Something about them triggered an old need and I suddenly felt vulnerable. I gazed up at his beautiful face and he bent over and kissed my forehead tenderly, as if he knew what I was thinking.

Well, apparently he does know what I'm thinking . . .

To give myself a moment to regroup, I decided to ask about his abilities. 'Can you really read the thoughts of everyone around you? Surely that would take the fun out of getting to know someone. Life could get very boring if you always knew everything in advance.'

He closed the curtains, clasped my hand, and walked me further down the hallway to a set of ornate double doors.

We paused there. 'Life can indeed become boring, which is one reason why I mastered the ability to read thoughts selectively. As I have said, your thoughts are private unless I actively choose to listen to them. The constant mental chatter is also very distracting, and often there are other matters that require my attention. I have responsibility for several large businesses, for example.'

'Oh, I see.' *So even though he can use his abilities all the time, he expects me to believe he doesn't.*

He used an old-fashioned key to open the door and ushered me into a huge room filled with lovely antiques, tapestries and artwork. The room was big enough to contain my entire townhouse with space to add a garage. Along the walls were beautiful candelabra holding lit candles which, combined with the prisms of light shining from an overhead chandelier, gave the room a soft illumination. The stone walls must have created natural soundproofing because I couldn't hear the music from upstairs any more. The silence was rich.

I scanned the room and noticed that all the modern office equipment one could need was there – computer, fax machine, printer – built into antique desks, armoires and tables interspersed among colourful couches and chairs. One half of the room was obviously used as a library, the walls lined with bookshelves holding thousands of books, some of which appeared to be very old.

'Welcome to my private office.' Devereux bowed. 'Make yourself at home.'

'Wow, this is amazing,' I said, mostly to myself, as I wandered around the room, exploring. He had marvellous taste in furnishings and a remarkable sense of colour.

Appreciating the care he'd put into creating his workspace made me remember my own sparsely appointed office and I vowed to give it more attention. If it was true that someone's outer world reflected his inner world, then Devereux was indeed a complex and multifaceted person.

When I turned back to him, it occurred to me that I hadn't seen him in bright light since he'd come to my office to interrupt Bryce's attack. As attractive as he appeared upstairs in the dim lighting of the club, now the combination of his shining blond hair and luminous blue-green eyes was almost overwhelming. He wore leather trousers that were a dark version of the colour of his eyes and a silk shirt of nearly the same shade. His boots had a full heel that made him even taller than he already was, which caused his lean, muscular body to look even more impressive.

I moved over to him, stood with our bodies almost touching, and gazed up at him. 'What do you want from me?'

'Everything.' He pulled me against him and his lips reclaimed mine.

My body came alive with sensations and desires. The longer we kissed, the more I became convinced I wouldn't survive the intensity of the feelings I was experiencing. My knees were weak and all my pleasure centres throbbed with need. I felt him hard and thick against the front of my blue jeans. He made sounds that were part moan, part growl.

My heart was pounding so loud and fast it took me a minute to figure out that both of our hearts were beating together in a synchronised rhythm. I could almost hear the blood pumping through my veins.

He suddenly jerked away from me and retreated a step,

observing me from beneath his dark eyelashes. Throwing back his head, he ran his tongue over his top lip and gave a quick glimpse of fangs.

I gasped in surprise, still lost in the web of desire we'd spun.

He closed his eyes and breathed out a heavy sigh. As he did that, the long canines retracted back up into his gums.

When he opened his eyes again, he studied me, his expression serious. 'It has been many years since I have lost control of myself that way. You do indeed have great power over me. I hope I did not frighten you.'

I knew that I'd just seen Devereux's teeth do the same curious thing Bryce's had when he forced me to put my finger on his tooth in my office, and I didn't have any better explanation now than I had then, but I really didn't care. I kept feeling that I should care, but I just didn't. I'd either have to accept his strange role-playing or walk away.

'You didn't frighten me,' I whispered.

'Come. There is something I wish to show you.'

He took my hand and drew me over to one of the bookcases, where he ran his fingers along the inside panel and pressed something that made a slight clicking sound. The large bookcase swung backwards, creating the entrance to an adjoining room. Devereux eased me through the opening in the wall of books into that other space, which was roughly half the size of the huge area we'd left, but still very large.

To say this was the most extraordinary room I'd ever seen would be an understatement. The floor was white marble etched with Celtic, astrological, alchemical, and other magical symbols in patterns of various colours. False walls of rich wood had been constructed over the natural stone, and paintings, which appeared to be the work of the same artist, covered most of the available space. The air held a subtle fragrance, a combination of incense and herbs. On one side of the room was a large antique bed, with bright-coloured bedding. Not a coffin in sight. At least he wasn't quite that delusional.

I had expected the bed to be our destination, and I felt both nervous and aroused about the prospect, but to my surprise, Devereux guided me to the other end of the room, which was filled with shelves and tables full of strange bottles, odd substances and peculiar items. In addition, there were candles of every colour, shape, and size. Further along the wall was an artist's easel, many canvases, and some paint supplies.

Devereux walked over to the easel. 'I want you to know me.' He held out his hand.

I joined him at the easel and let my eyes take in the lovely scene of a sunrise that was partially completed. He pointed to the rising sun in the picture. 'Perhaps we all want what we cannot have?'

'All these paintings are yours? You're an artist?'

'Painting is one of my passions.'

I moved around the room, closely inspecting the paintings hanging on each wall. There was a mix of breathtaking outdoor scenes alongside portraits of people dressed in clothing from other centuries. As amazing as the landscape scenes were, the portraits were even more spectacular. It was as if he'd captured the essence of each person's soul and added that mystical element to the final painting in some magical way.

'They're beautiful. You're very talented.'

He bowed. 'I have had a very long time to practise.'

One painting in particular drew me and I walked over to stand before it. The woman in the picture had the same hair and eyes as Devereux. She was dressed in a flowing white gown that made me think of angels, and around her neck she wore an exquisite pentagram on a silver chain.

'That was my mother,' he said, coming to stand beside me.

I noted the 'was' in his statement. 'I'm sorry. Did you lose her recently?'

'No.' He turned to me and smiled sadly. 'She died very long ago, but I still miss her. She taught me everything I know. She was an amazing woman.'

He walked back over to the shelves and tables of unusual objects.

'What's the stuff in the bottles? What do you do with all those candles?' I asked, moving over to explore the strange objects.

'Magic.'

'Magic? You mean magic tricks, like a magician?'

He pivoted to stand in front of me and met my eyes with his.

'They are not tricks, but yes, "magician" is one of the names those such as I have been called throughout the ages. We are also referred to as magus, shaman or wizard. I have a particular fondness for the title wizard because it honours the Druid lineage from which I descend.'

'What? You're a Druid?' I thought about the documentary I'd seen featuring robe-clad pagans celebrating the Summer Solstice at Stonehenge in England. Maybe that was where his role-playing originated. 'Wow. I thought the Druids died out after the Romans. Your family must go back for ever.' *He thinks he's a Druid. Can he tell the different between reality and fantasy?*

He winked. 'Yes, I can tell the difference.'

Annoyed, I crossed my arms over my chest. 'Stop reading my thoughts. It's rude. And you might hear things you won't like.'

'I apologise, and you are correct. I often hear thoughts I do not like. But in this case I could not resist. Your doubts about me are very strong. They scent the air. In response to your statement, my family *is* very old, and it is a commonly held mortal belief that the Druids disappeared after the Roman era. But many hidden tribes of Druids continue to thrive into the present, our existence unknown to human historians.'

'Unknown to historians.' I relaxed my arms. 'No offence, but that sounds pretty convenient.'

'Perhaps, but it is the truth, nonetheless. When we have been together longer, I will tell you tales of my life.'

'I see. When we've been together longer. It sounds like you have ambitious plans.'

He just smiled. My heartbeat stumbled and I felt suddenly hot.

This is not normal.

I fanned myself as his smile broadened. 'Er, what was it you said about wizards? You mean like the guys in the pointy hats in the fairy tales about King Arthur or Harry Potter?'

His expression turned serious, which surprised me and made me anxious. I shifted my gaze and nervously studied his collection of New Age paraphernalia on the nearby table.

'Ah, my dear Kismet, as a psychologist, you should know that all fairy tales contain a grain of truth. The actual stories of wizards are not commonly known, but they were indeed powerful beings. I do not expect you to believe everything – or perhaps even anything – that I will share with you, but I do ask that you keep an open mind. I want you to know why I am so drawn to you. Long before I became a nightwalker—'

I looked up from the crystal ball I'd been gazing into. 'A nightwalker?'

'A vampire, the undead, an immortal.'

I took a breath, preparing to ask more questions, but he held up a hand to stop me. 'Please. Let me finish.'

I nodded and picked up a crystal-encrusted wand.

'Since my human birth, I was schooled in the art and craft of magic. Generations of my family had apprenticed themselves to the witches and wizards who came before, and the skills and abilities of each ancestor were passed along the bloodline. By the time the gifts came down to me, they were extremely potent.'

He clasped his hands behind his back and paced to and fro, as if he were delivering a speech.

Why do I find his mannerisms so charming? If Tom did the same thing, I'd be irritated.

I followed him with my eyes. 'It sounds like you had an unusual childhood,' I said.

'Yes, in some ways. And in others it was perfectly normal. I was very fortunate. I had parents who loved me and who raised me in a beautiful place. In addition to my talents in the realm of the magical arts, I also inherited artistic abilities, which revealed themselves very early. It was not long before my ability to see the future blended with my love of painting to give me an extremely potent tool for expressing the prophecies and visions I sensed in my deepest mind. I became a seer.'

'A seer? Do you mean a psychic?'

He gave a quick nod. 'I suppose the word seer is old-fashioned and people today would call themselves psychic, or perhaps clairvoyant. My gift was only visual at first. I could enter into altered states and view the probable future. Now I have access to all the channels: visual, auditory, olfactory and others.'

'Wow,' I said. 'What's it like to be able to do that?' If he really could do all those things – and I was still a long way from believing he could – he had to be the most powerful psychic I'd ever heard of.

Sadness shadowed his features. 'Not as wonderful as you might imagine. The longer I have existed, the harder it has become to be aware of what is coming, to accept the poor choices made by most of humanity. My journey has been challenging. Lonely. Unfortunately, I cannot always see what is ahead for me – my vision dims when I focus it on myself. Had I known the true reality of becoming immortal in the beginning, I might not have made the same decisions.'

He suddenly looked like the lost, wounded child I had assumed he was when Midnight first mentioned him. My heart ached for the pain he had experienced. The loneliness. Obviously he'd had some trauma or crisis that precipitated his paranormal role-playing. I had just taken a step towards him to comfort him when he strode over to a large wooden cabinet and opened the wide double doors. Inside were scores of painted canvases, lined up next to each other like dominoes. He reached in and selected one particular canvas and drew it out of the cabinet, holding it carefully along the edge.

He carried the painting back to me, turned it around for me to see and held it up with both hands.

I gasped, staring. It was a portrait of me.

'Devereux! That's so beautiful. When did you have time to paint this? How could you have memorised my face so perfectly in the short time I've known you?'

I stood, speechless, taking in the details of the portrait. As I examined the exquisite artwork, something began to tug at my consciousness. There was something odd about this painting. I couldn't quite put my finger on what it was until it rolled over me like a wave.

'My necklace.' Suddenly I felt tense. 'You've never seen this necklace. In fact, this is the first time I've ever worn it, yet it's in the portrait. How can that be? And my blue blouse. How could you have painted me as I look tonight?'

But he did say he's psychic.

He propped the canvas on an easel. 'When I created this portrait, I did not know the woman in the picture or why I was compelled to adorn her with that particular piece of jewellery. As always when I am in the midst of a prophetic vision, I simply painted what I saw. Unlike the other visions that had been born on my canvases, this one would not release me after the image was complete. The woman in the portrait haunted me. She filled my dreams until I was sure I would go mad. She spoke to me in my mind and repeated one word, over and over again.'

'What word?'

He pointed to some writing at the bottom of the painting and I leaned in to read that single word.

Kismet.

'I thought the word meant the woman in the painting was my fate, my destiny. I waited patiently for her to find me, and after a time I locked the painting away. Until now.'

He closed the distance between us and grasped my upper arms. 'It was not a word at all. It was your name.'

I shook my head, searching the depths of his eyes for some clue to what he was talking about.

'I don't understand. Are you saying you didn't paint this recently?'

'Yes. Far from it.'

'When, then? When did you paint it?'

'More than eight hundred years ago.'

CHAPTER 12

It was official. Like Elvis, my brain had definitely left the building.

At some point during the last few hours I'd apparently fallen down the rabbit-hole. I didn't have a map of Wonderland, and nothing in my previous experience or education had prepared me to deal with the strange parallel universe I'd landed in.

Had someone slipped LSD into my Bloody Mary?

There I was, in the nether regions of Dracula's castle, staring at a gorgeous self-proclaimed immortal who insisted he'd painted my portrait eight hundred years ago, and I couldn't find the instruction manual to put the pieces together. I couldn't even find the box the damn thing came in.

Devereux seemed to have that effect on me. One minute I was ready to rip my clothes off, leap into his arms, and lose myself in a frenzy of body parts. The next minute I was rocketing between shocked horror, mind-numbing confusion, and righteous anger. My brain just wasn't equipped for that kind of neurochemical rollercoaster ride.

Then all hell broke loose.

I heard loud, angry voices out in the corridor and frantic

pounding on the outer door to Devereux's office. Evidently the villagers with burning torches had arrived.

'Master! Master! Come quickly. They're back and they've got Luna.'

Devereux grabbed the painting from the easel, shoved it at me and ordered, 'Stay here.' He moved so quickly through the opening in the wall of books that my eyes registered only a blur.

He must have opened the outer door because a cacophony of chaotic, fearful voices filled the air before the door clicked shut again, leaving me in eerie silence.

Stay here? I seriously don't think so.

I slanted another glance at the portrait then returned it to the cabinet. No matter when it had been painted, it was clearly high quality. Devereux was a talented artist. What was it with me? Why did I have to fall for brilliant men who were either egomaniacs, crazy, or both?

I hurried out of his secret room and crossed the main office area, heading for the door to the hallway. The closer I drew, the louder the sounds became. I put my fingers on the handle and gently pushed down, silently easing the door inward until I could poke my head out and view the area directly in front of the entrance. I half-expected to find a guard standing there, another of Devereux's motorcycle-gang thralls, who would keep me in my luxurious holding cell. However, this end of the hallway was empty.

Judging by the noise level, all the action was happening further up the corridor, in the area behind the velvet curtains. The sounds of crashing furniture, blood-curdling screams, Darth Vader-like rumblings, and screechings that had to be a demonic choir rehearsing the Satanic Mass for the Dead assailed my ears. Something unpleasantly red was oozing along the floor in front of that entryway.

The only way out of the basement was to pass the crazed circus carrying on behind curtain #1.

I tiptoed along the hallway and stood with my back pressed against the wall next to the entrance to the insane asylum. I peeked in long enough to see that all the people – if 'people' was the right word – crammed into the room were locked in combat with willing and enthusiastic partners. Devereux's assistant Luna had a huge hairy man wrestled down, her teeth shredding chunks from his neck as her victim screamed. A tall African-American male stepped near the doorway and turned his gaze in my direction. He opened his mouth, displaying long, bloody fangs, then reached into the chest of the man nearest to him and ripped his heart out.

Bile rose in my throat and my head spun.

The last thing I saw before I sprinted towards the stairs leading back up to the main floor was Devereux and Bryce, blood-covered, fangs bared, hair flying, levitating a few feet above the ground and clutching each other's necks.

That was it for me.

Holy shit! They really are vampires!

The volume of noise swallowed my unintended scream and I bolted from the totally unbelievable towards the merely improbable.

I ran up the stairs like I was being chased by the Hounds of Hell, pushed through the door where John the biker, the vampire addict, had abandoned his post, and smashed into Alan's chest. I screamed, instinctively tried to push away. He grabbed my upper arms and held me against him. I was shaking so hard my earrings rattled.

'Kismet! I've been searching all over for you. What the hell's going on here? What's all that noise down there? What happened to you?'

'They're fighting. It's a bloody mess.'

'Who's fighting? I'd better get down there—' He started to pull away.

'No.' I grabbed his arms. 'Wait. Trust me – you don't want to go down there. I can't believe I'm saying this, but this place really is filled with vampires, and I can say for sure that everybody is certifiably crazy. From what I just saw, you wouldn't last five minutes. Please, I want to find Tom and go home.'

'Okay, you find him. I'll call the locals.'

'No! Devereux wouldn't want you to bring the police into this. Let's just go.'

Alan tipped his head to the side and cocked a brow. 'Devereux wouldn't, would he? And how would you know that?'

'I'll tell you all about it – all of it – but right now, let's get out of here.'

His eyes bored into mine for a long moment, and then he nodded. Either I was sufficiently crazed-looking that he'd decided to humour me, or he'd read deeper between the lines and got that my terror was authentic. I could at least admit to myself that I'd never dealt well with violent psychotics, and everything about the scene in the basement triggered my worst nightmares.

He took both my hands in his and stared into my eyes.

'Okay. Just breathe. We'll find Tom. You go check out the dance floor and I'll see if he's ogling the bartender again. Let's meet outside in five minutes.'

I sighed in relief, pulled my hands free, and started off towards the crowded dance floor. After a few steps, I turned back to yell at Alan to hurry and saw him leap through the doorway to the basement. I should've known he'd have to be a one-man cavalry; an FBI agent, first and foremost. I filed away for future use the fact that he'd stared right into my eyes and lied to me.

Now more angry than frightened, I stomped off in search of Tom. Alan could flail around in the madness if he wanted to, but I was going to find my narcissistic ex-boyfriend, catch a cab and get the hell out of there. The further removed I got from everything that had happened downstairs, the more the idea of drugs in my drink seemed plausible.

I wandered around the club for several minutes, even going so far as to stand in front of the men's room, sneaking peeks inside whenever the door opened. That got me a lot of unwanted attention, suggestive comments and lascivious invitations. What it didn't get me was a glimpse of Tom.

Come to think of it, I hadn't seen Zoë either.

One good thing about being tall to begin with and wearing high heels was the elevated altitude. From my lofty vantage point, I was able to scan over the heads of half the blissed-out party-goers and save myself from unnecessary body-jostling.

If Tom was in the club, he had to be under a table somewhere because there was no sign of him standing or sitting anywhere. Alan hadn't emerged from the supernatural testosterone-fest below, so I was on my own. That was fine. I was used to being on my own.

It suddenly occurred to me that Tom might have gone outside, so I strode purposefully towards the front door and noticed the cadaverous bouncer was missing in action. I pushed through the heavy door leading out into the fresh night air and stood for a moment, coughing, as my lungs made it clear that I wouldn't be getting off so easily after spending an evening breathing in the chemical spewing of a fog machine.

I hadn't worn a watch, but I figured it had to be close to last call. Tom wasn't outside either, but he'd have to come out of the club eventually, so I decided to wait. Then it struck me that he'd probably left without me. There I was, waiting for him to make sure he got home safely, and he'd just gone on his merry way without giving me a thought. That would be typical Tom – not to mention typical of how I'd let him walk all over me. How could a supposedly bright woman be so dense at the same time?

Groups of people stood in front of the club in various states of inebriation, drug intoxication and passionate embrace, so I strolled further down the block. I rested against the building and sank back into the shadows while I took full breaths to clear out my lungs and appreciated the silence.

I mentally reviewed what I'd seen in the basement. Nothing fitted with any of my therapeutic experience. In all my reading and research, I'd never run across anything that included fangs, levitation, informal heart surgery and the kind of unearthly noises emanating from that room.

Vampires really exist. Devereux wasn't role-playing. What am I supposed to do with that knowledge? Where do I put it in my brain? If there are vampires, then I might as well pull up stakes – so to speak – and go and work in a fast-food restaurant somewhere, because everything I thought was true isn't.

I dropped my head back against the cool of the old brick and closed my eyes. The moment I did that, a wave of dizziness swept over me and I braced myself against the wall, feeling as if the ground had actually moved. I waited, locked my knees to keep upright in the midst of the spinning, and opened my eyes. Everything was subtly different. I blinked a few times to clear my vision but couldn't shake the sense that something was wrong. Something had changed. The darkness was deeper, more textured. The air felt thick, heavy, and was scented with a sweet coppery aroma. The smell got stronger until I could taste it in the back of my throat and I gagged.

'Come to me.'

I gasped. The voice was repulsive; it crawled over my skin with slimy fingers. I automatically jerked my head to one side, raising a shoulder to block the sound entering one ear.

What the hell was that? I'm really losing it. I willed myself not to move.

'Come. Now.'

I couldn't tell if I heard the voice with my physical ears or inside my mind, but it was unlike any I'd ever experienced. It was as if the words attacked my eardrums. The sound split into dissonant octaves again and again, until it filled the entire vibrational spectrum. It reminded me of those experiments where the government used audio frequencies to create madness.

I also had the sense of feeling the voice kinesthetically, of being able to locate places in my body where it resonated, pulsed, invaded. My bones and organs vibrated in time with a powerful rhythm outside of me. The pressure increased as the sound waves echoed around and through me, becoming more painful as they escalated.

'I am here. Come to me and I will show you miracles. I will grant all your earthly desires.' The voice tore at my ears, repeating the same message over and over.

I covered them with my hands and screamed, 'No!'

I felt myself moving away from the wall, as if pulled by a powerful magnet. My stomach tingled and ached and became hypersensitive. I had the bizarre notion that an invisible hand had attached to my midsection, physically compelling me. My head felt fuzzy, my mind disconnected. I couldn't stop myself. I couldn't resist. I walked away from the club into the darkness of the street beyond, the sense of dread and terror growing stronger with every wobbly step.

Then everything went dark.

I woke up in a coffin.

That might sound unpleasant, unsanitary, or maybe creepy to most people, but for me it was my worst nightmare.

This might be a good time to explain my greatest fear.

When I was young I saw an old movie called *Premature Burial*, where – due to a strange illness that caused complete paralysis mimicking death – people were buried before they were dead. The afflicted were put in boxes, placed in holes in the ground and were very aware of the dirt being piled on top of their supposedly deceased selves. They couldn't communicate their aliveness to any of the grieving mourners, so they slowly suffocated. When the illness was finally discovered and the Unfortunate Buried Alive were dug up, it became clear that at some point in the process the paralysis had worn off and the bloody fingernails of the Unwillingly Interred gave evidence of their vain attempts to escape. It was a hideous death. I couldn't sleep for weeks after watching that movie.

A psychic later told me that I'd died in a previous life due to being buried alive or maybe drowned or perhaps suffocated with a pillow – just choose one of the air-restricted methods – and that was why the movie had affected me so profoundly. I can't verify the accuracy of my previous causes of death, but I do know that anything dealing with being unable to breathe thrusts me into spasms of terror.

It was perhaps lucky that I didn't know right away that I'd woken up in a coffin. The first thing I noticed was a putrid smell, a unique stench consisting of backed-up sewer, rotted meat, blood, mould, mildew and death. The smell was so horribly potent that it caused me to become aware of the second thing: it was very dark. The reason the smell triggered me to notice the darkness was because as soon as I got a good whiff of it, my stomach heaved. I tried to sit up, or roll over, because I didn't want to throw up on myself, and I was certain that barf was in my immediate future.

My attempt to sit up caused me to bang my head against an unexpected barrier, which led me to discover there was a ceiling directly above my body. I began to push against it and quickly deduced it was an immovable object, or at least a very heavy one.

Then I panicked.

The feeling of my hands pushing against the resisting material immediately triggered a cellular memory of the aforementioned movie and I started to scream, which shifted my attention away from throwing up. This proved to be very helpful: fear is a powerful motivator. Like the mothers who lift multi-ton vehicles off their children, imagining myself locked in a box for my ride up the Entry Ramp to Eternity allowed me to become Hulk-like in my strength, and to force open what turned out to be the bulky lid of an old coffin.

I sat up, still screaming, the sound reverberating off the walls of the small, decrepit building I'd awakened in. A building that smelled extraordinarily bad.

Raising the lid on the coffin allowed me to see the sunlight filtering in through the broken front door. I couldn't tell how much time had passed, but it was obviously daytime. A chunk of my life was missing. I valiantly tried to reconstruct the chain of events that had brought me to this moment, and failed.

I stopped screaming – mostly because it hurt my throat – and let my eyes adjust to the dim light. Being able to see where I was made things worse. Instead of only suspecting I was up shit creek, I now had verification.

The building was an old, run-down mausoleum. Low spots in the cement floor were filled with stagnant, rancid water mixed with blood from several dead bodies. Even in the limited light, it was clear that no one in any state of aliveness could be the colour of the remains scattered around that room. The place looked like a human slaughterhouse. Back in a corner were bones and pieces of rotting clothing, which gave evidence to the likelihood that whatever was going on here had been going on for a very long time.

Needless to say, I had to get out.

I assumed that whoever had killed all those people was probably coming back to get me. I didn't have time to think about why I was still breathing, why the murderer had left me in the coffin instead of adding me to the collection on the floor. It occurred to me I was probably in shock, which explained the strange fuzzy feeling in my head.

Since the lid of the coffin had only swung back on its hinges and was still standing straight, I couldn't brace myself by holding on to both sides. Grabbing the available edge, I put my other hand down alongside my legs and felt it sink into clumps of dirt or sand. As I pulled my knees underneath me, I heard a soft clattering sound as something knocked against the inside of the coffin. I reached my hand out to find what had made the noise and closed my fingers around a long stick-like thing. I brought it up into the light and found myself in possession of a human bone. I had been lying on top of whoever had been buried in that coffin.

Holy shit!

My stomach lurched again and I rose to my feet as if pulled by ropes. Looking down, I could clearly see the remains of the original resident. With shaking hands I brushed off as much of the desiccated decomposed material as I could from the rear of my trousers and apologised silently to the person I had scattered into the air.

The coffin I was now standing in was situated on a pedestal about three feet off the floor. The area close around it was filled with dead bodies and pools of bloody water. I would have to jump, which under the best of circumstances called on grace I hadn't cultivated, and to jump while wearing four-inch heels would guarantee a painful outcome. But if my choice was to wait in the coffin for the psychopath to return or take my chances with a sprained ankle, I'd choose the sprain anytime.

Since I was far from adept in physical situations, it took me a moment to work out that I could sit on the open edge of the coffin, swing my legs out and scoot down, then find a small space for the ball of my foot on one of the few dry spaces on the floor and ease myself away from the pedestal.

Kismet the nerd who flunked gym class in ninth grade.

That's what I did, all the while listening for any sound that would alert me to the return of the monster who'd brought me there.

I walked on tiptoes through the carnage to the door, unable to avoid wading through puddles of slimy, bloody water, and finally reached the stairs leading up to the light. My stomach had been clenched so tightly I'd barely breathed since I left the coffin. I climbed up the stone steps and shoved the door. It swung open on rusty hinges, making that sound always present in horror movies. Then I stepped out into the sunshine and found myself in the middle of an old graveyard.

I heard sounds of traffic nearby and moved in that direction. I kept glancing behind me to see if it had been a trap, if someone – or something – was going to spring out at me from behind one of the huge gravestones and haul me back into the pit of hell, but I was alone.

Doubtless I must have been quite a sight as I walked out of the ornate cast-iron gates of the graveyard and crossed the parking lot of McDonald's.

CHAPTER 13

I had no idea where I was.

Another beautiful day in Paradise had got all dressed up and started without me. The sun beamed almost directly overhead, making it about noon. I shielded my eyes with my hand, spun in a slow circle, and searched for the mountains to give me a sense of location. Denver is a consistent distance from various distinctive peaks, and I always got my bearings by checking my position in relation to them, as well as the ever-present downtown skyscrapers.

Turns out I was within walking distance of Devereux's club. I never knew there was an old graveyard tucked away back behind Fast-Food Row. Well, you know what they say about learning something new every day ...

High-pitched giggles drew my attention down from the horizon and I found myself gazing at a gaggle of little girls. They all held dripping ice cream cones. As the children surrounded me, one sticky-fingered angel said, 'You're funny!' This caused another wave of gleeful laughter.

'I'm funny?'

That was apparently hilarious.

Another sweet cherub said, 'What are you doing in the

middle of the parking lot? Are you dancing? What's all that stuff on you?'

I looked down at myself and saw I was covered in samples of everything I'd found back in the death pit in the graveyard, including dried blood, which stained my hands.

With a gasp, I immediately leaped to the most drastic conclusion: that the blood was mine. I inspected myself, searching for wounds or cuts, anything that would explain the stains, but I found nothing. Since I had no recollection of what'd transpired during the missing hours – and at that moment I wasn't up for exploring the disgusting possibilities – I gave myself permission to stuff the entire matter deep inside my psychological Do Not Enter zone.

A pretty little brown-eyed tyke ventured a couple of tentative steps in my direction, pointed, and yelled, 'You smell!'

That was definitely some kind of cosmic cue. Simultaneously, anxious mothers scurried forth from everywhere, retrieved their children and whisked them back to the play area.

'What did I tell you? Never talk to strangers!' one mother scolded as she pulled her child away, tossing frightened glances back over her shoulder.

I raised my arm up to my nose and sniffed. Yuck. I did smell. In fact, I smelled worse than horrible. Just like that ghastly place. No wonder the moms had treated me like a carrier of the Black Death. I could only imagine what I looked like.

Wondering if my cell phone had survived the ghastly experience, I retrieved it from my pocket and hit the 'on' switch. It was as dead as the bodies in the tomb.

Shit! Perfect.

I fished in my pocket to see if the cash I'd put there the night before had survived my mysterious experience. I pulled out a handful of bills and coins. Even though I could've walked to Devereux's club, the memories of the previous night left a bad taste in my mouth. I had no desire to make a return visit. All I wanted to do was go home, take off the toe-smashing boots and crawl into a hot bath.

I'd just spied an old telephone booth and headed in that direction to call for a cab when a police cruiser pulled into the parking lot and blocked my path. Either I really did look suspicious enough to draw the attention of a passing cop car, or someone in the restaurant had alerted the police to deal with the crazy lady.

Two very young officers exited the car and walked cautiously over to me. One looked like a computer geek and the other a football player. I don't know what I expected, but it wasn't what I got.

'Are you Dr Knight?' the computer geek asked.

'How do you know that? I mean, yes.'

'Are you all right?'

'Yes. No. I'm not all right. I just woke up in a coffin in a graveyard and I'm covered in substances I don't even want to think about.'

'Are you wounded?'

'No. I don't think so. Not physically, anyway.'

'Is that your blood on your hands, Dr Knight?'

'I don't know.' I held my hands out and inspected them again. 'How do you know my name?'

'An FBI agent working with the Denver PD put out a red

flag on you, said you'd gone missing last night. Your photo's been running on the local TV stations all morning. You must be an important person because we're not usually allowed to act this fast on a missing-person report. It looks like you've had a rough time. If you'll come with us, we can sort everything out and get you some help.'

He took another step towards me and scrunched up his nose as he approached. 'Wow. Where did you say you've been?'

A quick visual communication passed between them, eye contact so covert that if I hadn't been trained to notice such things, I'd have missed it. The look said 'Potential Disturbed Person'. I knew that look well, having shared it with other professionals in various mental health settings. It was a shorthand code for a set of behaviours – behaviours that calmed the patient and encouraged cooperation. While I could understand why they might slide me into that category, I wasn't willing to assume the role.

I was in no mood to be cooperative or polite. My brain had finally kicked back into gear. Along with the fear and confusion I'd experienced since waking up in one of the levels of Hades, I was also pissed off – pissed off at whoever had dragged me to this place, and pissed off at being manipulated. The officers clearly thought I was hallucinating about waking up in a coffin in a graveyard so I decided to cut to the chase.

I'd been abducted, brought to a maniac's lair and who knew what else. Now was as good a time as any to take the cops on a tour of Horror Central. I pivoted and trotted back towards the entrance gate to the old graveyard.

'Hey! Stop! Where are you going?' the football player yelled.

'I'm going to show you where I've been.' I called on my

last reserves of glucose and sprinted through the gate into 'Capitol Hill Cemetery, an Historical Landmark' with the cops close on my heels.

'Dr Knight! You've obviously had some kind of trauma. You're not thinking clearly. Let us take you downtown. Stop or we'll have to restrain you.'

'Restrain me, my ass. You'll have to catch me first.'

If they were going to assume I was irrational, at least I could add some interesting fuel to the fire. I didn't like being treated as an incompetent – even if they meant well – and I never had played nicely with authority figures. It occurred to me that the officers might not know the old graveyard was back there either, since it was well hidden. If that were the case, it was little wonder my story sounded even more fantastic than it would've anyway.

My run through the graveyard was really quite impressive. I managed to find my way back to the ramshackle mausoleum without falling, being obstructed by the city's finest or turning an ankle. There was something to be said for adrenalin.

I heard one of the officers yell into his communicator, requesting backup, as they chased along behind me, dodging gravestones and statues.

'Dr Knight! Stop! We're only trying to help you!'

I skidded to a halt a few feet from the door of the death chamber and pointed. The police hadn't expected the race to end so suddenly, and they barely managed to avoid crashing into me as they slammed on their own brakes.

'There!' I jabbed my finger towards the mausoleum. 'Through that door is a stairway. There are dead bodies inside.'

The lean, cerebral-looking officer reached out and grabbed

my upper arm and tugged gently, coaxing me to accompany him as he started walking back towards the cemetery entrance.

'Come on, Dr Knight. No more games. Let's get you back to the police station and you can explain everything to the detectives. We've been instructed to bring you in immediately. The orders came straight from the chief.' He glanced at his partner. 'Did you know there was a cemetery back here?' The beefy guy shook his head.

For some reason, getting me back to the police station seemed more important than investigating my story, so I opted for drastic measures. I wrenched my arm out of his hand and leaped over to the door and pulled it open. The smell made my stomach turn. I doubled over and yelled at the cops, 'Go on! Nothing normal can smell that bad. You at least have to check it out!'

Each officer raised a hand up to his face, covered his mouth and pinched his nose, trying to stave off the odour. The larger one gagged. 'That is one god-awful smell. Maybe some animal died in there. Let's take a look.'

I moved away from the door and put as much space as possible between me and the stench. I bent forwards, bracing my hands just above my knees, still trying not to vomit.

'I'll go down and see what we've got. You stay up here with Dr Knight.'

The thin cop went through the door and down the stairs. Only a couple of seconds passed before he yelled, 'Jesus, Mary and Joseph!' and scrambled back up the stairs, his face gone pasty and his eyes wide.

'What's wrong with you, McCarthy? You're pale as a ghost!'

'Go down and see for yourself, Landers. A picture's worth a thousand words.'

Landers went through the door. Moments later I heard a gagging sound followed by 'Shit!' He raced back up the stairs and out into the slightly fresher air just as the requested backup arrived. They covered their noses, too.

A few minutes later, I was leaning against a large statue of an angel, drinking from the cup of steaming McDonald's coffee one of the officers had handed me while the new arrivals investigated the carnage inside the tomb. Finding something that grotesque had to be the worst part of police work.

McCarthy called for the officers whose job would be to get up close and personal with the contents of the gory scene. Then he turned to me and stared, appearing a little green around the edges. 'I apologise, Dr Knight. You were right – there are dead bodies down there. I haven't been on the force that long, but this definitely qualifies as the worst thing I've seen. Were you really in there all night?'

'I guess so. I can't remember. All I know for sure is that I woke up there this morning.'

'This place is going to be swarming with experts any minute, so it would probably be best if you let us take you downtown, away from here. You know the media's going to show up, too, and I don't think you want to face the world in that condition.' He pointed to my grisly attire and shook his head. 'Do *you* have a psychologist to talk to?'

I snorted. 'I'm not sure any of them would believe me. I'm not even sure *I* believe me.'

He signalled to a female cop who'd just arrived. 'Take Dr

Knight downtown.' Then he studied me again. 'I'm glad you were persistent.'

'That's a nice word for it.'

He walked away, talking into his cell phone.

Exhausted, my stomach churning, I followed the police-woman out of the cemetery and into her black-and-white. She opened all the windows, then glanced at me in the rearview mirror and said, 'No offence.' We pulled away just as the caravan of TV news vehicles arrived and I was grateful I didn't have to try to string two coherent sentences together because I would have failed. I hoped the process at the police station would be quick, but suspected I was doomed to disappointment.

Thanks to the manic media circus camped out around police headquarters, I had to be smuggled in via the underground parking structure and secretly ushered in through an old fire exit. My fifteen minutes of fame had apparently caused quite a frenzy. My abduction had been linked with the murder investigation, and the vampire theme was simply too rich for the tabloids to pass up.

My experience of sitting at the police station was like having one of those dreams about being in high school again, the one where no one talks to you and everyone walks wide circles around you while they stare, point, and laugh.

None of the cops was laughing, but anyone who got within ten feet of me cringed, recoiled, and rebounded away, giving me a wide berth. They were shocked to find their nostrils assailed by smells better suited to battlefields than to a psychologist whose face had evidently been on television all morning.

As one officer so succinctly put it, 'There just aren't words for that smell.'

It didn't take long for me to give my statement, because all I could remember was the last couple of hours. I didn't know what'd happened prior to my waking up and I had no clue about who'd brought me there.

As it turned out, I didn't have to worry about getting out of there quickly. In fact, taking my statement in the close quarters of the badly ventilated station proved to be such a challenge that my hosts eagerly arranged for me to finish up at the lab.

I'd expected to be headed off to the shower and outfitted with one of those delightful orange garments, but that didn't happen. In fact, ever since I'd arrived at the police station things had been strange. I'd been the focus of several whispered conversations, each containing the words 'the chief'.

Officers had escorted me to the lab and while I was waiting for a blood sample to be taken the double doors burst open and a heavyset, white-haired, fifty-something male strode into the room. Everyone around me froze in mid-action and came to attention. The new arrival signalled to the other officers, who scurried over to him immediately.

I would have just stared out the window, waiting for the bureaucratic huddle to end, if it hadn't been for the fact that various faces kept turning in my direction. It was entirely possible that I was still in shock, but I wasn't a complete vegetable. Clearly those people were talking about me.

For a brief moment before the older man left, all the eyes in the group turned to me.

What the hell was going on? What weren't they telling

me? I hadn't had much experience with the police, but being treated like a leper wasn't anywhere in my expectations.

The lab technician who'd been preparing my arm for the blood sample before the older guy arrived came back and I said, 'Who was that?'

He kept his eyes riveted on his task and said, 'Chief Cassidy.'

'Why was he talking about me?'

'There, all finished. The officer will take you back now,' he said, ignoring my question completely. He wrote my name on the samples, gathered up his materials, and nodded to a uniformed officer standing by the door.

A different officer led me back to the detectives' bullpen. I figured I was going there to answer more questions – not that I had any answers – and I mentally steeled myself for a long stay. I was surprised when they quickly said I was free to go. It appeared they were taking me home and that someone would come to my house later to pick up my contaminated clothing.

That piece of information drew several incredulous 'What?' responses from various detectives. I overheard one say, 'She must have powerful friends. Nobody rousts the chief out before the crack of dawn to start a search for a missing person, much less persuades him to postpone an interrogation and override all the proper procedures.'

Powerful friends? I was sure they had me confused with someone else, but that didn't matter. As long as this ordeal was over and I was being taken home, I'd claim to know the Queen of England. Hell, I'd claim to be the Queen of England.

In addition to everything else this situation was, it was humbling.

The pleasure of driving me home once again fell to the policewoman who'd brought me to the station, no doubt because the backseat of her unit was already tainted. I half-expected her to put down newspaper for me to sit on and, frankly, that wouldn't have been a bad idea.

'You're Dr Knight, right? I'm Officer Colletta. I saw your advertisement in the paper. The one they were talking about on TV this morning. The one that says you're the Vampire Psychologist.' She examined me in her rearview mirror.

'Yes. I'm Kismet Knight. I'm afraid to know what they were saying about me on TV, so I'm not even going to ask.'

She didn't volunteer the information. Instead she said, 'That must be an interesting job, being the Vampire Psychologist. I mean, what do you do, exactly? Are there really people who think they're vampires?' She lowered her voice and gave me serious eyes in the mirror. 'Are there *really* vampires?'

I shrugged and shook my head. 'If you'd asked me that question a week ago, I'd have said there are people who are disturbed enough to believe they're vampires, and that it's all mental illness and acting out. Now, after the things I've seen, all bets are off.'

'We've had murders lately.' She appeared almost magically able to keep the car on the road and watch me in the mirror at the same time. 'Murders where the victims were drained of blood. Do you know about those?'

'I heard something about that.'

'Maybe the murderer is one of your clients?'

One of my clients? Well, thank you for raising a horrible possibility I hadn't considered. 'I sincerely hope not.'

She made a wrong turn so I gave her directions and we rode in silence the rest of the way to my house. As we pulled up in front, Officer Colletta said, 'I'm surprised the cameras aren't here yet. The media's got your therapy office surrounded, as well as an apartment building listed as your home address. Maybe they don't know about this place yet.'

'I just moved recently.' I thought about my old neighbours and felt bad that they were being subjected to the paparazzi, but happy for my own brief reprieve. Apparently, not everyone had seduced an APA employee – yet.

'Yeah, well I don't think that's going to save you for long. Reporters are pretty resourceful. You'd better prepare yourself for a media blitz. You probably won't have much privacy for a while.'

'I'm afraid you're right.' I sighed. 'Thanks for everything.' She met my eyes again and saluted, touching two fingers to the visor of her hat. I hauled myself out of the cruiser and she pulled away.

I'd just stumbled up to my front door when I heard the screech of tyres and the slam of a car door. I assumed the news vans had caught up with me and was surprised to hear a familiar voice.

'Where the *fuck* have you been?' Alan demanded, bounding towards me. His face was red, deep frown lines etched the skin between his eyes, and the veins in his forehead bulged. 'I've been out all night searching for you. I told you to wait in front of the club. Where did you go? You look terrible. What's that stuff all over you? And what's that gross smell?'

He lurched away from me as if he'd received an electric shock.

As he yelled at me, the psychic numbness that had kept me from feeling the depth of the hideous experience receded, and I stood there trembling. The inner dam broke. Tears raced down my cheeks. I slumped onto the porch, tumbled over on my side, and started sobbing loudly.

Alan cursed under his breath.

'Geez, don't cry.' He knelt down next to me. 'I'm sorry, Kismet. I didn't mean to be a jerk. I was just so worried. I heard on the police scanner that they'd found you, and then something about dead bodies. I guess I added up the numbers wrong and overreacted. I felt responsible for taking you to that club and for whatever happened to you. And now you stroll up to your front door, obviously in one piece, and I'm so relieved to see you and so pissed off at myself for putting you in danger.'

'You didn't put me in danger,' I mumbled.

He sniffed the air. 'We need to get you into the house and out of those clothes, because I never thought I'd say this to you, but you stink worse than anything I've ever smelled. Plus the media vultures will be here any minute.'

The professional part of me knew that I was sobbing because it was a natural physical reaction to the kind of trauma I'd experienced, but the little girl part was simply crying because it had been a terrible night and she wanted to be held on someone's lap and rocked to sleep. She wanted to feel safe again. To feel normal again.

'Let's take these boots off out here, okay?' He slid them off my feet and tossed them next to the porch. Then he pulled me up, put his arm around me, asked for my alarm code and opened the door.

I still couldn't stop crying long enough to speak in full sentences, so I was grateful he was intent on helping me. Now that reality had melted through the defences I'd created to weather the nightmare, I was hanging by very thin threads and was happy to have someone running underneath me with a net. Hopefully the net wasn't accompanied by men in white coats.

Still holding on to me, he helped me up the stairs to the bathroom and propped me against the sink while he turned on the water for my shower.

'I'm going to leave the door open, if that's all right with you, because after you've undressed and stepped into the shower, I'm going to take these clothes and bag them up for the forensics team. They'll want to analyse all the various ... substances.' He shook his head. 'I can't believe the chief made them let you wear the clothes home.'

He really did look like he'd been up all night, and I was touched by the concern in his eyes.

'Sure.' I gave a limp shrug. 'Leave the door open. That's fine.' I sniffled as I started to peel off my clothes without waiting for him to leave the room.

'Uh, er, uh, yeah, go ahead and get undressed. I'm gonna go find that bag. I'll be right back.' He flew down the stairs.

Sometimes life gets very simple. Standing under that stream of hot water was the best thing I'd ever experienced. At that moment, not even chocolate or orgasms could top it on the list of wonderful things.

I washed my hair several times and used every good-smelling soap product I owned. I scrubbed my nails and finally just stretched out in the tub and let the water beat down on me. Bliss.

'Kismet? Are you okay?' Alan yanked back the shower curtain.

I stared up at him, unable to move even one muscle in response.

'I'm sorry.' He shifted his eyes to the side for a moment. 'I didn't mean to burst in on you like that. I couldn't see you in the shower and I thought you might have fallen down or something.'

I didn't seem to have any opinions about him opening the shower curtain or seeing me lying naked in the tub. Nothing was more important than continuing to enjoy feeling like a warm, limp noodle. I couldn't get worked up about my nudity or anything else. I was so happy to be home – to be safe, clean. It would have taken an earthquake to jar me out of my Zen tranquillity.

Now that I smelled better, I realised I'd shared my aromatic carry-out with Alan, and he was less than springtime-fresh himself. Whatever had been on my clothes was now on his.

I raised my arm. 'Give me a hand, would you?'

He pulled me to my feet, his eyes tracking slowly down my body.

I pinched my nose closed. 'Anything strike you about your state of hygiene since you helped me upstairs?'

He glanced down at himself, half-grinned and scrunched up his nose.

'I think you'd better add your clothes to the bag for the forensics team and step into the shower with me. That smell doesn't work any better on you than it did on me.'

Really? Did I just say that? Since when am I so bold? What's up with me? I must still be in shock.

His eyebrows shot up and then he shrugged. 'How can I refuse such an enticing invitation?' He sloughed off the fouled clothing and gingerly stepped into the tub, making sure he kept his back to me.

He had an astoundingly nice ass, firm, round, and begging to be palmed. I stood at the far end of the shower and watched the muscles in his back ripple as he soaped his arms.

After he'd washed everything he wanted to without turning around, he finally shifted his body and faced me, his compass enthusiastically pointing true north. My eyes feasted on the impressive erection and he stared at me as he lathered himself there.

I felt an earthquake.

'Oh my,' I uttered without thinking. I fought the urge to reach out and touch someone.

We admired each other in silence, eyes caressing where hands wished to be.

He turned off the water and ran his fingers through his wet hair, pushing the strands back from his face. His lovely purple-blue eyes sparkled mischievously and his cheeks were flushed. Moisture beaded on the muscles of his chest.

He stepped forwards, brushing my arm as he reached for the towels on the rack outside the shower. My skin tingled where he'd touched me and became the epicentre for waves of pleasure sensations. He handed me a towel, then slowly dried himself off and stepped out of the tub.

I stole another quick peek at his admirable erection and argued with myself about what I was thinking. I followed him, tucking the towel around me above my breasts, and moved over to the sink. I wiped off the mirror with my hand, leaned in and stared at my reflection. None the worse for wear, if you didn't notice my spacey, glazed-over eyes. The normally clear-sky blue didn't look so vibrant right then.

Alan made use of the extra toothbrush I produced and we stood side by side, silently gazing at each other in the mirror. I don't let just anyone watch me take care of dental business.

I brushed my teeth, flossed and used every kind of mouthwash I had in my medicine cabinet before I finally felt seminormal.

'What do you need now?' he asked.

Knowing exactly what I needed, I turned to him and met his kind eyes. 'I want to curl up in my bed, under my covers, and I want you to hold me.'

The corners of his lips quirked up in an amused grin, which I interpreted as an affirmative. I grabbed his hand, led us into my bedroom, and pulled down the bed covers. I dropped my towel and slid between the sheets. Giving him my best 'come hither' smile, I patted the mattress next to me and sent a clear message. I wasn't sure the Brazen Hussy part of my personality had ever had a chance to come out and play. She'd always been locked in the closet by Nerd Woman.

Wait. Do I have a Brazen Hussy part? Something has definitely juiced up my sexuality. Should I worry about that? Am I totally whacked? This is Devereux's fault, I just know it.

He stood and gazed down at me, hesitating only a few seconds before he joined me.

Pushing thoughts of Devereux aside, I wrapped myself around Alan, finally feeling safe, and sighed. 'Thank you for being here with me. You're a good friend.'

'A friend? You're giving me way too much credit. I'm not having very friend-like thoughts at the moment.'

I met his eyes. 'What kind of thoughts *are* you having?' As if I didn't know, even without the compass to point the way.

'I'm-in-bed-with-a-beautiful-woman thoughts. But I know this isn't the right time to be romantic because you need to rest and recuperate.'

'It's very sweet of you to take care of me.'

I didn't want to think about where I'd been all night, or what might have happened, or the media frenzy that was waiting for me. I absolutely didn't want to consider the probability that there really were vampires. And I especially didn't want to think about what it meant for the world if there were hidden monsters everywhere. All I wanted was to be held, touched, connected to someone who wasn't constantly probing my mind, without any expectations or rules or complications.

I brushed his lips lightly with mine and slid my hand down the muscled plane of his belly and along the warm, firm length of his erection. He moaned, grabbed a handful of my wet hair and pulled me tight against him as he closed his lips over mine with hungry need.

'I haven't even begun to take care of you yet,' he breathed against my mouth.

Our bodies melted into each other as we took the kiss deeper, allowing all the emotions and tensions of the previous hours to find release through the firestorm of our mutual attraction. We kissed until every nerve in my body sizzled and burned.

He pulled away, his breathing ragged and his voice husky. 'I don't want to take advantage of this situation. Tell me to stop and I will.'

All I could think about was how good he felt next to me, how warm and sweet his mouth was on mine. And after the freak circus I'd experienced the night before, the pleasure of being with a normal male felt overwhelmingly right. Safe. Pure, primitive desire with no insanity attached to it. No fear.

'Don't stop.' I ran my hands over his smooth chest.

He rolled me over onto my back and began to lick and suck my nipples as he trailed his hand down my stomach. His body was fever hot and his touch like liquid fire.

He brought his face up to mine. 'Your body is beautiful. I've imagined this since the first moment I saw you.'

'I've had some naughty thoughts about you, too.'

We kissed each other wildly, hands exploring. His erection rubbed against my leg rhythmically as he slid his finger into the hot wetness between my thighs. I arched my back and opened myself to him as a wave of ecstasy built inside me. He straddled me and licked his way down my body until his tongue finished what his finger had started. I screamed and dug my fingernails into his shoulders as he laved me over the edge. Quivering, I grabbed his hair and pulled him up onto me, aching for him to fill me, longing to be joined in that primal way. Wanting to give him what he'd given me.

Then there was loud pounding downstairs on my front door.

'Dr Knight? Denver PD. Your door was unlocked. We heard a scream. Are you all right? Do you need help?'

Alan leaped up and ran into the bathroom.

I sat up in the bed and yelled, 'No – everything's fine. Stay where you are. I'll be right down.'

Damn, damn, damn! That's twice I've left my door unlocked in as many days, and both times I got interrupted in the middle of something delicious.

Still revelling in the spell cast by Alan's magic mouth, the muscles between my legs contracted with desire as I breathed to recover myself. I heard the shower start in the bathroom and I was tempted to sneak in there so Alan wouldn't have to finish without me. That thought provided an unexpected orgasmic aftershock and I forced myself to swing my legs over the side of the bed and stand up.

If only the cops had waited ten more minutes. Nothing about my world made sense any more.

I walked over to the closet, pulled on my pink terrycloth bathrobe, tied the sash and shuffled down the stairs.

CHAPTER 14

'Dr Knight? I'm Detective Robles and this is my partner, Detective Nyland – we met at the station earlier. We have a few more questions for you, and the forensics team is sending someone by to pick up the clothes you were wearing last night. Do you have them bagged and ready?'

'Almost. I'll get them.' I pointed. 'Why don't you go into the living room and have a seat. Just give me few minutes.'

I returned to my bedroom, peeled off my comfortable pink robe, put on fresh underwear, and stood in front of the closet, trying to decide what would be appropriate dress for a police interview. I rifled through my professional clothes and debated whether a skirt or trousers would be better. Then I stopped and shook my head. Who was I trying to impress? The cops had seen me covered in blood and gore and smelling like an outhouse. I pulled one of my new sweat-suits off the hanger and slipped it on.

It occurred to me to run a brush through my hair, but it had already dried in long curls and sometimes it was better to leave well enough alone, otherwise all the curl would turn into frizz.

I listened for a few seconds and couldn't hear the shower

running in the bathroom so I approached the door and knocked lightly. 'Alan?'

'Yeah. Come on in.'

He sat naked on the edge of the bathtub, in the pose of that famous statue *The Thinker*.

Something about the incongruity of the situation made me laugh out loud.

He snorted. 'I'm glad someone thinks anything about this day is funny.'

I walked over, knelt down in front of him, and took his face in my hands. 'I'm sorry we got interrupted before. It was wonderful. You were wonderful. I'm upset you had to finish without me.'

He grinned. 'You might not have been in the bathroom with me, but – trust me – you were there.'

I shifted forwards and kissed his warm lips. 'Can I have a rain check?'

'You have a standing invitation.' He pulled me in for another kiss. 'I hate to change such a titillating subject but I assume the locals have come to collect your clothes. Before I got back into the shower I went through the pockets, retrieved everything and tucked your filthy duds into that yellow bag there.' He pointed and shook his head. 'Unfortunately, I should've been more careful when I was enthusiastically tearing off my clothes to join you in the tub, because my brand new Fruit of the Looms wound up getting tossed on top of a really nasty chunk of something on your jeans and they're trashed. There's probably nothing on my clothes that the lab won't get from yours, and I'd really prefer to keep the locals out of our personal business – it would only raise questions neither of us wants to answer. When the officers leave I'll use your washing machine, if you don't mind. Otherwise I won't have any clothes to put on.'

A tantalising visual formed in my brain. 'Wow. That raises all sorts of interesting possibilities. A stranded naked man in my house, at my mercy. Who said dreams don't come true?' I laughed. 'My appliances are at your disposal. It's the least I can do.' I waggled my eyebrows at him.

'It might be the least you can do, but it isn't all you can do ...'

I grinned at him. 'We'll have to talk about that later. I'd better get back downstairs.' I kissed him again, retrieved the sack and closed the door.

The detectives stood when I entered the room and I handed over the yellow bag. It resembled one of those biohazard containers from a disaster movie – an eye-searing slap of colour. All it needed was a skull and crossbones.

'Why don't I make us some coffee? Come on into the kitchen while I grind the beans.'

They accepted my offer and followed me into the kitchen. A few minutes later, a woman from the forensics team joined us and we all drank while the detectives asked me the same questions they'd asked earlier. I had little to add to my original statement and in less than a half-hour I was showing them out.

I walked them to the door and paused with my hand on the knob. 'Thank you for being so kind to me today and for coming over here to pick up the clothing.'

'Just doing our job. Your Mr Devereux can be very persuasive.'

Huh?

'My Mr Devereux?'

The detectives stole a quick glance at each other. 'Yes. It was at his request that the chief bent the rules for you. They seem to have an ... *unusual* relationship. Mr Devereux is a very influential man. By the way, you've got quite a bit of company out there. You might want to—'

I opened the door and was immediately overwhelmed by voices screaming questions, bright lights shining in my eyes and cameras thrust in my face. Even knowing I'd be the focus of attention, however briefly, hadn't prepared me for the reality of finding my front lawn filled with aggressive strangers who were competing to record my moment of infamy.

The street in front of my townhouse was lined with police cars as well as television news vans. Neighbours I hadn't had the chance to meet yet filled the perimeter.

And I really can't believe I left my door unlocked and forgot the media would be arriving. Something is definitely wrong with my brain.

The detectives took charge of the situation and strode down the path, reminding all the reporters that they were trespassing on private property.

I closed the door and pressed my weight against it. I'd learned my lesson. This time I made sure all the locks were securely engaged and the alarm was on. I didn't want any more private experiences thwarted by unexpected company.

After giving the detectives a couple of minutes to disperse the crowd, I peeked through the slightly raised slat of a blind and saw several uniformed police officers herding the reporters back towards the street. I hoped the media would lose interest in me before Monday because I had a full client schedule and I wasn't willing for my life to get any more out of control. Besides, what was I supposed to tell them? I had no idea what happened to me and I couldn't break confidentiality.

I cringed as I thought about Nancy's reaction to my situation. If she thought my writing a book about vampires was bad, I could only imagine how she was dealing with this insanity. I'd call her as soon as possible.

And what was that about Devereux? A relationship with the police chief? The thought of him reminded me of the violent scene I'd witnessed in the basement of The Crypt. It also reminded me of my overwhelming desire to crawl into his lap. Both those memories felt like they'd happened in another life. I didn't know whether to be disgusted with myself for letting my raging hormones get me into so much trouble, or be grateful that my long dry spell with men might be over.

But he's a vampire.

I decided all that was too much to deal with and I'd think about it later. Yeah. Me and Scarlett O'Hara. I might get tossed out of the Psychologists' Club for saying this, but a little denial never hurt anyone.

When in shock, keep busy.

'Hey,' I stood at the bottom of the stairs, 'they're gone. You can come down now. There's coffee.'

I returned to the kitchen to forage for snacks to serve with the coffee and then picked up the phone to check messages. I had no personal messages on my home phone, but when I dialled my business voicemail, a synthetic voice from the phone company notified me that my message queue was full and I'd need to delete some before I could receive any more.

The first few messages played and I saved them if they were from clients or potential clients. I deleted the ones from media outlets, and then heard the sweetly sensual voice of Vaughan the chiropractor saying something about our dinner date tonight.

'Kismet? This is Vaughan. About our date tonight. I heard your story on the news this morning – I hope you're okay. It sounded like a miserable experience. What a terrible thing. Anyway, I'm sure you want time to yourself, so we can postpone our dinner. Would you mind giving me a call later when you can, just so I can be sure you're safe and well? I'll talk to you soon.'

Shit!

I'd totally forgotten about Vaughan. It felt like weeks since I'd made the date – back when there were no men on the horizon, before Devereux did whatever he'd done to me – and now I couldn't even imagine keeping it. I didn't feel remotely like the same person any more. I wrote a note on the whiteboard on my kitchen wall to remind myself to call him.

I heard the sound of bare feet padding into the kitchen and turned, expecting to find a luscious naked man, and instead burst out laughing. Alan had rooted around in my closet and found an old pair of torn pink sweatsuit bottoms that rode up to his mid-calf and fit him like a second skin, and a very small, tight T-shirt that said 'Woman Power!' Even though he should've looked ludicrous, it was all I could do to keep myself from leaping on him and finishing what we'd started earlier.

He apparently enjoyed my reaction and strutted around in a circle so I could see all sides of the spectacular presentation.

'I didn't want to put on anything that I might stretch out and ruin, and I figured you probably weren't too attached to these. Besides,' he said, laughing, 'I look great in pink, and it takes a real man to be able to say that.'

'I think you probably look great in anything.' *Not to mention in nothing.*

'Thank you.' He gave a slow blink and sauntered over, his face serious. 'I believe you mean that.'

The close proximity of his body and the sudden shift in intensity surprised me and I felt myself melting into a puddle on the floor. I leaned against the counter and cleared my throat. 'Of course I do.'

We stared at each other for a moment, then I forced my gaze away. As delicious as it would have been to return to my bedroom and spend the rest of the evening exploring each other's erogenous zones, the shock and confusion of the morning had worn off and fatigue was setting in. It was time to face all the realities I didn't want to think about.

My stomach growled. 'Are you as hungry as I am?'

He grinned.

'For food, I mean?'

'Yes, as a matter of fact, I am. Shall we have something delivered? What'll it be? Pizza? Chinese? Mexican? Lady's choice.'

'How will the delivery person get through that horde of reporters out there?'

'I'll call in and request a police escort to the front door,' he said.

We negotiated the food and I went into the living room to collapse on the couch while Alan performed the phone duties.

'I'm going to put my filthy clothes in the washing machine, then we need to talk,' he said. 'Something traumatic happened to you last night. Obviously you didn't disappear of your own volition and I want to hear every detail you can remember, no matter how inconsequential.' He hesitated for a few seconds. 'And I have something to tell you.'

The tone of his voice indicated I wasn't going to like his news, so, being my usual impatient self, I abandoned the couch and followed him into the laundry room.

'What do you have to tell me?'

'Hold on a minute.'

I drummed my fingers on the counter while he loaded the washer. 'Hurry up.'

He shook his head and grinned. 'Such a control freak. Come on, let's go back into the living room.' He grabbed my hand, pulled me to the couch and we sat.

I didn't say out loud that I thought we had control-freak characteristics in common. Instead, I sighed impatiently. 'So? You're starting to make me nervous. Did something bad happen? I mean, something in addition to what happened to me?'

'Yes.' He nodded. 'Something bad happened. Do you

remember the call I got last night at the club? The one about another body being found?'

'I remember.'

'The body they found was Emerald Addison's.'

All the air leaked out of me like a punctured balloon and I sagged back into the couch cushions, speechless.

'I'm sorry.' He patted my hand. 'This must be hard to hear. She was your client.'

I still didn't correct him. 'What happened to her?'

'She was found in the alley behind an apartment building in Capitol Hill. The report said she had a friend living there named Eric Weiss. Her body was drained of blood, same as the others. It was a vampire attack, although the locals aren't seriously considering that angle.'

I stared at the wall in silence. Poor little Emerald. I wished she really had been my client so I'd have more memories of her than just our brief trip to the hospital. I wondered if Midnight and Ronald had been notified and how they were coping. If they'd heard about my situation, they were probably worried about me, too.

I jumped up and hurried to my desk, intending to search for my briefcase and my current client files.

Alan stood, looking alarmed. 'What's happening? What're you doing?'

'I've got to call a couple of my clients, friends of Emerald's – you saw them with me at the hospital. They must be feeling terrible.'

I sat at my desk, located their phone numbers, called and got their answering machines. I left messages giving them my cell phone number and asking them to return the call, no matter what time they got my message. I had to do something to help and I hoped someone would give me a clue as to what that might be.

Alan walked around behind my chair and rubbed my shoulders. 'Do you want to talk more about Emerald, or are you ready to tell me what happened to you last night?'

'Both, I think.'

He swivelled my chair around until I faced him, took my hands and guided me up from the chair and back over to the couch.

I studied him, searching for answers in his eyes. 'You said Emerald was killed by vampires. Do you really believe that? Are you telling me the truth? There really are vampires?' *Devereux is really a vampire?* I made one more feeble attempt at denial. I didn't want to believe, but that boat had sailed. I knew what I'd seen in the basement of The Crypt.

'Yes,' he said, 'I'm telling you the truth. Nothing in my background, education, or training prepared me to believe vampires really exist, but that's what I discovered. Beyond any reasonable doubt. For some reason I don't understand yet, more of the mindless, demented vampires are showing up in Denver.'

None of that made any sense to me. 'Why is this happening all of a sudden? Has Denver had other murders in the past where the victims were drained of blood?'

'According to my research, there have been sporadic deaths attributed to massive blood loss, but they were few and far between. It makes sense, because there've always been vampires, and some of them would have been the type who needed to kill. The death toll only became significant over the last few months.' He picked up our coffee mugs, refilled them in the kitchen, and brought them back. The pink sweatsuit bottoms were almost glued to his skin, leaving nothing to the imagination. The view, coming and going, was distracting, but then I remembered what we were talking about.

'Why Emerald?'

'That I don't know. But I promise you, I'll find out. Now, tell me – what happened to you last night?'

He stretched out his long pink-encased legs and crossed his ankles on the coffee table. I curled up, my legs tucked underneath me, at the end of the couch.

'Well, after I saw you in the club and we split up to find Tom ... Hey!' I sat up straight. 'That reminds me – you lied to me. You said you were going to help me search for him and then I saw you charge through the doorway to the basement. How am I supposed to trust you if you lie to me? And how do I know you're not lying about other stuff?'

He studied the carpet and shook his head. 'Spank me, I've been bad.' He shifted his eyes to gaze up at me from under his unfairly long eyelashes and grinned. 'I'm sorry I lied to you. But you need to know this about me: I'm dedicated to my work and it wasn't even in the realm of possibility that I'd go off searching for Tom instead of finding out what was happening with the vampires downstairs. It's part of the job description of being the kind of obsessive-compulsive I am.'

I frowned at him and relaxed back into the cushions, but had to admit to myself that I did understand what he meant. Having a curious mind had landed me into more sticky situations than I could count.

'What was going on with the vampires downstairs? Why

were they fighting? From what I saw, it was about to turn into a bloodbath. Talk about *Night of the Living Dead*.'

He scooted excitedly to the edge of the cushion, eager to share.

'By the time I got there, the chaos had started to wind down and the interlopers were gone. From what I could gather, some vampires are challenging Devereux's rule of the coven. Bryce, the one we talked about before, is determined to take Devereux down. It seems very personal to him – the two of them definitely have unfinished business. He and his followers threatened the club manager, knowing it would piss Devereux off, and the fun began. The room was one unholy mess after the combat ended.'

'Yeah.' I grimaced. 'I saw some of the body fluids oozing out from the doorway.'

He motioned with his cup. 'Vampire bodies heal very quickly, so even the worst injuries repaired themselves within minutes. If it hadn't been for the blood everywhere, you wouldn't have known a vampire war was being waged.'

'What did you do? Just run in and start swinging? Do you have a death wish?'

'No.' He laughed. 'I'm adventurous. I'm courageous. I'm relentless. But I'm not stupid. Besides, I'd found out from my vampire source Ian – Deep Fang, I call him, you know, like the Watergate informer – that when a vamp loses blood, the first thing he does is seek a donor. I didn't want to be anyone's dinner, so I kept my distance until Devereux was alone in the room.'

A little energy rush charged through my body. 'You talked to Devereux?'

As Alan started to answer, the doorbell rang. I walked over and peered through the peephole to make sure the visitor was welcome company. It was more than welcome. It was food – police-escorted food. I cracked the door, and was slammed by a wall of noise as hordes of reporters shouted questions from the road. I quickly handed over enough money to cover the bill plus a generous tip and reached out to grab the bag. I offered my thanks, then closed and relocked the door. I carried the large sack of Chinese food to the kitchen table.

'Do you want to wait on the rest of the story until you've eaten, or can you continue?' Alan asked.

The smell of the food was driving me mad and I moved around the kitchen in a blur, gathering plates, glasses and utensils. 'I'll bet I can eat and talk at the same time. Wow. You ordered lots.'

'Oh, did you want something, too?' He laughed.

'Very funny.'

I opened a new bottle of wine and poured some into each of our glasses, then we sat at the table and dived into the feast. Neither of us gained any points for table manners during the meal. The food was glorious and we ate with silent enthusiasm for a few minutes. There's nothing like stress and hunger to cause us to revisit our primitive roots.

For some reason I suddenly thought about the fact that vampires didn't eat food. I wouldn't ever be sitting at the table sharing a meal with Devereux. At least not any meal I could force myself to contemplate. Unless, of course, we'd all gone mad or there were hallucinogens in the water supply, and none of this had really happened.

I paused in the food-shovelling process and sipped my wine. 'You spoke to Devereux? What did you talk about?'

Alan had already cleaned up his first helping and was reaching for reinforcements.

'It was strange, actually. He was in the middle of telling me about his long-standing rivalry with Bryce and all of a sudden he stopped talking and closed his eyes. Then he said, "She is gone – he has taken her." I started to ask who was gone, and who "he" was, but before I could get the words out, Devereux vanished.'

'You mean he left the room?' I claimed seconds on the egg rolls.

'No. He literally vanished. Vampires aren't bound by the same limitations of time and space as we humans are. They can move through both with just a thought.'

'I don't understand what you mean. Physical matter has certain unarguable limitations – flesh-and-blood bodies can't just disappear from one place and rearrange their molecules in another. We haven't caught up with Star Trek yet.' Although I had seen Devereux and Bryce levitating. That was definitely strange.

Alan polished off his second helping and went for the championship round, adding an impressive third layer to the sustenance already on its way down to his deceptively flat stomach.

'Devereux would say there are limitations if you believe there are. But I've seen him vanish and reappear so many times that I don't have any problem accepting that vampires can travel by thought, not only in this dimension but in all the others.'

I pushed my plate away, finally satiated.

'Other dimensions? You know, every time we talk your stories get weirder and weirder. Are you going to tell me next that the vampires are really aliens, preparing to take over the Earth? Or maybe they're controlling us with their minds, and we'll be herded into holding pens – walking blood receptacles – to wait for an impending undead feeding frenzy?'

'No.' He chuckled. 'I'm not going to tell you any of that, but you have to admit they'd be interesting hypotheses to pursue. I'll make a note of them. Shall I continue telling you about Devereux, or would you rather make fun of my proclivities?'

'Oh, by all means, please continue.' I raised my wineglass in his direction.

'Anyway, after he vanished I went back upstairs and then outside, looking for you. Of course, you weren't there, but I found Devereux leaning against the building about a half-block down from the entrance to the club. He was just standing there with his eyes closed and when I approached he said, "The one who has her is not only evil, but he is also insane. His mind is splintered and he is more animal than vampire."' Alan had altered his voice, imitating Devereux's accent and unique speech patterns. 'At that point I still didn't even know who he was talking about. He said, "I am linked with her mind so I should be able to sense her, but he has done something to mask her energy signature. He has overwhelmed her mind with his and is keeping us from communicating with each other. I have met few others powerful enough to do that. She is in great danger. She must be found."'

I appreciated his clever Devereux impersonation and shook

my head. 'You actually remember what he said, word for word? That's quite the memory you have there, Special Agent Stevens.'

'Yes, it does come in handy. I have the auditory equivalent of a photographic memory. Remember that in case you tell me something and then say you didn't.'

'Okay.' I reached out and patted his arm. 'I'll remember that. Then what happened?'

We returned to the living room and reestablished ourselves on the couch.

He cleared his throat. 'A whole lot of nothing. Devereux vanished again and I went back into the club to search for you. I still thought you were in there somewhere. Just so you know, I kept an eye out for Tom too, but I never saw him. I ran into Devereux's personal assistant, a snarly vamp named Luna, and I asked if she'd seen you. She said she couldn't believe so many people were interested in one ordinary human and that Devereux was so beside himself that you'd been taken. That was the first time I realised they were talking about you.'

'I'm surprised Luna even deigned to acknowledge my existence.'

'She is a charmer.' He reached over and stroked my leg. 'I didn't want to believe you were missing – I'm stubborn that way – so I kept looking in the club and giving people your description and asking if they'd seen you. Finally, I drove back to the cop shop to see if there'd been any reports. I knew they wouldn't put out a missing-person report that soon, but I was rattling cages as much as I could. Turns out I didn't need to. A couple of hours later, the chief showed up in person and ordered that you be made top priority. All available units went out on the street, searching for you, then they alerted the media. I've never seen anything like it before. I still don't know what happened to get the chief riled up.'

'I was told Devereux called the chief.'

'Devereux? What would Devereux have to do with the police chief—?' He paused. 'Of course – I should've remembered. So much for my famous tape-recorder memory, eh? During one of our discussions, Devereux told me he'd used his ability to control minds to create relationships with several powerful people in town, people who could "smooth away any difficulties", as he put it.'

'What do you mean?'

'It makes perfect sense now. He simply called the chief, suggested he rally the troops and that's all it took. No one would question it, and the chief would always think it was his own idea. Ingenious, really.'

'Are you saying Devereux used mind control on the police chief?'

'Yep. The chief and a few other highly placed cops.'

'Doesn't it bother you that Devereux manipulated the police? What if he uses mind control on you?'

He grinned. 'I have a healthy respect for his abilities – he's the most powerful vampire I've ever run across. It might be worth it to let him take over my mind for a little while, just to see how that feels. You have to admit, it got the job done. The cops found you.'

'Actually, I found the cops. But I'll have to thank Devereux the next time I see him.'

And why does thinking about seeing him feel good and bad at the same time?

'Okay, stop stalling. Tell me what happened to you last night.'

I rearranged myself on the cushions. 'I'm not stalling.' *Yes, I am.* 'There really isn't much to tell. I went outside to wait for Tom – or you – and walked down the block and rested against the building. I suddenly had an overwhelming bad feeling, instant terror, and heard a grotesque voice calling me. I couldn't tell if the voice was coming from outside of me or inside my mind. It was like fingernails on the blackboard from hell times a thousand. The voice kept telling me to come to it. I remember thinking I just needed to stay where I was and everything would be fine. That I could just ignore it. That's the last thing I recall until I woke up this morning in the cemetery.'

I told him everything about the mausoleum, the coffin I'd awakened in, the dead bodies, and my encounter with the police. He sat silently while I spoke, shaking his head.

'I've had some horrible experiences since I joined the FBI, but none of them comes close to being worse than what you just told me. Now I'm really sorry I was such an asshole when you came home.'

'Apology accepted. We were both stressed out. I'm glad it's over. Well, except for the media fallout. I guess I can't avoid it any longer. Go ahead and tell me – how bad is it? What did they say about me on TV?'

'Pretty much what you'd expect.' He grinned. 'They played up all the occult aspects and continually referred to you as the Vampire Psychologist, with accompanying snickers. I think you'll have to make a statement when you feel up to it – they're not going away until you talk to them. I imagine this isn't the direction you envisioned your career moving?'

'No,' I said, frowning. 'I guess I'm a laughingstock now.'

He stared at me for a few seconds. 'I'm going to borrow your therapist hat for a moment and mention something you're working hard to ignore. You've been through a lot of bad shit in a short period of time and you're probably still in shock. It's okay for you to admit you're not doing very well, if that's true. What would you tell a client who was trying to keep a stiff upper lip in the face of so much insanity?'

I heaved a heavy sigh and my shoulders sagged. 'I'd say it was only delaying the inevitable.' I sat silently, studying his concerned expression. My vision swam as tears gathered in my eyes. 'It was horrible. I was so afraid when I woke up in that terrible place this morning. I'm still afraid. Not remembering what happened makes me doubt myself. Everything has been out of control for days. I don't know who I am any more. I don't know what's real–'

Alan reached for me. Suddenly there was a popping sound accompanied by a slight breeze, and Devereux materialised in the middle of my living room.

CHAPTER 15

'Kismet!'

I sat up straight, blinked to clear the tears from my eyes, and snapped my attention to Devereux. *What the hell? How'd he get here? And holy shit – would you look at him?*

Instead of his usual tight leather, Devereux was decked out in a luscious charcoal-grey suit and a magnificent turquoise silk shirt. The colour of the silk made his eyes appear even more spectacularly kaleidoscopic than usual. His hair shone like liquid moonlight. He could've stepped right out of the pages of a European high fashion men's magazine.

Since I had no idea what he actually did with his time, I couldn't begin to imagine where he'd been, spiffed up like that. I felt a brief twinge of jealousy at the thought of him dressing up for a woman. Maybe his assistant, Luna, or one of the other perfect female specimens he had working for him at The Crypt.

But who was I to be jealous when I'd spent part of the afternoon taking a shower and playing 'you show me yours and I'll show you mine' with a fixated, well-endowed FBI agent?

Devereux glided over to me, swung me up off the couch with his arms around my waist, and kissed me thoroughly. Then kissed me again.

I was stunned but apparently willing, because I looped my arms around his neck and kissed him back. Interesting to discover this entirely new set of instinctual behaviours I appeared to have acquired regarding Devereux.

I've lost my mind. I've never behaved this way with anyone.

He pulled back slightly, slid his lips close to my ear and whispered, 'I have never felt so helpless as when I could not find you. There would have been no end to my vengeance had you been harmed.'

My own personal avenging angel. He looks like a god but talks like a character from a historical romance novel. I can sure pick 'em.

'Are you well? Did the dark one harm you?'

'Uh . . .'

There it is again – that brain-melt thing that happens to me whenever I'm within ten feet of Devereux.

Alan leaped up from the couch, his face a mixture of confusion and outrage. 'Hey! Devereux! What's going on here? What are you doing?'

Despite the fact that it was difficult to appear threatening while wearing short pink sweatsuit bottoms and a decidedly feminist T-shirt, Alan managed to gather up sufficient testosterone to get his point across.

Apparently, Devereux wasn't interested in butting heads with anyone. He lifted me up into his arms, then glanced over at Alan and whispered gently in that amazing voice, 'You are tired, my friend. Lie down on the couch and sleep now.'

Damned if Alan didn't do just that.

He arranged himself into a foetal position, made a few soft snorting sounds and drifted off, smiling.

Wow. That's impressive. And disturbing. Shouldn't I be putting up some kind of fuss? Should I worry about getting used to being carried around like this?

Devereux refocused on me. 'You must come with me now.'

'I must?'

There was a swoosh of air, a sound reminiscent of the crackle of electricity and we were suddenly standing in the middle of Devereux's private room underneath The Crypt.

He released me and I stood, head spinning, stomach churning, trying to make sense of something that was impossible to make sense of. Whatever had just happened definitely messed with my equilibrium. I wasn't sure my legs were up to their usual task of keeping me vertical.

'Please, come and sit. You do not look well.' Devereux fetched a small chair, pushed it gently against the back of my knees and I sat. I scanned the room, recognising all the paintings on the walls, the art supplies and the stash of bottles and strange artefacts on the table.

As I perched there, trying to reclaim my balance, I became more and more annoyed. The journey through Devereux's invisible transporter – or whatever it was he'd used to get me from where I had been to where I was – had definitely rained on the good feelings that kissing him had inspired in me, and I was royally steamed. Not to mention extremely tired of finding myself in locations chosen for me by some male or another without my consent. Something in my brain snapped.

No. That's it! No more manipulating me and jerking me around.

I vaulted up from the chair with the fury of a woman pissed off, shaking with rage, and got right in Devereux's face. All the anger that had been repressed during the previous hours burst out like a five-alarm fire as I yelled at him, 'I don't *want* to sit. I *don't* want to be here. You had no right to bring me here. I didn't tell you to snatch me. I'm tired. I want to be in my *own* house, in my *own* bed, away from all your bullshit!' I punched his stomach with my fist, and then, outrageously shocked at myself, retreated a couple of steps. Definitely a case of temporary insanity.

He gasped and bent forwards slightly. He stared at me, shocked, his mouth hanging open, his eyes wide, eyebrows creeping up towards his hairline. 'Well.' He straightened, recovering his poise, and grinned at me. 'I wondered when you would let your feelings out. I am glad you have chosen to share them with me.'

I gave him a hard frown. I didn't appreciate his apparent enjoyment of my outburst. In fact, he was acting downright superior about it, as if he'd arranged it.

With that, the last remaining fragment of the dam burst. 'Share them with you?' I screamed. 'I'll show you how I'll share them with you, you pompous bastard!'

I had no idea how, but I managed to fling myself on him – flying through the air, as it were – my hands out in front of me, grasping towards his neck. It didn't occur to me that attacking a vampire might have bigger ramifications than I'd anticipated. There was still some part of me that continued to have a hard time accepting that Devereux could be something as horrible as a blood-drinker. Although he did seem to have an extraordinary amount of physical strength. Not to mention that travelling-through-thought ability.

In an effortless movement he caught my wrists in one of his hands, curled his arm around my waist and wrestled me down to the floor, laughing.

Of course, listening to him laugh only made me angrier, and being restrained pretty much undid any remnants of control I still pretended to have. I struggled to get away from him and screamed at his apparent amusement. He hadn't even worked up a sweat keeping me his prisoner on the floor.

'Are you laughing at me, you Fabio-wannabe?' It was great to see him be playful, but I wasn't in the mood for fun and games.

He laughed harder, and then stuck out his lower lip in a pout.

'Fabio? Is he still around? Surely he must be a senior citizen by now. My dear Kismet, you know very well that the two of us do not resemble each other. My hair is much lighter, my eyes more soulful. I have been told I am much more hand-some and desirable than that particular gentleman. In fact, some well-known young European musicians resemble me much more than that over-the-hill cover model.'

Okay, it was a cheap shot. Devereux is more beautiful than most men, a young Fabio included. But what arrogance!

I vainly struggled to get loose. 'Well, *you're* not conceited. Tell me more about how handsome and desirable you are.'

He shifted so he straddled me, still holding my wrists down against the floor. The bright turquoise of his eyes, already noticeably heightened by the colour of his shirt, now radiated a surreal glow, as if his irises were gemstones come alive. Long, pale hair fell across my face and he threw it back with a toss of his head. His signature fragrance wafted through the air and into my nostrils, caressing the pleasure centres of my brain.

It appeared that no matter what else was happening, my attraction to Devereux remained parked at the kerb, motor running.

He locked his gaze on mine. 'Shall I tell you how beautiful and desirable *you* are?'

That squeezed some of the juice out of my anger and I forced in a couple of deep breaths to keep my chin from quivering.

Well, I'm just pitiful. One compliment and I regress back to being a needy five-year-old. I must be exhausted. Or seriously screwed up.

Embarrassed by both my erratic behaviour and my sloppy wardrobe, I stared down at my crumpled sweatsuit. 'Oh yeah, tell me how beautiful I look and how arousing this outfit is, Mr Fashion Model.'

He studied me for a moment. 'You are indeed beautiful, and if you wish to dress accordingly, I can accommodate you.' He chuckled. 'Is it safe to let you up now?'

I snorted and tried to shake him off of me, which made him start laughing again.

How annoying that he has such a great laugh.

'I will take that as a yes.' With another burst of his inexplicable speed, he suddenly loomed over me, then reached down to take my hands to pull me up.

The temper tantrum had exhausted most of my remaining energy. I frowned and gave him my hands. 'What do you mean, you can accommodate me?'

After he assured himself I was up and steady on my feet, he glided over to the bed I'd seen during my first visit to this secret room. Spread out on it were several beautiful evening gowns in various colours and fabrics.

'I bought you a few gifts.' He pointed to the dresses. 'I hope you enjoy them. I would be pleased if you would wear one tonight.'

'Oh, I see.' I scraped the bottom of the energy barrel and revved my anger back up again. 'You have another plan for me to follow? Something else you'll manipulate me into doing, whether I want to or not?'

'Absolutely not.' He flashed a wide smile. 'If you prefer to wear your charming sweat ensemble, that is perfectly fine with me.'

I glanced down at the baggy sweatsuit again and then over at the silky creations on the bed, and was torn between wanting to touch them and not wanting Devereux to know how much the stunning dresses had captured my interest.

He waited silently while my inner demons wrestled with each other, and I saw the corner of his mouth twitch slightly as he fought to suppress a smile. I hated that my emotions and thoughts were so transparent to him.

I mumbled under my breath and inched over to the bed. The gowns were lovely, almost works of art. Even someone with my limited fashion sense could see they were amazing. My eyes were immediately drawn to a shimmering blue garment and I ran my fingers along the soft fabric with a sigh. The dress already felt as if it belonged to me.

'I love the dresses. They're beautiful. But I don't understand why you bought them for me. Where would I wear such things? And it isn't only the dresses.' I examined my bare feet. 'If you'd told me you were going to zap me out of my living room, I would've put on shoes.'

He strolled over to an ornate wooden wardrobe, opened the tall doors and pointed to boxes of shoes and drawers of exquisite lingerie. All conveniently in my size, no doubt.

He bowed from the waist, a sweep of his arm indicating the collection as if he was one of those game-show models. 'I believe we have everything you require.'

What is this? Vampire Cinderella? Should I be flattered or creeped out?

'Why did you buy all those things for me? And why do you want me to wear them?'

He sat on the corner of the bed near me. 'You are a beautiful woman. You should adorn yourself with beautiful things. It is appropriate for you to dress for the ceremony.'

'Ceremony?' I instinctively stepped back. 'What ceremony?'

Sacrificing a virgin? Not in this lifetime. Bride of Dracula? Dinner for the coven? Whatever it is, count me out.

'A ritual of protection. You have been taken by the darkest spirit I have ever encountered. I can feel his presence even now.'

'Ritual of protection? Wait a minute – how do you know who kidnapped me? Did you have something to do with it? What do you know about my ending up in a graveyard?'

He held up a graceful hand, palm out. 'I had nothing to do with your abduction, but as soon as I awakened this evening I reconnected with your mind, read your memories and discovered what had happened. You are in great danger, and I must protect you.'

I was torn between being frightened by what he was saying and annoyed by his bossiness.

'You know, this is sounding more and more like something from a horror movie, and I don't think I want to play. I want you to call me a cab so I can go home.'

I rushed towards the door and he was suddenly there, standing in front of me, blocking my path.

He placed a finger under my chin and lifted my face up so that we locked eyes, his expression very serious. 'I should have been more forthcoming with you from the beginning. I should have anticipated your need to understand and analyse everything. I did not wish to frighten you away by acting too quickly, but I see now that I have blundered. Please allow me the opportunity to make it up to you.'

He bent down and pressed his lips against mine in a sweet kiss and I took the first exit to Euphoria. Again. I reached up and held his face in both my hands and pressed my body against his, deepening the kiss.

First I punch him, then I kiss him. I've given new meaning to the words 'mood swing'.

We stood melded together for not nearly long enough. I let my hands slide down his face, then stepped back. It took me a couple of tries to find my voice.

'What is it you should've told me?'

'This might take some time.' He reached for my hand. 'It is better to be comfortable.'

Hmmm. The vampire version of 'Let's get in the backseat'?

He led me over to the bed, gathered up all the dresses and draped them across the back of a throne-like chair. He crawled onto the bed – which was itself a very arousing thing to watch – sat against the headboard and patted the space next to him, inviting me to join him. I did.

I had a brief thought about what it meant that I was in bed with another man after spending the afternoon in a very intimate encounter with Alan. Was I now being unfaithful to Alan even though we'd made no promises to each other? We hadn't pretended our sexual attraction had any future implications. Or had I been unfaithful to Devereux? For some reason, that concept felt more troubling.

Wait a minute! Am I channelling a soap opera or something? I barely know either of them and I haven't made any commitments to anyone. I'm a free agent and can do as I please. A curse on all those old Sandra Dee movies my mother used to make me sit through! Any minute now I'm going to get up and go home.

I immediately became distracted by the fact that the bed felt so soft and welcoming and I was half-tempted to close my eyes and drift away. I forced myself to open my eyes very wide and concentrate on the painting of Devereux's mother that was visible from my vantage point.

She was so beautiful. Almost as beautiful as her son. I think her eyes were slightly more greenish-blue and his more bluish-green. Or maybe not. They resembled each other strongly, but I couldn't quite put my finger on what made Devereux so masculine – perhaps his jaw was slightly stronger than hers, or his cheekbones more defined – but whatever it was, I couldn't ignore his pure maleness. Dangerous male. Yummy male.

I giggled, of all things.

'Kismet?'

'What?' I realised my mouth was hanging open and my eyelids were at half-mast.

'You are clearly more exhausted than I thought. Perhaps you should lie down and rest for a while.'

'No, really, I'm fine. Just let me catch my second wind.' I blinked my eyes several times and sat up straighter, then turned to him. 'Or coffee, maybe. Yeah, that'll do it.'

He crawled down to my feet, grasped my ankles, and tugged on them gently until he'd pulled me into a prone position with my head on the pillow.

'Hey, I don't want to lie down. I don't want to—'

Sleep must have ambushed me, because that's the last thing I remember.

Until the dream.

CHAPTER 16

I'm walking through a run-down old abandoned house. The darkness is relieved only by the full moon shining through the large broken windows. There's an unpleasant musty smell masking something metallic – sweet – something familiar I can't identify.

I hear a child crying somewhere in the house and I run towards the sound, yelling, 'Where are you?' The corridor stretches out ahead of me, extending itself as I stumble along, feeling like I'm wading through tar.

Now the child's voice pleads, 'Help me, help me,' and my feet become heavier with every step. 'Help me, help me.' A heart-wrenching cry.

'Please,' I scream, 'tell me where you are. I want to help you.'

My mouth is dry, my heart pounds, and I force myself to keep moving. I open every door along the unending hallway and finally come to a furnished bedroom where a sobbing boy sits on a huge four-poster bed next to a small table where a candle burns. The child reaches out his little arms as if to hug me, and I lean in to embrace him. His arms encircle my neck and he rests his cheek against mine. I rock him gently as he quiets, and then he resumes his chant, 'Help me, help me, help me . . .'

I ask, 'How can I help you?' and he suddenly rears back, exposes long, pointy fangs, and sinks the horrible teeth into my neck. I fight against him, trying to push him off of me, to break his vice-like hold, but he has strength beyond imagining.

Finally I fall back onto the bed, barely breathing, and another voice – a terrible, disgusting voice I've heard before – takes up the child's plea. 'Help me, help me, help me . . .' I close my eyes, expecting death, and the familiar voice says, 'Ah, we meet again.' My dream eyes fly open and I'm no longer lying on the bed in the old house. I'm buried alive in a rotting coffin . . .

'No! Let me out!' I screamed, struggling to sit up. My heart raced and my skin felt hot, as if I'd been heated by a fire.

Twin points of pain throbbed on my neck and my lungs ached as I gasped for air. The hideous tones of the voice echoed in my ears and slithered across my skin. The same repulsive voice I'd heard outside The Crypt before my brain shut down. I pushed and fought against the hands holding me as if my life depended on it.

'Shhh. Kismet, it was only a dream. You are here, safe with me.'

I gasped and forced my eyes open. Devereux was sitting next to me on his bed, holding me down, a concerned expression on his face. I realised I'd been flailing my arms and kicking my legs. My cheeks were wet, and my body trembled.

'It was only a dream. No one will harm you.' Devereux pulled me up into a hug, and rocked me as I'd rocked the child in my nightmare.

'Only a dream. I don't know what that means any more.' I didn't feel normal with my eyes open or closed, and somewhere along the way I'd lost hold of the thread of sanity I'd been clinging to.

I closed my eyes again for a moment and sank into the soothing motion, enjoying being close to Devereux. I burrowed my face into his silky hair, loving the spicy smell of it. I didn't know what it was about him that felt so right to me, so familiar. In the midst of the madness my life had become, I was almost willing to stop thinking and just trust.

He picked up a bottle of water, cracked the seal, removed the top and handed it to me. I downed half of the water in one long pull and only realised how dry my mouth had been after it wasn't dry any more. I set the bottle on the table next to the bed and suddenly felt awkward. There I was, in a magnificent bed being held by a blond god and all I could think about was that my sweatsuit was all rumpled and my mouth tasted sour, which didn't bode well for the state of my breath.

Devereux smiled and stroked my hair. 'Your breath is fine, but after you rest a while longer, if you wish to refresh yourself in order to feel confident, I can provide everything you need. Now I think you ought to lie back down. You still look pale.'

'That's something, coming from you,' I teased self-consciously, in an attempt to change the subject.

'Yes.' He grinned. 'I suppose you could say I have no need of suntan lotion.'

He put his hand behind my head, grasped it gently, and guided it down towards the pillow. It did feel wonderful to surrender into the soft mattress again. He stretched out next to me, our bodies touching, his head propped on his palm, facing me.

'Kismet, are you having more dreams lately? More than usual?'

I thought about the child's fangs in my neck and my skin went clammy.

'It isn't that I'm having more dreams. I always dream. It's that the dreams, the nightmares, are horrible. Graphic and bloody and violent. Completely unlike my usual dreams. Why do you ask?'

'The same thing is happening to me and many others of my kind – an increase in dark visions and nightmares.'

I lifted my head, stared at him. 'Are you saying that vampires dream?'

He opened his eyes wide and raised a brow. 'That is the first time you have referred to me as a vampire. Do you realise that you have just accepted what I am? What has happened to change your belief?'

'Well, it was mostly because of talking to Alan. And what I saw at your club last night.'

At the mention of Alan, a heavy feeling settled in my stomach. Chinese food with a side of Guilt poured over Shame. I hoped Alan was still sleeping soundly on my couch. I didn't know if Devereux was aware of my sexual interlude with Alan earlier, but I knew Alan wasn't aware of my relationship with Devereux.

What a tangled web we weave . . .

'Yes.' Devereux responded to my thoughts. 'I am aware of your time with Alan, but you are a grown woman and able to make your own decisions. As much as I wish I could have been there for you this morning, that was not possible. I am glad someone was. Of course, you will never find yourself in such a predicament ever again, so there will be no need for you to turn to anyone but me.' Then he chuckled. 'Feeling guilty? You surprise me. I would not have expected such a thing from a modern woman. Why would you feel guilty? You did nothing wrong.'

'Well, Mr Mind-reader, I don't really. It's just old programming, cultural baggage. Most women have some of it – the idea that we're bad if we express our sexuality freely. I know all the therapeutic reasons why guilt isn't useful, but I still feel it anyway.' I sighed. 'Yesterday Tom walked in on me in the bathtub and if he hadn't behaved extremely badly, I might have had sex with him. Then last night I just about tore your clothes off at the club, and today I was with Alan. After two years of celibacy, that's a lot to deal with. I really don't know what's wrong with me. I'm usually so repressed.'

His voice wrapped me in aural fur as he stroked my cheek with the side of his finger. 'It is not necessary for you to be so hard on yourself. You have had a lot of changes to integrate and understand. Being in the presence of a vampire has altered your normal behaviours. As I mentioned before, we have that effect on humans.'

'What do you mean? What effect?'

'Expanded appetites of all kinds. So turning to Alan for comfort was a natural thing to do. You had been through a terrible ordeal.' Anger flashed in his eyes. 'An ordeal that will never happen again, I promise you. You are *mine* to protect now.'

I felt the air crackle and my skin tingled. *Wow. He's capable of some impressive mood swings himself. This probably isn't a good time to talk about the 'mine to protect' thing.*

He took a slow breath and his eyes returned to their calm, magical turquoise.

The corners of his mouth curved gently. 'But we were talking about dreams. You asked if vampires dream. Yes. We have access to levels of consciousness that are unavailable to most mortals, and when we turn inward during the daylight hours, our minds – or souls, if you will – journey to other realms, dimensions that cannot be explained with words, worlds that exist beyond the waking and sleeping dreams that humans know. Are you willing to share your nightmare with me?'

'I thought you could read my mind. Why do you need me to tell you the dream?'

'For some reason, I can only sense it as a series of emotional impressions – fast-moving pictures. If you tell me what you experienced, perhaps I can help you understand what it is trying to communicate to you. That is what psychology teaches, yes?'

'Yes, that's true, but I still don't understand why you want to know.'

'Honestly, I am not sure. I simply feel compelled to find out. Unless it is too unpleasant to recount again so soon?'

'No. I believe that dreams are metaphorical messages, so I might as well figure out what this one really means.'

I gave him all the details of the nightmare, along with all the feelings it triggered in me. He listened quietly, his brows contracted, his lips compressed.

'We must make time very soon to discuss the symbols in your dream. It is fascinating that so many are having similar visions. It is also important for us to have a conversation about vampires and what acceptance of us will mean for you. I wish we had time to begin the dialogue now because I would have preferred to explain tonight's ceremony to you in greater detail, but we must hurry.'

'Wait a minute.' My stomach tightened. 'I don't care for the sound of that. What will this ceremony consist of? What would you have explained?'

A knock sounded at the door and a petite five-foot-nothing twenty-something woman stepped into the room. She looked more pixie than vampire, at least until she spoke and exposed very visible, highly distinctive fangs. She had bright red hair that curled around her shoulders, large brown eyes, and she wore a sheer black dress under which was, apparently, nothing but skin.

'Master, it is nearly time for the ceremony. The others are arriving.'

Master?

Devereux acknowledged her and she backed out of the room.

He climbed off the bed, stood next to it and held out his hand to me. 'I swear to you that no matter how strange the ceremony may appear to you, no matter how unfamiliar, no harm will come to you. A ritual of protection is one of the oldest, most potent types of magic. In its simplest form, it is a focusing of intention that surrounds the one who needs protection with a powerful aura of well-being that repels all energy unlike itself. It will be as if you are floating in an invisible bubble of safety. Not very different from current pagan rituals.'

Pagans with fangs?

I sat frozen on the bed, my mind spinning out ever-more-gory, blood-soaked scenarios about the mysterious ceremony. No matter how logical his explanation, I barely knew Devereux and had no reason to trust him. He was apparently a vampire, and I was at his mercy. What I'd observed about Devereux and his colleagues didn't fit into any reality I knew about. I had no frame of reference. I was completely at sea with no map or compass, and the lifeboat I'd been floating in up until then had sprung a leak. I had no idea if there were sharks in the water.

My stomach contracted so tightly I could barely breathe.

'No harm.' Devereux bent down and met my eyes. 'I swear.'

I gazed into his blue-green depths and believed him. *So the Head Shark just said he won't eat me. Should I laugh or scream?*

The door opened again. Several women, none of whom I'd ever seen before, entered the room and lined up a few feet away from the bed.

Devereux indicated them with a sweep of his arm. 'My companions have come to assist you with dressing. They will prepare you for the ceremony.' Then he kissed me lightly on the lips and turned to walk away.

My throat tightened and my voice came out like a squeak. 'Wait! What do you mean, they'll prepare me for the ceremony?'

Why does this remind me of the cartoon where the cannibals have a huge pot boiling on the fire, waiting for the hapless hunter to arrive?

I didn't see any ropes, chains, or anything else that could be used to restrain me. No cooking utensils or objects with an edge that could cause bleeding. But my imagination was working overtime, creating scary and unspeakable possibilities.

'Ah, my apologies. I forget that you have not yet given yourself permission to read my thoughts – although it is true that reading vampire thoughts takes practise, even for someone with natural talent. It is as if we are on a different frequency from humans. We will be able to share the ability in the future, but for now, there is no hurry. In the meantime, my associates are here to help you select one of the beautiful dresses and to make sure you have everything you need.'

He pointed to a tall, slender woman with long brown hair and golden eyes. Her rangy body was encased in a unitard, those one-piece body suits that were only worn for exercising until the disco era, when shiny skintight numbers showed up on the dance floor, along with six-inch platform shoes and big hair. Hers made her look like she'd been dipped in a glittering rainbow, since every colour imaginable was present. The form-fitting garment left no doubt about her voluptuous shape.

'This is Nola. She will see to your hair and makeup.'

I ran a hand through my tangled hair. *The disco queen will see to my hair and makeup?* 'My hair and makeup? I don't think so.' I rolled off the bed and walked a wide circle around the women standing between me and the door.

Devereux repeated his disturbing habit of suddenly appearing in front of me, gave me serious eyes and laid a hand on my arm. 'Why do you object to being adorned? You usually wear makeup.' He said the last with impatience in his voice. I guess my resistance had unpleasantly surprised him. Maybe he wasn't used to anyone saying 'no' to him. I wasn't the only one who had a lot to learn. I summoned my best no-bullshit facial expression. 'You need to fill me in on what's happening here. I'm not going anywhere or letting anyone do anything until I'm clued in.'

He heaved a heavy sigh and shook his head. 'As I have said before, you are the most stubborn woman I have ever known. Are you never willing to be spontaneous? Must you be in control at all times? Are you unable even to sense the truth of my words?'

Well, that stopped me. He'd managed to trespass into my psyche and find the hottest buttons to push. I'd often been accused of lacking spontaneity, and my controlling nature was legendary. How else is a woman supposed to rise to the top of her field if she doesn't take control of her reality? He had pulled the scab off a painful wound. I did wish that I was able to relax and trust more, that I could follow my intuitive guidance. That I wasn't so . . . anal.

It was the expression on his face that really turned the tide. In one breathtaking gaze he'd managed to communicate that he thought this ceremony was for my benefit. That he'd arranged it to keep me safe. That he was worried about me.

Shit. Now he's gone and done it. He's got me feeling guilty about letting him down. How did that happen? My shoulders sagged. I met his concerned eyes. 'All right. I trust you.'

Maybe. Where can I find some shark repellent?

He flashed a brilliant smile. 'Thank you.' He bowed from the waist and glided towards the door. 'I will return for you shortly. It will be an extraordinary evening.'

As soon as he left, the women surrounded me. Nola floated over to the chair where the dresses were draped. 'Which one do you prefer?' She smiled, showing even white teeth.

I expected her to have fangs and was surprised she appeared so normal. Except for the golden eyes.

She flashed another smile and her canines descended.

Can everybody read my mind?

She smiled. 'Probably.'

I'm in a parallel universe where everyone is telepathic except me.

'No. You will be able to do it in the future too. The Master told us. He said you are a special human.'

'Why do you call him Master? Is he holding you here against your will? Are you brainwashed?'

She cocked her head to the side as confusion flowed across her features. 'He takes care of us. He is more powerful than any who came before. We aren't prisoners here. We are privileged to attend him, to be in his presence.' Her face shone with rapture.

Eeewww. Devereux has a harem of bloodsucking handmaidens, worshipping devotees – disempowered females. If he thinks I'm going to join the cult, he's sadly mistaken. This is the twenty-first century, mister, and I'm a liberated woman. I wonder what other services they perform for him? What if this ceremony deal is some kind of bizarre sexual ritual?

'Can you tell me about the ceremony we're going to? What should I expect?'

She grinned, which confused me until I figured out that she'd obviously read my mind and knew about all my judgements and speculations.

She met my eyes briefly then shifted her gaze away. 'That

LYNDA HILBURN | 271

information is not mine to share. Have you decided on a gown?' She pointed to the dresses on the chair.

I'd felt a mild tingle wash through my body as she'd turned her eyes to me. I didn't know if all vampires could entrance with their eyes, but I had to admit I'd felt something.

I walked over to the chair. Remembering the beautiful shimmering blue dress I'd seen, I lifted the others out of the way until I found it. It was floor-length, with a plunging neckline, made of a soft, lustrous material that might have been woven moonlight.

'This one will be fine. You know, I'm perfectly able to dress myself, so you and your friends can go and do whatever you need to do now.'

'We are here to attend to you. It is the Master's wish. We shall remain.'

Okay. Maybe we could have an informal consciousness-raising group here. These women must have slept through the '60s.

Nola draped the blue dress over her arm and floated across to the wardrobe containing the shoes and lingerie. The other women, all dressed in flowing gowns, were posed like goddess statues in a semicircle, where they'd been since they entered.

My newly acquired assistant opened the drawers, pulled out the shoe boxes and rifled through them. She seemed to be searching for something in particular.

'Yes.' Her voice raised in pitch, sounding excited, 'these are lovely.' In one hand she held up a pair of open-toed high heels the same shade of blue as the dress, and in the other, a strapless satin corset with garters for stockings.

I stood next to her, watching. 'Just out of curiosity, how do you know what's in there? Did you buy this stuff?'

'Yes. The Master asked several of us to observe you and to discern your clothing sizes. Then he told us what he had in mind and gave us free rein to purchase all manner of clothing from the Internet. It was very entertaining.'

'What do you mean, "observe me"?'

'Physically and astrally, of course. We watched you in your home and joined you in your dreams. The usual ways.'

The usual ways?

My eyebrows shot up. 'You spied on me?'

'Oh, yes.' She nodded enthusiastically. 'You are very interesting. Come now – there is a room for dressing and hygiene.'

Why does everyone around Devereux speak so strangely?

She stepped over to the nearest wall, touched a symbol carved in the wood and a panel slid aside exposing an opening into yet another room: the 'room for dressing and hygiene', or more commonly, the bathroom. It was a very large, ornate bathroom.

She took my hand and pulled me as if I were her little red wagon. The rest of the team remained behind.

Gee. Devereux's private bathroom. Should I genuflect or something?

The room was big enough to be a public restroom, but much too luxurious for the masses. There was a faint hint of his scent in the air, perhaps more easily recognised because no incense was burning to mask the fragrance. Mirrors lined each wall and opulent silver-streaked marble counters were abundant. Multiple sinks with sparkling modern hardware were interspersed along the counters and the floor was pristine white marble.

A huge silver bathtub sat on a raised platform, enclosed

by glass etched with figures of nude men and women dancing. Next to it, in another glass-surrounded area, was a double shower.

Fluffy white towels sat in piles on the various counters and hung in artistic racks on the walls next to the bath and shower areas.

Painted along the top of the walls, like a happy little border, were more men and women frolicking in all their naked majesty.

This is unsettling. Devereux really seems to enjoy the nude human form. That makes me both anxious and excited at the same time. Back to my question about the nature of the ritual.

White leather chairs and a loveseat sat off to the side in an alcove, and a clothing rack stood next to a small mirrored makeup table with a fancy matching chair. On the table was a little box wrapped in shiny paper with a rose pinned to the top instead of a bow. A small card had my name on it.

Nola watched me as I opened the gift. She rocked back and forth from heel to toe, smiling a cat-who-ate-the-canary smile.

Inside was a black velvet jewellery box containing a gorgeous silver pentagram on a chain, identical to the one Devereux's mother wore in her portrait.

I was speechless. My mouth opened into an 'ah' that remained silent. The weight and craft of the piece suggested it was high quality and probably very valuable.

I turned to Nola and shook my head.

She looked surprised. 'Are you unhappy with your gift? The Master was very pleased to choose it for you.'

'No, I'm not unhappy – I'm confused. Why would he give me something so valuable? He barely knows me.'

She tilted her head to the other side and studied me. 'Perhaps that is not true. You must dress now. The night awaits.'

Just then, as if there'd been a silent signal, the other women filed into the bathroom. I decided to let all the rest of my questions wait until I could speak to Devereux.

After some initial stubbornness on my part, when I insisted on adjusting my own breasts in the cups of the corset, I finally gave up and let them take over. It turned out they were pretty good with makeup and hair, and when they finally stepped away to survey their work, it was declared good.

They'd managed to enhance my features through their cosmetic witchery. They had left my hair down, and subtle silver sparkles had been dusted on my curls. The lovely pentagram necklace was added as a last touch. It dangled in the cleavage created by the low-cut dress and tight corset.

Although cleavage was usually the least of my concerns. In fact, eliminating it had always been a thornier problem. Thinking about my genetic heritage from my mother made me wonder what she'd say if she saw me at that moment. If she and my father had considered me strange before, now they'd probably move to another state and leave no forwarding address.

Suddenly all the women raised their heads as if they were listening to something I couldn't hear, then Devereux's enticing voice floated through the opening of the door.

'Kismet? Shall we go?'

The sensuous sound of his voice sent a wave of heat through my body and caused my heart to stutter. Everything about Devereux fried my circuits.

My entourage escorted me back into the other room, as I wobbled a bit on my shoes' thin heels. They were not quite stilettos, but in the neighbourhood.

He literally gasped when he saw me, and I had the same reaction when I laid eyes on him.

He waltzed elegantly over to me, held out both hands and took mine. 'You humble me with your beauty. I am over-whelmed.'

'Uh . . .'

It's becoming annoying that my brain goes on vacation whenever I'm around Devereux. I had no idea lust could be so intoxicating.

He twirled me in a dancelike movement, causing my dress to spiral out around me, lifting off the ground.

He looked spectacular. Dressed in cream-coloured soft leather, his trousers were obviously cut specifically for his lean, muscular frame. They fitted his body like a perfect glove, the waistband riding just above his hips. A line of soft plat-inum hair snaked down his lower stomach and disappeared into his trousers. With the exception of those enticing little strands, his chest was smooth and hair-free. The state of his chest was apparent because he wasn't wearing a shirt. The muscles in his abdomen were toned and obvious, and his nipples peeked out occasionally from beneath the open floor-length duster, which moved like something much softer than leather. Or maybe that was how expensive leather moved.

Shining in the centre of his chest was the same antique medallion he'd worn the first time he'd come to my office.

The colour of his hair matched his clothing and it spilled down over his shoulders, long, soft and delectable. The blue-green of his eyes sparkled with a fire from within. They shone like the alchemical blending of emeralds and sapphires.

As he swayed with me in our inadvertent dance, I became entranced by the sight of him in all that leather without a shirt. The pink of his nipples peeped out from the edges of the duster, vivid against his pale skin, and captured my attention – and my imagination. A trick of the light made the medallion seem to pulse against his skin. I had to fight the desire to run my hands over his chest.

We stopped moving and I finally found my voice. 'You look amazing. I just want to run my fingers through your hair and lick your chest.'

My outburst startled me and I felt my face grow hot with embarrassment. *Geez, did I really say that out loud? Have I been sucked into the cult?*

He let go of me then took my face in his hands.

'Thank you for that. I have never been so flattered. I hope you will still feel that way when we are alone later.'

When we're alone later? At least he assumes I'll get through this ceremony in one piece.

He smiled. 'As I have said, I swear you will be safe.'

'And when did I give you permission to read my thoughts again?'

'My apologies.' He bent his arm at the elbow and lifted it for me to take. 'The journey to the ceremonial site might cause you to be dizzy and momentarily uncomfortable. It will pass quickly.'

What? Every time I start to acclimatise, he says another weird thing.

I had a brief panic attack and considered bolting out the door, but decided I wouldn't get far in the high-heeled shoes. I had to clear my throat a couple of times before I could speak.

'Where are we going? How will we get there?'

We walked into his main office and headed towards what appeared to be a solid wall.

'Our destination is another dimension, and we shall move through thought.'

Before I could complain or raise my hand up to keep my head from colliding with the physical boundary in front of me, I heard a swoosh of air again, as I had when Devereux brought me from my house. My hair was blown back gently from my face and my equilibrium shifted. I'd say we'd been moving, but it wasn't like any kind of motion I'd felt before. It reminded me of an experience I had in an elevator once, when the car plummeted down several floors in free fall before the automatic controls took over and stopped the downward motion. My stomach churned and if Devereux hadn't been holding me, my knees would have buckled.

I'm not sure when, but I'd apparently closed my eyes because when I sensed we were stationary I opened them.

And words failed me.

I was standing on a cloud in a huge candlelit room surrounded by what looked like hundreds of other people.

Devereux brushed his finger gently across my cheek and I turned to him. He took my hand and walked me forwards a few steps.

'It is my pleasure to introduce you to Lady Amara.'

A beautiful woman with long pale-blonde hair approached. She wore a breathtaking white gown and a warm smile and resembled Devereux so strongly she could have been his sister.

She moved in very close to me, lifted the pentagram necklace resting on my chest and met my eyes.

'Welcome, Kismet. You have come at last. I am Devereux's mother.'

CHAPTER 17

Devereux had been correct in predicting that I might feel queasy after our inter-dimensional road trip. My head felt fuzzy and a loud buzzing filled my ears. Part of me figured I'd fallen and hit my head and that was why I was having both auditory and visual hallucinations.

Talking to Devereux's dead mother? Walking on a cloud?

After I accepted my temporary madness I relaxed and enjoyed the experience. After all, it was obviously just a dream: a marvellous, esoteric, lucid dream. It made perfect sense to me that I'd called up the beautiful blonde woman's image from the portrait in Devereux's room and that the cottony feeling in my head might be symbolically translated into a cloud.

'Okay.' I gave what I thought was a supportive smile and trilled, 'Sure. Absolutely. Devereux's mother. It's nice to meet you, Lady Amara.'

'Amara, please.'

The two of them exchanged a look. Devereux stepped in front of me and raised my chin with a gentle finger so he could search my eyes.

'Kismet?' He frowned. 'Are you well? Your mind is racing like a film on fast-forward.' He removed his finger from beneath my chin but continued to stare at me.

'Oh, sure,' I said, dazed. 'This is a great dream. Much more fun than all the bloody, scary ones I've been having.'

He glanced at the blonde woman and they shared a smile. Devereux moved over to her and drew her into a hug. 'It is wonderful to see you, Mother. It has been so very long.'

They held each other tightly, both reluctant to let go.

Amara finally stepped away from his embrace, wiped a tear from under her eye and stood in front of us. Shifting her gaze to each of us in turn, she said in a trembling voice, 'My beautiful son, I am so happy you have found your mate and that your heart will be at peace. I cannot remain long, so we must begin.'

His mate?

Surprised by this confusing new development, I scanned the immediate area, searching for the mate Amara had referred to.

Before I could ask any of the multitude of disturbing questions that had commandeered my partially functioning brain, Devereux positioned himself between us. He offered us each an arm and we were suddenly in the middle of a cavernous room. The dreamy quality of the experience began to recede and the sounds, colours and sensations lost their vague edges and became hyper-focused. My sensing system shifted to high alert and my inner defences rallied the troops and pulled up the bridge over the moat.

My stomach turned and my breath went shallow. I was suddenly afraid. All around me were people I didn't know, and we were still walking on a damn cloud. Candles floated in the air of their own volition, just like in the Harry Potter movies, and the flames were overly large and multicoloured. Every few seconds each candle sent up a spark of mini-fireworks, but no one else paid any attention.

Maybe there was something funny in that water he gave me. Some kind of occult drug from one of those strange bottles he has in his bedroom.

The air was thick and heavy, as if it was very hot, but it wasn't. There was a wall of murmuring sound, which I soon discovered to be the whispered conversations around me.

Devereux guided us into a large, cloud-free open circle. As if on cue, all the other guests surrounded us, forming themselves into several concentric rings, one behind another. On the floor of the open area were symbols similar to the ones in Devereux's private room. An ornate, jewel-encrusted chair with a high back sat in the centre of the circle.

Amara grasped my hand and led me over to the fancy chair, indicating I should sit. I gazed into her eyes, searching for any sign that I was in danger, but all I saw was kindness, warmth and compassion.

Since I didn't know what else to do – or what else I *could* do – I sat in the chair. The moment my hind end touched the seat, the people in the circles began singing. Or maybe chanting would be a better word to describe the sound, some repetitious melody in a language I didn't recognise. The vocalising started out softly, harmonies flowing over and under the tonic, but as it went on, it got louder, then louder still, until I could feel the vibration of the sound in my bones.

The song was mesmerising, eerie and lovely. My eyelids drooped and my head fell forwards. I was still fully conscious, but had the distinct impression that my body had gone to a different time zone. I concentrated on lifting my head and was finally able to raise it just enough to have the motion cause it to flop back against the chair.

Out of the corner of my eye, I saw Amara step next to me. She took my hand and I tried to produce sounds, but nothing came out.

I don't know what Devereux had been doing all this time, but he suddenly appeared next to me in the centre of the circle and all the singing stopped. I mean everyone literally stopped chanting at exactly the same second. Devereux raised both his hands in the air.

'Welcome, my friends. I am grateful for your willingness to join us in this ceremony of protection today to hold the sacred space. It is truly a momentous occasion and a special time for me because my mother is here. Please welcome my mate Kismet to the circle.'

What? I'm his mate? When did I sign up for that? Why isn't my brain working properly?

He gestured towards me with a graceful, flowing hand-and-arm movement and everyone said words in unison in that exotic-sounding language.

Ever since the singing ended, my mind had begun to clear and my body was operating at my command again. Amara released my hand, but continued to stand next to me.

Devereux extended his hands out in front of him and a large golden chalice appeared from nowhere. He held the chalice over his head and moved around the inside edges of the circle, keeping up an ongoing monologue in that mysterious sonorous language. He was quite a sight to behold, gliding like a dancer, his duster billowing out behind him, his naked chest gleaming in the candlelight.

My mind was clear enough to find him compelling and my body was aware enough to be aroused – in fact, for some reason I was intensely aroused. My suddenly hard nipples thrust against the silky fabric of my dress, threatening to burst free from the restraining corset, and the area between my legs grew slick with liquid heat.

Then he came and stood in front of me, set the chalice on the floor at my feet, threw off his duster and, for lack of better words, performed an erotic dance for me.

Vampires dance? Who knew? Well, he did say it was a pagan ceremony.

His movements were totally unlike his usual elegant, contained presentation. His hips undulated, his stomach muscles rolled and his arms sliced through the air in deliberate, graceful motions. He threw his head back, his platinum hair flew and his face went slack, as if he'd got lost in ecstasy.

A potent energy sparked off Devereux as he danced. I felt the tension building inside myself and thought that if he didn't touch me soon, I'd literally explode. As I caught some of the expressions on the faces of the other participants, I saw I wasn't the only one having that reaction.

Devereux's skin shone with sweat, like liquid diamonds. He moved his hands seductively over his body, locking his eyes with mine. Bending towards me, he opened his mouth and slowly and deliberately licked his upper lip with his tongue. His canines were fully extended and he kissed me, catching my lower lip with his fangs, then backed away.

I gasped, thinking he'd bitten me, but I tasted no blood. All my erogenous zones were frantic with desire – literally aching with need – and my heart pounded double-time. I was so excited and aroused by his dance that I doubt if I'd have complained even if he'd taken a pint.

I scooted to the edge of the chair, ready, I supposed, to leap onto Devereux at the earliest chance. Oddly enough, thinking about making a public display of myself with Devereux didn't upset me. All that mattered was doing whatever I had to do to get him to touch me again.

He picked up the chalice, glided over to the circle of people and pandemonium broke out.

As Devereux approached the crowd a madness built. Excitement spread around the circles, and all variety of wails, moans, groans and howls rent the air. Some of the participants' bodies convulsed, limbs twitching and jerking in random spasms as their heads flopped back and forth on boneless necks. Others jumped up and down with manic intensity, as if they'd been taken prisoner by a sadistic puppeteer.

Holding the chalice in his left hand, Devereux magically manifested a knife or dagger in his right. He stared into the eyes of the woman in front of him in the circle and she offered her arm. Using the knife to make a small cut on her wrist, he caught the dripping blood in the chalice. A roar went up from the crowd.

Arms shot out from everywhere as the noise level rose.

Devereux navigated the ring, repeating the process with as many wrists as it took to fill the chalice with blood.

I'd been so shocked by Devereux's sudden shift from lust object to phlebotomist that I hadn't noticed the other really bizarre situation that was unfolding.

People were sucking on each other's wounds.

Well, technically, I guess you couldn't call them people.

Vampires were sucking on each other's wounds.

And not merely sucking – feeding frenzy would be more accurate.

I felt my jaw drop as I watched the bloodsuckers attach themselves to wrists and necks, some falling to the floor together in passionate mid-suck. A few of the revellers were so swept away by the feasting that clothes were discarded and other parts of the body were invited to play.

Vampire orgy. Perfect.

I instinctively sat back in the chair, hoping the lunacy wouldn't spread to me. Amara took my hand again and I turned to her. Her eyes were large and shining, greener than Devereux's, and she said, 'He would never hurt you. You must trust him.'

At that moment he stalked towards us, his hair fanning out behind him, holding the chalice in his hands. His eyes were feral, expressing a wildness he'd never shared with me before, and his face was startlingly beautiful. A fallen angel.

Clutching the chalice in his left hand, he held it away from his body and embraced his mother in a one-armed hug. He met her eyes and she tilted her head to the side. Devereux leaned in to her, exposed his fangs and sank them into her neck. She gasped and laid a hand on the back of his head.

I didn't know what to do with myself – where to look. Devereux had just assaulted his mother and she was apparently enjoying it. There was something very sensuous about him sucking on her neck and I couldn't imagine that was a psychologically healthy mother-son activity.

But then she's dead and this is a dream, so do the rules apply?

After a few seconds he raised his head, embraced her again, said something in that strange language and turned to me, licking blood from his lips.

Devereux raised the chalice into the air and the chanting started again. Vampires rose from the floor and disentangled themselves from each other, adding their voices as they reformed the circles. As the intensity of the sound increased, the curious entranced feeling overtook me again.

Devereux knelt before me, offered the chalice and said, 'One sip, my love.'

There was a major firestorm of resistance in my brain. One part of me was already struggling to get up from the chair, begging the muscles in my legs to report for duty one more time. But the muscles were hanging out with the other part of me that was fantasising about tearing off Devereux's clothes and jumping on him. One sip of blood wasn't much of a price to pay for being able to get my hands on this blond Adonis. Good thing this wasn't really happening.

My hands reached out for the chalice and he gave it to me. It was warm. I raised it to my lips, stared into his astonishing eyes over the rim and drank. For some reason I'd imagined blood would taste like tomato juice. It didn't. But by the time I discovered that the taste was thick and unpleasant, I'd choked and swallowed the entire gulp. I coughed and sputtered and finally stuck my tongue out, maybe thinking that would dissipate the taste.

Definitely a dream. I'd never drink blood if I was awake. Nothing to worry about. Just a dream.

He mouthed the words, 'Thank you,' retrieved the chalice from me and drank the remainder of the blood. Saying more of those unfamiliar words, he held the cup out in front of him and it vanished.

The chanting grew louder and another portion of my consciousness drifted away.

Devereux stood, pulled me out of the chair, wrapped his arms around me, and kissed me passionately. I made an effort to hold on to him, but my bones had mysteriously dissolved and all four of my limbs were now only useful as paperweights.

Bending me over backwards he whispered, 'No harm.' He kissed his way down from my mouth and along my neck, finally resting his lips on the fullness of my breast. The part of me that wanted to roll around with Devereux sighed contentedly. He planted little kisses on my skin, then there was a flash of pain, followed by the most blissful feeling I'd ever experienced.

After a few seconds he lifted me into his arms, brought his lips to mine and held me. I briefly wondered how someone who drank blood could have such sweet-smelling breath, but I decided to add that to the list of things to think about later.

Besides, this is my dream and I'm not likely to give my lust object stinky breath, right?

He returned me to the chair, kissed my cheek and walked out towards the vampire chorus. The chanting immediately ceased.

That was too weird. I'd sung in lots of choirs and I knew how hard it was to get people to all stop singing at exactly the same moment. There was always at least one person not paying attention or something. This was downright eerie, as if sound itself had disappeared.

Just as before, as soon as they stopped chanting I began to come back to myself. Not that I knew where I'd been prior to that, but I didn't know how else to explain it.

Immediately I noticed that my breast was throbbing with pain. One quick glance solved the mystery. Standing out against my very-white skin were two neat puncture marks surrounded by a sea of traumatised red tissue which would soon be a colourful blue-green-purple.

Amara, who still stood next to the chair, took my hand again. She inspected my chest. 'I will heal that for you before I leave. There will be no lasting mark. Devereux will explain.'

My eyes darted to her neck to see if her bite marks looked as bad as mine, but there was nothing to see. Her skin was smooth, white and flawless.

She nodded once. 'Exactly so.'

I didn't know if it was a flaw or a virtue, but I'd always had an innate need to be polite, to be a nice person. I couldn't blame Amara for what her son had done, but I had to turn away from her because it was temporarily impossible for me to pretend that I wasn't seething with rage. Something about the physical pain had jolted me into awareness.

Damn it to hell! This isn't a dream. It's a wide-awake nightmare. I can't believe the bastard bit me. He actually bit me. I'm probably going to turn into a vampire now.

Amara stepped in front of me, her eyes hard and serious. 'No. It is not that easy to become a vampire. It requires intention.' Her gaze went to the bite on my breast. 'This was merely a symbolic gesture. I wish there had been more time to help you understand, but no harm has been done. You will be as you were.'

I scanned the area for Devereux. He'd retrieved his duster and was moving slowly around the inside of the circle, pausing occasionally. Some of the words he spoke sounded like English and I picked up the phrase 'guardian of the four directions' along with a few others. I got the idea that each place he paused in the circle represented east, south, west or north.

He pulled a gem-studded wand from the pocket of his coat and held it in the air at each cardinal point. A burst of brilliant white light emanated from the tip at each location and hovered, forming a vertical line floating in space.

I was tempted to rub my eyes because I couldn't believe what I was seeing, but I remembered how much mascara Nola had insisted on plastering on my eyelashes, and I hesitated at the last moment. I didn't want to look like a raccoon.

By the time Devereux completed the circle, there were four beams of luminescence.

At a signal from him, all the vampires in the inner circle took a step forward, which put them in line with the hovering lights. As soon as the radiance touched the vampire closest to it, the glow began to spread around the circle, flowing out to each circle in turn. Soon the white incandescence transformed into multiple colours, shifting and changing every few seconds. The mini-fireworks put out by the candles became more pronounced and the medallion around Devereux's neck sparked like a floodlight.

I lowered my eyes to shield them from the bright glare but was able to squint enough to see that all the vampires in the circles had clasped hands. As they did that, the light began to pulsate and writhe, creating bursts of colour that completely enveloped everyone in the circle until there was only pure energy.

Devereux turned in my direction and held out his hand.

I looked anxiously at Amara.

My feet had a mind of their own and I found myself standing and inching over to where he waited. I stretched out my hand and the moment our fingers met there was a sharp sound that reminded me of the crack of a whip. The light exploded and engulfed us.

Then there was nothing.

CHAPTER 18

I woke up naked in my bed. Naked except for the pentagram necklace. At least I assumed it was my bed, because I couldn't open my eyes. I raised my hands up to investigate and found the source of the problem. All that mascara I'd worn the night before had somehow congealed into gummy clumps and hermetically sealed my upper lashes to my lower ones.

I spent a couple of minutes prising them apart, opening and closing my lids to test the equipment, and then discovered I'd apparently rubbed my eyes at some point because there was a big black stain on the side of my right index finger. I knew the mirror would present me with even more delightful news.

But thankfully, I was in my own bed.

Staring up at the ceiling, I listened to the sounds floating in through the window and appreciated the evidence that, for some people, normal reality still existed. Lawns were being mowed, dogs walked, greetings called out from yard to yard, cars driven. Music still blared from the radios of passing vehicles and children were playing. The everyday world that I used to belong to – that I took for granted – evidently continued as if nothing earth-shattering had happened.

Memory fragments from the night before bobbed like apples in the tub of my brain, waiting for me to capture one and take a bite.

Bite.

I bolted up, filled each hand with a breast and warily lowered my eyes, afraid to see what might be there. Instead of the torn, bruised and traumatised skin I'd anticipated, there was nothing but the white, lightly blue-veined expanse I'd always had.

Breathing a sigh of relief, I watched the patterns of sunlight play across the wall in front of me and felt numb.

There were only two possible explanations for what was happening to me. Either I was in the midst of a psychic melt-down, maybe even a psychotic break, and the entire sequence of events had only unfolded inside my fevered, twisted mind, or I had truly entered a monstrous world where vampires drank blood, levitated in the air, read your mind and seduced your body.

Quite frankly, I didn't know how to deal with either option.

My mouth was as dry as the lunar landscape and it tasted as if I'd scoured the floor of an ER with my tongue.

A wisp of memory floated into my brain and opened a Pandora's box of horrible possibilities.

There was no way in hell I'd drunk blood. Not one chance in this or any other universe. Not even if someone held me down and forced my mouth open. Yuck, yuck, yuck.

I raised the palm of one hand in front of my mouth, breathed into it and almost gagged.

No. I must just have eaten something funky. Something

gross. I hoped I hadn't shared this breath with anyone I actually liked.

The digital clock on my nightstand showed 1:00 p.m. That information didn't really tell me much because I wasn't even sure what day it was. Panicking, I picked up the TV remote control and clicked on CNN, assuming the data panel on the bottom of the screen would have the correct date. Sunday. Relief swamped me. I hadn't lost any more time than I already knew about and, more importantly, I hadn't missed any client appointments.

I swivelled my head around, stretching the tight muscles of my neck and shoulders, then swung my legs over the side of the bed. Turning off the TV, I forced myself vertical and walked over to the closet to fetch my comfortable pink robe. As I slipped it on and tied the sash, a sparkling blue fabric caught my eye. The lovely dress I'd worn the night before hung neatly in the closet, and on the floor underneath it were the matching shoes. I found the corset and stockings draped across the rocking chair in the corner.

I hoped it had been Devereux who'd brought me home, undressed me and tucked me into bed. The startling possibility that it might not have been him, or that things I didn't want to know about might have happened, froze me like a statue.

Laying a hand against the wall to brace myself, I closed my eyes and sent my awareness through my body. I'd always been able to use my intuition to test the state of my physical health and recently that ability appeared especially heightened.

Whether I wanted to know about it or not, I needed to find out if there'd been any sexual activity – either consensual or forced. I steeled myself for possible bad news and asked the silent question. None of my usual indicators fired a warning, so I asked again, just to make sure.

As before, calm silence.

I'd learned to trust the subtle 'yes' or 'no' reactions of my body and felt relatively confident that I hadn't been physically harmed while I was sleeping. Or unconscious. Or whatever I'd been.

Relief washed over me and I straightened, tightened the sash on my robe and headed downstairs for desperately needed coffee.

Halfway down the stairs I remembered that the last time I'd seen Alan, he'd been sacked out on my couch. It had been eighteen hours since I'd left him sleeping there. I couldn't imagine he'd still be snoozing. Then I remembered how his unnatural sleep came to be and decided that rational rules wouldn't necessarily apply. I figured he'd be rightfully confused and probably angry, and he'd want to know where I had gone.

Sure enough, the couch was empty. I walked around the room, checking for a note, but there was no sign of one. I scanned the whiteboard in the kitchen. Nothing.

Recalling that his clothes had been in the washing machine, I lifted the lid and there they were, still wet. He hadn't even transferred them to the dryer.

Why would he have gone out in those ridiculous pink sweatsuit bottoms? Unless he got another call from the police and had to hurry out. But even so.

I went over to the front window, lifted one of the slats in the blinds – just in case the media circus still had its tent erected – and tried to find Alan's car. It was still there, right where he'd left it yesterday. And, unfortunately, so were the media. Not only had they not gone away, but there were more of them than ever lining the street. It was probably incredibly naïve of me to hope they'd find something even more sensational to cover; that I'd be yesterday's news. Fat chance when anything vampire was involved.

Noticing the large police presence circling my home, part of me thought it was a waste of taxpayers' money for so many officers to be on guard duty, but mostly I was grateful. I knew the reporters wouldn't stay behind the barricade without strong incentives.

As I peeked out I noticed several men dressed in military-type clothing standing in a line between the street and my front door. What the hell? Who'd called out the marines? Did Devereux's influence reach that far? This entire situation was getting out of control.

I tore myself away from the window and did another walk-through of my house, calling Alan's name loudly, but I got no response.

Still trying to figure out the mystery of the missing FBI agent, I absentmindedly went through the motions of making coffee and then remembered the phone. I hadn't checked the messages yet, and if Alan'd had to leave quickly, he might have called. Plus I'd contacted Midnight and Ronald and had left – or been snatched – before they could call me back.

While the coffee brewed and sent its heavenly aroma directly into my nostrils, I punched in the retrieval code to listen to my business messages, then I checked my cell phone.

There were several from media outlets, a few from concerned clients, wondering about my safety, and one from a friend in Paris who laughingly said she'd seen a report on CNN about a flaky psychologist in Denver who worked with vampires. So much for my career.

Midnight had left a message saying she and Ronald were not dealing with Emerald's death very well, and they were worried about me. She wanted to know if I could possibly see them for a joint appointment on Sunday.

I was just about to hang up so I could call her when I heard the first couple of words of the next message and the hairs on the back of my neck rose.

Brother Luther's familiar Southern-accented voice screamed out of the earpiece, 'I know what you did. I know where you've been. Consorting with foul creatures of the night! You'll be punished! You'll burn in the fires of hell! Unholy Jezebel! Whore of Babylon! Suffer not a witch to live! No one can save you from the wrath of the Almighty! I am the messenger. You have been marked. You will burn.'

My eyes and my mouth were wide open, and after the message ended I felt slimed, contaminated, as if someone had thrown a bucket of psychic manure on me through the phone. The negative energy of the call hit my stomach like a fist. My knees went weak and I grabbed the edge of the counter for support. Was this sick fanatic stalking me? Was he dangerous?

I saved his hateful tirade because it was definitely time to report him to the police. The call had to be some form of harassment at the very least. Thankfully, he wasn't my client so I didn't have to walk any ethical fine lines.

Finally, there was a message from Alan. He spoke in a very soft, subdued voice, as if he'd just awakened. 'Kismet? You're probably going to think I'm insane, if you don't already, but I'm home and I don't know how I got here. The last thing I remember is being at your house and seeing Devereux appear in your living room. It's Sunday morning, the sun just came up and I'm still wearing your pink sweats. I went outside to look for my car and it isn't here. I think I left it at your house – along with my clothes – but I don't remember. You're probably thinking I had some kind of blackout or breakdown – and maybe I did – but I'd appreciate if you'd call me when you get this and help me figure out what the *hell* is going on.'

I disconnected, set the phone down and poured a cup of coffee. Then I plopped into one of the kitchen chairs. Sometimes there's just too much information for a brain to process.

Postponing the inevitable, I allowed myself the luxury of sitting still while I finished my first cup, then poured another and picked up the phone. I was so tired of all the drama.

I punched in Midnight's phone number and got her answering machine. 'Midnight? This is Dr Knight. I'm sorry I wasn't able to get back to you sooner. I had to take care of some personal business. There are no words to express my sadness about Emerald. I'm absolutely available to meet with you and Ronald. You have my cell phone number – call whenever you get this message and we'll schedule a meeting. Talk to you soon.'

Next, I dialled Alan's cell phone, and he must have been using it because my call went directly to voicemail. 'Alan, I don't think you're crazy. In the midst of everything that's going on, you might be the only sane person I know. Your car is still here, along with your clothes. I have a client session later, so just give me a call when you get this and we can arrange a time to get together. See you soon.'

I'm sure my voice sounded as tired as my spirit felt.

What I wanted more than anything was to do absolutely nothing. To sit quietly without thinking. Without trying to interpret, understand or accept. Without being afraid.

Since none of that was likely, I rinsed out my coffee mug and went back upstairs to take a shower, carrying my newly charged cell phone with me.

The view of my face in the bathroom mirror caused me to laugh out loud. I'd really done a job of spreading the mascara around my eyes and upper cheeks; I looked like a child had scribbled on me with a black Magic Marker.

Gorilla breath and raccoon eyes. See what happens when you stay at the ball past midnight?

I momentarily wondered if I'd made myself this appealing a sight before or after my pale knight dropped me off. Or should I say, my pale bloodsucker? I'd better get used to telling the truth, at least to myself.

As attracted as I was to Devereux, I wanted to keep my distance from him for a while, to pretend to be normal again. But how did one remain distant from something that could come and go through thought? Something that moved through time and space like walking from room to room? Something that didn't give a shit about anyone else's boundaries or needs?

I turned on the spray, dropped my robe on the floor, pulled the necklace over my head, laid it on the counter and stepped into the shower.

After blissing out for a few moments, letting the hot water cascade down my body, I poured shampoo on my hair and piled the soapy mass on top of my head. I picked up the plastic bottle of body gel and was spreading it across my breasts when my hand slid over something on my chest. The necklace. I'd forgotten to take it off.

Wait. No. I hadn't forgotten. I *did* take it off. I laid it on the counter.

I tugged aside the shower curtain, squinted through the fog that the hot water had created in the small room and scanned the counter. No necklace.

I placed my hand back on the pentagram and Devereux's voice whispered in my mind, 'This necklace is your protection. You must never remove it.'

What the hell?

Expecting him to pop in, I looked around, but nothing happened. I thought vampires couldn't go out in the sunlight, so where'd the voice come from? But then, after what I'd seen, I could testify that there was no rule book for what Master Devereux could or couldn't do.

I lifted the necklace over my head again and in the nanoseconds it took me to do that, the pentagram returned to rest between my breasts.

The same words floated through my mind. 'This necklace is your protection. You must never remove it.'

Apparently, Devereux had somehow implanted a message in the talisman that replayed any time the pendant lost contact with my skin.

Well, to hell with it. I'd leave the damn necklace on. It was just another way that Devereux had reached out to intrude on my life and I wasn't going to give it one more moment of attention than I had to.

I finished washing and rinsing, wrapped up in a towel and stepped out of the shower.

My cell phone rang – Midnight calling to schedule a time to meet. We set the appointment for two hours later, which gave me time to get dressed and eat something. My empty stomach echoed like an abandoned cave.

I made a sandwich, sat in the living room, and turned on the TV. I clicked through the channels until I came to a live news broadcast featuring an interview with my favourite detective.

'Lieutenant Bullock, can you give us an update on the case everyone is calling the *Vampire Murders*? Do you have any leads? Any suspects? Are you close to an arrest?' the young reporter asked.

'We're following several leads,' a very tired-looking Lieutenant Bullock said. 'I'm not at liberty to give any specific information at this time.'

'Is it true that the bodies were drained of blood? What kind of serial killer does that? Do you have any evidence that the killer actually drinks the blood?'

'That's sensational speculation, young lady, not good journalism. All we know now is that five people are dead.'

'Do you know how psychologist Kismet Knight is involved in the murders?'

'No comment. When we have more details, we'll schedule a press conference. That's all for now.' With that, Lieutenant Bullock stalked away from the camera.

Great. I'm a star.

I clicked off the TV, reflecting that Lieutenant Bullock was as rude to everyone else as she'd been to me. But she looked exhausted. She'd probably been working round the clock since the murders began. Five people dead. I wondered what Emerald had in common with the other victims. Alan probably knew. I'd have to ask him. The comment Officer Colletta made in the squad car came back to me, the one about the killer possibly being one of my clients. Chills raced up my body. What if it was true? I barely knew some of my new vampire-wannabe clients. Could one of them be responsible?

I pushed the thought away and went back upstairs to finish getting dressed. A short time later, I'd just picked up my briefcase and purse to head out the door when my cell phone rang again.

This time it was Alan. He sounded a lot more solid and had retrieved his usual cocky attitude. He launched right in. 'So, did I imagine it, or did Devereux plant a passionate wet one on you when I was there yesterday?'

'Uh, I seem to recall something of that nature.'

'You want to tell me what's going on?'

'No.'

'What?'

'Sorry, I don't mean no, I don't want to tell you, I mean not right now. I need to get over to my office for an appointment. Besides, I'm seriously burned out on talking or thinking about all the weird crap that's been going on. I'm running on empty. Could we discuss it later?'

'Sure.' He paused. 'I just thought maybe you and I had possibilities, but after what I saw, I don't know any more.

What do you think? Do we have possibilities?'

Ah, shit. This is exactly the messy kind of issue I don't want to discuss. The stuff I don't have one clue about.

I couldn't keep all the impatience and frustration out of my voice as I paced around the room. 'Can I waffle and say that I'm confused? That I don't even know my name right now, much less what's happening with my love life? Seriously, can we put a bookmark in this discussion?'

'Absolutely.' His voice became more formal, less friendly. 'We'll talk later. Things are still crazy for me, too – there've been some leads in the Emerald Addison murder case and I don't know when I'll have a spare minute. I'm going to have one of the black-and-whites drop me off at your place so I can pick up my car. I'll get the clothes some other time. I'm ready whenever you are – ball's in your court.'

Either he'd decided to humour me or he really caught the vibe. Or maybe he really didn't care all that much. Then the confusing possibility that he cared too much raised its scary head and gave me brain overload.

'Thanks.' I nodded, then remembered he couldn't see me. 'Talk to you soon.'

Feeling like I'd just dodged a very large bullet, I willed myself to relax.

I stole one more peek out my window to see how many media types were lurking before I made my escape. There weren't quite as many as the day before, but the remaining reporters appeared to be hunkered down for the duration. Officer Colletta told me yesterday that my office was surrounded and I assumed the situation there hadn't changed either. I needed a little help.

Cautiously I stuck my head out the front door. Various media representatives jumped to their feet and started yelling questions again, on-air personalities brushed dirt off the seats of their slacks. The military fellows were gone. One of the officers looked my way when the chaos started and I signalled him to come over. He trotted up to the door.

'Is there a problem, Dr Knight?' He removed his sunglasses. 'Do you need something?'

'No problem, officer. I have to go to my office to see a couple of clients. Could you help me get out of my garage without running over any cameramen or TV anchors? And could you alert your associates at the office building that I'm headed their way?'

'We'll take care of it. Will you return to home after that? We have orders to stay here indefinitely.'

Really? Indefinitely? I wonder what they'd do if they found out all this was because of a vampire whispering in the chief's ear.

'Yes, I'll be back after that. I really appreciate your help.'

'We'll clear the way.' He replaced his glasses and headed back to the line of police cars.

I waited a few seconds for the authorities to get into place then walked through the adjoining door from the kitchen to my attached garage, which opens onto a paved alley. I had no idea how many reporters were back there. I got into my car, clicked the door opener and startled a handful of men and women sitting on the driveway, playing cards, their recording equipment stacked up around them like an electronics garage sale. I revved the car motor as several offi-cers arrived, and luckily the squatters didn't stick around long enough to discover if I would have rolled over them. They scattered, yelling to their colleagues out front. One brave soul jumped on my hood with his video camera and managed to film a few seconds of me smiling and waving before the officer who came to my door pulled him off.

Even something as familiar and comfortable as driving required extra attention. I caught a glimpse of my eyes in the mirror, half-expecting to see a shell-shocked reflection, and was surprised to appear so normal. As if nothing had changed. As if I hadn't lost my mind. As if I still lived in a world where there were no such things as vampires.

I was more comfortable believing I was nuts.

My office was just a few minutes away and I managed to get there with only a small caravan of journalists on my tail. The parking lot across from the building was filled with the same assortment of vehicles and people as the street in front of my house. I had to drive a block down to find a place to park. I locked my car, grabbed my briefcase and made a dash for the entrance. Officers swarmed from all directions, holding everyone back and giving me the opportunity to make it inside the lobby, where it was strangely quiet.

Midnight and Ronald showed up right on time. Neither of them appeared to have slept in a couple of days, and their vulnerability made my heart ache.

'How are you holding up?' I asked.

Midnight started to cry and Ronald put his arm around her. 'Not very well. We just can't get a grip on how anyone could hurt someone as sweet as Emerald. She was the most easygoing, laid-back person we've ever met,' Ronald answered. 'Do you know if they caught the killer yet?'

'I don't think so,' I said, 'but every cop in the state is on the case – they'll find the sick person who killed Emerald and the others.'

Midnight pulled a tissue from the box and blew her nose. She had to clear her throat a couple of times before she could speak. 'I can't help but think this is all my fault. If I hadn't left her alone, she wouldn't have been hurt to begin with.' She gave a frustrated scream, which startled both Ronald and me. 'I'm so pissed off and I feel so helpless. The police aren't going to be able to find the one who killed her. It was a vampire. But they're not even taking that into consideration. How could a human drain all the blood from a body?'

That's a good question. Most humans can't.

'We're going to The Crypt tonight to talk to Devereux and ask him to find the vampire who hurt my friend.'

'I hope he can help.' I met her gaze. 'But Emerald's death isn't your fault, Midnight. She was just in the wrong place at the wrong time. If you'd been there with her, maybe both of you would have been harmed.' I paused. 'It's normal for you to be angry – that's one of the stages of grief. But you couldn't have known what would happen to her. There was nothing you could have done to prevent it.'

'That's what I told her,' Ronald said, squeezing Midnight's shoulder.

We spent most of the rest of the time processing the grief and anger they both felt.

They asked a lot of questions about what had happened to me – the abduction and waking up in a cemetery – and

I gave brief answers. I told them the truth: that I had no idea who had taken me there or what had happened.

Devereux said I'd been taken by a vampire, a *dark spirit*, but I had no comprehension of what he meant.

Midnight said she'd returned to her parents' house temporarily because she couldn't face Emerald's empty bedroom in their shared apartment. As he had before, Ronald showed great strength and compassion. He stayed close to Midnight, and had been her constant companion during the last couple of days.

In fact, at one point they kissed each other on the lips and the sense I got was that it was more romantic than friendly. There was obviously more to the soft-spoken guy than met the eye. Perhaps Midnight had radically misinterpreted Ronald's reaction to her relationship with Bryce. Maybe it hadn't been Bryce he was interested in after all.

Watching them together gave me a hopeful feeling.

I walked them out to the waiting room, feeling tired but thinking I'd done something useful. I came back in the office, sat down at my desk and rested my head on my arms. I must have dozed off because a sound caused my head to jerk up and it was no longer light outside.

The sound had been the throat-clearing of the individual standing in my doorway.

I tensed.

I hadn't turned any lights on in my office except the small desk lamp, so the room was mostly dark. As had become my careless habit, I hadn't closed or locked my office door after Midnight and Ronald left, thinking I myself would be leaving momentarily. Who knew how long I'd been sleeping?

I definitely had some karmic thing going on with doors.

The man standing in the entrance was very tall, but he stooped and his shoulders were rounded. The overhead light in the waiting room provided enough illumination for me to note that he had shoulder-length dark hair with a rapidly receding hairline. He wore a black suit, white shirt and skinny black tie. My visitor held his hands together at chest level and twisted them as if he was continually rolling a ball of clay or dough.

He edged forwards, still standing in the doorway, as if reluctant to enter. 'Are you the vampire doctor?'

CHAPTER 19

I rose from my desk, turned on another table lamp and walked slowly towards him, still straining to make out his shadowy features. My heart pounded and my stomach began to tingle gently. I rested my palm there while I determined if that familiar signal was simply information or a warning.

I kept a couple of feet of space between us. 'I'm Kismet Knight. I'm a psychologist.'

'Yes. You're the one. Can you help me?'

'I don't know.' *I don't even know what that means any more.*

Since I wasn't picking up any negative reaction from my sensing system and his uncomfortable, nervous gestures gave me the odd notion that he was more afraid of me than I was of him, I forced myself to relax. I pointed to the interior of the office. 'Would you like to come in?'

He nodded and lumbered – as if moving his body around involved concentrated effort – over to the couch and sat.

I hesitated for a moment and watched him.

So, should I leave the door open because I don't know anything about this fellow, or should I close it to give him privacy? Should I lock it so no one else can surprise me today? Which would also mean I'll have to quickly unlock it if I need to get out fast. I can't believe

I'm talking to myself about doors. In all my years of private prac-
tice, I've never given the door one thought. Never felt threatened. I
guess I can kiss those days goodbye.

I gently closed the door, leaving it unlocked, and eased
over to the dimmer switch on the wall. Rule number one:
Never make quick moves with a frightened client.

'Would you mind if I turn on a bit more light?'

He lifted his chin from where it had been resting nearly
on his chest and finally gave me a glimpse of his full face.
'I don't mind.'

I turned up the watts and claimed the chair nearest to
him.

He had a thin, cadaverous face dotted with deep pockmarks from a rough case of acne and lined with scars that
brought to mind the sewn-together monster in *Frankenstein.*
He sported a beak-like nose that took up lots of facial real
estate. His washed-out grey eyes were small and close together,
which made his dark unibrow stand out starkly against his
light skin.

He lowered his head again and twisted his hands in his
lap.

'How can I help you?' I asked.

'I heard that it's safe to talk to you. That you won't tell
anyone about us.'

'Who's "us"?' I sat back.

He raised his head, brows contracting in the centre. He
retracted his upper lip so I could see his long canines. 'Why,
vampires, of course.'

My breath caught and I straightened in my seat. 'Uh, yes,
certainly.'

Okay, Kismet. Don't panic. He's a vampire. A real vampire. You didn't think you'd be treating actual vampires, but you did ask them to come on down. That explains the stomach tingle.

I licked my suddenly dry lips. 'You can talk to me. How can I help?'

I hope this isn't the stupidest thing I've ever done.

The hand-twisting escalated and he lowered his head again. 'I have an unusual problem. You know that vampires drink blood, right?'

I cleared my throat, wondering if this was a trick question. 'Yes, I'm aware of that.'

This is so amazingly ludicrous. How can I sit here and talk with a vampire about drinking blood? Where am I supposed to put this in my brain? Is my intuition out to lunch? Am I in danger?

He swivelled his head around and scanned the room, as if he wasn't sure we were alone, then started, 'Well, I find the sight of blood disgusting.' His shoulders sagged and his chest became even more concave than it had been. He almost whispered, 'I avoid looking at it as much as I can. It's revolting.'

Holy shit, somebody help me. A vampire who doesn't like blood – is this a joke? Am I being secretly filmed for some reality show?

Suddenly I remembered Devereux's mind-reading tendencies and how he'd told me that all vampires are telepathic. Even if this was an individual of a different 'species' sitting across from me, I didn't want to have my rude thoughts announced through the vampire broadcast network. I needed to ask some questions and set some ground rules.

I held up my hand in a 'stop' gesture, and he brought his eyes to mine briefly before lowering them again. 'I'm sorry. I don't know your name.'

'Yes,' he said in a clear voice, 'I suppose you would need that. I'm Apollo.'

My face showed surprise before I could catch myself. 'Apollo? Like the Greek god?'

'The very same. I know I don't match my name very well – being decidedly un-godlike – but it was actually my last name when I was alive. Anthony Apollo. My human ancestors originally came from Greece. In the vampire world, catchy names are preferable to mundane, human-sounding ones, so I go by Apollo. Besides, it gives everyone quite a chuckle.' He smiled for the first time and relaxed his hands in his lap.

I returned his smile, pleased to see a lighter side of him, and hopeful that letting him into my office hadn't been yet another bad decision.

'So, Apollo, you probably know that working with vampires is a relatively new thing for me and I'm still finding my way around. I'd appreciate it if you could answer some questions. Would that be all right?'

He nodded. 'If I can.'

'I'd like you to tell me what powers you have. I mean, can you read my thoughts? If I look into your eyes, will I be entranced? That sort of thing.'

'I'm pathetically weak for a vampire. I haven't been one long – less than fifty years – and the vamp who turned me was rather insipid himself. You probably know a vampire is only as powerful as the one who created him. Add in my little "problem" and I can honestly say that I don't bring much to the vampire gene pool. But to answer your question, I can read some thoughts – specifically strong emotions. If you're worried about what you've been thinking so far, I can tell you it's all gone over my head. Same with the eyes. Although I can probably give you a headache if I really concentrate.'

I pressed my lips together, trying not to smile because I didn't know him well enough yet to decide if he'd be pleased I'd got his humour or offended that I found him amusing. In any case, I was impressed by his way with words. So many articulate vampires. Who knew?

'Well then, let's deal with the largest issue. You said that you've heard I'm safe, that you can talk to me. I want to know if I'm safe with you. How likely is it you'll become interested in my neck?'

Gee, Kismet, that was graceful.

He laughed awkwardly for several seconds, then surrendered to full-out laughter, deep lines creating bizarre shapes out of some of the pockmarks on his face, which appeared to be unaccustomed to that much frivolity.

'Forgive me for laughing, but if you'd heard the warning Devereux gave the coven about anyone harming you in any way, you wouldn't even ask the question. Trust me – no one wants to have Devereux as an enemy. I think you will find that most of us have tremendous self-control. That is one thing I can say about myself, so you can rest assured you are safe with me.'

Said the spider to the fly.

He pulled a tissue from the box on the nearby table and dabbed at his eyes. 'Ah, that felt very good. It's been quite a while since I laughed out loud.'

I gave him a few seconds to collect himself. 'I'm glad the laughing felt good. Perhaps we can encourage you to do more of it. And thank you for explaining about what Devereux said. I'm pleased to know I'm safe with you, otherwise we wouldn't be able to work together.'

Get a grip, Kismet. This isn't just another client you're setting boundaries with. This is a being who sucks the blood of people exactly like you. Is there no end to your political correctness?

'I noticed that your . . . er . . . fangs are descended. I understand that some vampires can will them in and out of their gums. Can you do that?'

'No, I don't have that kind of control yet, so my fangs remain in this position all the time.' He raised his hand to cover his mouth. 'I hope that doesn't concern or offend you?'

I shook my head. 'No, it doesn't.'

'That's good to know.' He lowered his hand again.

I wound a strand of my hair around my finger. 'Forgive the rudeness of this question, but I don't understand where vampires get the financial resources to come to a therapist. I'm pleased to speak with you this evening, but I usually require appointments in advance and some kind of payment arrangements. Will that be a difficulty?'

Aha! An escape hatch!

'No.' He smiled broadly and raised his eyes to mine. 'The members of Devereux's coven are well taken care of – money is the least of our concerns. I'll pay cash. The fee is irrelevant.'

Well, now, aren't those words that cause a therapist's heart to flutter?

'Thank you. Now let's talk about your issue. How does your disgust at the sight of blood complicate your . . . experience?'

'I'm afraid I'm going to have to be quite graphic. Are you sure you're willing to listen to this?'

I swallowed the lump that had formed in my throat. *No!* 'I'll do the best I can.'

I feel like a newbie, a brand-new therapist sitting with my first client, trying not to screw up. Trying to convince the bogeyman under the bed that there's no bogeyman under the bed.

'Since you're the vampire psychologist, you probably know there are people who enjoy hanging around vampires because they want to have their blood sucked. They crave it.'

Yuck.

I crossed my legs. 'Yes, I've heard that.'

He allowed his shoulders to visibly relax and inhaled a deep breath.

He's breathing. Do vampires breathe? Does Devereux? Why didn't I notice that small detail?

'So finding necks to suck on isn't my problem – people offer themselves to me all the time, and all I have to do is tuck in. As long as I can't actually *see* the blood, I'm fine. Like any other vampire, I love the taste of it, and the way it makes me feel is worth whatever it takes to get it. But it's impossible to suck blood without there being any . . . remains. Residue. Drops. Or, horror of horrors, actual uncontrolled bleeding. You see, sometimes in the midst of a feeding I can get carried away. It really is like having a whole-body orgasm, if you'll forgive my bluntness, and I've been known to enlarge the wound with my fangs when my body starts reacting to the . . . uh . . . stimulation. It can be an overwhelming experience. Anyway, if I see even one drop of blood I immediately throw up everything I just swallowed. Then there is *more* blood, which makes me retch until the muscles of my stomach scream with pain.' His eyes had gone wide and glassy as he told his story and he clasped his hands together so tightly that the white skin had become blue. He sat very stiff and straight.

The obvious terror the story stirred in him caused me to shift in my chair in anticipation of having to perform some vampire CPR. I'd seen clients with that expression on their faces as they described fears of being covered in snakes, eaten by a lion or burned alive. A phobia is a phobia.

Although I had to admit I wasn't really eager to put the vampire CPR option to the test.

I took a breath and sat back. I noticed that my own hands now clutched the arms of the chair so rigidly the veins stuck out. I consciously let go and wiggled my fingers to restore the circulation. 'That sounds very scary for you. I can totally understand why you'd avoid situations where you have to see blood. Do you remember the first time you had that reaction?'

'Uh, yes. Unfortunately, I do remember. I have to warn you that this might be difficult for you to hear.'

Uh-oh.

He paused and stared at me before he continued. I guess he was waiting for me to give an indication I was willing to proceed. I nodded.

'It was a few years after I became a vampire. Prior to the event I'm going to tell you about, I could swim in blood and it had no effect on me. It was the first time I drank from a child. A dying child. The little boy was near death from cancer and I heard him crying through the window. He said, "Please don't leave me." I don't know who he was talking to because no one was there. The child was all alone in that room, but I could see people moving around in the other parts of the house. He was all alone.'

He studied me silently for several seconds. Despite the controlled mask he'd made of his face, his eyes betrayed him by expressing the fear and self-loathing he usually kept locked away.

The words 'all alone' had been said with such raw misery that my heart ached. In that moment I understood how difficult it had been for him to tell his story to a therapist – or anyone. I had a clear intuitive sense that he was afraid I'd . . . what? Run out of the room? Condemn him for being what he was? Grab a stake and hammer and leap on him?

'I understand.' I gave him a gentle smile and nodded. 'He was all alone. Then what happened?'

'I waited until everyone else had gone to bed and then I went to the boy and held him in the dark. I don't know why I felt compelled to go to him – I usually have no interest in children. He was bleeding from his nose and mouth, and I licked the blood from his skin and rocked him. He began to remind me of myself when I was small. I could feel his pain building and as he was ready to leave his body, I drank him dry. At the last moment he put his arms around my neck and pleaded, "Don't leave me, Daddy." After his soul left his body, I stumbled out into the alley and threw up for the first time.'

Shit. Where do I begin?

I let him see the sympathy and compassion in my eyes and spoke softly. 'That's a heartbreaking story. Do you remember a time when you were small when you asked your daddy not to leave?'

He stared at me with horrified, pain-filled eyes. 'My father abandoned the family when I was five years old. I remember the night he packed to leave. I didn't understand why he had to go away – I was sure it was my fault, that I had done something wrong, something bad. I begged him to stay. He laughed and pushed me aside. That was the last time I ever saw him. The following years were very lonely.' After he finished sharing the memory, he frowned and stared down at his limp hands in his lap. A tear rolled down his cheek.

'Do you think my experience with that little boy has something to do with my blood phobia? Because of my own father?'

'I do, yes.'

He plucked another tissue from the box and wiped away the tears now streaming down his face.

'You must be right, because I already feel different. Would you mind if we ended our meeting for now? You've given me a lot to think about.'

'I wouldn't mind at all. You do have a lot to process.'

We both stood and he reached into the pocket of his jacket, pulled out an envelope and set it on the table. He sniffled a few times. 'I don't know what your fees are, but there should be enough in there to hold me for a while. Just let me know when you need more. I promise to make an appointment next time.'

He extended his hand and I took it. The coolness of his flesh surprised me and I caught my breath. He noticed my reaction and released my hand.

'I'm sorry. Since I don't drink enough blood, my skin is always cold. I hope I can do something about that. Thank you for today.'

'You're welcome. I look forward to our next session. You might want to consider hypnosis – perhaps we can gently uncover more of the memory that's causing the problem.'

He gave a quick nod.

I walked him to the door and opened it.

He blew his nose on a fresh tissue, and left.

I briefly considered sitting at my desk and writing up case notes for Apollo, but I was tired and wanted to go home. I'd write up the notes at home later with a glass of wine.

It wasn't likely I'd forget any of the details.

I thought about Apollo's story and the poor child who'd died in his arms. As sad as it was, I'd actually heard much worse from my human clients.

Who would've thought that a vampire would have the same issue as anyone else – the universal experience of a crappy childhood? Maybe vampires weren't really so different after all.

Yeah, right.

Chapter 20

It was a miracle. A quiet, drama-free evening.

The police escorted me out of the office and back to my townhouse without incident. After I wrote up my case notes for Apollo, I enjoyed a long, glorious, undisturbed shower, still wearing the necklace that wouldn't go away. I stood under the spray until the hot water cooled, which was saying something because I had a very large hot water tank. My skin had got satisfyingly pruned. I slathered myself with the exquisite and obscenely expensive skin moisturiser my friend regularly sent me from her European exploits.

I snuggled into my Sigmund Freud pyjamas – seriously, they're white silk with Sigmund's face splattered like black Rorschach inkblots all over the fabric. They were a hot novelty item at the last American Psychological Association convention in Las Vegas. If that wasn't cosy enough, I dug out my furry Miss Piggy slippers, complete with snout and curly tail, and covered up with my ever-present pink robe. I pulled my hair, which occasionally can feel very heavy, up into a pony-tail on the top of my head and let it cascade down around my shoulders in spiral curls.

I was in the midst of total and complete relaxation. Or total and complete denial, whichever you prefer.

I'd just poured a glass of liquid bliss in the form of white wine when the doorbell rang.

Cautious, I turned on the porch light and squinted through the peephole. Either there wasn't anyone there or my visitor was hiding from view. Or some other option I didn't even want to think about.

After the events of the last week, none of the possibilities was good news.

I chose the 'when in doubt, do nothing' approach and was rewarded by a repeat performance of the doorbell tones.

Leaving the chain engaged, I cracked open the door barely enough to scan a small area, which turned out to be not the least bit helpful. I still couldn't see anyone there. My intuition remained silent.

I was just about to close the door when it occurred to me I should ask an obvious question. 'Who's there?'

'It is I, Kismet – Devereux. Please let me in.'

Devereux? If it was Devereux, why was he ringing the doorbell? Why didn't he just pop in unannounced, uninvited, as always? Why didn't he simply swoop in like an intrusive bat and snatch me off to another creepy-crawly adventure?

'Why are you here?' I was batting a thousand with Questions for Dummies.

'I have come to make love to you.'

'What?' I croaked. Couldn't say I'd heard that one before.

Since I was still staring at the floor in front of my door I recognised the black leather boots that stepped into my line of vision. I raised my eyes but could only see more black and a flash of what might have been blond hair.

Apparently he could also see the floor on the other side of the door because he said, his voice oozing amusement, 'What are you wearing on your feet?'

I glanced down at the dual Miss Piggys and felt the need to defend them. Her?

'None of your business. What do you really want?' Although I had to admit I'd rather enjoyed the previous answer.

'I spoke the truth. I have come to make love to you. Please open the door.'

How arrogant! And you just assume that's okay with me? That I'm just going to open the door and make another deal with the devil? That I'm even remotely interested in having sex with you after our last trip down the rabbit-hole?

'Hold on. This is crazy. My street is filled with cops and reporters. Why don't they see you?'

'I have created an illusion in their minds. When they look at the porch, they see only what they expect to see.'

'Uh, huh. Likely story. How do I know it's really you? You usually materialise out of thin air.'

'As you wish.'

I heard that familiar little *pop* sound, felt a rush of air and suddenly knew he was behind me.

I closed the door and turned, hands on my hips. 'Hey! That wasn't an invitation!'

A dazzling smile spread across his face. 'You forget I have that handy little mind-reading ability.' He bowed from the waist and his platinum veil of hair flowed forwards then back as he straightened. Dressed in a variation of his usual leather-god outfit, he was a feast for the eyes. 'I rang the doorbell because I thought you would prefer me to enter your home the normal human way. I understand you are weary of the drama that has taken over your life. I do not wish to contribute any further to your discomfort.'

He brought his hands around from behind him. They held a huge bouquet of pink roses and a box of chocolates.

'Gifts for you, my love.'

He leaned in and brushed my lips lightly with his. The familiar, delicious scent of him filled my nostrils and my lips instinctively puckered in anticipation of more of the same.

Instead he burst out laughing. 'You have pigs on your feet!'

He thrust the roses and box of chocolates into my hands, scooped me up into his arms and walked us over to the couch. As soon as he was seated with me on his lap, he reached over and lifted my feet, inspecting the colourful porcine coverings.

'How interesting.' The longer he stared at the fluffy piggy slippers, the harder he laughed. He pinched the snout between his thumb and first finger and pulled on the tail.

'Hey! Are you actually going to tell me you never heard of Miss Piggy?' I said. 'If so, your contemporary education is seriously lacking. When I was young, she was one of the best-known television and movie characters. Kids loved her.' I *loved her. She was so audacious – everything I wasn't.*

'I see. Television.' He grinned. 'Let me ask you this – why would a vampire spend time doing human activities? How could those things possibly hold interest for such alien creatures as the undead? We might share the world with mortals, but not your reality. Not to be rude, of course, but most of the programmes I have seen on modern television leave much to be desired. Why sit and watch pretend people and situations instead of creating an exciting life? There is so much to know and discover in the world. I have never understood the human tendency to be passive observers.' He waved his hand towards my feet. 'But I must admit that your Miss Piggy sounds charming. I look forward to further education. There were no such things when I was a child.'

'Well, maybe I'll get you your own pair.'

'I would be honoured.' His eyes twinkled with amusement.

He was right about people spending too much time in front of televisions, as well as computers and other media. It had never occurred to me that his 'species' might be different in every way – living a parallel but separate existence. As annoying as it was to be laughed at, something about his mirth was infectious and I found myself chuckling in spite of myself.

Once again, whatever resolve I'd built up against Devereux had leaked away in direct proportion to the number of minutes I spent gazing at his perfect face. It was a waste of time for me to argue that I was immune to his charm, or his eyes or whatever it was that caused my normal inhibitions to catch the first plane out of town. For the first time, it occurred to me that I genuinely liked him. He had an adorable little-boy quality.

At some point I must have put the flowers and chocolates on the coffee table because my arms were free to ensnare his neck. Which quickly led to me being flat on my back in my Freud PJs and my piggy slippers with an absurdly gorgeous vampire on top of me, attached at the lips.

So much for a quiet, relaxing evening.

We made out on the couch like teenagers.

As always with Devereux, I couldn't stop touching him, couldn't run my fingers through his long, silky, aromatic hair enough. Couldn't feast on his lips even remotely enough. Couldn't imagine anything more important than having him inside me.

Even counting my close call with Alan, I hadn't technically had intercourse for two years and the muscles in my vagina contracted in gleeful, moist anticipation.

He lifted his warm mouth from mine long enough to whisper, 'Will you invite me to your bed, my love?'

Geez, the guy's voice should be a registered weapon. It could take you down in three seconds.

'What happened to all the mind reading? I've been sending out the welcome committee for the last twenty minutes.'

'I know.' He raised himself up just enough so I could see his pleased expression. 'But it is important to me to hear the words from your own sweet lips.' He somehow managed to lift himself off the couch in a flowing motion while scooping me up at the same time. 'Shall we?'

He carried me up the stairs, the twin Miss Piggys bobbing up and down. But my mind was no longer on footwear. In fact, my entire brain was focused on the fastest way to get us both naked.

We entered my bedroom and Devereux paused at the foot of my bed.

'You have not changed the sheets since you shared your

bed with Alan. I can smell him. I wish to be the only presence here with you.'

He set me down and stood in front of me.

I started to explain that I hadn't 'officially' had sex with Alan and there really wasn't any part of him left behind, but Devereux gently pressed a finger to my lips, ending the flow of words.

'None of that matters. Nothing that happened before me matters. I simply wish to make love to you right now in your own bed on fresh sheets. Yes?'

He removed his black leather duster and threw it in a chair in the corner.

Enjoying the view of the physique that'd been hidden under the coat, I moved over to him and lightly kissed his lips. 'Definitely yes.'

I opened a brand-new set of silk sheets I'd had for a long time but never used, while Devereux stripped off the old bedding.

Quite an efficient team, we smoothed on the new sheets, watching each other with hungry eyes.

'Do you have candles?' he asked.

Uh, did I? I thought for a moment and remembered which box in the closet I'd stashed them in. I wouldn't tell him that I'd only bought them in case the electricity went out and I needed emergency light. I was trying to learn to keep my unromantic, nerdy explanations to myself. At least under certain conditions.

While I was in the closet I stepped out of the Miss Piggy slippers and put them back in their special place, next to my Glenda the Good Witch sandals.

Okay. So I did let my inner child out sometimes.

He took the candles and the holders I'd also retrieved, placed them on the nightstands on either side of the bed and stood back, appreciating his handiwork. He pointed a finger at each of the candles and the wicks burst into flame.

He smiled at me and said out loud what I'd been thinking. 'Indeed – more parlour tricks.'

I turned off the light switch on the wall and basked in the lovely glow of the candles. The soft illumination was the perfect setting for Devereux. His eyes sparkled, his hair was a shining radiance and his skin assumed the hues of the candlelight.

He stepped over to the window and closed the blinds, then circled back around to the door and silently sealed it. Gliding over to me, he gently released my hair from the ponytail and eased the long curls down over my breasts.

'Your hair is beautiful.' He nestled his face in it and inhaled the fragrance, then ran his fingers through it. 'You are beautiful. I had given up hope of ever finding you. And now you are here. Now you are mine.'

'I'm yours? What does that mean?'

'It means we belong to each other. We always have. I want to share every part of myself with you, and I want to know every aspect of you. I am so happy you have finally come to me. I have been lost without you.'

I started to question his assumptions, and he silenced me with a kiss.

He reluctantly pulled away and leaned against the wall to balance himself while he removed his boots. He pulled his shirt off over his head in one slow, elegant motion.

Vampire Chippendales.

Even though I'd seen him without his shirt before, the effect in the candlelight was almost overwhelming. The muscles of his shoulders, arms and abdomen were perfectly chiselled, a magnificent work of art in flesh and bone. I started to wonder what the odds were of a human being so exquisitely built, then remembered he wasn't human. Not even close.

But that didn't matter. In a very short, intense time period, I'd gone from thinking Devereux was mentally ill – an unfortunate having psychotic delusions about being a vampire – to waiting breathlessly for that very same vampire to fill me with what was already making its presence known inside his tight leather trousers.

I splayed my hands on his chest, relishing the firm warmth of him, and moved close enough to take one of his nipples into my mouth. He moaned and relaxed his head back, embracing me with his strong arms.

I started to unbutton the waistband of his trousers and he covered my hand with his.

'Wait. We must remove your shirt first.'

Vampire rules? I didn't ask why. He lifted my hair back behind my shoulders and unbuttoned my pyjama top. Letting the slippery silk fall away, he used his fingers to guide the fabric from my shoulders and down my arms. He bent and slid his face over my breasts, taking one nipple at a time into his mouth with a gentle sucking motion. He cupped both breasts in his hands and laid tiny kisses all over them before using his tongue to harden my nipples to painful, throbbing points.

He straightened, lifted the pentagram necklace and brought it to his lips. He kissed the centre of the circular design then replaced it, all the time gazing into my eyes.

I already ached for him, and couldn't imagine being able to hold out much longer. My knees were barely functional.

He stepped away and studied me, the expression on his face reflecting the maelstrom of feelings and desires he couldn't hide.

He caressed my breasts again and said, 'You are very lush for such a slender woman. In all my eight hundred years, yours are the most magnificent breasts I have ever seen. I shall never tire of touching them, of sucking them.'

I'd say he hasn't got out much if my breasts are the cream of the crop, but that's probably not true. I'll just enjoy the ride.

He demonstrated as I fisted my hands in his hair. After a few delicious seconds, he kissed his way back to my lips.

Sliding his hands into the elastic waistband of my pyjama bottoms, he eased the material down my hips, leaving my white cotton bikini panties in place. He stroked and massaged me, running his hands up my back and down to the mounds of my ass, pulling my lower body tight against his hard, thick erection.

My fingers found their way back to the button on the waistband of his trousers and successfully opened it. The zipper slid down easily and I quickly discovered that Devereux was an *au naturel* kind of guy.

That realisation was outrageously arousing for me, and I enthusiastically shimmied his trousers down his hips, releasing the unexpectedly large organ jutting out from a thatch of blond curls.

I had a momentary thought about the myth that a man's feet or hands are correlated with the size of his penis. In Devereux's case, his normal-sized artistic hands and average-looking feet gave no indication of what had been sequestered away behind that zipper.

I sank to my knees, still pulling down the leather trousers, and gently nudged him to sit on the edge of the bed. I raised my mouth to his, ran my tongue along his lips, then kissed him while one hand stroked his warm, hard length. He moved rhythmically against my hand, moaning softly. I slid my finger up to the drops of liquid oozing from the opening, then stroked him again.

We used our tongues to taste and explore each other. I felt his fangs extend as I carefully avoided their needle-sharp tips. Running my tongue up and down the length of his fangs seemed to have the same effect as my hand on his erection.

I pulled away from his lips and kissed my way down his chest and his stomach until I reached his hard length and took it in my mouth. His skin was velvety soft over the taut muscle.

He gasped and held my head between his hands, moving gently to show me what he liked. I used my lips and tongue to taste every part of him, to drive him mad with desire. I was a quick study apparently, and he soon cried out and lifted my head from his groin.

'If you continue to do that I cannot hold back, and I wish for us to share our first orgasm together while I am inside you.'

Aching with desire, I was more than ready for him. He

lifted me up onto the bed as I kicked off the last clothing barrier between us.

Both completely naked now, we knelt on the bed, faced each other, and built the anticipation.

His body was magnificent, long, lean and muscular, with smooth skin and perfect features. The light-blond hair that trailed down his abdomen to his crotch was soft and slightly darker than his long platinum mane. Rising out of that silk was an erection that belonged on a statue of a Greek god. Or a Celtic god. A Druid god? I still wasn't sure which part of Europe Devereux came from originally.

We reached for each other at the same time and I palmed his buttocks, exploring the firm muscles there as I pulled him tightly against me.

We embraced and kissed passionately, taking the joining of our lips deeper and deeper until it felt as if we were one being – merged.

He spoke that strange, musical language in my mind, a soft melody of words and spaces. Even though I didn't understand what he was saying, the sounds felt right, as if my body remembered them in some mysterious way.

He gently turned me and guided me down onto the bed, bringing his mouth to my nipples again while his finger slid into the wet heat between my legs.

'I love that you are so wet for me,' he whispered in my mind. 'You make me feel alive.'

Using one fingertip in a featherlight movement, he caressed my clitoris, making little circular motions that caused me to arch my body and spread my legs wider, before he moved that clever finger up inside me. Then he added a second finger while still stroking me with his thumb. A wave of something powerful built within me and I made primal noises, instinctively moving my hips in time with the rhythm of his fingers.

I moaned and fisted my hands in his hair, lifting his head. 'Devereux, please – I want you inside me.'

He raised his mouth from my nipple, brought his lips near mine and whispered, 'Inside your body and your heart.'

Eagerly, I reached down and guided his thickness into my opening, wrapping my legs around his waist at the same time to take him deeper.

If I hadn't been so wet his size might have been uncomfortable, but under the circumstances it was as if we were made for each other. One lock with a perfect key.

I don't know which one of us groaned louder, but he swallowed the sounds with his mouth on mine. Still kissing, he thrust himself inside me, long, slow, deep strokes. His controlled movements drove me mad with desire. I didn't know if all eight-hundred-year-old vampires had such skill in lovemaking, but this one certainly did. I'm not sure if I screamed or only wanted to.

Then he raised himself up, grabbed my hands and lifted them over my head, holding my wrists. His mesmerising voice became lower-pitched and husky, sending waves of chills over my skin.

'Do you remember the moment in the club when you asked me to use my eyes to join with you? When we became one consciousness?'

I didn't want to talk. I wanted his mouth on mine, his hands in my hair, his hips thrusting against me. But his description of the passion that fired in me that night brought me back to the delicious memory and I had a body rush, causing me to gasp. The muscles of my vagina tightened around him involuntarily and he reacted with a deeper thrust and an intake of breath.

He smiled, obviously aware of my memory and the mental chatter. Or maybe it was just because what we were doing felt so very, very good.

'I will take that as a yes.'

I closed my eyes and mumbled something that could have been interpreted as an affirmative.

'Open your eyes, my love. Let me show you that everything before this moment was simply a small taste of what is possible.'

I opened my eyes, connected with his, and reality as I knew it faded away.

My world became the blue-green of his eyes, a spinning, shining universe of bodiless yet extraordinarily physical sensations – as if the pleasure volume on every nerve ending had been turned up while simultaneously having no awareness of being physical at all.

Floating in a stream of consciousness.

I hadn't done any experimentation with hallucinogenic drugs so I didn't have actual experience to base anything on, but from what I'd read, I was in the middle of an altered state. The vampire version of an LSD trip.

Time had no meaning, so I didn't know how long we'd been there. His penis still moved inside me as we kissed wildly. It could have been hours. Or seconds.

Devereux and I communicated purely telepathically now

and as the orgasm built inside us, it was impossible to tell if the wave of pleasure had a specific starting place, or if we'd simply become the wave.

We'd fallen into each other's eyes, and nothing else mattered.

Just as the peak of the orgasm began, Devereux pierced my neck with his fangs.

I gasped but there was no pain, only intense, reverberating pleasure.

Pleasure that was off the scale.

I screamed as wave after wave of bliss washed over me. Every muscle in my body – I think it was my body – contracted in ecstasy.

Somewhere in the midst of my own release I felt Devereux spasm inside me, his mouth still at my neck, his silky hair flowing across my breasts.

He brought his lips back to mine and kissed me with profound tenderness, our souls merged as completely as our bodies. I tasted the sweet, coppery tang of my own blood on his tongue and found myself savouring the experience. I sucked on his tongue and ran mine over his teeth, wanting to take in more of the salty essence.

It occurred to me briefly that enjoying the taste of blood probably wasn't a good thing, but I was still too lost in the rapture of the moment to care.

A soft groan from Devereux brought me back to sufficient awareness to notice that I'd been sucking on his fang, which he obviously enjoyed. His erection expanded inside me, apparently eager to continue, and I lifted my hips to take him deeper.

In another of his amazing seamless movements he raised himself to his knees, drawing me with him, and held me by my ass, our bodies still joined. We locked eyes as he pressed me back against the headboard, one of his hands still underneath me, the other braced against the wall.

As he pounded into me I heard a voice repeating, 'Yes, yes, yes,' and discovered it was mine.

I tightened my legs and arms around him. He held me effortlessly, as if I weighed nothing. He'd told me that vampires possessed unnatural strength, but I hadn't had much personal evidence until then. I think he could have held me there, giving me one orgasm after another, until I cried for mercy.

Which I finally did.

I clung to him as he emptied himself into me yet again, only then allowing him to slide out of me. Still straddling his lap, I snuggled into his warm arms and let myself be gently rocked.

He whispered lovely words, in English, French and what might have been Gaelic, and stroked my hair.

At some point I must have fallen asleep because he swept his finger gently across my cheek and said softly, 'I must go, my love – the dawn approaches.'

My eyes flew open and I noticed I was tucked into my bed, and Devereux was fully dressed. He sat next to me and brushed a lock of hair away from my face.

'For eight hundred years I have waited for this night. I am very much in love with you. I do not expect you to return my feelings right away – I understand that this is all new to you. I only ask that you give me a chance to win your heart.'

He leaned over, brushed my lips with his and vanished.

I fell back asleep with the lyrics of Heart's classic 'Magic Man' flowing through my mind.

CHAPTER 21

The screeching of the alarm clock dragged me, kicking and screaming, back to the land of the living. I groaned, rolled over and turned off the annoying siren.

I'd had the most amazing dream – or, to be more accurate, I was in the middle of it when the damn alarm went off. I knew I had to get up, but it was so tempting just to lie there and revel in the memories from the previous night and the remnants of the nocturnal fantasy.

In the dream I'd been with Devereux again, but this time we were outside, in the sunlight, on top of a beautiful mountain surrounded by other peaks. I could actually feel the breeze blowing through my hair and across my body. Which was naked, by the way.

As was Devereux's. Yum.

The muscles of my vagina contracted as I remembered Devereux, stretched out like an alabaster nature god in the vivid green grass with me on top of him, riding that impressive erection as we both screamed with pleasure.

It felt so real – the sun shining on Devereux's pale skin, the texture of the grass beneath my knees and lower legs as I straddled him, the fragrance of evergreen wafting in the air.

After sharing another cosmic orgasm I collapsed on his firm chest and felt his arms close around me as his lips passionately reclaimed mine.

With another of his smooth moves, he flipped me over so I was on my back in the grass and kissed his way down my body. Faster than I could see, he bent my knees, opened my legs, and began to lick my clitoris. His tongue was soft, relentless, and had homed in on the perfect spot. Impossibly, within seconds I felt another powerful wave of ecstasy building. After he pushed me over the edge, he angled his mouth ever so slightly and gently sank his fangs into the soft lip next to my clit. There was a fleeting sting as his needle-sharp canines pierced the tender skin and he began to suck, but that was quickly drowned out by the mother of all orgasms.

Waves of intense pleasure built, one upon the next, as I screamed words in a language I didn't know. Just when I thought I would go mad if the sensations didn't stop, he ran his tongue over the tiny punctures, kissed me there and sat up, a wicked smile on his amazing face.

That's when the infernal alarm clock rudely interrupted and forced me to resurface into consensus reality.

Damn if it wasn't the best dream ever. Even thinking about it gave me a hot body rush.

I shut down my newly reawakened libido with a sigh.

Back to the real world.

All it took was the simple act of sitting up to remind me that my physical body as well as my dream body had undergone quite a workout only a few hours before.

That realisation birthed a silly grin.

I guess it could have been the fact that, after two years,

I'd been royally pleasured by the best lover I'd ever had. Magnificently shagged. Awesomely boinked. Spectacularly screwed. We'd surely broken the world record for the number of orgasms a couple could have and still be alive to talk about it.

Well, one of us was alive to talk about it, anyway.

I sat back against the very same headboard that had been witness to the athletic portion of the performance and sighed happily, still unable to stop grinning.

It occurred to me that I'd never asked Devereux where he went during the daylight hours. Did he sleep in a coffin? Maybe 'sleep' was the wrong word. But he'd told me he dreamed, and how could he dream if he didn't sleep? How could he dream if he just died when the sun came up?

Now that I'd actually accepted the ludicrous idea that not only did vampires exist but I was having a mad, passionate sexual relationship with the Grand Pooh-bah, I realised I was very curious. If I was going to counsel real vampires, I needed to ask lots more questions and get much better answers. It was important that I didn't simply shift from a total refusal to believe anything paranormal to a complete acceptance of any and all vampire weirdness. That was just too extreme for me, and not in the least scientific.

I threw the covers back, heaved my legs over the side of the bed, stood and attempted to stretch. All the major muscle groups in my body ganged up on me at once and started whining. If it hadn't been for the fact that I had a full client load for the next twelve hours, I'd have considered diving back into the bed and pulling the covers over my head. With any luck, I'd fall back asleep and have the mountain dream again.

Instead I promised the complaining muscles a long hot shower and I propelled myself in that direction.

I hoped I'd be able to wipe the goofy grin off my face when I got to my office. On the other hand, it might do my clients good to have their notions about me confounded, to help them realise that change really could happen. Even to me.

Nerd Woman joins the twenty-first century.

Walking to the bathroom reminded me again what happened to muscles if you didn't use them. The area between my legs was tender and sore, which was to be expected considering the size of the object that'd been in there.

I started the shower, adjusted the water temperature and stepped in. The soothing water flowed down my body, miraculously easing all the tight muscles while relaxing me into a boneless state. I washed my hair, then soaped the rest of me. The lathering came to an abrupt halt when I reached the area between my legs. Not only was it tender, but the soap caused a sudden burning pain.

'Ow, dammit! When did that happen?'

Not sure who I was asking, I put the soap down and felt around the sore spot with my fingers. Beyond verifying that it was indeed uncomfortable, the examination didn't give me much additional information.

Finding wounds on my body that weren't supposed to be there had started to be a regular occurrence. It didn't take a psychic to figure out that the feeling of déjà vu I experienced was because I'd been through this same routine just a few days earlier, thanks to Bryce.

Bryce. How weird that an entire vampire war had started over a broken heart. Not to mention the fact that the vampires in question supposedly *had* no functioning hearts. No heart-beats unless they chose to have them. I guess love, or in this case *unrequited* love, transcended life and death. Bryce wanted to destroy Devereux and the coven because he was a blood-sucker scorned. The therapist in me wondered if Bryce had ever been sane, even as a human. The idea of creating so much drama and trauma over a spurned relationship struck me as dysfunctional, but in the big picture, what else did vampires have to do to fill the millennia? Since he saw me as a threat to his *happy-ever-after* with Devereux I doubted he would lose interest in his vendetta before anyone else got hurt.

Finished with my shower, I towelled off and grabbed a hand mirror from the top of the vanity. Angling it so I could examine my nether regions, I ran a fingertip gingerly along the tender skin, but still couldn't make out anything in particular.

Maybe we'd just rubbed the poor little thing raw with our callisthenics.

But when I pulled back the lip, clearly visible on the inside were two not-so-tiny holes floating in a sea of angry red skin.

'What the hell?'

I reached over, opened the medicine cabinet above the sink and retrieved the tube of antiseptic salve that I'd used for my last bite wound.

Dotting it carefully on the sore spots, I struggled to remember any time during the night when Devereux had bitten anything but my neck.

Instinctively I lifted my hand up to my throat, checking for evidence of what I clearly remembered, but I felt only smooth skin. I raised the mirror, shifted my neck around to display all sides, then shook my head.

Nothing. No sign of the sensuous nibble. Not even a pink spot.

Either I'd blacked out and missed a very erotic chapter in our book of carnal knowledge, or something altogether different had happened.

Then, as if someone switched on a movie, I remembered the last scene of the mountain dream. The labial feast.

'It was not a dream,' floated through my mind in a familiar voice.

'Devereux?' I jumped up and ran into my bedroom.

'We were in another dimension and I was careless. My heartfelt apologies, my love. I will heal your wound tonight.'

'Dever—' I almost got his name out before I realised the voice was coming from inside my head. Or at least I was pretty sure that no one else could hear it.

At least, not anyone I could see.

I'll never get used to this.

I paused for a moment, waiting for any remaining astral proclamations, but the voice remained silent.

Well, that's great. Now even my dreams leave scars.

I didn't know whether I was being open-minded or stupid, but one thing was certain: nothing surprised me any more.

Well, almost nothing. With help from the police, I made it out of my house and into my office later that morning. As soon as I stepped off the elevator, I knew something was wrong. Not only did my intuitive radar system send up a warning, but my regular senses shifted into overdrive. I'd learned from recent and past experience not to ignore those kinds of signals.

I walked slowly along the short hallway between the elevators and my waiting room, steeling myself for what I'd find. That usually closed door was now open and a horrendous stench wafted from my inner office.

I set my purse and briefcase against the wall opposite the entryway, gingerly pushed the waiting room door open with one finger and discovered that the main door was not only open, it was off its hinges, lying on the floor in front of my desk.

All the chairs and tables in the waiting area had been overturned, some of them broken, and everything was coated with a dark reddish-brown substance. On the wall someone had scrawled, in childish print in that same horrible colour, 'i will not suffer a witch to live' and 'you will be washed in the blood'.

As bad as that was, my intuition told me it was only the prelude to the main concerto.

Holding my breath, I picked my way through the debris to the doorway of my office and surveyed the scene.

Compared to the condition of this larger room, the mess in the waiting area had been child's play. Perhaps that wasn't an inaccurate diagnosis of the perpetrator's developmental level.

I shuddered out the breath I'd been holding.

Someone had taken a knife – clearly a honking huge knife – to all the couches and chairs, slashing wide gashes through every cushion. Then, just to make sure the destruction was complete, the furniture had been tumbled over and liberally daubed with more of that reddish-brown stain.

All the files in my locked filing cabinet had been shredded and strewn around the room. Some appeared to have been partially burned, which explained one small portion of the odour, and the metal file cabinet itself was oddly twisted, as if hands had pulled it apart. The drawers in my desk were open and they, along with the top of the desk and my computer, were saturated with what could only be sticky-looking pools of congealed blood. The stunted artist hadn't spared the walls in this room either. Scrawled across all four were various obscenities, threats, and a few phrases I vaguely registered as coming from religious sources.

Actually, I recognised everything that was written on the walls because I'd heard it all before. Brother Luther had screamed every word of it at me in one or other of the enraged messages I'd saved in my voicemail system.

As astounding as the damage was in both rooms, I still couldn't figure out the source of the ghastly smell. Had Brother Luther broken into my office and left a dead animal? Excrement? If it had been him, he must be a very large, strong man. Or maybe he brought somebody with him. In any case, the destruction was violent, thorough and personal. I wasn't sure how much good it would have done, but I should've told the police, or at least Alan, about the telephone threats right after they started. Maybe Brother Luther, if he really was responsible, had done something similar before. He might even have a police record. Hindsight is always crystal-clear.

I scanned the room again for the cause of the smell and noticed that the door, which had been torn off its hinges, was lying strangely on the floor – not flat but at an angle, as if there was something underneath.

My stomach tightened and my heart pounded. My brain gave me a high-speed presentation of all the worst-case scenarios I could imagine.

I moved slowly and carefully through the debris, not wanting to disturb any more of the evidence than necessary, and knelt down near the dislodged door. A wave of nausea hit me. I lifted up one corner, which was all it took for me to discover the source of the smell.

A slender young male lay underneath – deathly white, clearly no longer alive, and drenched in blood. I guessed he'd been there for several hours.

Startled, I pushed the door off of him and jumped when it bumped into a still-upright end table, sending the lamp that had miraculously survived the onslaught crashing to the floor.

I was still staring at the unidentified young man when I heard someone gasp. 'Dr Knight! What happened? Are you okay? Oh my gawd! That's Eric!'

I turned so quickly I lost my balance and went down hard on my butt in a puddle of thick blood.

Midnight and Ronald had scheduled another joint appointment and they were right on time. We all stared at each other for a few endless seconds, and then Ronald stepped forward, offering his hand.

'Let me help you up, Dr Knight.'

Midnight had locked both hands over her mouth and was standing rigid, eyes wide.

I accepted Ronald's help to rise and moved away from the

young man Midnight had identified as Eric. The apprentice who'd crafted the little knives for blood-swapping.

After helping me up, Ronald went back to Midnight. He put his arm around her and stroked her hair, but she didn't respond.

I noticed a fine trembling in her body. One of the first signs of shock.

'Ronald, would you help Midnight out to the hallway, please? I need to go out there and make some phone calls.' I kept my voice as calm and normal as possible.

He understood what I hadn't said and pushed Midnight gently in the direction of the door, holding her by the shoulders to keep her from stumbling or tripping over the chaos on the floor.

Once out of direct sight of her friend's body, Midnight lowered her hands away from her mouth and began to cry silently, her head on Ronald's shoulder.

I left them huddled together long enough to retrieve my purse and fetch my cell phone. The expressions on their traumatised young faces were heart-wrenching, and I wished they'd been late for their appointment – that I'd been able to meet them out in the hall instead of involving them in more psychotic madness.

But ruminating about what should have been didn't do any of us any good. I joined them and rested my hand on Midnight's arm. 'I'm sorry, Midnight, but the police are going to want to talk to you and Ronald since you knew Eric. Why don't you sit down and relax until they arrive?'

They both nodded and lowered themselves to the floor.

I leaned back against the wall and closed my eyes, taking

a moment to sort out my emotions. Oddly though, instead of feeling frightened or upset, I felt calm. I'd been making the assumption that all of the terrible things that had happened – Emerald Addison's death, my kidnapping, and everything else – had something to do with the vampire community. I'd finally started to believe there were super-natural forces at work, that somehow the vampires were involved. It was almost a relief to come to the realisation I had a common-or-garden-variety psychopath on my hands. No doubt this serial killer had abusive childhood experiences, linked with religiously instigated guilt and shame. I'd hazard a guess he wasn't fond of women either. Classic. Textbook. A mentally defective, wounded child acting out in the most hideous ways.

Now *that* was something I knew how to deal with.

How convenient that he seemed to have taken a personal interest in me.

I walked down by the elevator and dialled 911 on my cell phone. I explained there'd been a death in my office and returned to the other end of the hallway where Midnight and Ronald were sitting to wait for the police to arrive.

The calm before the storm.

I glanced down and noticed my clothes were trashed. Again.

My bloody cream-coloured trouser-suit was a miserable reminder of the night I'd spent in the mausoleum. Since I didn't have any spare clothes to change into, I had little choice but to ignore the psychic flashbacks and distract myself by thinking about ways the police could use me as bait to catch the killer. By the time they arrived, I'd concocted some creative and audacious scenarios in which Super Psychologist would save the day.

I heard the *dings* of the elevators just before the doors opened and I instinctively moved a few steps in that direction. A dozen uniformed officers swarmed out, followed by a forensics unit.

At the tail end, preceded by heavy footsteps, came a familiar voice. 'Well, well, Dr Knight. We meet again.'

Lieutenant Bullock strolled over to me, clasped her hands behind her back and walked around me in a circle. The edges of her mouth were quirked in a grim sort of smile. She raised her eyebrows when she noticed the large, messy bloodstain on my trousers.

'Up to your ass in blood once more, eh? Or should I say twice more, since I last saw you? I heard about the cemetery deal, and your influential friend making sure you didn't have to go through normal channels. Oh yes. Why so surprised? I make a point of keeping track of "interesting" people, and you, Dr Knight, strike me as very ... "interesting". Funny how often death follows you around.'

She ran her fingers through her short greying hair and shifted her attention to Midnight, then Ronald, then back to me. She pointed at the couple huddled on the floor. 'I'll send some officers to begin their interviews and to get preliminary details from you. Then, after I do my job inside, I'll be back.' Her smile brightened. 'I'm going to handle your statement. Personally.' She took a couple of steps towards my waiting room door, then partially turned, her face devoid of emotion. 'Don't go anywhere.'

She pivoted and strode into my office, bellowing out orders to the officers already inside.

Surprise in his voice, Ronald said, 'Wow, that policewoman really doesn't like you, Dr Knight. What did you do to piss her off?'

I almost responded by saying, 'What do you think I did to piss her off?' but caught myself before giving the automatic therapy reply to a patient's question.

Instead, I shrugged. 'I honestly don't know. Something about me bothered her from the first moment she laid eyes on me. Maybe I remind her of someone else.'

'Or maybe she knew you in a past life?'

I turned towards the voice and was grateful and relieved to see Alan approaching. He covered the short distance between us quickly and put his arm around my shoulders.

'I couldn't believe my ears when I heard the address of the homicide on my scanner. What happened? Did one of your clients go berserk?'

'No. Someone broke in and destroyed my office.'

He tightened his grip on my shoulders. 'Well, your trusty FBI agent is always here for you. Who died?'

The shoulder resting against him relaxed. 'A friend of Midnight's. A boy. One of the other vampire apprentices.'

'This is a vampire thing?' He unceremoniously dropped his arm and sprinted off into my office, leaving me with my mouth hanging open.

So much for being here for me.

I sighed and backed up against the wall to wait for whatever Lieutenant Bullock had in store.

*

True to her word, she sent officers out to interview Midnight and Ronald, and a detective to talk to me.

The detective politely asked questions that I only had one answer for: *I don't know*. With each similar response from me, he appeared more frustrated.

I couldn't blame him for being sceptical. This was the third police interrogation I'd participated in during the past week and even I had trouble believing that I had no worthwhile information to share.

How had I managed to involve myself in so many situations where I felt like a chess piece being moved around on some cosmic board by unseen hands?

Somebody had obviously delivered the blood-covered material in the manila envelope. All I did was open it and report it to the police. To the best of my knowledge, I hadn't purposely lost my memory, strolled away from The Crypt and crawled into a disgusting mausoleum to take a nap in an occupied coffin. And unless I'd been abducted by aliens, causing me to have missing time, all I had done this morning was come to my office.

All the same, I realised my protestations of unaware innocence might be wearing pretty thin for the authorities right about then.

Finally Lieutenant Bullock emerged from my office, motioned to the ever-patient detective who'd continued to rephrase his questions in ways he thought might elicit additional information from me, and they shared an animated whispered conversation.

The detective ambled over to the officers still questioning

Midnight and Ronald. Lieutenant Bullock approached me, frowning.

'I'd like a private word, Dr Knight. Is there a lounge area or break room on this floor?'

I'd prepared myself for many possible opening lines from her, but that one took me completely by surprise, which must have been written all over my face.

'There's a small lounge area inside the women's toilets. Will that do?' I pointed past the elevators.

She launched herself down the hallway, indicating I should follow.

When we reached the toilet door she paused, pivoted and called to a uniformed officer standing in the hall, 'Greenfield!' She beckoned him over with a peremptory hand gesture, then pointed to the floor at her feet. 'Stand here. No one comes in.'

We waited while the officer dutifully stationed himself outside the bathroom.

Lieutenant Bullock pushed open the door, held it while I entered and surveyed the small lounge area.

My curiosity had morphed into nervousness when she'd assigned the officer to stand guard at the door. At least that was what it appeared he was doing. She hadn't mentioned it specifically, but if no one could come in, it wasn't likely I could leave without obstruction either.

'Sit,' she ordered, pointing to a red leather couch.

I sat. The dried blood on the seat of my trousers crunched like cardboard.

She paced in front of me for a few seconds, her hands clasped in back, then stopped. She assumed a military-style stance, feet so many inches apart, shoulders back.

The situation forced me totally out of my depth, and out of my comfort zone. I had absolutely no idea what we were doing in the women's bathroom, or why she'd taken me aside. I wasn't sure where to look so I focused on her sturdy black shoes.

When she finally spoke, her voice quiet, I met her eyes. 'This is awkward for me because it flies in the face of everything I believe in. Not only am I about to give police information to a civilian, but I also intend to raise an issue that will sound crazy and might reflect poorly on me as a law-enforcement professional. Although being a psychologist, I suspect you're used to having people tell you questionable stories.' She was silent again for a few seconds, then loudly cleared her throat. 'Stevens has been spinning some wild yarns about vampires, or "wannabes", as he calls them. He says there's quite a community of them here in the central Denver area. He's got some bizarre theories, but he keeps the details to himself because he thinks I won't believe him. What he doesn't know is that I've been following the same trail of deaths that he has, and I've come to similar outrageous conclusions.'

She believes in vampires? No way.

'If he's keeping his theories to himself, how do you know what conclusions he's reached?'

She lifted her chin. 'Let's just say I stumbled upon his notebook one day when he was downtown using the computer and eyeballed enough pages to get the drift. I've also overheard enough of his strange telephone conversations to whet my appetite for more information.'

'So, basically you're saying that you read his private papers?'

She made a swatting-away-a-fly hand motion. 'Don't go
there. The bottom line is that he believes there are actually
such creatures as vampires, and insane as it sounds, the
evidence I've seen supports it. Stevens thinks my interest in
this case is due to the fact that my friend was the first Denver
victim, and he's right – Webster's murder does play into it.
But that's not where it started for me.'

'Where did it start?'

She crossed her arms in front of her chest.

Hmm, arm-crossing. She feels the need to defend herself. Interesting.

'I was a cop in New York City ten years ago when these
murders began to pop up. Long story short, I found my
partner's body drained of blood and riddled with pairs of
puncture wounds. The perpetrator was never apprehended.
The victim in your office was killed by the same method as
all ninety-six others. He was drained of blood.'

'Ninety-six others?' I blurted, and sat up straighter. 'I haven't
heard anything about *ninety-six* murders. You said on the news
there were five bodies, and there was no mention of the
cause of death.'

'Yeah.' She nodded. 'Ninety-six altogether – ninety-seven
now, twenty-seven of them in Denver. We haven't released
that information to the public – I'm sure you can appreciate
how the average citizen might react to finding out there's a
serial killer who somehow removes the victims' blood while
they're still alive. But there's another piece to this sick puzzle,
and that's what I want to talk to you about.'

'Me? I've already told the detective everything I know.'

She pulled a small chair from the corner, set it in front

of me and sat. She leaned back and rested one ankle on the opposite knee.

'Let's just call this a consultation between a law-enforcement professional and a psychological expert. A psychological expert who calls herself "the Vampire Psychologist".'

I realised I'd scooted up to the edge of the couch cushion and forced myself to slide back. All the muscles in my neck were tight and I rotated them in an attempt to relieve the pressure.

'Okay, we're having a professional consultation. Go on.'

She studied me, her face blank. I wondered if she played poker, because no one would be able to read her if she didn't want to be read. 'Remember I said that all the bodies had been drained of blood? In almost all the cases there wasn't a drop of the victims' blood to be found at the scene. Out of the ninety-seven cases, only two bodies were covered with blood. The first was the body of Emerald Addison and the second, the young man lying on your office floor.'

She cocked her head, put both feet flat on the carpet and leaned forwards. 'Any thoughts about another thing both those murders have in common?'

I didn't care for the direction the conversation was taking. 'You're saying that I'm the common denominator?'

'Very good, Doctor. But that's not the really interesting part. The blood found all over Emerald Addison wasn't hers. I'm not sure if I could even call it human.'

'Are you saying she was covered in animal blood?'

She stood, replaced the chair in the corner, and began pacing again. 'That's what we initially thought. Whatever the blood-like substance is, it doesn't have the necessary ingredients to be classified as mammalian. I'd be willing to wager that the blood all over the victim in your office isn't his. I think we'll discover it's a match to what we found in the Addison case.'

I rose and paced in the square she hadn't claimed, making 'I don't know' gestures with my hands. 'I don't understand. Where would the blood come from if not from the victim or an animal?'

'Well, Doctor, that's where you come in. As a psychologist, give me your professional opinion about why a killer might leave his own blood, or some synthetic liquid that looks like blood, at the scene of his crimes?'

I paused and thought for a moment. 'It would be symbolic. Metaphorical. If it only happened in two of the ninety-seven cases, then something about those two cases was more personal for the killer. There was a reason for the killer to either spill his own blood or give that impression. Maybe something religious . . .'

My voice froze in midsentence and I stared at Lieutenant Bullock. I tried to wrap my mind around the notion of Brother Luther as the murderer of ninety-seven people. The same Brother Luther I had initially written off as a harmless windbag. But if Brother Luther was the murderer, what about the bodies being drained of blood? That fitted more with a vampire than a religious fanatic.

Maybe Brother Luther had a partner who was a vampire.

No. His telephone rants all centred on his hatred of vampires. None of it made any sense.

Frowning, Lieutenant Bullock stepped in front of me.

'What? Why did you stop talking? Did you think of something?'

'Yes.' I sighed. 'I think you and Special Agent Stevens and I need to get together right now for a serious talk. I want to tell you about some phone messages I've been receiving, and you and Alan have to come clean with each other.'

She narrowed her eyes and studied me for a few seconds, then bounded towards the exit. 'This way.'

CHAPTER 22

The next few hours were madness.

While I was in the bathroom with Lieutenant Bullock, the police had sealed off my entire office building.

I didn't have to imagine the reactions of the other occupants to the news that their Monday-morning schedules had been completely disrupted, because they informed me personally in no uncertain terms.

The normally sedate building manager had bolted up the stairway before the police blocked it off and he was livid. He blustered over to me, shook his head emphatically and wagged his index finger in the air. 'This won't do, Dr Knight. Everyone is very upset. This is the second time in a week the police have been called to your office. This is a reputable building and I have other tenants to consider. I'm sorry, but I'm going to have to terminate your lease and ask you to vacate immediately. I haven't been allowed inside your office yet, but from what I've been able to determine, the space is no longer in the same condition as when you rented it. I hope for your sake that your insurance is up to date and sufficient.'

I opened my mouth to protest, but the words died in my throat. He was right on all counts. I just stared at his red face and watched the veins pulse on his forehead as he launched into the second act of his diatribe and felt very sorry for myself.

Two weeks ago I was a successful, respected psychologist with a calm, predictable life. Things might have been boring, but they were sane. No vampires, religious zealots, quest-obsessed FBI agents, mausoleums, dead bodies or ruined offices. Why couldn't I have taken up yoga or belly dancing? Something that didn't come with an outrageous dry cleaning bill?

'Are you the building manager?' Lieutenant Bullock barked from a few feet away as she marched towards us.

He pursed his lips.

She handed him a business card. 'If you have complaints about the way this investigation has been handled, please register them at this phone number. Dr Knight was simply being a law-abiding citizen reporting a crime. I think you might want to consult your attorney about the legality of evicting her.'

She turned her attention to me, placed her hand on my upper arm and eased me away from the trembling manager. 'Please come this way, Dr Knight – some of the clients you had scheduled for this morning are waiting downstairs. One of the officers will walk down with you.'

I didn't know which amazed me more: her lecture to the building manager, his barely repressed rage or the fact that she was being nice to me.

After giving an explanation to my anxious clients, telling them I'd call to reschedule as soon as I had a new location and facilitating several mini-therapy sessions to ease their immediate concerns, I contacted the rest of the clients I'd scheduled for the afternoon to fill them in on the situation.

In the middle of making those calls, I thought about the two new vampire clients on my schedule for that night. I had no way of contacting them. They'd only left messages on my voicemail informing me of their intention to come.

Maybe I should drop by The Crypt and leave a message for Devereux. Who knew if the place was even open during the daytime?

That would have to wait until later. First, I needed to go back upstairs to check on Midnight and Ronald.

They'd been thoroughly and persistently questioned and now had the dazed appearance of abandoned puppies waiting to be rescued.

Since their interrogation was complete for the moment, Lieutenant Bullock arranged for them to be taken home. I accompanied the couple downstairs and suggested we meet at my townhouse the next day.

They both nodded, and Midnight gave me a quick hug.

As they drove away in the backseat of the black-and-white, Lieutenant Bullock and Alan entered the lobby. He'd retrieved my burgundy handbag and matching briefcase from the hallway and had draped the long strap of the bag over his shoulder. He rested his hand on the top of the bag as if carrying a handbag was a normal, everyday thing. Observing the nonchalance with which he carried the fashion accessory made me chuckle for the first time in hours.

An eternity later, I sat in my living room, stretched out in my incredibly comfortable oversize chair, my lower body attired in the finest orange police-issue trousers, the latest in paper footwear dangling from my toes. I thought about the events of the last few hours.

My trip to the police station had been the second in as many days and I could say with complete certainty that I'd rather be sucked on by vampires than return there again. Well, one vampire, anyway.

The chief hadn't intervened this time. As soon as we reached her office, Lieutenant Bullock snagged a passing officer, pointed to my trousers and ordered, 'Get Dr Knight some clean clothes and shoes, show her where to change, bag what she's wearing, then bring her back here.'

I caught Alan's trademark smirk as the officer guided me down the hallway.

When I returned to her office in my neon bottoms, Lieutenant Bullock and Alan were in the middle of a shouting match, precipitated, I gathered, by her disclosure about his notebook. They stood nose to nose, enjoying the verbal equivalent of a pissing contest.

After they zipped up and called a truce, I recounted everything I could remember about Brother Luther's telephone calls, then forwarded copies of the toxic harangues to Lieutenant Bullock's voicemail. The preliminary lab report came back verifying that the blood in my office didn't belong to Eric. As before, its origin couldn't be identified.

We argued for and against various theories and hypotheses, going nowhere fast, until it was obvious that we'd exhausted the productive possibilities for the day and we were all tired and hungry.

Lieutenant Bullock waved us out, said she'd be in touch, and Alan walked me to my car.

'Well, you've had a crappy couple of weeks, wouldn't you say?'

I shrugged, not sure if he was kidding or attempting to be supportive. 'I guess the dead people have had a crappier time than me.'

He grunted some variant of 'huh' or 'hmmm'.

I retrieved my keys from my purse and toyed with them, checking out the asphalt near my right foot.

'So, can I come home with you?'

'What?' I was sure my face clearly indicated I hadn't seen that coming. 'Why do you want to come home with me?'

'I think we have stuff to talk about.' He grinned and stepped closer. 'Things to clarify. Questions to be answered. You know, the usual. Maybe you'd like to have your back scrubbed in the shower. Or maybe your front.'

I laughed and shook my head. 'I can't really blame you for running hot and cold, because you probably think that's what I did. And I can't say I don't find you attractive, in an obsessive-compulsive sort of way, because I do. But I spent four years with a man who kept me very low on his priority list, and something about you reminds me of him. Been there, done that.'

His sapphire eyes darkened and he wrapped his arms around me and planted his very soft, warm lips on mine.

I kept my arms at my sides, but felt my lips opening for his tongue as my mouth welcomed the pressure of his. My body responded to the unexpected move by putting out the chemical welcome mat. I moaned softly.

After a few seconds, he released me and stepped back, leaning against the car next to mine. 'I've known lots of women in my life. I seem to be the kind of guy women make up stories about, attributing my loner tendencies to some kind of yearning that only they can heal. They think if they have sex with me I'll suddenly be different, not as work-obsessed, not as crazy. But they all find out quickly that what you see is what you get. So I've managed to have lots of experience with women, but zero success with relationships. I just don't know how to do them. I'm not even from Mars.' He laughed ruefully. 'There's no name for the planet I'm from.'

He studied me as if he was waiting for something, and I found myself doing the 'therapist nod' – the gentle, slow up-and-down head motion, not unlike one of those toy dogs you see in the back windows of cars, that most counsellors unconsciously perform while listening to someone's story.

'I'm not sure why you're telling me this.'

'You confuse me.' He sighed. 'Sometimes I think I've blown it and that you're unavailable, so I back off. Then other times I get the idea that our attraction is mutual, like the way you just responded to my kiss, so I take a chance. Now I'm just asking, flat-out: do I have a chance with you?'

I decided to be as honest as I could. 'I don't know. Right now, I feel emotionally connected to Devereux, though I'm not sure if that's because I really care about him or if he's zapping me with vampire juju and I'm a puppet on his string. The truth is that I met Devereux before I ran into you at the hospital. I don't know why I didn't tell you. Maybe it was because I thought the whole vampire thing was bullshit and Devereux

and you and all my wannabe clients were deluded and confused. It wasn't until all the insanity at The Crypt that I actually
forced myself to accept what my eyes were telling me. I was
already interested in him before I met you, but it's also true
that I'm very attracted to you. But I've had such poor experiences with men that all this attention has thrown me for a
loop. I suck at everything about relationships. So I guess I can't
tell you anything helpful. I simply don't know.'

He pulled me into his arms again and whispered into my
hair above my ear, 'I'll play my hunch, then.' He kissed my
cheek and said, 'Cover your back, Dr Knight.'

By the time I reversed my car out of the space and turned
to wave goodbye, he was already gone.

I tuned in to the local evening news on TV for the company,
poured a glass of wine and sat at my desk. It was time to
make a new plan.

Even if the building manager didn't evict me, it would be
quite a while before the police would let me back inside my
office and even longer for the space to be repaired. I'd have
to check online for cleaning companies that specialised in
bloodstains. Was there such a thing?

In the meantime, I needed to find a place to meet with
my clients. Having a home office wasn't appealing at the
best of times, and I certainly wasn't going to give a blanket
invitation to every vampire in Denver. Even if Devereux said
the needing-to-be-invited-in thing was a myth, I wasn't taking
any chances. Just because Devereux could come and go as
he pleased didn't mean that other vampires could. He seemed
to be the Grand Pooh-bah.

Hearing my name mentioned on the news jarred me out of my thoughts. I picked up the remote control and turned up the volume. The station was airing a story about the body found in my office. They replayed a video clip from my last trip to the police station while the voice-over speculated about my 'alleged vampire clientele'. At the end of the story, the reporter gave us his best stern expression and said, 'This reporter wonders how Dr Knight always appears to be involved in these murders. Maybe the police should be checking her alibi.' His lips spread in a lopsided horse-smile. 'Wes Carter, live in Denver. Back to you in the studio, Bob.'

'Thanks, Wes. It sounds like there's more to Dr Knight than meets the eye. We'll be following the story 24/7 until we get to the truth.'

If you find out the truth about me, I hope you'll tell me.

I jumped up and made sure all the doors and windows were locked and the blinds and curtains tightly closed. The police had been great about keeping the media at bay, but what would happen if something more pressing occurred and they had to leave?

Just then somebody pounded on the door between my garage and kitchen. 'Shit! Did some reporter sneak in?' I said, wishing my trusty intuition had put in its two cents a bit earlier. I hurried over. 'Who is it?' My midsection tingled.

'Oh, get over yourself. Open the door.'

The voice was familiar. I unlocked the door and cracked it just enough to see X-rated Luna standing in the garage, unaccompanied by reporters, cameras or microphones. The light in the garage was motion sensitive so I could view her in all her vampiric glory.

'Luna?' I swung the door open. 'This is a surprise.'

She was dressed in a low-cut black top, tight black jeans and pointy-toed black high-heeled boots. Vampire dominatrix. The dramatic makeup artistry on her pale skin was even more striking than the first time I saw her. Her silver eyes were embellished with Cleopatra-like wings. Very exotic.

'Yeah, well, don't count on it ever happening again. The sooner he tires of you, the better. But I told him I'd come to your house and that I wouldn't just pop up in your living room, so here I am. He can't give me any more grief about you. It was a pain in the ass avoiding all those humans cluttering up your street. I'll never get why anyone would be interested in you.'

Luna's distaste for humans, and me in particular, was easy to read, even without my intuition.

'And to what do I owe this honour?'

'You've got that right. I have a message from the Master. He has serious business he must attend to tonight and he won't be able to see you, but he said he'll visit your dreams and explain. He said I had to tell you that you're in danger and not to let anyone remove your protective necklace.'

'What does he mean, I'm in danger?'

'Hey, I just deliver the messages, I don't explain them. But I will tell you that something's up – vampires are swarming into Denver in droves, and some of them make even us tough vamps nervous. Something dark and heavy is in the air, so to speak.'

'Where's Devereux?' I asked.

She glared at me. 'Not that it's any of your miserable human business, but he's off on some kind of inter-dimensional rescue mission. He's always saving somebody.' She pursed her lips and brought her face closer to mine. 'He simply can't resist a hard-luck case.' She stepped back. 'I'm guessing it has to be something big for him to tear him away from his human plaything.' Her lips relaxed into a wicked smile, displaying fully descended fangs. 'But who knows? You might get snatched away by the Dark One again and I won't have to hear about you any more. Wouldn't that be great?'

With that she laughed and vanished.

I wasn't sure what to make of her attitude towards me. Clearly she didn't have much use for me, but I knew she'd follow Devereux's orders. I was sure she wouldn't hurt me. Probably.

Leave it to Devereux to choose a pissed-off beauty queen for his personal assistant. No bug-eating, rotted-tooth Renfield for him.

I relocked the door and returned to my desk.

The next task on my list was to contact all my clients, cancel or reschedule any appointments set for the next couple of days and assure them I'd be functioning again as quickly as possible. I spoke with all but a handful and left general messages for the ones I hadn't reached, asking them to contact me.

Tired, I rubbed the back of my neck to ease the tight muscles. I shuffled over to my comfortable chair, found the remote control and clicked through the channels, searching for mindless entertainment.

I landed on a well-known national discussion programme. The show's host was an abrasive, politically dogmatic, argumentative bully who only had guests to give him someone to shout over. I usually didn't have much time for television, and this show was particularly worth avoiding, but something about the topic caught my attention.

A diverse panel was talking about the end of the world. Normally discussions about that topic have a decidedly religious flavour and don't appeal to me, but this group appeared to be comprised of all kinds of people: scientists, psychics, spiritual leaders, law-enforcement officials and politicians: quite an unexpected amalgam of opinions.

An old white-haired woman on the panel moved to the podium and spoke. 'The world is being contaminated by a growing darkness, a cumulative negative energy so strong that it's eliciting the worst from all the Earth's inhabitants. The idea that thoughts and emotions hold certain vibrations is no longer speculation. According to the Law of Attraction, like attracts like, and we are witnessing clear evidence of that all over the world today.'

Where had I heard that before? It sounded so familiar. Then I remembered – Cerridwyn the tarot-reader had said almost exactly the same thing. I hadn't realised the end of the world had become such a hot topic.

The speakers droned on and I listened to the panel's discussion, waiting for the voices of ridicule and condescension that usually follow such proclamations, but none came. Everyone on the panel had a unique angle on this 'growing darkness' to share.

My ears pricked up when they mentioned Denver as one of the cities on the leading edge of the escalating negativity. According to a dark-skinned man wearing a turban, unexplained deaths and all forms of violence had increased in these cities at a higher rate than the national average. They devoted the next few minutes to comparing ideas about why those particular cities and areas of the country had become the focus of evil, and decided it had something to do with a psychic buildup of toxic human emotions: hate, fear, blame, guilt, rage, shame – conditions that prepared the ground for increased violence, manipulation, intolerance, control and destruction.

The white-haired woman explained, 'People's focus on fear, hatred, and violence has caused a greater vibrational accumulation of those emotions in places across the country where there are powerful concentrations of hopeful, optimistic, and enlightening energy. In other words, everything and its opposite exists equally – and in these locations, they are *both* increasing.

'We are called to make a choice between love, compassion and tolerance and hate, fear and war. A true archetypal Armageddon.'

The discussion sounded so New Age, I was shocked by the host's uncharacteristic lack of reaction. Strange. I'd never heard him be polite with anyone before. I guessed his behaviour was as clear an indication of the impending end of the world as anything. Or maybe hell had frozen over.

I thought about the reading Cerridwyn had given me and all the weird situations I'd found myself in since then. I was no longer the same person who had concrete answers about what was and wasn't real. Maybe I should go and visit her again.

Wow. Did I just seriously consider going to a psychic on purpose?

The programme went to commercial and a group of children in costumes screamed, 'Trick or Treat!' as an advertisement for Hallowe'en candy filled the screen.

Hallowe'en? Was it Hallowe'en already? I didn't even know what day of the month it was, although I'd vaguely been aware it was October. Turned out today was the thirtieth, so tomorrow was Hallowe'en.

I'd loved the holiday as a child. It didn't take a psychologist to figure out what metaphor I was acting out by dressing up as a princess every year. Damn those Disney fairy tales!

In graduate school, I studied Samhain, the old pagan holiday that pre-dates our current consumer-driven observance; it celebrates the time of year when the veil between the worlds is most transparent – when magic is afoot.

Unfortunately, our culture became suspicious of true magic and has shrouded the holiday in fear, superstition and nonsense. I'd attended a Wiccan coven's ritual once and walked around hearing bits of people's thoughts for a week afterwards. Powerful stuff.

I'd read something in the newspaper recently about a big party or gathering on Hallowe'en, a yearly event. Not that I intended to go – my life was bizarre enough without voluntarily adding more occult madness.

A sudden pain shot across my forehead and my stomach seized.

The lightbulbs in both the overhead fixture and the table lamp simultaneously exploded, leaving the room illuminated only by the eerie glow of the large TV screen.

'Harlot! Whore!'

The screeching voice from behind me startled me so badly

I leaped out of the chair and landed on top of the coffee table, knocking over my glass of wine.

Creeping towards me, circling in front of the table I was crouching on, was an emaciated-looking male. The sunken cheeks of his white, cadaverous face appeared blue in the shadowy light and his floor-length black coat hung loosely on his tall, wiry frame. His head was a luminous egg, hairless, with crisscrossing veins. His coal-black eyes were rimmed with swollen red tissue, something foul and thick oozing from the corners. He looked like an experiment gone wrong. A body in search of its grave.

He pointed a finger at me, the elongated fingernail ragged and stained. In his other arm he clutched a huge battered black book. He snarled, displaying yellow and brown teeth. And fangs. I recognised the Southern drawl from the phone calls.

Is this Brother Luther? He's a vampire?

The degree to which I'd missed the boat blew me away.

'Evil Jezebel!' he screeched. 'You will burn in eternal damnation! Consorting with Satan's minions!'

His breath was horrible, reeking like a sewer. It provided nauseating contrast to the rancid odour wafting from his clothing.

I scanned the area, weighed my options and the distance to the nearest phone, then leaped off the table, landing as far away from him as possible.

There wasn't any way I was going to make eye-contact with him, so I focused on his nose, which was a mass of bumps and missing skin. 'Are you Brother Luther? What do you want?' I asked, using my least threatening therapy voice. My heart was running a marathon.

As if he hadn't heard my question, he continued slinging vile epithets. 'Whore! Sinner! Evil temptress!' He stared at me with his glassy dark eyes, tiny droplets of spit flying as he ranted.

Shit! What the hell's going on? How can this be Brother Luther? I thought he hated vampires.

Simultaneously, I reached for the cordless phone and he lunged at me. I grabbed the phone, managed to punch in nine one, then lost my grip on it when he jerked me towards him by the fabric of my blouse.

My eyes watered as he held me close to his face. It was almost impossible to breathe while being bathed in the noxious stink radiating from his mouth. I pushed against him and had the clear impression that my wrists would break before I'd budge him an inch.

He was staring at me but his eyes were unfocused.

My bowels threatened to liquefy and I fought to turn my head to get away from the worst of it.

'She must be punished,' he bellowed in my face, gathering more of my shirt in his grasp. His head suddenly jerked down, his vacant eyes locking on something he now held in his palm. He screamed as the necklace Devereux had given me lit up the room, burning his hand. He dropped his book and released me, and I fell to the floor.

I speed-crawled a few feet away from him and slowly stood.

Evidently the necklace had done more than scorch him, because he put both hands on his bald dome and whimpered in a weak, shaky voice, 'Don't hurt me, don't hurt me, please don't hurt me, help me, help me . . .'

Something about his words reminded me of the dream I'd had about the child in the house.

He lowered his arms, then clutched his stomach and rocked up and down, sobbing loudly.

I became momentarily confused and almost made a move towards him.

Suddenly he jerked upright and rose to his full height, which looked taller than before, and held his arms out on either side of him. He closed his eyes and slowly let his head drop back, his mouth falling open.

It wasn't possible, but it looked as if the coat that had hung loosely on him moments before now stretched taut across his chest, shoulders, and upper arms. As he spread his arms out, the coat flapped open, exposing his scarred, festering naked frame. His chest was a mass of oozing sores surrounded by coarse, filthy body hair, which trailed down to a thick patch sprouting a huge reddish erection.

His head snapped up as if a spring had been released and the black coals in his eyes ignited into flames. He eased his hand down his abscessed stomach, grasped his penis and began stroking its length, groaning.

'Come to me. Touch me.' He gave the worst smile I've ever seen. Thrusting his foul erection towards me, he laughed, his voice burrowing holes in my ears, making my knees weak.

I backed as far away from him as I could.

What just happened? What is this thing? Why does his voice sound familiar? Where's his Southern accent? Why does he look different? He obviously did something to cause me to believe he's physically bigger than he was just a few moments ago. Some mind-control ability. And what about the protection ritual? I guess it didn't work.

He began moving the hand on his penis faster and became momentarily distracted by what I guessed was an approaching orgasm. I didn't want to be standing in front of him when he got to that point.

I dropped to the ground, crawled towards the front door as fast as my hands and knees would carry me, and cringed when I heard him scream his release. The cry sounded more like pain than pleasure. Almost immediately I felt myself being lifted up by the waistband of the orange bottoms.

That hideous laugh washed over me again. Just as I was wondering if my death would be quick and painless or drawn out and torturous, the front door burst open and a whole flock of vampires swept into the room.

Several of them leaped on my captor, causing me to be flung against a wall, where I sat, semi-dazed, watching my vampire cavalry getting thrown around like sponge toys.

What the hell is going on? Is he some kind of vampire demon?

Brother Luther, if it really was Brother Luther, seemed to be able to control vampires as well as humans with his mind, but there were too many for him. Or else he simply lost interest. He threw down the hulking vampire whose neck he was sucking on, turned his red eyes to me and shrieked, 'Soon.'

Then he either disappeared or moved so quickly there wasn't even a blur, because one moment he was there, the next he wasn't.

The vampires lay around the room, scattered like bowling pins after a strike.

The silence was broken by a deep male voice saying, 'Get the fuck off me,' as a short, rotund man sprang up.

I didn't recognise any of the blood-covered warriors except one, the last one I expected to see. Still in shock, I crawled over to a woman sprawled out on the floor between the living room and the kitchen. Her long black hair was matted with blood from several head wounds and two large holes gaped at the top of her left breast where fangs had torn the skin. The wounds had already begun to heal.

'Luna? Is that you?'

'No, it's the Avon lady. Are you always this dim?'

'What are you doing here?'

'Saving your unimportant ass.'

I nodded and smoothed a clump of her long hair away from her frowning face. 'Believe me, I appreciate that, but how did you know that – whatever he was – was here?'

She slapped my hand away. 'Devereux expected trouble tonight and ordered me to keep watch on your house as well as the vampires he already had guarding you. He said I should bring more reinforcements, just in case. I thought he was overreacting because of his unfathomable attachment to you, but I hung out, watching you through the window. I saw the skuzzy guy appear, summoned the others, and the rest is history.'

She sat up. I tried to help her, but she slapped my hand away again.

'Who is that guy? Or, better yet, *what* is that guy?'

She shrugged. 'I don't know – he was your gentleman caller, not mine – but whoever he is, Devereux's going to rip him a new one. I hope I get to watch.'

'How was he able to control you and all the other vampires like that? I thought mind control only worked on humans?'

She nodded while tapping her index finger on her chin in thought. 'It usually does only work on humans. It takes one hell of a powerful vampire to control other vampire minds, and the only one I've ever seen do it is Devereux. He's definitely going to go ballistic. Whoever the guy with the boner is, he's gonna find out what happens to vampires who mess with the Master's property.'

Master's property?

I was way too exhausted and traumatised to open up that coffin of worms, but Devereux and I were definitely going to have to come to an understanding.

'Wait a minute,' I said, glancing towards the front door. 'How could you use my front door without the media seeing you?' I listened to the heavy silence. 'Where are they? Where are the cops? We should have been invaded by now.'

'Yeah, that's another weird thing about the bald guy. As soon as he materialised inside, the mortals ran away. Gross dude has one helluva nasty vibe. It saturated the air and terrified the poor little humans. They shot outta here like missiles, and they won't even know why they bolted.' She gave an evil laugh. 'I'll bet they all pissed their pants.'

I know the feeling.

During the short time we'd been talking, the wounds on all of the vampire bodies had healed, and if you didn't count the blood splashed all over every part of my living room, you wouldn't have known a life-or-death situation had just occurred. That I'd almost been dinner for a crazed vampire zealot.

How can Brother Luther have festering sores on his body? Why doesn't his body immediately heal them? Why didn't it occur to me he could be a vampire? Not too bright, Kismet!

There *was* blood all over my living room.

A trashed office and a living room that smelled like a used sanitary pad.

Luna rose in a fluid motion, without the aid of bones, and brushed off her black ensemble.

I scrambled to my feet, not nearly as gracefully, and noticed all the vampire eyes staring at me.

I was in room filled with vampires. Blood-drinkers. Children of the night.

Well, hell. What am I supposed to do with a roomful of vampires?

I couldn't offer them coffee and bagels. Should I offer them the use of my shower? My washing machine? Should I open up a vein?

The problem was solved when one of them – the huge one the crazy vampire had sucked on – stalked over, bowed from the waist and said, 'We serve the Master. We will hide ourselves outside again and keep watch over you until sunrise. I will send someone to replace your door lock.' He raised his hand, made a 'come on' gesture, and a dozen undead walked out of my front door.

Luna surveyed the wreckage of my living room and said, 'Do you want to stay here, or would you rather spend the rest of the night at The Crypt?'

On automatic pilot I'd already started picking up papers and books that had fallen off my desk. I was too emotionally wiped out to deal with her prickly attitude. If anyone was in dire need of psychotherapy, it was Luna. Anger and hostility rolled off her in toxic waves. It was a good thing there were rules against doing therapy with someone you know, but even if there weren't, I wouldn't be caught dead having her as my client. Oh, wait. Bad choice of words. I probably would be dead.

I sighed, my voice shaky. 'I'll stay here. There's no blood upstairs and I need a shower.'

'Then I'll stick around, too. Devereux would stake me if I left you alone tonight.'

Swell.

She walked to the kitchen door and looked around. 'Where's your washer and dryer?'

I pointed, and reached down to retrieve another pile of papers. When I turned to see if Luna had figured out how to operate the washing machine, she was walking back into the living room, naked.

She put her hands on her hips. 'Do you mind if I take a shower first if you're going to clean up down here?'

'Uh, sure. That's fine. Make yourself at home.'

And it just keeps getting weirder.

I heard the little popping sound that indicated some vampire or another had just made an unscheduled arrival or departure, and then the sound of the shower running.

What was up with all the naked vampires? Was nudity a requirement to join the club?

The mentally ill sometimes act out childhood shame issues by getting naked and being sexually aggressive. Masturbation as an anxiety-relieving and self-soothing technique was common. That didn't surprise me.

And I wasn't a prude. I'd spent as much time as any other woman in health club locker rooms, making small talk with other naked women. Still, a naked vampire built like a silicone-enhanced supermodel calmly cruising around my kitchen was a little out of my comfort zone.

It was natural to be curious about a body that perfect, but actually gawking at it had to be out of the question. What was I supposed to look at while I spoke to her? I wondered how many times Devereux had seen her naked. Geez. Together they'd look like a god and goddess.

Insecure? Me?

CHAPTER 23

It probably made sense that a vampire wouldn't worry about human rules. I mean, once you were undead, who were you trying to impress? Who would get in your face about anything, anyway, if the result would be having your throat torn out?

Luna glided down the stairs, moving with feline grace. Her calm exterior only partially camouflaged the power and violence lurking just under the surface. She was still naked. She strolled over to the washing machine, noted the cycle wasn't complete and sat down at the kitchen table.

How weird was it to have a sky-clad vampire wandering around your house?

I'd replaced the lightbulbs and done everything I could in the living room. Now it would be up to the cleaning crew. I heard the washing machine spin cycle click off and walked over to shift her clothes into the dryer.

Like the moment in a horror movie when the forest goes strangely silent and we know the monster is watching us through the trees, a chill ran through my body, sliding an ice cube down my back. I turned to look at Luna.

She was watching me, eyes narrowed, the tips of her fangs peeking out through parted lips. 'I need blood.'

Terror took me hostage. In three seconds, I'd gone from being in denial about the predator padding around my kitchen to having every ancestral alarm bell in my psyche clanging madly. My stomach contracted, I felt hot and cold at the same time and my knees were suddenly rubber.

Smart-mouthed, cynical Luna was gone and in her place was a vampire. A creature that drank human blood – a hungry predator.

I only had one card to play. My mouth had gone totally dry and I was only partially successful at keeping the fear out of my voice. I knew she could sense it, anyway. 'If you're thinking about having my neck as your entrée, you'd better consider what Devereux will say. He is, as you said, some-what attached to me.'

My anxiety escalated. Her intention saturated the air. I knew exactly what she meant to do.

She stood and stalked very slowly across the room, closing in on me. She locked her eyes on mine, which caused me to get the fuzzy, floating feeling that meant she was pulling me into her gaze, taking control of my mind.

I visualised the protective wall that usually kept me from drowning in other people's energy and felt it collapse. Nothing in my repertoire could hold up against the kind of power Luna wielded.

This wasn't vague energy. It was laser-sharp mind control.

I threw my hands up, palms out, in a reflexive action which did nothing but give her something to grab.

Pinning me against the washing machine with her lower body, she ran her hands up and down my arms, holding me still. Her silver eyes were large and foggy, as if the lights were on but no one was home. Her pointy fangs elongated as she caressed them with her tongue. She leaned in and slowly licked the side of my neck.

I braced myself for the shock of pain I was sure would come and was surprised to hear a scream.

She'd slid her hand across my chest and encountered the necklace. It had the same reaction to Luna that it had to the bald lunatic. There was a flash of light and a sensation strong enough to cause her to drop the necklace and leap away from me.

As she stood snarling, the fog in her eyes cleared and her fangs retracted into her gums.

I wrapped my arms around myself and trembled. The part of my brain that had wanted nothing more than to do whatever Luna commanded threw cold water on itself and woke up. I stared wide-eyed at the creature in front of me. She'd known about the necklace, but the bloodlust apparently didn't waste time on frivolous details.

It was impossible for me to truly understand the craving for blood, to have blood obsession to the point of being enthralled by the need. But I'd just got a psychic encyclopaedia full of information from Luna's mind that horrified and sickened me. Mental postcards of all the bodies she'd drained, all the destruction she'd caused, slammed into my brain.

She might not have wanted to kill me, but she would have – even if it meant Devereux would destroy her.

My body was shaking, a delayed reaction to my second near-death experience of the night.

Luna backed away and reclaimed the chair at the kitchen table, still watching me, her fists clenched. She was clearly struggling to regain control. Her eyes were dull with dark smudges underneath, her skin pasty-white.

She cleared her throat then spoke, her voice husky. 'You're lucky Devereux gave you that necklace. If you hadn't been wearing it, I'd have bled you. I would've tried to take only enough to sustain me until I could find another source, but I probably wouldn't have been able to restrain myself. Hunger after being wounded is the worst. There's nothing in the human experience that comes close to being as overwhelming as the need for blood. Not even a heroin addict's craving for a fix. I have to go and feed.' She sighed and licked her lips. 'Until I do, I'm a danger to you. Not that I care, but Devereux does.'

'You're right,' I said, my voice still weak, 'Devereux does care.'

Holy shit. I'm glad to have the necklace, but I'd be a fool to put all my faith in it – or in Devereux's protection. Note to self: buy wooden stakes.

She sneered, 'Necklace or no, even now I can't think of anything but the taste of your blood and the pulse pounding in your neck. I'll go and find one of my regular sources, one of my vampire addicts. It won't take long. Then I'll come back.'

Is that a promise or a threat?

It was probably stupid to question a hungry vampire, but I couldn't help myself. 'Do you mean you're going to go kill someone?'

'No.' She shook her head. 'I'll find one of the humans who regularly donate blood and sex. Getting both my needs met at the same time seems to take the edge off.' She stared at me with cold eyes, her voice deep and serious. 'Don't make the mistake of thinking that vampires are just eccentric humans who simply have a nasty little habit or two. We're not human. We take blood from willing and unwilling victims alike. Killing is what we do. We enjoy it. All of us. You might be surprised to know what pleasure it brings me to fantasise about draining you dry.'

She rose, sauntered over and gazed at me through her thick eyelashes, a cold grin on her face. 'In fact, you could say you and I have a date the moment Devereux dumps you.'

I started to ask another question, but she flicked her fingers dismissively and said, 'That's enough. If I don't leave now, you'll be sorry.'

She blinked out and I slid to the floor, my back against the washing machine. Exhaustion swamped me.

I woke up in sunlight, lying on top of the covers on my bed, Devereux's voice an echo in my mind.

'My love, Luna told me what happened last night. I am sorry I was not there to protect you. Something very strange is happening. I was tricked into journeying into a difficult reality and was intercepted once I arrived there. The power necessary for someone to deceive me is beyond any I have seen before. We must be vigilant. I will come to you as soon as I rise. Oh, yes – here is the address of your new office: 984 Lincoln Avenue, Number 505. The building manager is expecting you. Until tonight.'

A phantom vampire lover, a religious fanatic killer, and a beauty queen predator.

Just another day in undead Oz.

*

My first glimpse of the emergency room décor in my living room was depressing. For one brief moment I had hoped it was a bad dream and I'd find my living space just as normally cluttered and blood-free as usual.

But no.

As promised, my front door now had new locks and my illusion of safety was restored.

I spent a few minutes on the phone, interviewing cleaning services, being very up-front about the bloodstains, and settled on the one that specialised in taking 'the jobs that nobody else wants'.

The woman started to tell me about the last crime scene they'd been hired to restore and how no one would ever have known that an entire family had been brutally murdered there and I cut her off, saying I was sure they could handle my situation. Too much information.

They agreed to come later that day.

Once showered and dressed, I decided to focus on finding another office. I wanted to make a change regardless of what my current building manager chose to do.

Unfortunately, I discovered immediately that my infamy had spread and suddenly none of the vacancies in the paper were still available after they heard my name. I couldn't really blame them, because what property manager in her or his right mind would want to rent to someone who'd had her office recently trashed by a murderer?

Then I remembered Devereux's mental memo. Had he said something about an office?

I closed my eyes and allowed the address he'd imprinted in my memory to resurface, then I grabbed my purse and keys and headed out, wondering briefly if my guardian vampires had really spent the night out in my yard, and if it had been Luna who'd carried me upstairs.

Cold chills ran through my body as I imagined myself sleeping and vulnerable as Luna crouched over me, maybe thinking about which vein she'd puncture first.

I drove to the address Devereux had given me, which turned out to be only a block away from The Crypt. The building was spectacular: delightfully old, it had been lovingly restored and remodelled, and now it was the crown jewel of the neighbourhood. A garage, built to blend in with the architecture of the antique building next door, sported a sign that said, 'Parking for The Crypt and Lady Amara Only'.

The building is named after Lady Amara – Devereux's mother?

Come to think of it, Midnight had mentioned that Devereux lived in a loft near the club. It looked like he owned the whole building.

Damn. I'd been so caught up in trying not to believe Devereux was a vampire that I hadn't given any thought to the fact he was also a *rich* vampire.

I pulled into the parking garage, then walked around to the lobby entrance and stepped through the wood-framed stained-glass double doors.

Breathtaking. Gold-etched marble floors stretched out for hundreds of square feet, and just past the bank of elevators stood a large reception desk. Plush leather couches and chairs were scattered throughout the room, Devereux's artwork filled the walls and relaxing music flowed from invisible speakers. Still gawking at the beautiful lobby, I walked to the reception desk and asked for the building manager.

The woman seated behind the desk smiled brightly and asked my name. Upon hearing it, she rose and held out her hand. As I shook it she introduced herself. 'I'm Victoria Essex, building manager, receptionist, troubleshooter and all-round *Wunderkind*. I've been expecting you.' She sailed her arm through the air in the direction of the elevators. 'Right this way.'

The elevator was a mirrored affair: lovely to look at, but it might be annoying to have nothing to rest your eyes on but yourself during your ride in the box. Unless, of course, you had company, and then you had total licence to indulge your people-watching desires to your heart's content.

I'd just given myself permission to study my companion in the mirror when the ding sounded, the door opened and we stepped into a lushly carpeted hallway. The ice-blue of the floor matched the colours in the elegant European-style wallpaper. I could easily have imagined myself in a luxury old-world hotel.

Pausing in front of a hand-carved portal, Victoria slid a keycard into a slot near the handle, the red light changed to green and the door clicked open.

There had to be some kind of mistake. This place was big enough and extraordinary enough to be Oprah's Denver corporate office. We wandered through a space that would make a great waiting room, then entered a large, multi-room suite.

'Isn't it incredible?' Victoria beamed. 'Devereux designed the renovation of the building himself and chose the interiors for every suite.'

'So Devereux owns this building?'

'Yes.' She nodded. 'This one and many others, including the gothic wonderland down the street. Have you ever been to The Crypt?'

'I have. It's really something. Does he live in this building?'

'I'm sorry. Devereux gave me the impression that you two are close friends, so I just assumed you were aware of his personal details. Then again, he did tell me to answer all your questions, so yes, he keeps the penthouse as his residence.' The charming expression returned to her face as she opened a set of double doors that led to a lovely full bathroom.

'On the other side of the suite is a smaller bathroom, which would be perfect for your clients to use. Would you care to see it?'

He must have filled her in about my line of work. I nodded and she guided me across the expanse.

'What other kinds of businesses have their offices here in the building?' I asked.

'All the businesses here belong to Devereux and his associates – they run several international corporations. Yours will be the only outside business in the building. Well, what do you think? Would you like to move in?'

'You bet.' I chuckled. 'In a heartbeat. But affording the rent is another issue.'

'Devereux told me you'd say that – he said to tell you he'll discuss the details of the rental agreement with you personally, and I should assure you that you can easily afford the space. I'm going to leave you here for a few minutes by yourself so you can get a feel for the place.' She took a couple of steps towards the door, spread her arms wide and spun in a circle, pointing around the empty space as she twirled. 'Start imagining where your furniture will go. Enjoy the view of the mountains from your windows.'

'Thank you.'

'Oh, by the way, he also asked me to tell you that you can have the suite unfurnished or furnished. He has a huge warehouse full of couches, chairs, desks, tables, lamps, anything you might desire. Exceptional pieces. He said to let him know what you require and it will be delivered immediately.'

She stopped spinning, walked through the suite and closed the door behind her.

I laughed out loud at her joyful free-spiritedness and threw my arms out as she'd done, then let them return to my sides. If I'd ever managed to learn how to turn cartwheels in elementary school, I'd have been tempted to turn one now.

I strolled through the spacious rooms.

Of course, it was out of the question. There was no way in hell I could afford this place. The bathroom fixtures alone must have cost more than I paid for my townhouse.

But wouldn't it be great if I *could* afford it? Furnished or unfurnished? I hadn't even started to figure out how I was going to acquire new furniture to replace the broken stuff in my office. My insurance would probably reimburse me, but that could take months.

On the downside, if I moved into Devereux's building and let him give me a rent break, I'd be obligated to him. I was sure that's what he wanted. Where was the line between taking advantage of a good deal and losing my autonomy? What happened if I decided I didn't want a vampire boyfriend? What if Luna was right and he dumped me? I'd have to move again.

Thinking about all that made my head hurt.

I glanced down at my feet, which had sunk deep into the rich pile of the carpet, and wondered if a rug this thick had to be vacuumed or mowed.

Then the view out the windows drew me like a magnet. From this suite's row of windows I had a panoramic view of Colorado's Front Range, the mountains that skirted the metro area all the way from south of Colorado Springs up to the Wyoming border. Wind clouds hovered along the tops of the peaks, signalling that the Denver area might be in for some of our famous one-hundred-miles-per-hour window-rattling, roof-lifting air blasts. If this building had been here as long as I suspected it had, it wasn't likely to get blown away anytime soon.

Giving in to temporary insanity, I'd just dropped down onto the floor and was flailing my arms and legs and giggling, making a snow angel in the carpet, when Victoria reentered and clapped her hands.

'I knew you'd love it!'

I was outrageously embarrassed. I was halfway to my feet when I realised she was lying on the floor with me, following my example. We laughed at ourselves and each other, spent a couple of minutes being five years old again and finally got off the floor. Then we grinned at each other. After all, our inner children had bonded.

She handed me the keycard and a business card with her information on it.

'Devereux said I should give you the keycard so you could spend as much time in the suite as you wish before you decide one way or the other.' She started towards the exit then turned, a wide grin on her friendly face. 'I think he really likes you. I look forward to having you here. If you need anything just call me, any day, any time. Blessed be.' She waved and left.

Blessed be? That was a Wiccan greeting and parting, wasn't it? Of course Devereux had a witch as his office manager.

Did she know everything about Devereux? He must have told her something to justify the fact that he was never here during the daylight hours. He did tend to surround himself with people who were devoted to him. Maybe he secretly slept in a coffin in the basement?

I wandered around the suite for a few more minutes, stared out the window, then forced myself to head back out to the hallway. I'd apparently decided to take him up on his offer. Providing, of course, the true cost wasn't higher than I was willing to pay.

Hallowe'en. The big news story in town was the yearly bash, which turned out to be called The Vampires' Ball. How could I have lived here so long and never heard of it?

The event was the topic *du jour* on the radio. According to the legend, twenty years ago, in the foothills west of Denver, an eccentric billionaire had built a monstrously huge hotel that was designed to resemble the rich guy's favourite Scottish castle. He'd even had a chunk of the Celtic original dismantled and shipped over for his masterpiece, in the hopes that a ghost or two might tag along for the ride.

There are lots of stories about those ghosts, which might have contributed to the failure of the hotel as a successful enterprise. Or maybe the hotel went belly-up because the billionaire lost interest in it and didn't continue all the maintenance and upkeep required for a castle in the foothills of the Rocky Mountains. Whatever the reason, the castle languished – until ten years ago, when it was purchased by yet another eccentric billionaire and transformed from a hotel to an event site.

Specifically, the site for The Vampires' Ball.

Gee. I wonder if I know any eccentric billionaires who might be attracted to a ghost-filled castle as the location for a celebration dedicated to vampires? Hmmm. Let me think.

It wasn't enough that Devereux was a vampire who could move through thought, a wizard who travelled to other dimensions and a gorgeous hunk of godlike masculinity. Now I had to deal with the fact that he was rich and owned half the world.

I didn't know whether to laugh or scream.

Devereux's involvement aside, the gala sounded like it would draw every vampire, vampire wannabe and fan of the paranormal on this side of the Mississippi. It occurred to me that the ball would be a great place for the police to use me to capture Brother Luther.

Or whoever the hell he is.

But why would I want to do that? I wasn't the brave type. If I couldn't use my therapy skills to resolve a situation, I was pretty much out of my league. Now that I'd actually seen the monster up close and personal and witnessed his madness firsthand, why would I want to put myself in danger again?

Because until he was caught and put away, I was a prisoner. He could show up anytime and destroy as many offices as I could move into. In fact, that reminded me – I needed to talk to Devereux about whether or not he really wanted me in there if his incredible building could be wrecked by Vampire Satan at any moment.

Still, weighing all the pros and cons, I thought the idea of my participation in the capture was worth a phone call to Lieutenant Bullock.

Chapter 24

The first thing I noticed when I returned home was that the media and police were still missing in action. What kind of monster could cause humans to run in fear just from his physical presence? Why hadn't I felt whatever made the others head for the hills? Apparently, it doesn't affect everyone.

Within minutes of pulling into my garage, the cleaning crew showed up and my townhouse became a flurry of activity.

While the professionals put my living quarters back together, I sat at the kitchen table, deleting and saving voice-mail messages.

I'd made the big time.

In among the calls from current clients, prospective clients, babbling psychotics, New Age seekers, *Twilight* fans, hopeful romantic partners – mostly prisoners or the recently released – and local media, there were messages from all the major networks.

I'd been invited to appear on every late-night, early-morning, afternoon and prime-time interview programme on the TV schedule. The segment would probably be called 'Let's ridicule, harangue and generally humiliate the allegedly professional woman calling herself the Vampire Psychologist'.

Turns out that not all advertising is good advertising after all.

The one exciting message was from a well-known publisher, asking if I'd consider writing a book. That was definitely a keeper.

Tom would be so proud of my fifteen minutes of fame and fortune.

Thinking about Tom's shallow tendencies reminded me I hadn't heard from him since Zoë pulled him onto the dance floor at The Crypt several nights ago. From past experience I would've said disappearing that way wasn't his style, but I really didn't know him well enough any more, if I ever did, to guess what he would or wouldn't do. Especially if there was a woman involved. In fact, now that I thought about it, taking off with a gorgeous female was exactly something Tom would do.

I saved all the messages from the national media, just in case I ever did finish the book about vampire wannabes – or was it about vampires now? – and needed some New York and Los Angeles contact numbers.

Being productive felt good. I called all my current clients, told them I'd have a new location soon and arranged for telephone counselling sessions in the meantime. The prospective clients were willing to wait until I set up my new office. I was surprised by how many of them hadn't been put off by the gruesome publicity surrounding me. In fact, thanks to the national obsession with celebrities, some of the callers sought me out because they'd seen my face on the local news. Maybe I would come out of this mess with some parts of my life still intact.

By late afternoon the living room sparkled and silence reigned supreme. I'd left a message for Lieutenant Bullock outlining my offer to be bait tonight at The Vampires' Ball, but hadn't heard back from her. Taking advantage of the quiet, I drifted into a catnap on the couch and was startled when the doorbell chimed me into wakefulness.

I bolted up, heart pounding, and immediately checked the window for signs of sunlight. I was relieved to find the sun hadn't gone down yet. I was safe. Maybe. It wasn't healthy to make assumptions about the limitations of the undead, but I hoped the not-being-able-to-go-out-in-the-sun thing was true.

I crept over to the door and yelled, 'Who is it?'

'It's your trusty FBI agent.'

I huffed out the breath I'd been holding and stared through the peephole. Alan's smiling face filled the view.

The vampire handyman had installed additional locks on the door – not that locks would keep undead visitors out, but I had to do something – and going through the unlocking process took a bit longer than before.

'Hey, you added more locks.' He pointed back over his shoulder. 'Where are all the news vans and cop cars?' He hugged himself, running his hands up and down his arms as if he were cold. 'Shit. I don't know what the hell is going on, but as soon as I pulled in front of your house, my stomach cramped and I had a strong urge to jump back in my car and drive as far away from this place as fast I could. I almost did. It felt like something really horrible would happen if I got any closer.' He pressed his palm to his chest. 'Damn. My heart's going nuts. What the fuck?'

I tugged him into the room. 'Come in and sit down. You don't look so good.'

He gave a weak grin. 'Just what a guy wants to hear from an attractive woman.'

After carefully relocking everything I led him into my disinfectant-scented living room and offered him a seat on the couch.

I sat in my fluffy chair and explained the events of the previous evening as he recovered himself and wrote in his dog-eared notebook.

When I finished, he frowned and smacked a hand down on his leg, the negative effects of Brother Luther's energy waning. 'I knew I should've come home with you. None of that would've happened if I'd been here. Why didn't you call me? You know I've been on this case for months.'

I did the therapist nod and spoke in my most reasonable voice. 'Well, first, you wanted to come home with me so we could have wild and crazy sex, so I might've been even more vulnerable when the maniac showed up if I'd been on my back, screaming Johnny Depp's name.'

He snorted out a laugh.

'And second,' I continued, 'I don't have to tell you what violent psychopaths do to people who stand in the way of their object of fixation. If you'd been here, even if we were just talking in the living room, he'd have seen you as a threat and taken you out. For some reason I've become important to him.'

'You don't have to worry about him taking me out. I could've handled myself.'

'Maybe.' I wasn't convinced. 'I didn't call you because it

simply didn't occur to me.' I tucked my legs underneath me and sighed. 'From the moment Brother Luther showed up 'til Luna's vampires arrived and the room got too crowded for him to the second I fell asleep on the floor, I was on automatic pilot. Actually, by not letting you come home with me, I probably saved your life. Therefore, clearly, you owe me.' I gave him my sweetest, most innocent smile.

He chuckled and slouched into the couch cushions. 'Let's entertain the possibility that your suppositions are correct and he would've torn my throat out if I'd been with you. That makes what you proposed to Bullock even more dangerous and lame-brained. How many people would he take out at a huge gathering in order to get to you?'

'Well, that's why the police would be there. Don't you think it makes sense to call him out? If I don't, I'll be looking over my shoulder every day until he either loses interest in me or gets caught. And what's the likelihood that a psychopath will lose interest?'

'Okay, I hear you.' He folded his arms across his chest. 'But I can tell you that Bullock won't go for it. She can't put a civilian in danger – it'd mean her badge. Personally, I think having the cops show up at the ball is a great idea.'

'Tell that to Lieutenant Bullock. Are you going?'

He grinned. 'Would I miss an opportunity to schmooze with every vampire in the western USA? After all these months following the trail of bloodless bodies, I might be in on the takedown. That's definitely worth the price of admission.'

That gave me the opportunity to ask him the questions I'd wanted to ask since I met him. 'Why are you so obsessed with this case, and vampires in general? What do you really want?'

He lowered his head and got very quiet. It wasn't only that he didn't speak. It was as if he stilled his body to the point that I was tempted to get up and put my hand on his chest to see if he was breathing.

After a few seconds he raised his eyes to study me, then he sat up straight, brushed off some imaginary substance from the front of his shirt and spoke, his voice low. 'I've never told this to anyone. Not anyone. Ever. I'm not sure why I'm telling you. Maybe it's because I really do want to have that wild and crazy sex you were talking about, or maybe it's because I just want to tell someone. Finally. And you've got that mystical therapist vibe going for you.' His smile didn't reach his eyes. 'I wouldn't have been able to tell you this even a week ago, but after everything you've seen and heard, my story won't sound so far-fetched or delusional. Maybe.' He stood and paced around the room for a few seconds then propped himself against a far wall, his arms folded over his chest again.

'Ready?' He stared at me. 'Wait for it.' He paused. 'My mother is a vampire.'

I opened my mouth but no sound came out. My brain spun for a few seconds, trying to concoct the perfect response, and failed. Was this his way of telling me he wasn't going to answer my question? Was he trying to be funny again to deflect from whatever the truth was?

He returned to the couch and sat, reading my face. 'You're trying to figure out if I'm kidding or messing with you, or if I've gone barking mad, right?'

'I always did great on multiple-choice tests.'

He hand-combed his thick chestnut hair, which left a couple of the shorter bits on top sticking straight up. 'Okay, let me rephrase. My mother *might* be a vampire.'

'I'm all ears, Special Agent Stevens.' I sat back in my chair and almost reached for my pad and pen before I caught myself.

He sighed and ran his hands over his face, like he'd splashed water on it and was wiping it with a towel. 'It happened when I was twelve. My father had taken off for parts unknown a few years before, leaving Mom and me by ourselves. Mom was great. She worked two jobs to keep the roof over our heads. She never complained. One of those jobs was tending bar at an upscale watering hole in Manhattan.'

He got up and started pacing again, as if the very telling of the story required movement. 'My mom was beautiful – I mean, *seriously* great-looking – and she was very attractive to men, but she always picked the wrong ones. She was too soft-hearted for her own good. She used to take me to work with her sometimes and I washed and stacked glasses behind the bar. It was illegal to have an underage kid there, but everyone was cool. No one would've turned my mom in. They loved her.'

'It sounds like you loved her, too.'

He ran his fingers through his hair again, strode to the window, and peeked outside. He was giving off so much nervous energy that I could've asked him to hold the plug end of my portable razor and shaved my legs while he talked to me.

'Yeah, you could say that. About a month before she disappeared she started hanging out with this slick guy – you know the type: expensive clothes, big car, diamond-stud earring. He seemed okay at first. I thought he might be sick because he was so pale, but he was nice to me when I saw him.' He walked into the kitchen and I heard the cabinet open and the faucet run. He carried his glass of water back to the couch and sat.

Patience, Kismet, patience. Wait. Some stories are hard to tell.

He rubbed the palm of his free hand repeatedly against his thigh. 'I was happy for her: she really liked him, and he treated her well. But she started staying out all night, then ignoring the alarm clock when it went off in the morning, and she wound up losing her day job.' He set the untouched glass of water on the table. 'Then she started looking different. I was just worried about her, I didn't know what was wrong – now I'd call it anaemic. One evening when I came home from my after-school job, I found her still in bed, barely breathing, with two hellacious holes in her neck. I ran out to get help and when I came back with the nurse who lived next door, she was gone.'

He slumped into the cushions, his chin almost resting on his chest.

I joined him on the couch, and laid my hand on his forearm. 'You made the vampire connection because of the holes in her neck?'

'Not for a while.' He shook his head. 'I thought she'd been kidnapped or ran away or that she died and someone snatched her body and didn't tell me. The police investigated, but it went nowhere. I was sent to live with my mother's sister in Jersey. I didn't make the undead association until I saw my mother again.'

Whoa! That came out of left field. I paused long enough to stifle my initial knee-jerk reaction, forcing myself to remain companionably calm, detached. 'You saw your mother?'

'Yeah, during college: a bunch of us guys went out drinking in Manhattan at this new trendy bar. I got up to go to the john and I saw the guy – the slick guy my mom had been dating before she disappeared. He looked exactly the same. I was ten years older than the last time he'd seen me, but there was a spark of recognition . . . and surprise. Just then the person sitting next to him at the bar turned in my direction and it was my mom, looking very pale and not one day older.'

He leaped up and paced again. I was getting tired just watching him.

'What did you do?'

'I yelled, "Mom!" and before I could say another word, the slick guy pulled her by the arm and they were out of the bar faster than it was possible to move. I bolted after them, but they'd disappeared by the time I got outside. I ran first in one direction, then the other, desperately hoping for a glimpse of the long red dress she'd been wearing, but there was nothing. My friends came piling out, thinking I was drunk, and crammed me into a taxi.'

He plopped down next to me again, and sighed. 'Of course, nobody believed me. They wouldn't even check out the possibility that she'd been abducted and held against her will. I didn't begin to explore the vampire angle until I read a couple of small articles in the New York paper about dead bodies with holes in their necks. Then it clicked.'

I took his hand. 'So you're searching for your mother?'

He gave a sheepish smile. 'Pitiful, eh?'

'No.' I shook my head. 'Not pitiful. Understandable. What will you do if you find her?'

His eyes welled up. 'I just want her to tell me why she left me. She loved me – I know she did.'

I gathered him into my arms and gently rocked him.

He let me hold him for a few minutes, then pushed away and plucked a tissue from the nearby box. 'Some FBI agent I am, eh? Blubbering on your shoulder like a kid. I'm sorry. I didn't mean to turn you into my therapist.'

I stroked his cheek, letting him see the compassion in my eyes. 'You didn't come to me as a therapist. You came as a friend. And as someone said to me recently, "I'm here for you".'

He blew his nose and smiled. 'I guess the wild and crazy sex is out? I'd be willing to settle for pity sex.'

I laughed and took his hand again. 'How about a chaste platonic kiss?' I bent in and pressed my lips to his.

He pulled away and whispered, 'How about this instead?'

He used his body to shift me backwards until I was prone on the couch. His lips were soft and warm as they captured mine. He gently rubbed his groin against me and teased his tongue into my mouth.

My arms tightened around him, and I felt his excitement.

He broke the kiss and slowly sat up. He wore the expression of a man who was certain of his sexual charm.

'Yes. When it finally happens, it will be very good.' Then he nodded and stood.

I sat up, relieved I didn't have to enter the murky territory of Alan versus Devereux, but aroused all the same.

Men were so good at disguising vulnerability with sex. He straightened his clothes and nonchalantly ran his fingers through his hair as if he hadn't just reintroduced me to Mr Happy. The physical contact had done what he wanted it to do: it distracted us from the hurtful topic.

'I'm going to go home and put on my costume for the ball. Do you want me to come back and pick you up?'

Driving up to the mountains alone was always fun in the daytime, but at night, with more vampires afoot than usual, company sounded like a good idea. Besides, I didn't have any idea where the ghostly castle was or how to get there. 'I'd appreciate the ride. What are you wearing?'

He grinned. 'Guess.'

'Common-or-garden-variety vampire, or something unique and interesting?'

'I'll surprise you. Is an hour enough time?'

'Sure. I'll just throw on a low-cut black number, put on some white makeup, false eyelashes and red lips and I'm good to go.'

He headed for the door, and glanced back over his shoulder. 'Okay, then – it's a date. Be back in an hour.'

Before doing anything else, I followed him to the door and locked it behind him.

I raced up the stairs, started the water in the shower, then went into my bedroom to discover what kind of long black dresses might be hiding in my closet. It was entirely possible; I'd accumulated dresses that I wore for one professional event or another and had then forgotten about. As I'd suspected, pushed against the far wall of the closet was a plastic bag stamped with the name of an expensive chain store, which contained the perfect black dress.

Finding the price tags still attached meant I'd never worn it, or I'd gone out in public with the tags flapping underneath my arms. Unfortunately, both options were possible.

Well, I couldn't help it if my inner world was more interesting to me than most of the mundane details of the outer world. Would I trade my expertise in the emotional, psychic and psychological realms to be less socially awkward? No. But I wouldn't mind giving my Inner Nerd a break. Maybe I just needed a wife? Yeah, that was it, someone to do all the stereotypical things we attribute to wives.

Or maybe a harem. Yum, a male harem.

I imagined Devereux, Alan, Tom, Vaughan the chiropractor, and the cute doctor I'd met in the ER all dressed up in slave costumes. I spun the wheel of various scenarios and envisioned them feeding me grapes, rubbing my feet and carrying me in one of those Egyptian-style chairs. Immediately I became totally distracted by a quick visual of the six of us having a private party in a luxurious curtained bed.

Maybe a cold shower would do me more good than a hot one.

But it's a good sign that I'm having normal sexual urges, right?

I laughed out loud, removed the dress from the plastic bag and spread it out on my bed.

I even clipped off the price tags.

An hour later my makeup was done and the curls of my hair were combed into a long shining thickness. I was perfumed, high-heeled and poured into a slinky floor-length, cleavage-exposing black dress.

The ever-present, recently life-saving necklace was nestled in the valley.

Not too shabby.

After checking out the pale hue of my natural skin tone against the black of the dress, I'd decided against putting on even whiter makeup. Sometimes having a ghostly complexion came in handy.

Right on time the doorbell sounded and I scoped out the peephole.

I turned on the porch light and felt a ripple of dread fan through my body.

What now?

Standing on my porch was Dracula strolling the streets of London, à la Gary Oldman: top hat, long curls, blue-lensed glasses and a silver-knobbed walking stick.

But there was no mistaking that charming smile.

'Alan!' I opened the door. 'You look amazing!'

He strutted into the entryway, preened and bowed. 'This time I was prepared for the nightmare energy out there, so I used my vast intellect and a little self-hypnosis to counter its effects.'

'Really? That's good to know. I'll have to teach the mailman to put himself into a trance so I can get my mail delivered. Enter, Count Dracula.' I swept my arm through the air in invitation, then closed the door.

Adopting a thick Transylvanian accent, he said, 'Mina, I mean, Kismet, I vant to drink your blood. But I could be persuaded to do something else instead.'

He stepped around behind me, lifted my hair away from my neck and ran his teeth over my skin. He sported the same kind of tiny fake fangs Midnight had worn.

The touch sent goosebumps across my skin and I turned to face him. 'We'll never get out of here if you keep on doing that.'

He slid his fingertips down my arms, still speaking in the thick accent. 'It vould be my pleasure to rip off this incredibly sexy dress and ravage you right here on the floor. Do you prefer to be on the bottom or the top?'

'Oh, Count, you take my breath away, but I fear we'll be late for the vampire-staking if we dawdle.'

He lifted my hand and kissed the palm. 'Then I shall come to visit you in the night.'

We both laughed.

'Aren't they adorable, Raleigh?'

Alan and I both jerked our heads towards the voice.

Once again, my living room hosted unexpected visitors. Bryce stood in the centre of the room, his long dark hair resplendent against a blood-red floor-length velvet coat. White ruffles peeked out of the lapels and sleeves. Black leather trousers hugged his well-proportioned lower body.

It had to be some kind of cosmic injustice that such an evil being was so devilishly handsome. He could've been a candidate for Vampire Pinup of the Year if it hadn't been for the struggling human he held under his arm in an effortless headlock.

I recognised Ronald's auburn hair immediately; he was being held in a chokehold so tight that only grunts emanated from the young man's lips.

My stomach contracted and I gasped. Could this day get any worse?

As he'd done before, Raleigh laughed maniacally while parading, Munchkin-like, around the room. Instead of the sleeveless muscle shirt he'd worn last time, in honour of the ball he was decked out in a miniature version of traditional movie vampire garb: slicked-back burgundy hair, white shirt and long, sweeping cape with a raised collar. He'd painted black circles around his icy blue-white eyes.

Creepy.

Alan dropped his walking stick, pulled a gun from somewhere under his jacket and pointed it at Bryce.

'That's enough. Release him. Now.'

'Well, well. Things just keep on getting better. I do love a good drama.' Bryce ignored the gun and, moving faster than we could see, planted himself directly in front of Alan, surprising him. He gazed into Alan's eyes, which fluttered then closed completely, his chin nodding against his chest.

Alan's arm fell to his side. The gun slipped from his hand onto the floor with a thump.

'What a disappointment.' Bryce kicked the gun aside. 'Not a worthy adversary after all. Just another squawking blood-sack.' The handsome demon turned and moved towards me, dragging Ronald along like a crash-test dummy.

He gave his favourite evil smile. 'But I must admit, I'm surprised to find Devereux's paramour indulging herself with another man. I wonder if he knows? What a shame I'm so bad at keeping secrets.' He smiled wider. 'It will give me great pleasure to be the one to tell him that the pathetic human woman he rejected me for is being unfaithful.'

'Really?' My mouth dropped open. 'All the fighting, violence and drama are because you're *jealous*? You want to take over the coven and hurt Devereux because he doesn't share your feelings? Seriously? Are you twelve?'

I immediately regretted my outburst. *Not a very savvy therapeutic intervention, Kismet. Never agitate the predator.*

His face contorted with rage. He stepped forwards and leaned towards me, the epitome of pure malevolence. 'Shut the fuck up, human. You know nothing about me. Devereux and I were together centuries before you were born. It was only ever a matter of time until he came to his senses. After I dispose of you, everything will be as it should be.' He straightened and gave what he probably considered to be a charming smile. 'I see you're all ready for the festivities. Excellent. We have a special room reserved just for you.' He jostled Ronald. 'I'm afraid your little friend here had quite a hissy fit when I sucked most of the blood out of his girlfriend Midnight's body. He insisted on coming along to tell you all about it. Unfortunately, he seems to be a little tongue-tied at the moment.' He laughed robustly, tightening his grip on Ronald's neck.

Ronald gasped for air. He wasn't going to make it if Bryce didn't release him soon.

I didn't know what to do, so I did something stupid. I took a step towards Bryce, got in his face and screamed, 'Let him go, you bloodsucking coward! Showing off is for idiots and children. We'll see how big and bad you are after Devereux gets through with you!'

Bryce flinched; he didn't like that. His handsome features contorted into a ghastly mask, his eyes narrowed and grew darker. He growled, showing razor-point fangs.

I figured mentioning Devereux's name would push his buttons, but I didn't think it through beyond hoping he'd turn his rage on me and drop Ronald.

So much for that.

Bryce simply appeared at my side, circled my waist with his free arm and yanked me against his body. He jerked his chin in unconscious Alan's direction and said to Raleigh, 'Bring Dracula.'

CHAPTER 25

Travelling by thought might be miraculous, but it certainly messed with my equilibrium. When Bryce suddenly released me I stumbled backwards, straining to catch my balance.

We'd materialised or metamorphosed or whatever the hell we'd done, in the centre of a lavish balcony.

I shuffled a few steps towards the railing and my mouth fell open.

We were definitely at high elevation.

I reached that conclusion because mountain peaks were visible through high-placed windows, and from my vantage point the angels with fangs painted on the vast ceiling looked close enough to touch. I'd never even imagined such a place. It reminded me of a photo of a European opera house I'd seen in a magazine, except much bigger.

Was this the famous ghostly castle?

The walls were lined with ornate balconies, one underneath the other, each filled with people in costumes. The terrace we'd popped onto seemed to be the only one with limited occupancy.

Stretching out below me was an extraordinary ballroom. Everything was gold, sparkling gold, from the designs in the antique wallpaper to the water fountains strategically placed throughout the room to the nude sculptures. Dazzling chandeliers burst down from the painted ceiling, dangling like mammoth crystal earrings.

It wasn't an exaggeration to say there were thousands of people milling about in the main area. The costumes were incredible – assuming they were costumes.

An amplified voice floated through the air: 'Welcome to The Vampires' Ball.'

I raised my arms over my head, signalling, calling to the party-goers across the stadium-size space.

A commotion behind me caused me to turn my head in time to watch Bryce pull a screaming Ronald by his hair towards a door in the far wall. Raleigh followed, dragging the still-unconscious Alan, whose wig, glasses and hat were missing in action.

I guess Bryce didn't care if I yelled or drew attention to myself by waving my arms madly. He left me standing against the railing, turning back once to sneer at me before disappearing through the doorway.

The noise level told me why he didn't care. Even if I set myself on fire and screamed, no one would've taken it seriously. I couldn't be heard over the ear-splitting music or the hysterical frivolity, and if I'd been inclined to turn myself into a human torch they'd probably think it was part of the night's entertainment.

Jumping from the balcony wasn't an option, either. Even if I made it to the next level down, the distance was great enough that I'd kill not only myself but the unlucky soul I landed on.

After making one last futile effort to communicate to anyone that I needed help, I gave up and followed them through the door.

I felt numb. I didn't know if I was getting used to being terrified, or if my adrenal system had simply gone into overload and shut down.

Under any other circumstances, the beauty of the room on the other side of the doorway would've taken my breath away. As it was, words failed me. All the walls of the expansive room were mirrored. Several large chandeliers, like lightflowers in bloom, hung from the hand-painted ceiling and reflected the never-ending glow of the clusters of illumination. Instead of angels with fangs, the painting overhead depicted fanged Greek gods and goddesses playing musical instruments.

I wondered if the original owner of the castle had been the one to order the vampire-inspired artwork or if it was a more recent addition. There hadn't been anything like these fanged characters in Devereux's art gallery under The Crypt, but it wasn't beyond the bounds of possibility that he'd painted these, too.

The exquisite music room contained several grand pianos, each a different style, forming a widely spaced square around the perimeter of the room. Harpsichords, antique harps and other instruments filled the spaces between the pianos. Music stands holding what appeared to be handwritten scores waited patiently for musicians who might never arrive.

In the centre of the room Midnight was lying, deathly white. Bryce must've released Ronald when they'd entered because he was sitting on the floor next to Midnight, his legs underneath her head. He gently stroked her hair, murmuring softly.

I rushed over to the couple, knelt and felt for a pulse in Midnight's neck, which was dotted with fang-sized holes. The beat was there, faint, but present.

Ronald and I shared a look that communicated relief, frustration and fear.

Bryce swaggered into the centre of the room, his crimson coat and dark hair reflected in every facet of the mirrors. Once again I was struck by evil's ability to be beautiful.

'Is she going to die?' I asked, standing.

Bryce walked a circle around Midnight, studying her as if she were a mildly interesting display, smiling. 'Perhaps. Perhaps not. It all depends on whether or not I choose to finish what I started.' He raised his eyes to mine. 'Maybe I'll give her the immortality she's always wanted.'

I remembered what happened the last time Bryce pulled me into his eyes so I didn't meet his gaze, but instead focused on a spot between his eyebrows. Even being in that close proximity to his dark-green orbs caused a fuzzy, tingling feeling in what Devereux had called my 'third eye'.

For some odd reason, Cerridwyn's words floated through my mind: 'Don't be afraid of your abilities. They will save you.' Her words didn't make any sense to me, but they sounded important, comforting.

I knew I had no chance of doing anything physical to get away from Bryce. Even if I managed to escape, I couldn't leave Ronald, Midnight and Alan behind. My only hope was to use my mind. Maybe if I could get him talking, I could discover something helpful. 'Why have you brought us here? What do you want?'

'You, my dear Dr Knight, are bait.'

Bait? Was he trying to catch Brother Luther, too?

'Bait? For what?'

He hesitated. 'Well, I guess since the curtain is about to rise on the first act, it's prudent to tell you. Lucifer seems to want you for some reason, so I brought you here for him. Then he'll get me what I want.'

'And what do you want?'

He licked his lips and ran one hand slowly down the zipper of his leather trousers, cupping himself. 'I thought I made myself quite clear – I want Devereux.'

Something about the way he said Devereux's name sent chills up my body. My pulse quickened and my stomach contracted. *Where is Devereux, anyway?*

'You aren't strong enough to do anything to Devereux.'

He gave a Cheshire-cat smile. 'Perhaps not. But Lucifer and me together – well, let's just say we're an unbeatable team.'

That was the second time he'd mentioned that name. Was he talking about the Devil? 'Who's Lucifer?'

He laughed and uncupped himself. 'You'll find out soon enough.'

Suddenly the air was filled with the familiar popping sounds and at least two dozen vampires materialised into the room. They carried bottles, carved boxes, enormous gemstones, ancient-looking books, statues and swords. A couple of the new arrivals resembled the old bearded characters in *The Lord of the Rings*.

Somehow I didn't think they were there to hold a Renaissance Fayre.

Bryce nodded, pleased. He grabbed my arm and pulled me towards him. 'We'll go and enjoy the party while the ritual is prepared.'

'What ritual?'

'The ritual of High Magic that will render Devereux helpless long enough for me to take control of him. Lucifer already began the binding process in Devereux's dreams. Even now his power weakens.'

Devereux had mentioned he'd been experiencing strange dreams, and he'd said something about being tricked into entering a 'difficult reality', whatever that was.

Until that moment, I hadn't seriously tried to contact Devereux telepathically. I still had a hard time believing I could call up my supposed abilities at will. Pushing the doubt aside, I put everything I had into sending a burst of thought to him, and for a second I could've sworn I *heard* him say my name.

I didn't know if that was good news or not. It certainly would be great for me if he turned up – but if he did, he'd be the guest of honour at the Ritual from Hell. I didn't care for the sound of this Lucifer guy.

'What about Midnight and Ronald and Alan?'

'They're perfectly fine.' Bryce spoke pleasantly, nonchalantly waving a hand in the air. He lowered his chin and whispered. 'For now.'

'Can you save Midnight?'

Harsh laughter burst from his mouth. 'Silly human.' He addressed his pint-sized servant. 'Raleigh, drag the girl and her saviour over to the corner with the FBI agent. We need the space in the centre of the room to cast the circle.'

Raleigh gave a dramatic bow and skipped over to Midnight. He pulled her by the arm and her head slammed onto the floor as it fell off Ronald's lap.

'Please! Don't hurt her!' Ronald's eyes glistened with tears. It feels horrible to be helpless.

'Get over here under your own steam or I'll be happy to drag you, too,' Raleigh yelled at Ronald. 'Of course, your arm might accidentally be pulled out of its socket, but by that time you'll have passed out and won't notice.' He made a braying sound that was probably laughter.

Bryce beamed like a proud parent watching a precocious child. He appeared to be having a very good time. He turned to one of the bearded vampires who'd brought over a jar of something for him to inspect.

Movement in one of the mirrors caught my eye. A man dressed not in vampire regalia but in an old-fashioned waistcoat and breeches stalked across the room and stood at the edge of the activity, watching. In his hands he carried a violin and bow. He began gesturing angrily with the bow, his face contorted, his mouth forming soundless words.

None of the vampires in the middle of the room responded. Apparently they couldn't hear him either. I shifted my head so I could see the man directly instead of reflected in the mirror. He wasn't there. Turning back to the mirror I found him right where he'd been before.

I tried the experiment again, with the same result. What the hell? Was I the only one who was able to see this guy?

It was obvious from his body language that the violinist was becoming progressively more upset the longer he was ignored.

He moved towards Raleigh, who was hefting a large black stone into place in the circle, and poked him with the bow ... which passed right through his body. Not getting the result he desired obviously enraged the man further. He stamped his foot and threw his bow on the floor.

When he bent over to pick it up, his eyes met mine in the mirror. Surprise flashed across his face and he disappeared.

No. I didn't just see that. Bryce must've messed with my brain again. No more supernatural weirdness. I refuse to believe one more unbelievable thing.

At that moment, Bryce dismissed the bearded vamp and turned to me. He closed his arm around my waist. I felt a feather's breath of air against my face, then we were down on the main floor, in the middle of the party.

I almost asked him how he managed to come and go without smashing into or landing on top of anyone, but caught the words before they left my mouth. I didn't want him to mistake my nervous chatter for actual interest in anything about him.

I craned my neck, searching the area for Brother Luther, and was relieved to come up empty. Since I hadn't heard back from Lieutenant Bullock and Alan was incapacitated upstairs, I hoped the lunatic wouldn't show up. According to what Bryce had said, there was already a full dose of misery on tap for the evening.

Misery, and a ghost in the mirror.

A velvet voice floated through my mind. 'My love.'

I started to say, 'Dev—'

'Speak to me silently, in your mind. Bryce is not very good at telepathy – he lacks discipline – but we do not want to draw his attention.'

I didn't waste any time questioning whether or not I could communicate telepathically. I sent him a bundle of thoughts, emotions and pictures, sharing everything I knew about Brother Luther, Bryce's intentions, the ritual to trap him and someone named Lucifer.

'I will not allow harm to come to you. Do not let anyone know you have spoken to me. I will be close by. No matter what.'

I felt an odd emptiness and knew he was gone.

Bryce's mouth was moving, so I assumed he'd been talking to me. I focused on his words, hoping he'd provide more useful information.

'—why he would be interested in someone like you.'

'What?' I blurted, annoyed that I'd missed the first part of his sentence. I held my hands over my ears, pretending I hadn't heard him because of the loud music.

He scowled and raised his voice. 'Devereux knew when he brought me over that I'd be powerful. He also knew how I felt about him. I don't care what he says – he's as bisexual as the rest of us. I never did believe his song and dance about waiting for some soulmate or whatever. It's bad enough he's making a fool of himself over a woman, but a *human* woman is beyond belief.' The evil grin slid across his face again. 'He'll have a long time to regret and reassess his choices. I might still take him back. If he begs. Let's dance.'

Before I could protest, or think of a way to avoid the close contact, Bryce had pulled me onto one of the table-free areas where couples were slow-dancing. He put his hands on my bottom and ground his lower body against mine.

I struggled to free my arms from his rigid embrace. He didn't even notice. He was busy studying my cleavage in the low-cut dress.

'I might just have to sample the goods Devereux is so hot for before the night is over. You've got big tits. I like that.' He reached a hand around, grabbed my breast, squeezed it and laughed. 'More than a handful.' He slid his hand from my breast to the hair resting beside it and lifted a curl. 'Your hair is long. It's almost as pretty as mine. Almost.'

If he was waiting for me to compliment his hair, he'd be a rotted corpse in vampire hell before that happened.

Thankfully, he didn't react to my lack of response.

He palmed my butt-cheeks again and moved us assertively through the crowd. He clearly fancied himself as the vampire Fred Astaire. As we circled the dance floor, I searched for familiar faces.

I thought it might be easy to pick out the vampires in the sea of wannabes, but it turned out to be more complicated than I expected. The high quality of the costumes, makeup, wigs and fake fangs made identifying the real vampires more challenging. Everybody looked like an authentic bloodsucker.

The longer we danced among them, however, the more I began to notice the familiar tingle in the solar plexus when I was in the vicinity of a vampire. Not only that, I found I was able to intuitively sense the level of the vampires' powers. Some of them barely sent out enough buzz to charge a flash-light battery, while others came across like a mini-cattle prod to the midsection.

My stomach muscles had repeatedly contracted since Bryce had kidnapped us out of my living room – fear tends to do that – so it was a good guess he belonged in the second category.

Apollo had told me that a vampire was only as powerful as the one who made him, so if Devereux was Bryce's maker, his abilities were probably beyond the norm. Or whatever passed for normal in vampire reality.

Vampire. Reality. Two weeks ago I'd never have put those words in the same sentence.

The slow song ended and the band launched into one of those World Beat compositions that combined African and Latin rhythms. The primitive drumbeats called to the celebrants and the dance floor filled.

I had to admit, most vampires might be sick puppies, but they could dance.

Bryce flipped me around so my bottom nestled against his groin. His arms encircled my waist, pulling me tighter against his apparently ever-present erection as he propelled us through the cavorting masses. He boogied, shifting his hips from side to side, forcing me to mimic his movements.

Ever since we'd popped onto the main floor, I'd been so occupied with Bryce, spotting Brother Luther if he arrived, and trying to communicate with Devereux that I'd missed some interesting developments.

I'd always thought most men were overly fond of their penises. They were always ready, willing and able to talk about them, show them to you, touch you with them or try to sneak them into any warm, wet, available place.

Vampires had apparently elevated penis fixation to an art form. Sexual activity surrounded me on the dance floor, with penises being stroked by either the owner or a willing partner of either sex.

I'd stumbled into a vampire porn video.

Was that what being immortal meant? Bloodsucking and masturbation? Why was it only the male vampires? Did something weird happen to testosterone in the transformation? Was that the best they could do with eternal life – perpetual sexual adolescence?

Devereux was right. Vampires are a completely separate species. And apparently most of them are insane.

Lost in thought, I was startled when a woman screamed a few feet away from me. I was only able to hear it because the tone of her cry was higher-pitched than the music. I jerked my head in the direction of the scream and saw a woman pinned to the floor by a vampire whose fangs were embedded in her neck.

I guessed she wasn't a willing donor.

None of the bystanders offered to help her. In fact, the attack only excited the strokers more.

I struggled to get out of Bryce's grasp and he clasped me tighter, rubbing himself against me and making soft moaning sounds. It was completely stupid of me to think I could do anything to make the vampire release his victim, but I absolutely couldn't just stand there and watch. I stomped down hard on Bryce's foot with the heel of my shoe and he relaxed his arms enough for me to slide down through them. I don't think he let go because I hurt him but because I surprised him. He was obviously distracted.

I leaped onto the back of the sucking vampire, who turned out to be a very large, muscular, smelly bloodsucker who flicked me off without even lifting his mouth from the woman's neck.

Laughter echoed around me as I fell to the floor on my back. A hand reached out of a full-length hooded robe to help me up and I caught a glimpse of a familiar face inside the hood. Even the clown-like vampire makeup couldn't disguise Lieutenant Bullock's distinctive features. I started to acknowledge her, but she stopped me with the slightest shake of her head.

Bryce's arm snaked around my waist again and he jerked me up off my feet, holding my back against his chest. 'Ordinarily I'd punish you for your absurd actions, but I still need you for a little while longer. You're lucky Lucifer wants you. Playtime's over. Let's go back upstairs.'

The woman on the floor had stopped screaming and was clearly dead.

The crowd actually applauded.

Vampires suck. In more ways than one.

I managed to catch Lieutenant Bullock's eyes and shifted mine in the direction of the high balcony, showing her where we were going. She replied with an almost invisible nod, lowered the hood over her face and merged into the crowd.

Just before Bryce popped us out, I caught a glimpse of several robed figures heading towards a doorway.

The music room had been transformed into the Church of Satan, or the setting for a Black Sabbath concert, something that required lots of black draperies, upside-down crosses and pictures of ugly guys with horns. A large circle containing an inverted pentagram had been drawn in the centre of the room and the massive gemstones placed in presumably meaningful positions. Some of the mirrors were now decorated with elaborate symbols and the light from the chandeliers had been replaced by the soft, eerie glow of black candles.

When we materialised in the room, Raleigh scurried over to Bryce. He frowned as he noted that Bryce was holding me off the ground, tight to his chest, and that one of his hands had moved from my waist to my breast. Raleigh shot me a dirty look and snarled, showing his pointy fangs.

Jealousy?

I knew I should be terrified, but instead I felt numb. After so much horror my brain had simply shut down.

Bryce noticed and enjoyed Raleigh's reaction. He laughed out loud and removed his arms from around me and I fell in a heap on the floor. Raleigh clutched Bryce's hand like a child.

It took a minute for my eyes to adjust to the dim light, but I was finally able to make out the shapes in the corner. Ronald was cradling Midnight in his arms and Alan was sprawled next to them, still as a corpse.

I hadn't allowed myself to consider the possibility that Alan was actually dead, but now that it had occurred to me, I had to know. I started crawling in his direction.

I'd just reached him, picked up his wrist and detected a light pulse when the familiar limb closed around me again. Bryce held me under his arm like a rolled-up newspaper.

'Playing Florence Nightingale, Dr Knight? Trying to save the handsome FBI agent? My, my – how many men are you servicing these days? But you mustn't rattle the blood-sacks. I need at least one of them for the ritual. Maybe two.'

'What are you talking about? What do you need for the ritual?'

'Blood.'

'Do you mean you need to drink blood?'

'You really are a tedious human. Of course I need to drink blood. But this blood's for the ritual. It's the final step – we're going to smear it all over the circle. Quite a waste of food, if you ask me, but the wizard geniuses say it's necessary. It will be worth it to have Devereux under my power. Finally, after all those centuries, he'll be forced to do my bidding, in every possible way.'

He carried me near the circle and set me on my feet. Then he positioned himself in front of me, shoved one of his hands down the front of my dress and roughly grabbed a breast again. 'You didn't answer my question, Florence. How many men are you servicing?'

His grip on the tender flesh hurt, but I didn't want him to know that. I breathed in slowly through my nose, trying to use a relaxation technique to lessen my awareness of the pain. 'None of your business.'

He squeezed harder and I yelped. It hurt like a mammogram times a thousand, and he wasn't even trying. My entire breast was going to be black and blue. If he didn't rip it off. Apparently the protective necklace only worked if it was touched directly. What kind of magic talisman was that?

Smirking, he released his hold, pulled his hand out of my dress and let me fall to the floor as my knees gave out.

Standing over me, he unbuttoned his trousers and slid down the zipper of his fly. Mercifully, the silence that had fallen around us was suddenly shattered by an extremely loud pop, and Brother Luther appeared.

CHAPTER 26

Bryce physically jumped back a few inches, visibly startled. 'Lucifer!'

Lucifer? This isn't Brother Luther? Then who's Brother Luther?

The tall, bald vampire growled, his discoloured fangs bared. He stepped over me and stalked towards Bryce, whose eyes had gone wide. It didn't take a psychologist to figure out that Bryce was afraid of the foul-smelling creature backing him into a corner.

'Lucifer, I wasn't really going to do her.' Bryce's voice quivered. 'I was saving her for you, just as we agreed.'

Lucifer picked Bryce up by his throat, piercing his neck with long, filthy fingernails. Bryce struggled uselessly as rivulets of blood trailed down his neck and Lucifer licked them with his long tongue.

Bryce screamed, 'Dammit, Raleigh! The song! Play the song!'

Raleigh sprinted over to a boombox propped on a chair. He pressed a button and Brahms's 'Lullaby' floated softly from the speakers.

Lucifer continued to suck on the wounds on Bryce's neck.

'Crank it up!' Bryce yelled.

Raleigh turned the music up eardrum-shatteringly loud and Lucifer pulled back, dropped his hand from Bryce's neck and let him fall to the floor. He shuffled over to the boombox and sat in front of it, swaying to the music, humming tonelessly.

Bryce leaped to his feet, massaging his neck.

Raleigh rushed to him. 'I did good, didn't I, Master?'

Bryce kicked the small man in the stomach, causing him to double over.

'You almost fucking got me killed, you moron. You should've started the damn CD the moment Bizarro-Man showed up. You know that's the only way I can control him, otherwise he goes fucking ballistic.'

Raleigh, who wasn't even as tall as Bryce's waist, hugged him. 'I'm sorry, Master. Don't punish me!'

Bryce hesitated for a few seconds, appearing to consider the possibilities in the location of Raleigh's face, then peeled the mini-vampire off his body.

I'd got to my feet during the chaos and retreated behind a spectacular mahogany grand piano. I studied the bald vampire who'd inexplicably ceased his rampage and sat hypnotised in front of the CD player.

Shit! Lucifer's affected by the music. Not only affected, but manipulated, controlled. I've never seen a reaction that strong before. He transformed from being a dangerous predator into an almost childlike state. I never would've suspected. This is one for the psych journals. If they believed in vampires, that is.

My silent diagnostic session was abruptly interrupted.

Bryce scanned the room, shoved Raleigh out of his way and quickly found me. He stalked over, grabbed my upper arm forcefully enough to leave bruises and pulled me to the circle. The pain of his fingers burrowing knifelike into my arm was so intense I gasped, struggling to catch my breath.

He bellowed, 'That's enough bullshit. On with the show.'

Several vampires had been busy placing objects inside the circle and drawing geometric shapes around the outside. Others were working in a different part of the room, blending the contents of small bottles into a silver cauldron that bubbled over a fire. All of them came to attention at Bryce's command.

I hadn't noticed before that each wore a black robe. Vampire monks? Vampire devil worshippers?

Lucifer swayed gently, oblivious.

Except for one of the bearded vampires, who scooped thick liquid from the cauldron into a black cup, everyone else assumed their places in the circle and began chanting.

The sound of the chant was different from what I'd experienced with Devereux. That had been melodic. This was more like a deep rumbling sound. It reminded me of a performance I'd attended by a group of Buddhist throat singers. They had the ability, through years of training and practise, to sing two, three or four distinct low tones at the same time, a technique they used for meditation and trance induction. It was eerie and powerful. These guys were doing the same thing, and it sent chills through me, just like it had at the concert.

The other bearded vampire walked the circle, holding a sword straight up over his head. The blade sparkled in the candlelight. He mumbled words under his breath and paused at regular intervals to lower the sword's tip to the floor and lift it up again.

He came to a stop at the point nearest to where I waited with Bryce, whose claw-fingers were still cutting off the circulation in my arm. Using the sword, the vampire made a downwards swipe, and reached his hand through an invisible slash in an imaginary entryway, pretending to hold something open.

Bryce dragged me through. The growling chant rose in intensity.

If I hadn't participated in the Wiccan coven's ritual years ago, I'd have been surprised by the energetic change I experienced inside the circle. The air felt thicker, as if it exerted more pressure on my skin. My body seemed to move in slow-motion and candyfloss filled my head.

Bryce released me with a push and I crumbled onto the floor.

Again.

Not only were my arm and breast throbbing, but my hip was screaming. I must have fallen on it earlier. I kicked off the only shoe that had made it into the circle and stood.

Bryce yelled to Raleigh, 'When I tell you, turn off the music.' He studied me, amused. 'I'm going to summon your blond vampire lover now. Fix your hair – you're a mess!'

I rubbed my arm and gave him a blank stare.

He can't really force Devereux to appear, can he? He's acting very smug and arrogant, even more so than usual. What if all these vampires together have more power than Devereux?

Bryce strutted over to the invisible opening where the bearded alchemist who'd been stirring the foul-smelling brew at the table handed him the black cup. Bryce muttered something that sounded like strings of vowels and drank whatever was in the cup.

He grimaced, and bellowed, 'Devereux! Come to me!'

There was a moment of unnatural stillness, then my skin itched as currents of air gathered in the ring. The velocity increased, blowing my hair back from my face as the light flickered and became suddenly brighter.

A sound – not a pop this time but a full-fledged sonic boom – resonated only seconds before Devereux's shirtless body burst into the circle. The momentum was powerful enough that he landed on his hands and knees.

Bryce dropped the cup he'd been holding and clapped his hands delightedly. He bowed to the circle of chanting vampires.

'Bravo, gentlemen! You've exceeded all my expectations and will be abundantly rewarded.'

Whatever had happened to cause Devereux to arrive had clearly taken a toll on him, because he struggled to get to his feet and appeared dazed.

Bryce watched his guest, who'd finally managed to rise.

Devereux glanced in my direction, and I instinctively moved towards him. His eyes held an emotion that almost looked like fear. 'This is impossible,' he whispered in my mind.

Bryce intercepted me and stepped between us. He gave me his back and ran his hands over the muscles of Devereux's chest.

'Don't look at her.' He frowned. 'Look at me. I told you what would happen if you didn't cooperate. This is all your fault.'

Devereux rubbed his eyes. 'What is this spell? You are not powerful enough to summon me.'

Bryce swung his arm flamboyantly in a wide arc, indicating the robed participants. 'When you have the right bargaining chips, anything is possible.' Then he hollered at Raleigh, 'Now!'

Raleigh hit the 'stop' button on the CD player and the lullaby abruptly ended. I hadn't realised how loud it had been – what a counterpoint the lullaby was to the chanting – until it was gone. I had a vague idea of what Bryce had in mind, but I couldn't figure out anything I could do to help Devereux. Or myself. Part of me still couldn't believe it was actually happening.

'Raleigh, bring me one of the blood-sacks. Now! Move it!'

Raleigh, who enthusiastically enjoyed his role as Bryce's flunky, smiled – or more accurately, leered – as he scurried over to the corner where Midnight, Ronald and Alan waited. He grabbed Alan by the neck of his shirt and pulled him to the edge of the circle, then dropped his head with a loud thump.

I was glad Alan was unconscious because that had to have hurt.

The bearded vampire with the sword reached his hand through the invisible entrance and mimed holding a curtain open.

Bryce seized Alan and dragged him inside, then picked up a ceremonial knife, an athame, which had been placed strategically in the ritual space. The confident, wicked smile on his face faltered as he darted a glance in Lucifer's direction and found him standing. Moving towards us.

I wished there was a volume-control knob to turn down the chanters, because the repetitive sound was giving me a headache.

Devereux's voice whispered in my mind, 'Stand back.'

Bryce was distracted by Lucifer's approach and finding the

knife to bleed Alan, and he'd underestimated Devereux's powers of recovery. He knelt down next to Alan, raised the athame and chanted some words in Latin. Before the blade reached Alan's skin, Bryce was forcefully lifted into the air by Devereux's arm around his neck.

The blade flew from Bryce's hand and clattered to the floor. The two of them tore at each other, snarling and swearing. They levitated, then wrestled down to the floor, pounding on each other like human fighters on angel dust.

I stood frozen, feeling like a helpless idiot.

As Devereux and Bryce flailed they crashed into the chanters, who had nowhere to go because the circle was protected by its own weird forcefield. Apparently, the only way in or out was through the imaginary opening. The fighters struggled back to their feet, separating long enough to hiss and growl at each other.

Devereux spoke, deep and slow. 'You are the mistake I have paid dearly for. It is finished.' With a ferocious roar, he launched himself at Bryce and ripped his throat out.

Bryce crashed to the floor like a felled tree.

Blood spurted everywhere, drenching the circle. A sizzling sound, like butter in a hot pan, could be felt as well as heard. Faint static electricity raised the hairs on my arms and tiny sparks ignited around Devereux.

I pulled Alan as far away from the oozing blood as I could.

Although copious amounts of blood still flowed from the wound, the skin of Bryce's throat had already begun to knit itself back together.

I shifted my eyes away from Bryce in time to see Lucifer plough into the circle and grab Devereux.

On a good day I was sure Devereux could hold his own against the ghoulish vampire, but he was weakened, and the outcome looked bad. Lucifer lifted Devereux into the air, holding him by his hair as he tried to sink his fangs into Devereux's neck.

Bryce's throat was healing so quickly he'd be back on his feet within seconds, and I didn't think Devereux had a chance of fending off both his enemies together.

I cast around frantically, searching for anything I could use to help Devereux.

My eyes caught movement in the mirror. The waistcoated violinist, still holding his instrument and bow, was waving his arms excitedly to get my attention. He moved his mouth, offering more silent words, and pointed his bow at something on the floor.

My eyes tracked where he was pointing, but I didn't see anything except the sword.

I glanced back at the image in the mirror; he nodded and mouthed, clear enough for me to understand, *Yes! Pick it up!*

The sword!

I really am dense.

What happened to the ZZ Top vampire who was guarding the opening?

I scooped up the blade, which was much heavier than I had expected. I intended to stick it in Bryce's chest, because everyone knew you could kill a vampire by puncturing his heart. I hoped that wasn't another movie myth.

Bryce's neck was almost completely healed. He had just lifted his head off the ground when I brought the sword down, aiming for his chest.

I whacked his head off instead. This time the blood oozed instead of spurted.

'Bryce!' Raleigh screamed.

The collective gasp of the now-silent chanters made me raise my head. All their surprised eyes were on me. A few of the vampires moved a step forwards, as if they intended to take the sword away.

I didn't care about that. My brain had clicked onto 'automatic'. All I knew was that I'd missed my target. Before they could do anything, I raised the sword again and plunged the tip directly into Bryce's heart, holding the hilt with both hands.

The Sword in the Stone in reverse.

In my prevailing shocked and traumatised state, that decision made perfect sense. I'd never again scoff at a story of a mother lifting a car to save her child. That was one heavy sword, but I'd wielded it like it was made of aluminium foil.

The electrical sensation increased and the sparks of light surrounding Devereux ignited with the sound of crackling fire. Bryce had said the blood was the final part of the ritual. He just never thought it would be *his* blood. But what would it mean for Devereux that the circle had been saturated with the thick red liquid?

He'd managed to prise Lucifer's hands off his hair, but he wasn't making much progress in getting free.

'Kismet?'

I turned to find Alan sitting up, staring at me, his mouth open. He was still wearing the fake fangs. He shifted his eyes to Bryce's body – both parts – then to the sword, then back to my face.

I could only imagine how I must've looked.

Well, I probably looked like what I was: a blood-soaked, traumatised, barefoot, ghost-seeing vampire slayer.

In my demented state, I wondered if I should add 'vampire slayer' to my business card, but then I figured it wouldn't do much for my vampire therapy business.

I wasn't even particularly surprised that Alan had rejoined the land of the living. Since Bryce had been the one to put the whammy on him and he was now undergoing an accelerated decomposition process, it made sense that Alan might be released from his evil eye.

It's funny how lucid you can become in the midst of a psychotic break.

Bryce's handsome face had regressed to his true age, and the massively wrinkled skin slowly began to crumble like ancient papyrus, exposing his skeleton. Chunks of his now-grey, brittle hair blew across the floor in the air currents caused by Devereux's continuing struggle with Lucifer.

I turned towards my ghostly helper in the mirror and mouthed the words, *Thank you.* He bowed from the waist, raised his violin to playing position and moved the bow vigorously over the strings. I wished I could've heard the tune.

Apparently, seeing ghosts is another one of my skills. Who knew?

A groan from Devereux brought him back to centre stage in my attention. Something was happening to him. He stumbled, unable to remain erect. His eyes met mine and I saw fear again before he collapsed on the floor.

Lucifer loomed over him, slowly bending down.

'I love you,' Devereux whispered in my mind.

Something about the hopelessness and finality of the

feeling he sent along with the words terrified me. A bone-chilling cold that rose from the horror of killing Bryce and the possibility of losing Devereux washed over me. I dropped to the floor and crawled to him. I stroked his cheek. 'Devereux, please wake up. Don't leave me.' He didn't answer.

Alan grabbed the athame from where it had fallen on the floor, leaped up onto Lucifer's back and stabbed him repeatedly. Lucifer looked more annoyed than injured and flailed about, trying to dislodge the irritant between his shoulder blades.

Finally he reached over his shoulder, grabbed Alan by his thick hair and threw him into the former chanters. One of the vampires held on to Alan for a few seconds, a confused expression on his face. Maybe he wasn't sure where his loyalties belonged since I had killed Bryce. He must have decided that it wasn't wise to be on the losing team, so he let Alan go.

Grasping at straws, I screamed up at Lucifer, repeating all the words he'd said to me as one of his other personalities: 'She must be punished. You are the warrior of God. The redeemer of lost souls. She's a harlot! Jezebel! Whore!'

Lucifer froze. He reached down and grabbed a big chunk of my hair, pulling me up as he straightened. He locked his red eyes on mine and I felt my brain slide out of my ears.

I closed my eyes to break the eye-contact and kept repeating the words, trying to remember everything else he'd said, until I felt him relax his grip on my hair. Even before I opened my eyes I could tell he'd transformed. I knew for sure when he launched into his familiar Southern-accented rant.

'Whore! Jezebel! You'll be washed in the blood!' He seemed to shrink before my eyes, the stained, horrible-smelling black coat now larger than his shrivelled frame, his eyes black coals again. He backed away from me, clutching his coat around him, rocking slightly.

I became aware of Alan standing next to me, his eyes wide, fascinated by the spectacle unfolding in front of him.

I hoped the transformation from one of the split-off person- alities to another might release Devereux from whatever power-hold Brother Luther – or Lucifer, or whoever he really was – had on him, but Devereux lay still as death.

The ritual Bryce had set in motion had taken on a life of its own and fulfilled the original intention: to control Devereux.

Then several things happened at once. A loud noise drew my attention to one of the mirror panels on the other side of the room, which turned out to be a hidden door. Lieutenant Bullock's costumed police officers stormed the room, yelling, 'Police! Freeze!' The human rescuers were followed by Luna and too many vampires to count.

The arrival of Devereux's coven caused the vampires who'd been involved in the ritual to dash through the imaginary opening in the circle and pop out of the room.

Luna barrelled towards the ritual space and smashed into the invisible forcefield.

'Fucking magic bullshit!' she screamed. 'They had the whole building protected so we couldn't enter through thought. We had to follow the stupid humans who'd found a way in. Now we'll have to erase their memories.'

Her expression became suddenly serious as she got a closer

look at Devereux lying helplessly on the floor. Then her face contorted. Enraged, she screamed at Brother Luther, thinking he was Lucifer, not realising that for all intents and purposes he was a different person – er, different vampire.

Trying again unsuccessfully to enter the circle, Luna vented her anger and frustration on the stooped, pitiful vampire standing over Devereux.

The longer she yelled, the more upset he became, until eventually he covered his face with his hands and sobbed loudly.

I knew what would happen if he reached a breaking point, so I tried to convince Luna to stop haranguing him. 'Please, Luna – you've got to stop. He's calm for now. Trust me, if you keep screaming at him, something bad will happen. He's sick.'

'Fuck that! This asshole did something to Devereux and I'm going to find out what it was. Take your human psycho-babble somewhere else.' She'd been prowling around the perimeter of the circle, testing for an opening. Not finding one made her even angrier.

I stared down at Devereux's beautiful face and remembered the music.

Keeping the dangerous, psychotic vampire subdued so we could remove Devereux from the circle was the highest priority. Maybe when he was freed from the influence of the spell, he'd revive.

Playing the lullaby, which would make Brother Luther shift into his child personality, seemed to be the best temporary solution. Perhaps he'd be immune to Luna's threats in his regressed state.

All I could think about was saving Devereux, so I didn't consider the repercussions when I sailed through the opening in the circle, heading towards the CD player.

'Where are you going?' Alan called out.

'No time to explain.' He'd missed the musical portion of the evening.

When I got there, the little CD drawer was open and empty. *Where was the CD? Where was Raleigh?*

Luna yelled, 'About fucking time,' and leaped through the opening I'd shown her. She strode towards Brother Luther, snarling, fangs bared, a true vampire Amazon on the warpath.

Too late, I realised my mistake and ran after her. I tried to step in front of her and she pushed me aside effortlessly, shoving me into Alan so hard we both hit the floor.

The sight of her caused Brother Luther to shriek in terror. He clutched his stomach and performed the same up-and-down rocking motion he'd done at my house. Between sobs he begged, 'Don't hurt me, don't hurt me, help me, help me.'

Luna kicked him, screaming, 'What have you done to Devereux, you festering piece of shit?'

He whimpered, 'Mama!' then dropped to his knees, covering his head with his hands and arms. A physical spasm rocked his body. He threw his head back and gave an ear-piercing primal scream.

As before, the transformation was rapid and astonishing.

Alan and I stood and watched Lucifer.

Shocked, Luna backed away. 'What the fuck?'

He rose slowly to his feet, his no longer emaciated body filling the previously loose coat.

Alan sucked in a breath. 'Jesus Christ!'

Somehow Brother Luther's body had become taller, bulkier, more muscular. His actual bones had shifted. His eyes were on fire.

He advanced menacingly towards Luna, his mouth gaping, exposing his still-elongating fangs. She assumed a fighting stance, crouched low, waiting.

Several of the vampires Luna had brought with her crowded into the circle. They growled deep, flashed their fangs and surrounded Lucifer.

He took a step towards Luna, hand reaching for her throat.

Just then, Lieutenant Bullock crashed into the circle, gun pointed. 'I said *freeze!*'

All eyes turned to her for a split-second, and in that tiny window of opportunity Lucifer scooped up Devereux and they both vanished.

We all froze for several seconds, stunned.

Staring down at the empty space on the floor, my brain finally registered that Devereux was gone and I lost it. I screamed like the Banshee from Hell. The walls reverberated as all the pain, fear, confusion, and grief I'd tried to hold inside burst forth in one long, gut-wrenching, soul-shattering cry. Then the tears began. I dropped to the floor and pressed my forehead on the spot where Devereux had been lying.

Everyone was silent while I sobbed.

Alan knelt down beside me and stroked my hair. 'I'm sorry, Kismet. We all tried to save Devereux. He's very powerful. If anyone can get away from that lunatic, it's him. You've got to keep hoping.'

I raised my head and met his eyes to see if he believed what he'd said or if he'd chosen that moment to dredge up his unused therapy skills. His warm eyes beamed sincerity. And compassion. I sat up, exhausted, tears streaming down my face. I was grieving for his competition and he was being remarkably understanding.

Luna snorted in disgust. She narrowed her eyes, pressed her lips together tight and covered the few steps to where Lieutenant Bullock stood, still pointing her gun. She knocked the weapon away, growling, and brought her face nose-to-nose with Lieutenant Bullock's.

'Bitch! You distracted us. I almost had the fucker. I'm trying to decide if I should kill you now, or wait until we find Devereux so he can do it himself.'

Lieutenant Bullock retreated a couple of steps. 'You are interfering with police business. Step away.'

Luna turned to the other vampires. 'Police business? Gather round, everyone. This cow thinks she has something to say about what's happening here. She thinks she knows one fucking thing about anything.'

Lieutenant Bullock still didn't seem to understand who, or *what*, she was talking to. She might've understood vampires in theory, but she had no personal experience with them. She probably thought all the bloodsuckers in the room were humans dressed in their ball costumes. It's likely she didn't know she was conversing with the real deal.

'There's a body on the floor and blood everywhere. You bet your ass I have a lot to say about it.'

Luna plastered on her most evil smile. 'And what kind of body do you think is on the floor, human?'

Alan rightly sensed that things were going south at the speed of light, and he jumped up and squeezed himself in between Luna and Lieutenant Bullock. But instead of helping, he leaped into the fray. The three of them started arguing at the top of their voices.

The other cops and vampires lined up on opposite sides, facing each other like the Sharks and the Jets in *West Side Story*. Though I doubted they'd break into a dance routine.

I tried to intervene a couple of times, but I didn't have the energy to involve myself in anything as meaningless as blame or police protocol or whether vampires existed. Devereux was gone, maybe dead. That was all the pain my heart could hold. If I'd had any doubt about my feelings for him, losing him made things crystal-clear.

I staggered out of the circle and walked aimlessly in no particular direction. The sound of someone crying penetrated the fog in my head.

'Shit!' How could I have forgotten about Midnight and Ronald?

I raced over to where Ronald was still cradling Midnight in his lap and knelt. He was crying, his shoulders shaking. 'She's so cold – she's dying, Dr Knight. I'm losing her.'

I stroked his cheek with the backs of my fingers. 'Hold on, Ronald. It's not over yet.'

I leaped up and hollered, 'Someone call an ambulance!'

That stopped the argument.

Everyone ran over to see what I was yelling about.

There'd been enough death and loss for one night. Midnight wouldn't be on the list, not if I had anything to say about it.

*

Having a positive goal seemed to galvanise everyone. Soon Midnight and Ronald were being carried on stretchers out of the music room to a Flight for Life helicopter waiting on the castle's roof.

I noticed that everyone in the room was taking turns watching me, as if they expected me to pick up the sword and behead someone else. Since I hadn't known I was capable of that kind of violence to begin with, I couldn't give anyone any guarantees about my future actions.

With Devereux gone, I didn't know what to do.

After the medical tech got Midnight prepped and stabilised, he told me her vital signs were incredibly good for someone who'd almost been drained. I don't know why he spared the time to talk to me again and be so encouraging. Maybe he saw something in my eyes. Anyway, he said her outlook was great.

Except for some missing hair and scalp, a nasty souvenir of his first ever Vampires' Ball, Ronald was completely fine.

I was morbidly drawn to the edge of the circle, which no longer held together, where I stared obsessively at the partial skeleton wearing a red velvet duster. The sword still rested nearby, clear evidence of something I knew logically but was resisting emotionally. I sat down, trying to feel bad. Trying to feel ashamed. Trying to feel anything. But I was still utterly numb.

Alan had finally got across to Lieutenant Bullock that it was a vampire body rotting on the floor in the Dark Magic circle, so no forensics team would be arriving to collect evidence.

'Lieutenant, if you tell anybody you spent the last couple of hours with vampires, you'll be taken away by the men in white coats and put in a straitjacket. Is that how you want to end your career?'

Luna was still prowling the area, mumbling under her breath about the stupid humans and what she wanted to do to Lieutenant Bullock. We each deal with pain in our own way.

I wasn't sure how I was going to deal with mine. I rested my forehead on my bent knees as another river of tears poured down my face.

It wasn't fair. I'd just accepted that Devereux was a vampire and that I had strong feelings for him, then he was gone. We'd known each other less than two weeks. My brain still hadn't processed all the chaos and horror I'd experienced since I first met Midnight. Did the idea of working with real vampires even remotely appeal to me any more? Why would I want to involve myself with such a violent, irrational group?

Devereux dead? My mind couldn't accept it.

Weren't vampires supposed to live for ever?

I knew that after the shock receded, I'd have to deal with all the stages of grief. Was I supposed to move into an office in Devereux's building, seeing constant reminders of him every day? I'd have to be a glutton for punishment to do that. I shook my head, unable to believe that I could even think about something as meaningless as office space or buildings. Maybe I'd take a sabbatical from my practice. Hide away. Go to Paris to visit friends.

I don't know how long I sat there in front of Bryce's remains, but for some reason I had an urge to raise my head. The ghost in the mirror was once again working hard to get my attention.

Nobody else has the ability to see this ghost but me?

He was beside himself with joy. He smiled very wide, danced in circles and thrust his bow vigorously in a pointing motion towards the far end of the room.

Since he'd been such a reliable resource, I rose and shifted my eyes in the general direction the bow indicated.

There was something on the floor, half-underneath one of the grand pianos.

My heart pounded and I gasped. My body knew before the rest of me did.

I ran flat out across the room, skidding to a stop a foot away from flowing platinum hair.

Devereux looked like he'd been hit by a truck. Or exposed to the vampire equivalent of kryptonite.

I screamed again, this time with pure joy, which was quickly followed by the sound of running footsteps and excited voices.

He lay sprawled on his back, his hair partially covering his face.

I dropped to my knees, held his face in my hands and kissed his parched lips. His skin felt icy-cold to the touch. Suddenly terrified, I feared that Lucifer had sent Devereux's dead body back as a sadistic parting shot.

I checked his pulse points for a heartbeat, but couldn't detect anything. But if he was dead to begin with, did it matter that he had no heartbeat? I knew so little about vampire mortality that I had no idea what signs to look for.

Luna, who'd dropped down next to Devereux across from me, closed her eyes and pressed one hand against his forehead and the other to his chest.

I watched her, not sure what she was doing, but hoping

she knew some kind of vampire trick that would bring Devereux back to consciousness. I couldn't help myself. I started crying again.

'I can feel him.' She glanced at me. 'He's in there.'

'What does that mean?' I choked out between sobs.

'Stupid human,' she said gruffly, and then cleared her throat and spoke more softly. 'Take his hand and find out for yourself.'

I picked up his hand and held it in both of mine, waiting. I didn't know what I was supposed to be listening for, but touching him felt wonderful. Even if his skin was as cold as marble. I closed my eyes and clearly *heard* him say my name. His finger twitched almost imperceptibly.

I burst out laughing, still crying, and a joyful roar rose up from the bystanders.

My vampire was alive.

Or whatever.

Epilogue

Luna transported Devereux back to his underground room at The Crypt. He didn't really regain full consciousness for three weeks. He spent most of that time comfortably tucked into his huge, luxurious bed, surrounded by various devotees and well-wishers. I sat with him, held his hand and talked to him, as often as I could. Luna humoured me. She assured me he was aware of my presence, even though he couldn't communicate beyond an occasional telepathic whisper of my name or a tremble of a finger. She even kept me company once or twice, if you could call sitting with her back to me while she filed her long, sharp fingernails company. She chuckled darkly occasionally, so I was pretty sure what she was thinking about as she honed the lethal points. She said she had a good time wiping the memories of all the police officers involved in the showdown at the Ball. I didn't ask what she meant.

It turned out that the magic Bryce and Lucifer had used was ancient and powerful, and had been stolen from the same line of wizards Devereux claimed as his ancestors. Maybe that was why it had worked so well. When he awoke, Devereux did everything necessary to ensure no such mystical ammunition could ever be used against him again.

I asked Devereux how he was able to return to the music room in the castle after Lucifer abducted him. Apparently it was because of me. My desire for him, fuelled by our connection, my strong emotions and whatever mysterious abilities he insists I have – not to mention the magical pull of the pentagram necklace – functioned together as a beacon to call him back to my 'plane of reality'. I still have lots of questions. Seems there's no limit to the strangeness of vampire metaphysics.

While he recovered, I read the entire *Harry Potter* book series to him, not only because I thought he'd enjoy it, but because the books are the written equivalent of a teddy bear for me.

All of Devereux's inter-dimensional caregivers told me he'd recover completely. Whatever 'recover' means for a dead guy.

It was weird watching Devereux feed while unconscious. A steady parade of human blood donors visited his quarters and offered wrists for the cause. Apparently the rooting instinct that causes infants to turn towards your finger when you rub the corner of their mouths works in a similar way when a mortal body part is pressed against a hungry vampire's lips. Under normal circumstances, no human would have been able to pull her or his arm away from Devereux's grip if he wasn't finished with it – he was simply too old and too strong. But that never became a problem. At a certain point, Devereux's fangs simply retracted and he opened his mouth, releasing the donor.

Of course, the general consensus among the healers was that Devereux could do things other vampires couldn't because he was just that evolved an individual.

The fact that Devereux was physically incapacitated didn't keep him from pursuing me romantically and sexually while I slept. In the dream realm, he swept us off to intimate rendezvous all over the world, where we made love, and talked for hours. I told him things about myself I'd never shared with anyone, and he did the same. And he educated me about the strange parallel world of the vampires. I now know things human brains aren't really equipped to know.

My private practice is busier than ever. Moving into the new office in Devereux's building was the best thing I ever did. All my old clients returned, as well as a full evening caseload of vampires. Thanks to the ads I ran offering therapy for vampires, my waiting list for both humans and the undead is long. I'm still adjusting to the special needs of my blood-sucking clientele. If I'm honest with myself, I have to admit I'm still terrified most of the time. But nobody has gone for my throat. Yet.

Tom really did run off with the gorgeous woman – er, vampire. He left me a cryptic voicemail message saying Zoë had accompanied him back to California, but that they'd be returning soon. He said he needed to speak with Devereux about living for ever. Hopefully Zoë's long life had equipped her with the infinite patience required to spend time with narcissistic Tom. Maybe he'd learn some humility. Yeah, right.

A few days after the madness at The Vampires' Ball, the terror-provoking energy must have dissipated enough for the media to return to their stakeout of my townhouse. It was like a carnival without the rides: food trucks, balloons for the kids, vampire tattoos, even a resourceful entrepreneur selling T-shirts featuring a photo of me with fangs (I managed to persuade a friend to drive over and buy a couple for me as souvenirs). Lieutenant Bullock surprised me by turning out to be very helpful. We held a joint press conference about the 'vampire murders', where she did most of the talking. She said the City of Denver was still actively following leads, but that there had been new deaths in other cities, which shifted attention to the next bloody chapter of the story. My part consisted of saying I really didn't remember being abducted, and I couldn't answer any other questions without breaking client confidentiality. Rather anti-climactic, actually. According to reports, I was a huge disappointment. But the good news is I'm a blissful nobody again.

The lieutenant started visiting me for 'professional consultations' about all things vampire. She said she'd made mistakes because of her lack of knowledge, and she wanted to rectify that situation. We had an unofficial therapy session about her friend who was killed and I think she gained a lot from our time together. She asked me to call her by her first name, which turned out to be Amy. I never would've guessed; she definitely doesn't look like an Amy. It has been nice, though, having another human around who knows the truth. She's asked me to consult on several of her cases and I've discovered I enjoy the work. It's possible we could become friends.

And speaking of friends, I made another appointment with Cerridwyn the tarot-reader, who is close with Devereux's building manager and resident witch, Victoria. Small world. She said my challenges with the vampires aren't finished yet, but that I'm up to the task. I hope she's right. She also warned me again about the psychic darkness growing in Denver. I still don't know what that means.

Midnight spent less than a week in the hospital and was released to her parents, who made some changes of their own. The three of them came in for family therapy sessions, and Midnight was able to talk about the pain of her mother's emotional abandonment, as well as her father's alcoholism. As a result, her mother reordered her priorities, cut her weekly hours at work back to forty and has been spending regular time with Midnight, who has begun to blossom. Her father went into a recovery programme and, as of today, has had thirty days of sobriety. He also switched psychiatrists and is exploring a new medication for his schizophrenia. So far, things look promising. Midnight grieved the loss of Bryce, or the idealised version she thought she knew, but she's making good decisions. She's still seeing Ronald, and she admitted that whilst being with a human male isn't quite as exciting as the chaotic life she had with a member of the undead, she's adjusting. She hasn't given up the vampires altogether, but our therapy sessions are more about her now and less about her fixation on vampires. She's making plans to attend college, and is content to live at home for a while.

Brother Luther/Lucifer hasn't contacted me. Yet. Discovering a vampire with Dissociative Identity Disorder – what used to be known as Multiple Personality Disorder – has piqued my interest in the diagnosis and I've been doing some research. It's clear we haven't heard the last of the demented bloodsucker, so I want to be armed with as much information and as many skills as possible when he circles back this way. I still have nightmares about him. According to the reports of blood-drained bodies, he's moved on to another one of those pockets of escalating good and evil: Sedona, Arizona.

So has Alan.

He stopped by to say goodbye one afternoon about a week after the insanity at the haunted castle. After a couple of awkward moments, we practically leaped into each other's arms. I don't think either of us expected that. His lips were as soft, warm and inviting as always, and I don't know what to do with the feelings I have for him. He plans to follow the monster's trail wherever it takes him. I've had a few emails from him since he left, reporting his progress in the hunt for the killer – and his search for his mother. He'll never give up on finding her, either. He said he plans to visit Denver in the near future, which makes me excited and nervous.

After my lifelong awkwardness with relationships, I'm grateful for all the 'normal' feelings I'm having. Even if they make me uncomfortable.

I can't be in love – or lust, or whatever it is – with two men, can I?

I don't know. Stranger things have happened. But I do know that vampires exist. Vampires, and ghosts, and who knows what else.

What does that mean for me? Hell if I know.

But I'm ready to find out.

The End

Acknowledgements

This book has had a long journey and many incarnations. I'm very grateful to everyone who helped along the way: the friends, generous authors, readers, critique groups, writing groups, plotters and brainstormers who gave ongoing support, suggestions and encouragement (and chocolate). Special thanks to Thalia Andrews and Deborah Snider, who provided love and positive motivation, and Esri Allbritten and Laurie Hawkins who spent lots of time in restaurants with me, discussing plots and sharing publishing stories. Couldn't have done it without you! Much appreciation to all the wonderful professionals at Quercus Books and especially my editor, Jo Fletcher, who believes in me and my strange vampire world. I'm very lucky to have her. Hugs to my agent, Robert Gottlieb of Trident Media Group, and his vision for me and my books, and to Elaine English who steered me through some choppy legal waters. It's been an amazing experience.

Follow the adventures of Kismet Knight, Vampire Shrink,
in the next exciting instalment:

Blood Therapy